MW00364188

# THE
# NORTH
# WIND

BOOKS BY ALEXANDRIA WARWICK

THE FOUR WINDS SERIES
*The North Wind*

THE NORTH SERIES
*Below*
*Night*
*Hunt*

STANDALONES
*The Demon Race*

# THE NORTH WIND

## ALEXANDRIA WARWICK

ANDROMEDA
PRESS

Published by Andromeda Press

Copyright © 2022 Alexandria Warwick

All rights reserved. No part of this book may be sold, reproduced, or distributed in any form without written permission from the author.

This is a work of fiction. Names, characters, places, and incidents are either products of the author's imagination or are used fictitiously. Any resemblance to actual persons, living or dead, events, or locales is entirely coincidental.

ISBN 978-1-7330334-7-3
First Edition

*For the lovers and the dreamers*

# THE
# NORTH
# WIND

# PART 1

# HOUSE OF THORNS

# CHAPTER

## I

The sky foretells a coming tragedy.

It is the palest of grays, yet a red stain clots the eastern horizon—evidence of the rising sun. The stain expands, sopping the clouds and dripping farther westward, puddling in dark splotches among the lingering shade of night. Huddled in the thicket of snow-laden trees, I watch the day waken with fear running cracks through my heart. The sky is red, like bloodshed.

Like revenge.

I have been expecting such a sight for days now. It is as the stories claim. First comes the budding of leathery cones from the old cypress tree growing in the town square. Three decades the tree has lay dormant, and the emergence of new blooms sent the townsfolk into a frenzy, the women into hysterics, the men stoic with grim-faced defeat. The buds, then the bleeding dawn. At this point, there is little I can do. Because if the sky is to be correct, Edgewood is expecting a visitor, and soon.

A harsh wind rattles the bare, finger-bone branches. I tug my patchwork coat tighter around my body, yet the invading cold always manages to slip between the openings.

Encased in its white, icy skin, the land lies in muted silence, the snow soft, fresh from the storms that blow in as frequently as the moon cycles. For now, I will not think of what may come. My task lies here, in this uninhabited stretch of wood, with the black trees and their rotted cores spreading around me, and my stiff, gloved hand clasped around my bow.

Peering around a trunk that has long since been stripped of bark, I scan my surroundings. Two weeks of tracking and I had all but given up hope. Three days prior, however, I stumbled across a game trail, still fresh. The tracks led me here, fifteen miles northwest of home, but I've yet to spot the elk.

"Where are you?" I whisper.

A gust wails in response. The forest, a labyrinth of frost and snow, seems to shudder around me. Starve-edged desperation sent me deeper into the forest's heart, beyond that small pocket of civilization—north, where the River Les gleams, where no one dares dwell. The fear is never far, but I'll be damned if I let it show.

Movement catches my eye. The animal limps into sight, alone, separate from any herd. That is the way of the Gray. Its slow, laborious gait is evident in the dragging hooves, the twisted left foreleg. The sight sickens me. It's not the animal's fault it suffers. That responsibility belongs to the dark god who squats beyond the Shade.

Hardly daring to breathe, I pull an arrow from my quiver, fingers curled around the bowstring. One seamless pull, a full draw, and my hand grazes the underside of my jaw, the string brushing the tip of my nose as an additional reference point. The elk paws at the snow, seeking something green, something that is like hope but that never will be. It won't have to suffer for much longer. My kills are immediate and clean.

But I am not alone.

There is a scent that does not belong. A deep breath drags traces of the forest into my lungs. Ice. Wood.

*Fire.*

A smell of burning. An ashen forge bloated with heat, acrid and unclean. It coats the back of my throat and swells in my nasal cavity with each inhalation. It is a warning, and it comes from the north.

My senses still. My ears strain for any unusual sound. Tension winds knots through my limbs in preparation for flight, yet I force my mind to calm, to return to what I know, and what I know is this: the scent is faint. Enough distance separates me from the darkwalker that I have time, but I'll need to move quickly.

When I return my attention to the elk, I notice it has shifted far enough away that the likelihood of hitting it on the first strike has drastically decreased. I can't risk moving closer. If the animal flees, I'll never catch it, and I haven't enough supplies to extend this trip any longer. Back home, the bread grows hard as tack, the last of the jerky reduced to crumbs.

*So don't miss.*

I adjust the angle of my bow, the arrow tipped a few inches higher. Exhale and—release.

The arrow screams against the frigid air. The elk's head snaps up. Too late. The arrow lands true, burying itself deep into living flesh and a still-beating heart.

Today, my sister and I will live to see the morrow.

Hurrying to the animal's side, I check to make sure it's dead. Its massive rack of velvet-coated antlers weighs down the magnificent head. Large, liquid eyes stare unseeingly, and its snout is soft despite the cold-riddled air.

The last of the elk herds vanished decades ago, yet this one managed to wander back into our lands. The poor animal is naught but skin sagging off warped bones, and I wonder when it last ate. Little flourishes in the Gray.

Quickly, I begin skinning the animal with the knife I am never without, the last of Pa's possessions. Steaming chunks of meat hacked from the carcass, packed as tightly into my satchel as I can manage. Blood saturates the hide and drips from the smallest openings. It smells of copper. My mouth pools with saliva, and the pit that is my stomach gnaws relentlessly. Every so often, I glance over my shoulder, scan my surroundings. The sky's red tinge has cooled to blue.

The smell of a forge still lingers beneath the copper stench. Or is it growing stronger? Reaching into the body cavity through the split stomach, I slice another chunk free, pack it with the rest. Hot blood coats me from fingertips to elbows.

I'm severing the liver when a distant howl lifts the hair on my body. I cut faster. With the abdomen hollowed out, I shift my focus to its flanks. I've a small pouch of salt hanging from my beltloop, but that will only protect me from one darkwalker, maybe two if they are small. Except that howl mutates into a roar, so close the trees shiver, and my entire body stiffens, my heart leaps and plummets in the span of a breath, my pulse races with panic, on the crest of a black wave.

I'm out of time.

A glance at my front shows I'm drenched in the elk's lifeblood. Despite darkwalkers' aversion to salt—and that includes the salt in one's blood—the scent will draw their attention, for they feed on the living, rasping their serpentine tongues to gather the life of one's soul.

A paralyzing cold creeps through me. *Flee.* Flee fast and far. But the blood . . .

I scrub the snow against my arms with jerky movements. It's not coming off. Harder, frantic now, as the breeze carries that woodfire warning of approaching peril to me. It's not working. The snow has absorbed the top layer, but not whatever has dried against my coat and gloves.

In a single motion, I peel my heavy coat from my sweat-soaked body, then my blood-stained gloves. My teeth clench as a painful shudder runs through me. It's too damn cold. A killing cold, if I'm not careful. I unwrap a dry woolen tunic from where it protects a flask of wine inside my pack and tug it over my head in rough pulls. The air, prickling like shards of glass, hastens my actions. By the gods, I did not travel two weeks in this barren wasteland just to die. If I do not return with this food, Elora will meet a similar fate.

With my soaked clothing removed, I stuff everything beneath the bleeding carcass, then scramble up the highest tree I can find. The frozen bark bites into my already chafed palms. Up, up to the tallest branch, which groans beneath my insubstantial weight. I suppose that is the bright side to starvation, however morbid. The multitude of branches, as well as my brown tunic, provide adequate camouflage.

The darkwalker lurches into the dell moments later, though I'm not given a clear view of its form. Snatches of shadow. Black wisps that bleed against the white. It investigates the fallen elk for a time before prowling the surrounding area. Sounds of snuffling pin me in place. I clench my jaw shut to contain the chattering of my teeth.

The Shade—the barrier separating the Gray from the adjacent Deadlands—is supposed to keep the darkwalkers bound to the afterlife. The townsfolk speak of holes in the barrier, splits that allow the corrupted souls to reenter the land of the living, to feed off those who still breathe. I've not seen these holes myself, but if it is true, I can't say that I blame them. You do what you can. You lie and you thieve and you don't apologize for it. I certainly don't.

My fingers grow stiff and pained in the passing minutes, stinging at the tips. They creak as I curl them into fists and shove them against the warmth of my stomach.

The darkwalker noses the open pack stuffed with meat. The beasts are not alive, not truly, not enough to need food and sleep, but it does not stop a barb of fear from pulsing through me, for that elk is my salvation. It will ease the tightness in my belly. The hide will make a new coat for Elora, despite the torn seams in mine. The antlers—tools. At least, that was the plan.

Eventually, the beast moves off. Ten minutes I wait, breath held. The burning air clears. Only then do I scramble down the tree, don my coat and gloves, rubbing my hands together to bring warmth to the deadened flesh.

Half the meat still awaits severing from the steaming carcass. Two months' worth of food. As much as it pains me to leave anything behind, I can't risk taking the time to finish the job. One month of food will have to do, and if we're careful, Elora and I can make it stretch further. Maybe another half-starved animal will stumble across the remains.

Heaving the satchel across my back, I begin the fifteen-mile return trek to Edgewood, grunting beneath the weight of my cache, punching through the soft ground with my fraying boots. By the third mile, my feet, face, and hands have lost sensation. Tears freeze at the corners of my eyes, which ache fiercely. The wind does not relent no matter how many gods I pray to, but they must know of my lost faith. A dull ache worms its way into my legs. The cold is so absolute it kills the breath before it is able to escape my body.

It takes the day. Evening darkens the world and slides into rich, violet-tinged twilight. With less than two miles remaining, I hear it. A low, lamenting bleat of a sheep's horn that climbs through the valley and kicks my pulse into a perilous sprint. The sky foretold a coming tragedy, and it was right.

The North Wind has come.

# CHAPTER

## 2

Long ago, the Gray was known as the Green. Three centuries prior, the land, this earthen ground, was an image of vitality: lush and verdant, with clear water singing over smooth rocks, and herds of elk and deer, and wild hare, and songbirds like the wren from which I was named. Hunger did not exist, for there was no famine. Cities prospered, and that fortune spread to the outlying towns. Even the rivers were plentiful, the currents rushing south to the lowlands, swollen with trout and freshwater clams, which were caught and sold along the banks. And disease? There was none. The people grew old and fat and happy, and died in their sleep. I do not remember that time, for I had not yet been born.

The change did not occur all at once. It was like the moon, ripening, then waning, dwindling to an extinguished light. Over the years, the summers grew short and winter stretched and deepened. The sky blackened. The ground froze to stone. The sun slipped behind the horizon and was not seen for months.

Then the Shade appeared, as if having been erected by phantom hands. No one knew of its origins or purpose. The darkwalkers materialized, nightmares made flesh. We drove them off, yet they returned in droves, in hordes, in amassing shadows. Eventually, winter encased the land, and not even the sun could thaw its icy exterior.

And so the Green was abundant no longer. Edgewood and the surrounding towns starved, for their crops withered, the rivers hardened to ice, the livestock perished. Supposedly, a god lived in those tangled Deadlands beyond the Shade, having been banished, along with his three brothers, to the outer edges of our world. The Anemoi, they are called—the Four Winds—who bring seasons to the land. The rumors grew hearts and drew breath and came alive in those darkening years. He calls himself Boreas, the North Wind: he who calls down the snows, the cold. But to all who live in the Gray, he is known as the Frost King.

I reach Edgewood within the hour. A low stone wall heaped with snow encloses the humble town: a sprinkling of thatched roofs and frozen, mud-packed abodes. As well, a thick ring of salt tops the wall. Darkwalkers may roam the forest, but so long as I am inside the protective ring of salt, I am safe.

Nothing stirs inside the barrier. The shutters have been pulled, the lamps doused. Shadows pour into the cracks and in-between places of the rutted stone road, spreading as twilight slips into the true black of night. As I pass one of the communal salt buckets hanging from a post, I quickly replenish my supply. Then I am past, moving up the road, the pack squelching against my back from the blood seepage. The horn was the initial warning. My sister and I don't have long to prepare.

The lane empties into the square where the cypress tree grows. The sight of those round cones has me hastening across the deserted area. Narrow walking trails snake through the snow surrounding the cleared square, the earth gray and wet with frequent tread.

Our cottage perches atop a knoll partially shielded by long-dead trees. I hurry through the entrance, calling out as I kick the door shut behind me. "Elora?"

Heat from the burning hearth thaws the stiffness in my face. The wooden floorboards groan beneath my boots as I deposit my bow and quiver at the door and move through the cramped space. Since the cottage is only three rooms, my search ends in less than ten heartbeats.

The house sits empty.

Sometimes Elora spends time at our elderly neighbor's plot, helping with small tasks around the house. But when I peer out the door, I see the windows are dark. Asleep, or no one is home.

I move to the kitchen and lean against the scuffed, wobbly table for support. The blood-soaked satchel hits the floor with a wet thump. The sound is distant. My body is distant. The Frost King could not have arrived yet. It is too soon.

The first call announces the king's crossing into the Gray. The Shade is hours away, even on horseback, and our cottage is farthest from the town entrance, small and overlooked. Unless I am mistaken? If he took Elora, then I am left with nothing.

It's as though my mind has frozen over. A cold, black, glassy terror roots my feet to the floor. If he chose Elora as his victim, how long ago did he arrive? When did they depart? Why is this town not in upheaval? They would have traveled north. I could still reach them if I run, though there is always Miss Millie's horse. I have my bow. Five arrows in my quiver. Throat, heart, gut. If I shot them simultaneously, would it be enough to kill a god?

The back door opens, and in steps my sister, shaking snow from her woolen hat.

My relief is so monumental my knees fold, cracking against the floorboards. "You—" The word deflates. "Don't do that!"

Unsurprisingly, Elora has no idea what I'm talking about. She pauses in the middle of closing out the cold, her sweet round face wrinkling in puzzlement. "Do what?"

"Disappear!"

"Nonsense, Wren." She sniffs, brushes flakes from her shoulders. A long, messy braid the color of pinecones hangs halfway down her back. "I went to gather more wood for the fire, but we're running low. The ax is still broken, by the way."

Right. Yet another task on my list. It needs a new handle, but in order to cut the handle I need a working ax . . .

Exhaling loudly, I drag myself to my feet, glance at the shut cupboard. At Elora's look of disapproval, I turn away from the sight, though my throat feels so dry it aches. "Promise me you won't disappear without telling me." My legs carry me to the opposite wall. Pacing. Something to do. A way to feel in control. "I thought he'd taken you. I was prepared to steal someone's horse. I was considering the most effective way to kill a man who cannot die."

"You're so dramatic."

As if fearing for my sister is a meaningless thing. "I'm not. I'm . . ." *Livid* comes to mind. According to Ma, I didn't enter this world quietly. No, the wet nurse had to yank me bodily from the womb because I fought so hard against it.

Dramatic is for the unimaginative.

"Purposeful," I finish smoothly, tucking a lock of dark hair behind my ear.

Elora scowls. I'm almost positive she learned it from me. We are the same, yet our hearts sing to different beats. Her dark eyes are life-giving coals. Mine are cold, mistrustful, wary. Her skin, a deep umber, is physically flawless. Mine is interrupted, puckered from the pale, raised scar mutilating my right cheek. Elora's hair is straight as a pin while mine has the frustrating habit of curling. She is my twin, and she is the opposite of me in every way, despite our nearly identical appearances.

Looking at Elora is like looking into a mirror—one that shows the person I used to be, prior to finding ourselves orphaned. And now? Well. I've had blood on my hands more times than I care to admit. I've killed men, I've sold my body, I've thieved time and again, all for a bit of food or warmth or coin, or the dried herbs Elora loves to cook with so much, so small a thing, but rare and precious to her.

Elora knows none of this. She would never survive the Deadlands. She is too soft for this world, too good. She is my little sister, she is light, and she must be protected at all costs.

"The point is," I say firmly, "we can't stay here." It won't take long to pack our bags, for we own little to begin with.

"What?" She rears back. "When did you decide this?"

"Just now." It could work. We'll travel south, west, east. Anywhere but north, where the Deadlands lie.

A wan smile touches her mouth. "Of course you did."

"Come with me." I pivot, reaching for her slender hands. "We'll leave this place for good, leave it all behind, start over somewhere new—"

"Wren." Calmly, Elora unknots my fingers from hers. She has always been far more levelheaded than I. "You know we can't do that."

Any woman who flees the North Wind will be put to death. It occurs every few decades, his arrival. He comes, steals away another of our women, takes her across the Shade for reasons unknown. Sacrifice, the stories claim. One woman to suffer so that others may live. There is little I love in this life aside from Elora. And I wonder if I will soon face yet more suffering.

"I don't care," I hiss, tears pricking my eyes. "If he takes you—"

Her gaze softens. "He won't."

"Then you are a fool." A silly, naïve fool. Elora is the loveliest of all the women in our village. Every other week, a man asks for my sister's hand in marriage. She has yet to accept an offer for reasons unknown to me. That she does not worry as I do about the approaching threat shows just how different our priorities are, and clarifies the roles we have fallen into after all these years. Why should she worry when I am here to protect her? But even I cannot stand before a god and win.

Elora moves to a crate where we keep our stores of salted meat. Prying open the lid, she reveals its meager contents—a few days' worth of meals, if that—and shoves a few jerky strips into my hand. "Please eat something. You must be hungry after the journey."

"I feel ill."

"Then sit. Mayhap that might help."

It's not a chair I need.

The tension has burrowed so far inside me it's impossible to separate myself from it. And so I reach for the cupboard that contains the wine, snagging one of the bottles and uncorking the top. The moment the drink wets my tongue, the snarling knot at the base of my spine unravels, and my mind regains a bit of clarity. Two more gulps and I'm steadier.

"Wren." Quiet.

My fingers tighten their vise around the neck of the bottle. I take another sip, baring my teeth in a grimace as the burn sharpens, searing a path straight to my stomach. "I don't need your judgment. Not now."

"It's not healthy."

She dares speak about what is healthy? I scoff. "Neither is sacrificing our women to a vengeful god. We do what we must."

She sighs as I angle away, returning the wine to the cupboard. I ignore her. This is the conversation that never changes. Elora asks for things I cannot grant her. She asks too much of me.

Deep down, I know she's right. I'm a mess. I can hunt and chop wood all day, but when it's time to talk about feelings, I turn to the bottle. That's how it went following the death of our parents, and that's how it's been every day since.

Reaching into the inner breast pocket of my coat, I pull out a folded length of wool colored like the sky. "I passed a tradesman on my journey. You mentioned your scarf was wearing out."

Her eyes brighten at the gift. We have so few possessions as it is. "What's this?" She gasps in delight upon unraveling the scarf and discovering the intricate threading on either end of the fabric. It bears the image of large waves on a great sea, though we've never seen any large body of water save the Les, the river that separates the Gray from the Deadlands, and that's perpetually frozen.

"This is beautiful. Thank you," she gushes, wrapping it around her slender throat. "How does it look?"

"Lovely." Is there any other word to describe my sister? The blue complements her coloring. "Is it warm enough?"

"Very." She adjusts the fabric, then pauses. "What's that?" She gestures to the palm-sized book poking from my front coat pocket.

I go still, racking my head for a possible explanation. "That? That's nothing."

Elora plucks it from my coat, studies the slender volume. It's so old the cover clings to the interior pages by mere strands of thread. She flips to a page at random. "A romance?" She grins. "I didn't know you liked romance novels."

Color pinkens my cheeks. "I don't, actually. But he offered me a fair price." The explanation paints a picture that is not even close to being true.

"Ah," she says. *That makes more sense.* Elora can believe what she wants. I've never given her reason to think otherwise. The majority of the books in this house are mine. Nearly all are romance. Seeing as my sister rarely reads, the solid cloth covers do an adequate job at hiding the stories tucked inside the pages. The last thing I want is Elora discovering *The King's Passion*, or whatever my current read is.

For a second time, the horn wails, shaking the walls of the cottage.

I stare at Elora. She stares at me.

"It's almost time," she says hoarsely.

My hands curl into fists to halt their trembling. I think of the stories. I think of how, after tonight, one less woman will inhabit

Edgewood. The Frost King has taken so much from me, and he dares threaten to take one more most beloved thing. "Elora, please." My voice cracks. "You don't have to do this."

I bend a knee for no one, but I will beg for my sister and her life. Mine is irrelevant. I'm not one of the women being offered to the king as sacrifice. My scars mark me as undesirable.

"Everything will be all right." Coming around the table, she pulls me into her warm embrace. Sage, sweet and earthy, perfumes her hair. "You'll see. Tonight, after the king has gone, you and I will bake a cake to celebrate. How does that sound?"

I fix my narrowed eyes on her. "How can we possibly bake a cake when we're out of flour?" And sugar. And, well, everything needed to bake a cake. Snow and rocks does not a cake make.

Elora only smiles secretively. "There are ways."

I do love cake, but it's not enough to banish my unease. The air is foul this night.

"I don't like this," I mutter.

Elora's laugh sounds like a windchime. "Wren, you don't like most things."

"That's not true." I'm selective in what things I show enthusiasm for, is all.

"Come." She tugs me toward the front door, replacing the hat on her head and drawing my hood up around my ears. "Miss Millie will need help with last-minute preparations, I expect. Everything must be perfect."

$\sim$

The North Wind's welcome involves a grand feast held in his honor. In theory, there is to be a decadent, multicourse meal, as if to be chosen, stolen away to the Deadlands, is cause for celebration. Perhaps there was, once. The reality is Edgewood fades year after year. Nothing grows in the frozen earth. The bread is tasteless. The livestock, except for a few malnourished goats, have all perished.

Thus, this *grand feast* is only slightly better than paltry. Edgewood bears no massive ballroom to host him, no suckling, spit-roasted pig or extravagant spread of candied meats or diced roots. Hard, pitted evergreen berries are collected and mashed into a tart, acidic sauce the color of blood. There is soup: salted water flavored with wilted herbs. The meat—old goat—is the most unappetizing thing I've seen in my life.

I hope the king chokes on it.

The fare may not be to his liking, but he doesn't come for the food. Seven unmarried women between the ages of eighteen and thirty-five, all lovely and pristine, gather in the town meeting hall, where a long table has been set for the evening meal, a fire warming the stone hearth. They are dressed in their finest: woolen gowns cinched at the waist; hair washed and combed and braided; long, thick stockings and tired dress shoes. They have smoothed over their wind-abraded skin with oils and colored creams to conceal their imperfections. I smile wryly. My imperfection can't be so easily hidden.

"How do I look?"

I turn at Elora's voice. A dark blue, knee-length dress I stitched a few years ago hugs her slender frame, and black stockings showcase her willowy legs. She is stunning. Always has been. The curled, dark fringe of lashes. That rosebud of a mouth.

Despite my attempts to steady my voice, it croaks out, "Like Ma."

At this, her eyes fill. Elora nods, just once.

The longer I stare at my sweet sister, the more intensely my stomach cramps. He will take her. She is too lovely to escape his notice.

Miss Millie, a middle-aged woman who loves her gossip almost as much as she loves straying from her husband, emerges from the kitchen carrying two wooden pitchers. Bloodshot eyes and ruddy cheeks reveal she has been crying. Her eldest daughter is one of the seven. "Glasses," she snaps at me.

I fill the glasses at the table with water. My hands tremble, blast them. The women huddle in one corner like a herd of deer left out to cold. They don't speak. What is there to say? By the end of this meal, one of them will be chosen, and that woman will not return.

Miss Millie's youngest, a boy of twelve, lights the last of the candles. Beyond the shuttered windows, the townsfolk clump in the square, awaiting the king's arrival. His last visit occurred more than thirty years ago. He took a woman named Lyra across the Shade— meek, ginger-haired. She was only eighteen.

It's as I'm smoothing the wrinkles from the white tablecloth that I hear it—the clop of hooves on stone.

The silence is thick enough to choke on.

The clustered women press closer, grabbing each other's hands. No one utters a sound. Even their breathing has ceased. Elora's gaze meets mine across the room.

I could do it. Take my sister's hand, flee through the kitchen door in the back. The dark god would never know of Elora's existence.

"Places," Miss Millie hisses, motioning for the women to take their seats at the table. Suddenly, the air clangs with noise—shifting chairs and whispering cloth and the dreaded *clop, clop, clop,* closer and closer. Somewhere in the room, I hear a softly uttered, "Please."

I'm halfway to Elora's side when Miss Millie snags my arm. The woman's fingernails bite painfully. I can't pry them loose. "Let me go." White rings Elora's dark eyes, which are locked on the front door.

"It's too late," she breathes. Clumps of her gray-streaked hair stick to her round, sweaty face. The lines around her mouth deepen.

"It's not. There's still time. Lend us your horse. I'll take your daughter with us. We'll return once—"

Footsteps.

Miss Millie swings me around, shoves me into a corner as the front door opens. The hinges squeal like a mutilated animal. Around the table, the women flinch, shrinking back into their chairs as a gale bursts through the doorway, guttering half the lamps and plunging the room into near-darkness. I freeze against the back wall, mouth dry.

In steps a towering figure, etched black against the shadows. Cloaked, hooded, alone.

He has to stoop to enter the room, for the buildings are constructed with low slanted ceilings to conserve heat. When he straightens, the top of his head brushes the rafters, darkness coiling inside the cowl of his hood. Two pricks of brightness, the sheen of reflected light against his eyes, are all I see. I'm not sure of their color. His head turns slightly to the left—a brief perusal of his surroundings.

Miss Millie, bless her heart, shuffles forward. Terror has bleached her face white. "My lord?"

The sucking void that is his hood opening shifts in her direction. He lifts his hand. Someone gasps.

But he only pushes back his hood with a gloved hand, revealing a countenance of such agonizing beauty that I can only look at him for so long before I'm forced to turn away. And yet, only seconds pass before my attention returns, drawn by some unnamed compulsion to study him in greater detail.

His face appears to have been hewn from alabaster. Low lamplight illuminates the smooth plane of his forehead, his angled cheekbones, that straight nose, the space beneath his cut-glass jaw darkened by shadow. And his mouth . . . well. I've yet to see a more feminine mouth on a man. The coal shade of his hair drinks in the light where it's pulled into a short tail at the back of his neck. His eyes, the wintery, lambent blue of glacial ice, glow with penetrating intensity.

My hand clenches around one of the serrated knives piled on the small side table where the water pitchers rest. I dare not breathe. I'm not sure I can, given the circumstances. A stillness like agitation swathes the room.

The Frost King is the most beautiful thing I have ever laid eyes on, and the most wretched. I was only fifteen when Elora and I, newly orphaned after our parents died from starvation, learned the true weight of loneliness, those frightening years stretched before us in an unending black road. It was then I took up the bow. It was then I slaughtered the darkwalkers so Elora could sleep with death clear from her conscience. It takes everything in me not to drive this blade into his heart where I stand. Assuming he has one.

Another step farther into the room, and the women scramble to their feet. The Frost King has yet to speak. There is no need. He has the women's attention, and mine. We have prepared for this.

Judging by the cool disgust curling his upper lip, he is displeased by the lack of welcome. Tight black gloves encase his large hands in smooth leather. His wide shoulders stretch the heavy material of his cloak, which he removes to reveal a pressed tunic the color of a rain cloud, silver buttons stamping a line all the way up to where the collar strangles his neck. Beneath, he wears tight, charcoal breeches. Weathered boots cling to his calves. A dagger hangs from his waist.

My attention drifts to his right hand. It's curved around the haft of a spear with a stone point. I'm positive he wasn't holding that a moment ago. When it vanishes a second later, a few of the women sigh in relief.

Releasing my grip on the knife, I let the utensil drop onto the ground.

The clatter startles Miss Millie into action. She takes his cloak, hangs it on a peg beside the door, then pulls out a chair at the head of the table. The legs scrape against the floor, and the Frost King sits.

The women sit as well.

"Welcome to Edgewood, my lord," Miss Millie offers in a frail tone. Her attention flits to the woman sitting on his immediate left—her daughter. The women drew sticks to determine which unlucky souls sat closest to him during the meal. Elora, thankfully, is at the far end of the table.

"We hope you enjoy the meal we've prepared for you." The king scans the fare, unimpressed. "Our harvest has been lean in recent years, unfortunately."

What she means is *nonexistent.*

"The soup is one of our specialties—"

He holds up a hand in silence, and Miss Millie's voice peters out, the skin of her jowls wobbling as she swallows. And that, he decides, is that.

It is the longest, most painful dinner in existence. No one speaks.

The women I can understand. No one wishes to draw the king's attention. But our guest has no excuse. Can't he see how we have given him what little food we can provide? And not even a word of thanks?

Prick.

Elora barely touches her food. She hunches over her plate in an attempt to make herself smaller—my recommendation—but she does not escape the Frost King's notice. For that is where his gaze alights, time and again.

Nausea twists my gut into knots. My nerves are in a state of ruin. There is nothing I can do, absolutely nothing. When the pressure on my chest threatens to squash my lungs, I retreat to the kitchen, fumble for the flask tucked into my waistband, and take a healthy swallow. My eyes sting from the burn that feels like deliverance, like salvation. We should have run when we had the chance. It's too late now.

As the dinner crawls by, I pour the wine. The women guzzle it down, glass after glass after glass, red droplets slicking their bloodless lips, cheeks stained with flush. My throat begins to ache with its violent craving. Less than halfway through the meal and my flask is already empty.

At one point, I'm sent to retrieve more wine from the cool underground cellar. I use the brief reprieve to just . . . sit. Think. I'm even desperate enough to send off a short prayer. The dusty bottles are arranged in neat rows. How long have they been sitting here? Centuries? This wine is wasted on the Frost King. These should be used for celebration, a wedding or birth. Not a funeral dressed as a party.

"Wren." Miss Millie's stocking-clad legs appear atop the stairs. "What is taking so long?"

"Coming."

Her footsteps fade.

I return to the meeting hall to refill drinks. The Frost King barely touches his wine. It's just as well. I have absolutely zero desire to serve him in any way, shape, or form, unless it's to show him the door.

Miss Millie doesn't share the sentiment. "My lord, is the wine not to your liking?" The concern in her voice makes me want to vomit. I'm sure she believes if she treats him kindly, he'll pass over her daughter for another.

In answer, he brings the deep red liquid to his mouth and drains the glass. His eyes flare dully above its rim. It is as though his pupils hold a remnant of light, rather than light itself.

That leaves me to see to his needs. Moving to the Frost King's side, I begin refilling his glass. In the process, our arms accidentally collide, and the wine slops onto his lap.

Blood turns to ice in my veins.

The Frost King's gaze is a slow, crawling thing that drags from the spreading stain on his tunic to the pitcher I still hold, before eventually locking onto my face. His pale blue eyes exude a devouring, lifeless cold that creeps across my puckered skin. The scar tissue has lost sensation, but I swear it prickles then, as though his attention is a physical touch.

"Apologize to the king!" Miss Millie demands shrilly.

What is a little wine compared to the loss of a life?

No, I think I will keep my apology to myself. I can't imagine it's worth much to him anyway. "Only if he apologizes for stealing our women."

Someone gasps. It sounds like Elora. The king studies me as he would a small animal, but I am no prey.

"My lord, I apologize for her absolutely *wretched* behavior—"

He lifts one long-fingered hand. Miss Millie falls silent, the pallor of her skin like that of a fish's belly.

"What is your name?" Quiet.

The title he bears extends to his voice as well. It is low, deep, yet riddled with a chilling lack of emotion.

At my answering silence, a few of the women shift uncomfortably in their chairs. The walls creak in the wintry gales. The temperature continues to plummet despite the fire. The North Wind may be a god, but I will not break. If nothing else, I have my pride.

"I see." He taps a fingertip against the table. The woman to his immediate right twitches.

"Wren, my lord. Her name is Wren!"

The outburst comes from Elora. She leans forward in her chair, fingers gripping the arms, distraught.

My teeth click together in frustration even as my stomach hollows out. This is exactly what I was afraid of: Elora and her soft heart. If I hadn't let my emotions cloud my judgment, this could have been prevented.

"Wren," he says. Never have I heard so elegant a word. "Like the songbird."

There are no more songbirds in the Gray. They all perished or flew elsewhere.

After another lingering study of my face, his attention shifts to Elora. I want to claw his eyes out from how he drinks her in. "There is a certain likeness to your features."

"Yes, my lord." Elora bows her head in a gesture of respect. I could slap her for it. "We are sisters. Identical twins. I am Elora, and that is Wren."

A slight, peculiar tilt to his head as he compares us. I am sure he finds me lacking, in more ways than one.

"Stand up," he demands.

Elora pushes back her chair when my voice whips out. "Sit."

She stills, her hands curled around the edge of the table. Her attention flits from me to the Frost King and back. Meanwhile, Miss Millie appears on the verge of passing out.

An unbalanced light flickers in his narrow pupils, like a candle wavering in darkness. He straightens in one fluid motion, startling me. I imagine no one has challenged his word before. No one has been foolish enough to try.

"Come," he says in a voice like thunder, and Elora shuffles toward him, meek and spineless. The sight of her defeat rips through me, because how dare he? We are not chattel. We are people with beating hearts in our chests and breath in our lungs and lives we've managed to carve from this frozen existence he has cast upon us like a curse.

As Elora stops in front of him, he lifts her chin with a finger and says, "You, Elora of Edgewood, have been chosen, and you will serve me until the end of your days."

# CHAPTER

## 3

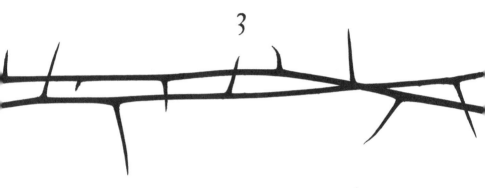

At once, I storm across the room and shove Elora behind me. "You can't have her." I am falling, I am plummeting at alarming speed, and there is no bottom, and still I fall.

Some part of me knew this would happen. My sister is the epitome of life, and the Frost King has little of it in his realm. I'd managed to convince myself there was a more suitable candidate, perhaps Palomina, with her doe eyes and gap-toothed smile and skill with a needle. Or Bryn, quiet and demure, whose laughter can lighten the most dour of situations. But no. He was always going to choose Elora, the fairest of them all.

The king surveys me as though I am a fly that has yet to be swatted. "You have no choice over the matter. She is my prize. She comes with me."

"She goes nowhere."

The other women, though clearly relieved they weren't selected, shrink further into their chairs as the conflict sharpens to a point. The air crackles, and for a moment, I swear something black slithers across the king's gaze, momentarily blotting out the slender blue rings.

"Wren." Elora touches my lower back. "It's all right."

"No." My voice cracks. "Choose someone else."

The Frost King's expression darkens. His height seems to expand, despite not having moved. Instinct screams I make myself smaller, less of a threat. A harsh gust slams open the window shutters, and the smell of cypress engulfs the space, chasing out the warmth. I blink stupidly. His spear has made a reappearance. Its stone tip thrusts upward, the butt of the haft resting against the bowed floorboards.

"Take care, mortal," he warns softly, "or your insolence will bring misfortune upon this town. I have chosen. My mind will not be changed. Now stand aside."

The refusal tries to cram itself back down my throat. I force it out. "No."

His mien remains a slate of blank emotion. The spear, however, begins to hum, the point brightening with an eerie glow. Elora retreats a few paces behind me. What power resides in that weapon? What ruin will he render should I continue to deny him?

"For every minute you delay my departure," he says, "one of these women will die."

He reaches for Miss Millie's daughter, who screams, attempting to lunge over her chair, but his fingers curl into the collar of her gown, and he drags her backward over the table. Food and wine smear the fabric of her dress. The chair crashes onto its side. Dishware slides off the table's edge, shattering.

"Please," Miss Millie screeches. Her eyes roll with the terror of the hunted. "Please, not her! Please." That plea joins the rising shouts. Through the now-open windows, I spot the townsfolk, their pale, ghostly faces as they witness the young woman struggling desperately to free herself from her captor's grip. She writhes, managing to wrench free, yet he catches her around the arm a moment later.

Using her momentum, the king swings her toward his front, lifting the spear with his other hand. Its point blazes with a pearly light.

"Stop!" Elora's voice, breathless with terror. She shoves around me. "Don't hurt her. I'll come with you." Her wide, dark eyes meet mine. She has made her decision, and silently pleads that I do not stand in her way. My chest caves.

The Frost King glances at my sister, then at me. "You will come quietly?" The question is for Elora, but his gaze never leaves my face.

"Yes. Just don't hurt anyone." To her credit, she manages to speak all this without stumbling over her own tongue.

"Very well." He releases Miss Millie's daughter, who falls in a heap onto the floor. Miss Millie rushes forward, taking her daughter into her arms, sobbing hysterically.

The Frost King offers his hand, palm out. "Come."

Shaking, Elora places her hand in his. He begins drawing her toward the door.

One moment, I am calm. The next, I am consumed by a hatred so devouring, it shreds through the remainder of my self-control. I move before I'm aware of it, snagging a knife from the floor, my revulsion toward this creature channeled into the single arcing motion of a knife spearing toward the king's unprotected side. The blade plunges into his lower abdomen.

A shared gasp rings out.

Warm liquid pours onto my hand. It gleams black in the low light, and patters onto the floor in fat droplets that spread through the cracks.

What have I done?

Everything fades but the Frost King. The collective angles that shape his face come into sharper focus. He stares at me like . . . well. Like he's never experienced anything like this before. He came here under the pretense of being fed, catered to, leaving with his prize, and instead, someone stabbed him with a dinner knife, of all things.

My fingers twitch around the wooden handle. He is the Frost King, the North Wind, whose power drags winter onto the land, but I'm surprised by the heat rolling off him in waves of sharp, unadulterated fury.

His fingers curl around mine, breaking the direction of my thoughts. Cool black leather presses against my feverish skin as he guides the knife from his body, his taciturn gaze unyielding, and forces my grip open so the weapon clatters onto the ground. In seconds, the blood clots. The skin knits together. A wound, fully healed.

The king didn't flinch when the knife entered his body. He didn't react *at all*. Because he expected retaliation? Because he can't feel pain?

The stillness is sundered by a punishing wind, a great clap of thunder, and somehow a blizzard beats inside these walls. The sound is so excruciating I clap my hands over my ears, screaming. When the king next speaks, his voice floods my mind with its indomitable presence. "Let me remind you, mortal. I am a god. I *cannot* die." He lets that knowledge settle. "But your sister surely can."

Drawing his spear, he yanks Elora back by her braid, baring the curve of her throat, the skin pale and unmarred and so thin it reveals the translucent blue veins beneath.

"Wait!"

Elora trembles. My knees knock together as the wind fades to a lull. One of the women has fainted. The ability to speak without gasping eludes me.

"Please," I say, the word like gorge in my throat. "Please don't hurt her. Take me instead."

The edges of his mouth curve slightly, and I flinch at the underlying violence there. "You are perhaps the last woman I would ever take, for you are neither beautiful nor obedient."

Since I have heard it all before, it doesn't stop me from shuffling forward on leaden feet. "Tell me what to do. Tell me how to make amends."

The Frost King considers me, unruffled and unmoved. I have made a mess of this evening, but if there's a chance I can make it right—

"Kneel."

My lips pinch. "Excuse me?"

"You ask for my forgiveness? Kneel. Demonstrate your remorse to me."

I look to Elora. My throat burns from how heavily I drag in air. Tangled strands of her hair dangle from the king's gloved hand, like fragments of a broken spider web.

"Wren," Elora whispers, tears tracking down her cheeks.

My sister's plea causes an instantaneous and almost violent reaction in me. The Frost King orders me to kneel, so I do. My knees knock against the floor. My head hangs. Insurmountable rage ignites my skin to a dull, spreading flush that warms me from belly to face. For Elora. No one else.

For a time, all is quiet. One of the women sniffles in an attempt to muffle her sob.

"Go," he hisses, shoving Elora toward the door, "before I change my mind. I depart within the hour. I expect her back by then."

We flee as if the gods themselves have lit a fire beneath our heels. Wind slices my exposed skin as I haul Elora through the snow toward our lonely cottage. The sky was clear hours ago, but a storm has rolled in and squats over Edgewood as though in punishment.

Once inside, I drag her toward the fire, my fingers digging into her frozen flesh hard enough to bruise. Quickly, I grab some cut logs from the dwindling stack outside, toss them onto the smoldering coals, and poke them until they catch, the fire climbing to a roar. "Elora." I give her a shake. Shock has whitened her lips. "Look at me." When there is no change in expression, I slap her across the cheek.

That snaps her free of the stupor. "Wren." Shock gives way to confusion and, lastly, horror. It's terrible to watch.

Deep in my heart, I knew this would come to pass. Elora hadn't thought beyond this night, never contemplated the worst possible outcome, but I did. I asked myself if the Frost King arrived and *did* choose my sister as his captive, what would I do?

Anything. I would do anything.

Grabbing her hand, I lead her into the kitchen. She moves woodenly. It's as though a part of her has already disappeared beyond the Shade.

Gently, I lower her into a chair and grab the spare coat, draping it across her shoulders. We left so quickly we didn't bother to grab our outerwear from the meeting hall. Her dark eyes stare straight through me. They are like shuttered windows, no flame to light them.

While Elora sits, I boil water and pull dried lavender from our pantry, along with a fine powder called maniwort. Once the water boils, I steep the herb and open the jar of powder. A small dose will send someone to sleep for an hour, a large dose, half the day.

A large spoonful it is.

Whatever horrors await in the Deadlands, Elora will not witness them. She is too soft a thing. Our home, the townsfolk, they are everything to her. Elora dreams of marrying a man she loves, tending a home, raising children. To snatch that opportunity would surely kill her.

But me? No one will care if I'm gone. And maybe it's better this way. Elora can be free of the sister who is too weak to overcome this toxic addiction. She can be free of the sister whose vomit often splatters the floorboards, forcing her to clean up yet another one of my messes after a night of binge-drinking. She can be free of a sister whose days are marked by that sweet haze, whose breath is never clean, and whose usefulness seems to wane in the passing years. I have seen the shame on her face, the resentment, the disgust. This choice is for the best.

"Drink." I pass the mug into her trembling hands.

She takes a swallow, wrinkles her nose, and downs the rest.

Beyond the cottage walls, the wind moans, thumps against the roof. There is not much time to set things right, but there is enough.

Eventually, clarity returns to her gaze. "Wren, I don't know what to do. He— I don't want to go." She shakes so severely the mug slips from her grip and shatters at her feet. "I should have listened to you. I'm so sorry." Her face folds and a sob rips from her throat. "It's too late now. It's too late."

My own eyes flood with the hot, stinging sensation. It's been years since I've cried. Not since our parents passed. I grip her hand tightly in mine. Her skin is like ice.

Air wheezes from her lungs. She stares straight ahead, a few tears clinging to her eyelashes. "Did you see him? He was so callous at that dinner. His eyes were like . . . like pits."

Yes, they were. Nothing but cold, dark eternity. Everything lives and everything dies, except for a god.

Another sniffle. "He didn't even thank Miss Millie for the food." She sounds appalled over this.

"Horrible dinner guest," I agree.

"I can't believe you stabbed him."

"The man is an absolute prick. He deserved it."

Elora snorts, her eyelids beginning to droop. "You always were far more reckless than I."

That stings. Maybe my actions had been reckless, but it was only to protect her.

Clear fluid drips from her nose. Kneeling in front of her, I use an old cloth to wipe her face, as I did when we were children. In a hoarse voice, she wonders, "What's going to happen to me?"

I do not want to lie to her, but I cannot reveal my intention. Elora must live, and live freely. "Nothing will happen to you," I soothe as her chin dips toward her chest. "I swear it."

"Don't leave me here alone. Stay . . . until it's time."

"You're not alone, Elora." Though I will be gone, the townsfolk will make sure she is cared for.

"Promise me," she whispers.

Somehow, I manage to choke out, "I promise."

In moments, she's asleep.

I catch my sister as she slumps forward, hefting her into my arms. From there, it's a short distance to the bed we have shared all our lives. The shape of her limp form sits as a darker shadow against the collective dim. She is alive. She is safe. By the time she wakes, I will be long gone. My only regret is that I will be unable to say a proper goodbye.

"I love you," I whisper into the half-dark, brushing a kiss across her cheek. "And I'm sorry."

Working quickly, I remove the coat from around her shoulders, as well as her dress. I pile the blankets atop her body and stoke the fire until it chases back the chill. Then I remove my own clothing, don the dress Elora wore, and wrap a scarf across the lower half of my face so it conceals everything but my eyes, including my scar. The Frost King will never be able to tell the difference, as long as I'm able to keep my temper in check and my mouth shut.

Our bureau contains four drawers—the top two for Elora, the bottom two for me. One holds my clothes, the other my possessions. I've two daggers, one of which I slip into an arm sheath, the second one tucked snugly against the small of my back. The salt satchel goes around my waist. My flask, tucked into my coat pocket. My bow I'll leave behind. Too unwieldy, and Elora will need it more than I do, despite her lack of skill with a bow. Maybe she will find some other use for it. Wood for the fire, perhaps. I never did fix our broken ax.

Rising from my crouch, I move toward the front door. After one last glance at my sister, I step out into the cold.

Wrapped tightly in my coat, I return to the meeting hall where the king and his horse await. Fresh snow blown in with the wind crunches beneath my boots, frost clinging to the thick fur encasing my calves. The Frost King stands by his steed, which, upon further inspection, is not a horse at all. I halt in place.

The beast lacks skin or fur. It appears as a semi-translucent, equine-shaped shadow with insides like shifting dark clouds, a tapered snout, an arched neck, holes for eyes that flare with a smoldering glow.

"Darkwalker," I whisper, and the sound catches fire, leaping through the gathered crowd. The beast tosses its head, pinning me with one pitted eye. It stamps one of its forelegs, and despite the transparent quality to its form, the knock of its hoof against the stone rings out clearly. Unconsciously, I reach for my salt satchel.

"It is a waste of salt," informs the king, gripping the reins in one hand. Though I do not speak the question aloud, he elaborates, "Phaethon is under my protection and cannot be harmed."

That must be how the creature was able to pass inside the ring of salt encircling the town. The odd thing is, the darkwalker takes the shape of a horse rather than the usual grotesque, misshapen appearance.

Its nostrils flare. They can so easily scent fear. The massive beast shifts to the right, sending anyone in the vicinity scrambling backward.

The Frost King takes in my hunched appearance with all the emotion of a hairpin. Here, in the dark and the cold, he is absolutely in his element.

"I'd like to say my goodbyes," I tell him in a noncombative tone, and he nods.

I go to Miss Millie, gather her in my arms. "I'm sorry," I whisper into her ear, and she stiffens upon realizing I am not Elora. "I hope your daughter is well. Be safe. Take care of my sister for me."

She nods, and I pull away.

I've no one else to say farewell to. I haven't any friends, only acquaintances. Elora has friends, but they are noticeably scarce at present. Not that I blame them, but it is a reminder of why I keep to myself. Still, I will miss this town. My throat swells with the painful emotion of leaving a place I have lived for the last twenty-three years. My entire life exists inside this crumbling wall and the surrounding lands. Edgewood is full of hard, toiling memories, but they are mine.

The king tosses me into the saddle as if I weigh nothing. When he settles behind me, the motion drags me back against his chest, my backside cradled by his hips. I stiffen, leaning forward in an attempt to separate our bodies.

He nudges the beast into a walk. The townsfolk watch our departure in silence. After passing the wall, Edgewood and its thatched rooftops vanish from view. And that's the last I'll ever see of my home. Gone, just like that.

We travel north. Mile after mile, rocked side to side in the saddle, we cut through a land steeped in silence. I don't speak. Neither does my captor. I'm afraid if I open my mouth, I'll retch all over my lap. If I'm to die, I'd like to do so with dignity.

After crossing yet another frozen stream, the Frost King tugs on the reins, and his beast slows as we break free of the forest.

The Shade.

The glittering line of the Les curves ahead: the outermost boundary of the Deadlands. Atop the frozen river squats an opaque veil, well over a hundred feet tall, which follows the shape of the river in either direction, concealing sight beyond.

A pulse ripples through the barrier as though a heart beats within. I can be brave, but only for so long. The last time I set eyes on the Shade, I was twelve, foolish and proud, unwilling to step down from a dare given by one of the village boys. This was as far as I got before terror sent me fleeing back to town. The substance shifts like drenched cloth in the breeze. The sight is so eerie it pricks my skin.

"How is this to go?" I ask in what I hope is my sister's gentle tone. The words themselves taste of grit. "If it's a sacrifice you want, make it quick. I'd like to think you were a man of mercy."

"I am no man." There's a pause, during which my pulse accelerates. "Sacrifice?"

As if he doesn't know. "What will it be? Will you shoot me through the eye? Poison?" My breath wavers on an exhale. Whatever pain I am to suffer through, it can't last long.

Again, a pause, yet I sense the king's deepening confusion at my back. "Your words are unclear to me."

Turning in the saddle, I'm given a partial glimpse of the king's face, which is shadowed by the cowl of his hood. His beast paws at the snow. "Everyone in the Gray knows you sacrifice our women. Only, we don't know how it's done. Or why."

Flat eyes regard me coolly. "Do you think I would travel all this way to kill a worthless mortal, whose life will surely end sooner than not?"

My, how the Frost King loves his insults. Unfortunately, I'm impersonating Elora, and Elora wouldn't punch the king in the mouth. "If I'm not your sacrifice, then why am I here?" Is it possible something worse awaits me in the Deadlands?

"It's your blood I need, not your death. Your oath, not your lies. In one day's time, we will be wed."

# CHAPTER

## 4

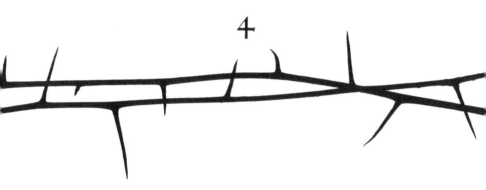

*Wed?*

I'm sure I misheard him.

No, I'm absolutely certain I misheard him. That is not what the stories claim. The North Wind takes a woman captive across the Shade. He takes her heart, her liver, her bones. He inflicts terrible pain, unspeakable pain, upon his victim. There are no stories about being wed.

Horror twitches through me. "You're joking."

He nudges his mount forward. The beast snorts, and its breath steams against the chill air. Somehow, despite the insubstantial appearance of the darkwalker, it bears weight, hoofprints trailing back to the forest's edge. "I am not."

"You're telling me every woman taken captive was made your wife?"

"No."

"So you do sacrifice our women!"

"I did once, but no longer."

He speaks stiffly, as though it pains him to speak so many words in one breath.

In Edgewood, matrimony bears certain expectations. A woman must, above all else, be obedient. A woman must place her husband's comfort above her own. A woman must accept any punishment received. If I had a choice between marrying the Frost King and being sacrificed . . . I think I would choose sacrifice.

"I'm not marrying you." The charade peels away. I'm supposed to be Elora. Meek, demure, obedient Elora, but that was when I believed to be walking toward my death, not a life of imprisonment.

He tugs the reins, maneuvering the beast toward a bend in the river. "You don't have a choice."

Choice.

Wed . . . or sacrifice?

With every approaching step, my freedom slips farther from reach. The Shade looms, a stretch of darkness so potent I am convinced it birthed the world. It clots like blood at the corners of my vision, and the terror rises, hooking claws into my soft innards. There is screaming on the wind.

My elbow snaps back into the Frost King's stomach, a soft *oof* expelling as my unexpected blow knocks him off balance, allowing me to slide free of the saddle. As soon as my feet hit the frozen ground, I bolt.

This near the Shade, the trees crumple and spiral into grotesque shapes, blackened leaves clinging stubbornly to the boughs. Rot and decay seep into the air, and my gut lurches as I pass what I believe is a pile of bones. I'll never be able to outrun the king's mount, but I can attempt to slow it down. The stand of dead, broken foliage I charge through is too dense for it to pass through. It will have to find another way around.

My skin tightens, my legs strain, my heart careens as my boots strike earth. I will not go quietly. I will not go at all. If I can lose the king and find shelter, maybe a cave or an abandoned burrow . . .

The ground slopes steeply. Slipping, skittering down the icy ground, into a valley where boulders have tumbled from an old landslide. I leap from rock to rock, scrambling up the incline.

A mighty roar ruptures the eerie silence of the wood.

Springing over protruding roots, clambering over fallen trees—on and on and on. I'm certain I've lost him when hooves pound suddenly to my right. My head whips around. He breaks from the trees, bearing down on me, and I have never witnessed a more terrifying sight as I do now, looking upon those pale features frozen over with an inhuman blankness.

The moment his hand begins to close on my hood, I drop and curl over my knees. Air stirs overhead: the tips of his fingers skimming the crown of my skull. He sits too high in the saddle to reach me. It is the smallest of miracles.

The Frost King curses, but there's too much momentum for him to slow. He's past, and I'm up, switching direction as he tries to pivot the darkwalker in the dense brush.

The uneven ground poses a threat to his mount, so I keep to the slopes and crags, scrambling up and down and toeing perilous drops to maintain a lead. When I reach the next valley, I follow it south, clambering over the boulders as often as I can so as to not leave any tracks. Night makes traveling treacherous, but I'll risk a sprained ankle so long as I'm out of reach. The moon provides patched light in darkness as I continually scan my surroundings.

A hollow at the base of a fallen tree catches my eye. Adequate. A short crawl on hands and knees, down into the cramped, darkened opening. There, I curl into a ball, and I wait.

Hoofbeats ring atop the frozen earth. The darkwalker stamps the ground right over my head, then stops. The king has pulled his mount to a halt.

I cover my mouth to muffle the coarseness of my breathing. My body shakes so hard I'm convinced my bones will rattle apart. As long as I'm quiet, I will be safe. I'm tucked deeply enough in the burrow that I'm hidden. Unless the king physically crawls into the tunnel, he can't see me.

He dismounts. Snow crunches beneath his boots.

My tracks are nonexistent. I made sure of it. I'm not sure how skilled of a tracker the king is, but my assumption is not very skilled. Granted, I know nothing of the king. Could his powers somehow flush me out of hiding?

The silence stretches before he moves off with a muttered, "Damn."

Once the hoofbeats subside, I slump against the wall at my back, teeth chattering. Instinct deems I run, but I force myself to remain in place until I'm certain he won't return.

It doesn't take long for my body to cool, the chill to invade. Admittedly, I didn't think this through. Edgewood calls to me. Elora calls to me. But I cannot go back. If I flee, I risk the Frost King returning to Edgewood for another woman, in which case he might choose Elora—the real Elora. A moment of fear could have ruined everything. So where does that leave me?

*It's your blood I need, not your death.*

It is the only clue to my future. I will not die on this day. Instead, I am to become the North Wind's prisoner, bound to the Deadlands until . . . what? I die of natural causes? Why does he need my blood? How much? And what are the parameters of my captivity? All things I should consider before making my next move. I have time. I'll find a way to change my doom. Until then, if that is to be my fate, then so be it. I'll need to return to the river.

My stiff muscles throb as I crawl from the burrow and pick my way around the thickest of the snow mounds. Every so often, I stop to listen. No sound but the wind.

I've barely gone half a mile when I spot the darkwalker and its rider through the trees. The king eliminates the distance between us with every eating stride. My legs tremble with fatigue. I've exhausted what little energy I have. But I have decided not to run.

I kneel. Bow my head. He pulls his mount to a halt a few paces away.

The voice that drifts from behind the scarf concealing my face is Elora's, not mine. "I apologize, my lord. I was frightened. It is a difficult thing, leaving one's family." Taking a breath, I lift my gaze. "But I am ready now. I can be brave."

His narrowed eyes rake my hunched form. I drop my gaze to the ground. It's what Elora would do. And she would wait, so I do as well. I'm surprised that, instead of stabbing me in the back, he offers a hand, helping me into the saddle, and wheels us in the opposite direction. Soon, we break from the forest where the Shade looms.

The Les is poured wide and frozen in the flat plain before me, with the protruding earth crowned at its back. When someone dies, their spirit is expelled from their body. It then passes through the Shade via the Les to await Judgment. But I am very much alive. So what does this mean for me?

The pit in my stomach twists as he sends his beast to the river's edge. Ice has crept onto the curved, shallow banks, glittering and white, and the water's surface gleams like glass under moonlight. Once he dismounts, he pulls me from the saddle as well.

"This is the part where you drown me, right?" I'm still not entirely convinced his marriage comment was genuine.

He flicks me a wordless glance, as if he can't bring himself to answer such a ridiculous question.

Bending a knee, he touches the ice with the tips of his fingers, and I watch in marvel as it thaws, hissing and spitting and bounding downstream.

A small boat emerges from the barrier, the bow pointed, the hull curved and full. I frown as the current carries the bobbing vessel to where we stand. "I thought we were riding your . . . horse?" If an equine-shaped darkwalker can be considered such a thing.

"Every spirit must enter the Deadlands via the Les. That includes you. Phaethon will pass through without us."

"But I'm not a spirit."

"Do you want to be?"

My, my, my. How quickly his patience frays. "Is that a threat?" He doesn't respond, which is perfectly fine, as I didn't expect him to anyway.

Water laps against the wooden hull. It's small, barely large enough for two people, and rocks from side to side. "I can't swim."

"Unless you plan on jumping into the water, you need not worry."

As a matter of fact, I was considering it. It might be a preferable way to go.

Brushing past him, I climb into the vessel and clutch the raised edges as he follows, the hull tipping sharply to the right. I gasp, grabbing the opposite edge, but then the boat levels out. Still, my heart pounds.

The Frost King is so large the only available space for me is the narrow bow, unless I want to spend this trip pressed against him. My knees dig into the curved wood, and I remember something I read in a book once.

"Isn't there supposed to be a giant, three-headed dog somewhere?"

He appraises me as though I've officially gone mad. Maybe I have.

"You should not believe everything you hear," says the king, pushing back his hood. "There is no such creature." A momentary pause. "When we pass through the Shade, you'll likely experience a range of sensations like hunger, fear, grief. Do not believe the things you feel. It is merely the last opportunity for the souls leaving the realm of the living to remember what it felt like to be human."

He couldn't be more wrong. I am hungry. I am grieving. But I nod, because what else can I do? Ask him for comfort?

The Frost King touches the water again, and the current miraculously changes direction, pulling us upstream.

The fabric pulses like a heartbeat, hungry and sinister, as we draw nearer to it. I am brave. I am *brave*, damn it.

Darkness. A void. An ageless, formless shroud. The Shade is alive, and I feel as though I'm drowning. Cool substance slides over me. It is twitching, burrowing, stinging, burning—

My mouth opens on a scream that never comes.

Teeth, tongue, throat—all coated in an oily black substance that seeps through my body. Agony flares through my arms, the base of my neck, my lower spine. Then it is gone. Emotions in their cruelest forms barrel through me. Anguish, grief, fear, and hunger, mindless hunger. My stomach is a hollow gourd, cramping so fiercely I curl up on the bottom of the boat, waiting for it to end.

Yet there is no reprieve. I am nothing but skin. I am disintegrating. I am crying out in my soul, trying to take a breath and confused as to why my sadness runs so deep. I am heavy. I am aggrieved. My chest clots with the feeling. Another lash of pain strikes my spine, and I flinch, releasing a cry that never reaches completion.

I feel the lapping water through the curved hull. And I can't help but wonder what would happen were this flimsy wood to suddenly snap. Already, the sound is in my ears. The boat shudders, and I reach out my hand. Planks of wood. Fabric stretched over warm skin. My hand fists around the material—an anchor.

"What's happening to me?" I whisper. My eyes are open, but all I see is black, black, black.

A voice drifts above me, low and flat and distant. "It's not real."

What's not real? The boat? The river?

Beneath me, the water sings.

If I focus on the trilling pitch, the void around me begins to retreat. The Frost King shimmers into existence at my side. I realize I grip a handful of his breeches and promptly let go. Beyond the vessel, the river gleams a stunning turquoise, the current bending far into the distance with strips of darker blue. *Come*, it whispers. *Let me offer you sanctuary from the darkness.*

Strong fingers lock around my wrist. "Don't touch the water!" he snaps.

I glance at him over my shoulder from where I lean over the boat, panting. His face drifts in and out of focus, though the brightness of his eyes is strangely grounding. My mind feels as though it's being stretched in five directions at once. "Why? You did."

"The Les would not affect you were you to touch it, but we are now traveling via Mnemenos—the River of Forgetting. If even a drop splashes your skin, you will lose all sense of self."

It takes a moment for his words to penetrate. That obdurate focus remains riveted on me. "I wouldn't remember who I am?"

"No."

My left hand tightens around the edge of the hull. The water shifts hues once again, an aqua so brilliant it hurts my eyes. Clear enough for a swim. Clear enough to drink. "Pull me back," I say as the crooning grows louder. "Hurry!"

A hard tug topples me onto my backside, the Frost King's unexpected warmth at my spine. I'm shaking so intensely my teeth chatter. To lose all sense of self—nothing could be more absolute. This place must know I am not dead. Not yet.

The darkness lifts. At last, the Shade is behind us, and I can see. The land is carved from rock and ice, puddled in watery moonlight. A single elm tree curves over the river to my right, but it is concealed by something resembling fog. It is the only living thing. Whatever color once existed here has been leached away. The rest is but gray, starving earth.

Wooden shards push upward from the ground like broken teeth, sparsely scattered. It is my belief they were once trees. The flat land rises in the distance, leading to an enormous citadel chipped from a granite rockface, shielded behind a dense wall of naked, sentinel-like trees. Turrets and ramparts and balconies and stacked halls of black stone pierce the roof of the world, a messy tear in otherwise smooth midnight fabric. No stars wink overhead. No clouds. Just blank canvas.

The boat knocks against the bank. Once we disembark, the river refreezes, and the beast he calls Phaethon reappears. The remainder of the journey is spent in the saddle. By the time we emerge from the wall of surrounding trees, my fingers are practically frozen in my gloves.

I have never felt so small as I do now, swamped in the shadow of a towering stone wall, the mammoth, iron gates barring our entry, the ends like teeth. The gates open with a harsh shriek, and we trot through, snow exchanged for a massive courtyard of gray stone. There are stables to the right, at least ten times the size of my cottage. A fortress of this magnitude, I would expect more activity, but there is not a soul in sight.

The king directs the beast up a set of stairs leading to twin doors of oak. Handles of intricate, twisted metal shine dully. He dismounts, as do I.

"Come," he says, as if I am a dog called to heel. My teeth grind together from the effort it takes to hold myself back from doing something foolish, like stabbing him again. The scarf concealing my face is all that stands between the king and my secret.

The handles twist of their own accord. The North Wind's power, it seems, can shape the air at will, and he uses that ability to push open the doors. A darkened mouth, the sprawling interior of the fortress, and then I am inside the beast's throat, the jaws snapping at my back.

Blood thunders in my ears. It takes a few moments for my vision to adjust to the vast entrance hall. The inside of the citadel is, if possible, drearier than the surrounding landscape.

It's dark, oppressively so. Heavy curtains cloak the windows. The air pulses with the saturation of the king's power. It tickles the back of my throat and tightens my skin. It tastes, dare I say, sweet, yet it moves with lethargy for how contained it has been. Watery lamplight offers little reprieve from the shadows.

I was so focused on doing whatever was necessary to spare Elora from this fate that I never thought of where the Frost King dwelled. This is where I must live? This oppressive, bleak, barren place?

He leads me down a passage to the left. Once my eyes adjust, I'm able to navigate without tripping over anything. What little furniture is present is covered with sheets that may have once been white, but that are now coated so thickly in dust they appear gray.

"Do you live here by yourself?" These deserted halls and abandoned rooms are but a shell. Had there once been life here, as there had once been green things?

"Yes," he responds without turning around, "though I have an extensive staff that cares for the upkeep of the citadel." We reach a wide staircase with a curved railing. Dust clouds the air as his boots make contact with the steps, my eyes watering in irritation. How can anyone live like this? And extensive staff? I've yet to spot another soul.

We reach a lengthy hallway on the third level, which leads us deeper into the shadowy interior. Doors upon doors line the walls. They are of variable height, width, material, and décor. Some handles are pure silver. Others are round knobs, caked in rust and appearing centuries old. One door with peeling white paint has a glass knob shaped like a diamond. Ten paces down, another is covered in small colored tiles in shades of yellow.

"What are all these doors for?" We pass one that is intricately carved plaster. Its neighbor is painted in blue and white stripes.

"They lead to other continents, other realms." The king sounds bored, or maybe that's his normal voice. "You will not find a way out of the Deadlands through the doors, so I wouldn't bother trying."

Hm. "So they're off limits?"

"No. You may explore what lies behind them, if you wish."

The idea intrigues me. I've never had the opportunity to travel. I've always been curious of what lies beyond the Gray.

After countless twists and turns, he stops at the end of a hall. Torches bleed shadow onto the blank stone wall. I hear what sounds like a scream, but it is faint, and perhaps I only imagine it.

"Orla will see to your needs," he says, producing a brass key and unlocking the door. "These are your chambers. Once you're settled, you may roam the citadel freely, but you may not pass beyond the wall."

"You don't trust me?" I already know the answer. I'm just curious of his reaction.

"No." His eyelashes lower, dark fringe upon pale cheekbones. "Run, and you will not get far. The forest dislikes my presence as it is. The citadel is the safest place for you."

He speaks as though the forest is sentient. I tuck that piece of information away to examine at a later time. "And where are your rooms?"

"They are located in the north wing, which you are not to enter."

He pushes open the door, but I hesitate in stepping across the threshold. "What happens after we are married? Am I expected to share your bed?" I'm not even sure he would be gentle in his bedding. I can't forget that slithering black emotion I glimpsed back at Edgewood, something feral lurking in the background.

"You will not need to worry about that. We keep separate chambers." With that, he nudges me through and snaps the door shut behind me. Soon enough, his footsteps die. I try the ornately carved handle. It doesn't budge.

I'm locked in.

"You bastard!" I scream, pounding the solid wood. My sedate mask slips free, and I grow wild, slamming my fist against the barrier.

Breathing hard, I step away to study the room. *My* room. Chambers, rather, with their vaulted ceilings and distant walls. Enormous, like the rest of this place. And cold. It is like a corpse, the ribs pried open, the cavern empty where a heart once thrummed. The furniture all but sags under the dripping opulence, heavy, solid-colored fabric in saturated reds and golds to match the bedding. Gilded mirrors. A gleaming four-poster bed frame, dark red wood. A fireplace with a wide, empty mouth. Rugs, so many rugs, exquisitely plush. Doorways that lead to interconnecting rooms.

A sudden wave of fatigue drags me down, and I sag onto the mattress, scrubbing my chapped hands down my equally chapped face. The chill air scratches at my skin, and I am alone.

I am alone.

My teeth begin to chatter. Curling my arms around my cramping stomach, I hunch forward, rocking back and forth, yet comfort evades me. I am a mortal woman in a dark god's realm. I have no family, no support. Am I to remain here for the next forty, fifty, sixty years? Is this how I will die? A prisoner, an animal in a cage? I'll never be able to return to my old life. Not while the Frost King lives.

The rocking motion slows, and I stare at the curtain-veiled windows with a frown. Something compels me to stride toward them and take the thick fabric in hand. With a mighty yank, I tear the curtains from their rods.

The sudden brightness makes me flinch. I assess the moonlit courtyard below with a critical eye, noting the stables to the left, the thick, towering wall, the black iron gates, the barren landscape beyond the enclosed grounds.

*Not while the Frost King lives.*

I came here expecting to die. But I have never been, and never will be, weak.

And so I return to books. I return to knowledge. I return to what I know, information gathered over the years, the tales and stories passed down.

This is what I know: the North Wind is a god. His power is limitless. He is immortal, can live forever, unless he is killed. But a god cannot die by a mortal-made weapon.

It's why the knife in his gut didn't kill him. Only a god-touched weapon has the power to end an immortal life, a tool created by the gods, for the gods. There is the spear he wields, its strange, alien power. The dagger sheathed at his hip.

He cannot know of the serpent he has released from its nest. For years I have suffered, my people have suffered, but now I am in the unique position to sever this snake at its head. If the Frost King dies, so does his eternal cold. So do the darkwalkers. So, too, does the Shade.

Only then will I be free.

~

Hours later, a tentative knock raps at the door. "My lady, are you decent?"

I'm lying on the massive bed. It's large enough to fit a family of four and is the most comfortable thing I've laid on in my life.

I hate it.

Pushing up onto my elbows, I take in my rough, dirty coat sullying the clean sheets and pillows. My stomach clenches in hunger. At least I had the decency to remove my boots before climbing into bed. Despite my exhaustion from the journey, I wasn't able to sleep.

"Yes," I call out, adjusting the scarf around my face.

The lock tumbles. A pleasantly plump woman steps into the room, dressed in a stained apron atop a simple woolen dress the color of heavy storm clouds, stockings, and black slippers. It's been years since I've seen anyone with extra padding on their frame. The body of one who does not know hunger. I can't help but stare.

Her eyes immediately lower in my presence, and she curtsies. Round face, wan skin, washed-out eyes, an upturned nose, and graying hair pulled into a bun.

"Hello, my lady. I'm Orla, your maid." She bustles to the fireplace to start a fire. Light chases back the insufferable darkness.

I scoot to the edge of the mattress and plant my feet on the ground. At least the rugs are warm. "What time is it?" Saliva cakes a ring around my lips. My throat is parched, crying out for a drink. I fumble for the flask tucked into my coat pocket and take a fortifying swallow. It is strange, but for once in my life, I am warm.

"It's almost noon. I must get you dressed and ready for the ceremony."

Dread, my old acquaintance, returns. Oh, how I hate it.

Moving to the window, I glance at the courtyard below, the

curtains I removed earlier piled at my feet. It's a long way down, with nothing to break my fall except the stone. I suppose there's little point in escaping if I'm going to break my legs in the process.

"How did you come to work for the Frost King?" I ask, turning back around.

"My lady. The ceremony."

Damn the ceremony. The king has an eternity. He can wait a few extra minutes. "While I understand we hardly know one another, I've just been stolen away from my home, forced to live out my life in the Deadlands, forced to marry the man whose cursed winter killed my parents, and I want answers. Now sit." With a little needling, I manage to maneuver her toward a vacant armchair, then take the opposite seat so we can converse properly.

Orla fiddles with the dirty apron tied around her waist. "Forgive me for saying so, but you are quite insistent."

"I'll take that as a compliment."

She sighs. "It was a long time ago. The Frost King made a deal with my town, Neumovos. Some of us were given the option to live in his fortress and work for him."

Option? Seems to me like she never had a choice in the matter. That a human establishment exists in the Deadlands is strange enough. I've never heard of it.

"Have you ever tried to escape?"

She struggles to neutralize her expression, as though not wanting to offend me. "Escape? N-no, my lady. Where would I go?"

That's an odd question, but I don't press her for more information. Anywhere but here, is my thought.

Orla glances at the dirt-smeared sheets atop the bed. "May I?" she asks.

I don't need someone cleaning up after me, but since she appears pained by the sight, I shrug. As the woman moves through a patch of weak sunlight lightening the floor, suddenly her figure fades. I'm staring *through* her body. She's completely transparent. Like a layer of fog.

"By the gods!" I shriek, leaping to my feet so quickly my foot catches on the leg of the chair and I crash into the floor. Pain ruptures where my elbow slams into the stone. "You're . . ."

"Dead, my lady?" Orla's kind face wrinkles in unhappiness. Resignation sits heavy upon her sloped back.

Perhaps that was a little insensitive. The woman can't help if she's dead. "Sorry. You startled me, is all." Pushing to my feet, I perch on the edge of the cushion, back straight, hands clenched around my knees. "I assumed—" No, that sounds insensitive as well. I will not make unnecessary enemies if I can help it, especially if I might need her help later on. She'll never speak freely if she believes my motives to be nefarious. And I'll never be able to gain her trust or learn the king's secrets, should that be the case.

"It's all right, my lady. The light shows what I am."

"A spirit."

"Yes. A specter."

"Are there others as well?"

"The entire staff. Everyone who hails from Neumovos."

"But—" Insensitivity aside, without questions, I'll receive no answers. "How was I able to touch you earlier?" I'd pushed her toward the chair. Orla's body had felt solid. The fabric of her clothes held texture and shape. Though, thinking back, I can't remember if I sensed any body heat.

She stays quiet for a noticeable length of time, her answer

curiously short. "Because we have not passed on yet, not truly." A harsh tug removes the sheets from the mattress. She bundles them up, drops them in a basket at her feet.

I see. Because without the staff, the Frost King's citadel and, to an extent, his realm, would not function.

"I'm going to ask you another question that is probably rude, but do you eat? Sleep?"

"Yes, I eat. Yes, I am able to sleep." If I'm not mistaken, her wan complexion fades, her outline growing faint. Now that I know she is incorporeal, it's impossible to overlook. If I stare closely enough, I can see the room's backdrop through her body. "But food tastes like ash in my mouth and my sleep is constantly plagued by nightmares. It is the same for every specter. As well, I am burdened with memories of my old life. Generally, when someone passes on, they shed those memories. The people from Neumovos do not."

Why make his staff suffer? Is there a reason for it? I mean to ask her to elaborate, but Orla grows twitchy. For now, I set aside my questions and steer the conversation to the matter at hand.

"Let's say I skip the wedding. Theoretically, of course. What then?"

"No, my lady, you *must* attend the ceremony." With a sound of distress, she returns to the fire, poking the logs with more force than is necessary. Stabbing them, to be certain. Flames lick the wood hungrily.

"What will he do?" I say, rising to my feet and planting my hands on my hips. "Lock me away in punishment?" He has already done that. He has taken me from what I love most.

Orla grows quiet. "No, my lady."

My gaze sharpens as the woman's head dips, an attempt to make herself small and unnoticeable. That is how prey behave when in the presence of an apex predator.

Kneeling in front of her, I gently pry her fingers from the fire poker and set it aside. Over the years, my memory of Ma has faded, but Orla reminds me of her. Rough hands, soft heart. My knowledge of the Frost King is sparse. I must build a picture piece by piece. "What will the king do, Orla? Will he hurt you?"

She pales, drops her gaze. "He has never laid a hand on a staff member, but he has a temper. It doesn't often appear, but when it does, it is . . . frightening."

"I see."

Wedding it is.

"All right, Orla. You win." I stand, arms spread at my sides. "Do what you will with me."

She strips me like a madwoman before dumping me into the roomy tub behind the divider, the water steaming. Scalding heat eats away the dirt and grime coating my skin, and I groan, loud and long.

I scrub myself from head to toe—twice. By the time I'm done, the bath water is an unpleasant, murky gray. Well, it's been some time since I've had a thorough washing. I step from the tub and dry myself with a towel. At this point, the scarf seems pointless, since Orla isn't aware of my deception, so I leave it off. The chilly air drags bumps across my skin.

As I step around the barrier, I go still. "What are you doing?"

Orla holds my clothes over the fire, as if preparing to toss them in as fuel for the flames.

She snatches back her hand, shame coloring her cheeks. "They are so filthy, I thought—" Her eyes dart to my scarred cheek, then away.

"It's all I have left of home."

Orla's shoulders droop, and she nods. "Once they're washed, I will return them to you."

The remainder of the hour is spent in preparation of the approaching ceremony. My maid tugs a simple dress over my head. Long-sleeved, thankfully, and a dark midnight blue that complements my brown skin. It fits quite well. I'm assuming this was worn by a former wife, which is rather dismal when I think of it, for the woman is, in all likelihood, dead. At least the dress isn't white. I am not that pure a woman.

Gold slippers and a matching headband complete the ensemble, my hair plaited down my back, clean and glossy. While Orla busies herself smoothing the wrinkles from the skirt, I slide on my arm sheath and dagger. Lastly, the veil. Once the Frost King removes it, he'll learn of my deception. The time for hiding, however, is past.

"This way, my lady."

Down the stairs, left, left again where the air is so cold my teeth begin to chatter. Every fireplace sits empty, and yet, sweat dampens my hairline. Endure. Survive. Fight with everything I have. It is all I can do.

The labyrinthine passageways empty into a cavernous hall studded with many hundreds of lamps. The light flickers and the shadows twitch where they clump in the forgotten corners. The room is empty but for the Frost King and another man—specter. They stand on a dais located in the center of the dusty room.

The king's gaze falls to me as I move toward him, drawn by some unnameable force. The North Wind, ancient and undying. The pale smoothness of his countenance holds not one imperfection. He is, externally, flawless.

I'm surprised by the hand he offers to help me onto the dais, the black leather cool against my skin. We face one another: a mortal woman and the immortal North Wind. He, wearing black breeches, black boots, a tunic of midnight blue with gold-threaded cuffs and collar. Our outfits match. How quaint.

The man, who I assume is the officiant, begins to speak.

"Today, let us witness this union . . ."

Sound fades. The world darkens.

My pulse is a drumbeat, a sluggish throb that hits low in my ears. The skin on the back of my hand prickles, and I frown, staring down at it. A strange black shape appears. A tattoo.

"—in times of struggle, in times of need—"

With each word, the tattoo darkens. When I attempt to wipe it away, nothing happens.

It must be a way to bind me. A vow is not enough. A vow can be broken. The tattoo, imbued with its enchantment, ensures the marriage is unbreakable.

The Frost King takes my hand then. My eyes lift to his. It's unsettling how intensely he stares at me. Since I entered the room, I don't think he's blinked once.

The officiant goes on, mentioning promise and commitment, while wrapping our hands together in a scarf. He is wasting his breath.

And then it is done. With the scarf wrapped around our joined hands, the Frost King and I are wed. I am his wife. He is my husband. We are bound in matrimony, and I have vowed to end his life.

"You may look upon your bride, my lord."

The Frost King catches the edge of my veil.

So it begins.

Carefully, he draws the fabric away from my face, revealing the brutalized flesh on my lower right cheek and jaw, the puckered terrain of old scarring, pale mountains against the darker, earthen skin tone.

Emotion. That is what I've been missing. A mien of heartless cold, yet here is a chink, shock he is unable to conceal, for I've burrowed underneath that hardened exterior, if only for a moment.

A breeze stirs the flyaway strands of my hair. Every facial muscle of the god standing before me tightens. Boreas, the North Wind, bares his perfect white teeth. For I may be a woman from Edgewood, but I am not the woman he chose.

"You," he hisses.

My smile curls nastily. "Surprise."

# CHAPTER

## 5

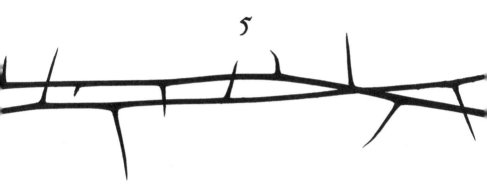

The Frost King's mouth pulls into an ugly sneer. "You."

"Yes, you already said that," I drawl unhelpfully.

"Where is your sister?" He wraps his hand around my upper arm. His strength overpowers mine ten-fold. I'm not sure I could pull free even if I tried.

"Back at Edgewood, I suspect." *More importantly, far away from you.*

His lips compress so severely it etches a white line across his pale skin. "Do you know what you have done?"

"Outmaneuvered you?"

He hisses in the lowest, coldest tone I have heard yet, "You have made the gravest of errors."

We stand nose to nose. Not many people can make me feel small, but I stand only as tall as his chin, and the air scratching at my back reveals how quickly his temper flashes to the surface. I am reminded again of who the North Wind is: an immortal who has lived to see a thousand beginnings and endings, while I am but the last leaf clinging to the autumn branch.

I do not want to be afraid of him.

I am a fool to be anything but afraid of him.

"No," I whisper, closing the last of the distance. The heat of his breath prickles my chilled lips. "You have."

Tension hits an unseen peak. His nostrils flare in response to my challenge, a gauntlet I have tossed down.

This is not a marriage.

This is war.

He steps back, and frost rushes between us, driving back the warmth that had gathered from our proximity. My heart pounds sickeningly.

I am not Elora. I am not gentle. I am a creature whose teeth were sharpened on suffering, and above all else, I will survive.

"Get her out of my sight!" he roars.

Two specter guards drag me from the room into a narrow and crooked passage with identical blue doors. With a burst of strength, I ram my body against the man to my right, crushing him against the wall. The grip on my arm loosens. I pull free, tearing down the long, darkened vein of the neglected citadel.

The men's shouts grow distant. One hallway bleeds into the next. Yellow doors and glass doors, screened doors and lopsided doors. One of these must lead to the outside. I choose one at random—pale wood capped with a round top, a square-shaped knob—and push inside.

The room is dusty enough to rival the rest of the fortress, but it can't possibly belong here, for the walls are wooden, and the floor, the ceiling. A large square window sits watchfully over rolling farmland, crops lined in rows. Not a speck of snow in sight.

"—think she went this way—" The voice dissolves in its own echo.

I rattle the window pane to no avail. Locked. There must be something— Ah. This chair will do splendidly.

With a mighty swing, I slam the piece of furniture against the window as hard as I can. My arms jar from the impact, the crash deafening. Not even a scratch on the glass. How is that possible?

"I heard something. Down here!"

Useless room. I make a hasty exit, turn down another hallway, and enter a door at random.

Only quick reflexes save me from imminent death. A spill of unbroken sky pools so near I might reach up and touch its star-flecked surface. Beneath, waves ram into cliffside walls. And I stand on the very edge, toeing the damp, crumbling rock.

Rough, salt-soaked winds pluck at my hair and dress. I've never seen the sea. I've never seen water this vast, free of winter's frozen trappings. But that life is not for me.

Something slithers around my ankle and yanks me upside down. My dress skirts fall around my head, revealing my undergarments. "What is this?" I struggle against an unseen captive.

The Frost King's boots enter my line of vision. "These doors lead to many places, though I have told you before, they will not lead you to escape. You are stuck here. You might as well get used to it."

"I despise you," I spit.

My derision leaves naught a mark on him. He is quite calm as he replies, "You are neither the first, nor the last."

My fury tastes alive, and I would see him experience it, too, if only to witness that iron control fracturing.

I drift back across the threshold, where the two guards I managed to evade earlier wait. The Frost King waves his hand, and I slam into the ground as his power vanishes around my ankle. The guards grip my arms so tightly they're sure to leave marks on my skin. Fooled them once, but no more. I'm dragged backward by the arms, through a locked door, down and down and down a set of stairs.

Black, frozen soil rises as high walls. Then a ceiling. Underground, the silence is so absolute it crushes my ear drums. Not a single candle or lamp. Only cells, so many cells. Empty now, but what manner of prisoners once occupied them?

At the very end of the tunnel, they open one of the barred doors and toss me inside. Keys rattle as the lock thunks into place.

"Wait." I lunge, catching the bars. "Please, help me."

The door slams shut, and I'm left to darkness.

∿

Being imprisoned in a hole in the ground is about as unpleasant as one would expect, my heartbeat my only companion in the lengthening hours. Worse than the killing cold is the thirst. The initial prickle in my throat morphs into an ache, then fierce agony. I demand wine. They bring me water. Soon, a sheen of sweat coats my skin.

My eyes adjust to the blackness quickly enough. The cell is tiny, nothing but packed dirt on three sides, with the door serving as the fourth wall. If I stretch out my arms, I can touch both walls with my fingertips, bits of soil crumbling free.

It feels as though I left Edgewood a lifetime ago. Elora—dear, sweet Elora. Missing her is a wound that might never heal. I'm sure she's furious with me. Few know of Elora's temper, but oh, it is stunning when she lets it loose. What did she think when she awoke, shaking free of the maniwort's effects? An empty cottage. Her sister, gone. The Frost King, gone. Her only remaining family, gone.

I made her a promise, and I broke it. But without the threat of the Frost King, she is free to pursue her dreams. I take comfort in that.

Days pass. I lie in pools of my own sweat, curled up in the back corner of the cell. Again, I ask for wine. Again, they bring me water. The stew I'm served is cold, the fat having congealed into an oily layer atop the surface. By some miracle, I manage to keep down what I eat.

In sleep, nightmares skulk and slither through me. Cold, blackened flesh and a hissing, spitting voice in my ear. Pain ruptures through my chest, and I wake with a start, breathing hard, my muscles contracting uncontrollably.

Someone stands outside my cell. A figure, shadow upon shadow, little more than a phantom. Every few moments I'm able to catch the outline of that staggering frame, shoulders all breadth, before it melts away and becomes dark.

My clammy skin stings in the stale air. With some effort, I drag myself back into the world of the living, far from whatever creatures await me in dreams. Acknowledging the Frost King feels like defeat, so I ignore him. He can stand there for the rest of his immortal life for all I care. Turning my back to him, I rearrange my limbs, my head supported by the crook of my arm.

"Have you learned your lesson?" His deep voice floats from out of the void.

My mouth twitches wryly at the game he plays. Perhaps it's time I make myself a willing participant.

"If you're asking whether I regret my actions, the answer is no. I'd switch places with my sister a thousand times if it kept her away from you. But how generous of you to show up. Had I known you'd grace me with your godly presence, I would have dressed for the occasion." The pretty dress I wore for the wedding is coated in grime, the hem torn. I daresay it is symbolic.

"You brought this upon yourself."

A slow exhale helps center me. I curl into a tighter ball, stare at the wall inches from my nose. Nothing the Frost King says can affect me. His opinion means little. He is the wind, insubstantial and fleeting.

Something scuffs against the ground, as though he takes a step forward.

"Had you kept your mouth closed, had you better control over your emotions, you could be safe in bed right now, back at your humble village with your sister."

As if he knows anything about me. "See, that's where you're wrong. Nothing would have stopped me from keeping Elora safe."

"Keeping your mouth shut would have kept her safe." As if sensing my confusion, he tells me, "She was not my first choice, but you drew my attention to her. You switched places. And you deserve this suffering."

I'm on my feet despite the body aches, stalking to the front of the cramped cell. Bars of iron sever his form into long slits. Shadows wreath his throat and rest opaquely upon his shoulders, in direct contrast to that skin of purest alabaster.

"I'm not even surprised you would say that," I snap, curling my fingers around the chilled metal. His attention shifts to my hands, then to my mouth, my scar, before returning to my eyes. "The gods blame misfortune on mortals time and again. You are so concerned with the symptoms, you do not ask what disease blackens the flesh. You are too selfish to do otherwise."

His fingers wrap around the bars, those large hands resting a hairsbreadth above my own. "How quickly you judge," he whispers. The blue rings around his pupils are the only color belowground. "You do not know me."

"Says the man who threw his wife into a *dungeon*." I rattle the bars for emphasis. And what a thought that is. The deeper I contemplate it, the more I wonder as to the purpose of these cells. Holding pens for his past wives?

"Why are you here?" I step back under the pretense of appraising him in a scathing manner, but truthfully, standing so near him makes me nervous. "Have you come to gloat?"

"I've come to release you."

My brow furrows. "Is this a trap?"

He cuts me a bland look before unlocking the door.

"You know—" A laugh rasps out of me. Nothing about this situation is funny, but if I don't laugh, I'm positive I'll crumble, and I refuse to let the man who ruined my life witness that private moment. "I think I prefer isolation."

The door opens with a harsh shriek. "I chose your sister as my bride, not you. Switching places was your choice."

"If you knew what it felt like to love someone with your entire being, you'd know I never had a choice."

I'm not sure what, exactly, changes. I only know the air stirs when he is displeased, and it currently rustles the hem of my dress. The Frost King's expression, however, remains neutral. "Your attendance is required at dinner tonight."

If he thinks I'm going to share a meal with the person I despise most in the world, he has a lot to reconsider.

"Unfortunately," I say, my smile oozing false charm, "I'm busy."

"With what?"

I make a show of considering his question. "Anything. Everything. There are so many possibilities. Choose one that satisfies you."

Two strides bring him into the cell, the scent of cedar trailing him. Pain pulses through me in a hot wave, and I have to fight to remain standing. It's been years since I've gone without the bottle for this long. It feels like an age. "You may be my wife," he murmurs, and I swear something wails in the distance, a child's scream, however faint, "but nothing says I have to house you. I'm happy enough to chain you outside, since you insist on acting like an animal."

I expel a furious breath. "Animal?"

He studies me dispassionately.

"How dare—"

The hand at his side lifts, fingers curling inward as if crushing an unseen object in his palm—my throat, I quickly learn. My breath wheezes as I inhale sharply, struggling to suck in air through the sliver of an opening.

"Stop. Talking." His cool, whispered breath wafts across my face. "You will attend this dinner. If you decide to forgo your duties, I will have you chained outside. I hear it's uncomfortable at this time of year."

My face grows hot, yet I step closer. He eases the pressure around my throat, perhaps in surprise, perhaps in curiosity.

"Unhand me," I say, the words crisp and precise despite the fog gathering in the corners of my vision, "or I will castrate you, immortal or not."

The tip of my dagger, which was hidden in my arm sheath, slides out to rest against his groin.

The Frost King goes still.

In curiosity, I watch his eyes darken with emotion. Shock? That I would threaten him, slip beneath his guard undetected. For half a heartbeat, he is unbalanced.

"I will not repeat myself." I shift the blade closer in warning, and he flinches. "An eternity is a long time to be deprived. I know how you gods love your sex."

The Frost King could easily disarm me, but this is not about strength of power. This is about respect. He *will* respect me. I may not be Elora, but I am a person, and I will not be mistreated.

Eventually, he steps back, lowering his hand. The pressure around my throat vanishes.

"Dinner will begin at sundown. I expect a prompt arrival." Turning heel, he leaves me with the lingering press of his hand at my throat. Only when the echo of his footsteps has faded do I slump against the cell wall. My hand shakes as I return my dagger to its sheath. Never again will he gain the upper hand. From this moment forward, I must utilize every weapon at my disposal. Mind, body, blade.

The North Wind will rue the day he decided to cross me.

# CHAPTER
## 6

Hours before dinner that night, I raid the wine stores. The guards, mindless fools that they are, were happy to point me in the right direction. If I'm to suffer through a meal with the Frost King, then I need to be sufficiently drunk.

With two wineskins in hand, I teeter back to my rooms and plop onto my ridiculously expansive bed. Eight pillows for one person? Pointless. Tipping back my head, I drink straight from the container. The liquid burns going down and sets fire to my belly.

"No, Husband," I whisper to myself, gulping more wine and swiping the back of my hand across my mouth, "I will not attend dinner with you." A hiccup squeaks out of me.

*Husband.* I gag on the word. The Frost King is no husband of mine. I am an obligation. He is an inconvenience. That I must remain here until the end of my days weighs like a stone around my neck.

Oh, I'll figure out a way to steal that spear of his. Or the dagger. Kill him, and freedom is mine. One thrust through the heart should do it.

That's how Orla finds me hours later, my boneless form poured out across the pillows, one skin of wine already empty.

"My lady?" She rounds the mattress, leaning over me in worry. My eyes cross in an attempt to focus on her face. The gray curls of her hair remind me of a rain cloud. "Are you ill?"

It takes me a moment, but I manage to right myself, the wineskin clutched to my chest. "The Frost King is a—" I burp. "—monster." My eyes fill and my breath hitches. What kind of man locks his wife in a prison cell? I take another swallow, and another. The wine won't fail me.

My maid stares at me as though I've grown a pair of antlers in her absence.

"Orla." Spittle drips down my chin. "You have to help me." A wave of dizziness sucks me under, and I lean back against the headboard. "He said . . ." What did he say?

"My lady!" The shrill cry makes me wince. I'm not sure when my head started pounding, but pressure throbs behind my eyes at full force. "Please." She snatches the wineskin from my grip, or rather, she attempts to. I cling to the container like the lifeline it is, and Orla has to peel my fingers free of the neck. She then marches to the open window and upends the remainder of the liquid outside.

Alarm hammers through me with increasing strength. "What are you doing? I need that!"

"What you need is to get dressed." As she hauls me off the bed, I nearly slam my face against the bedpost. I'm stripped down in seconds, dropped into the tub, and scrubbed clean. While my hair dries, Orla selects an ivory dress that complements the darker tone of my skin and brown-black of my hair. Pretty it may be, but I'm tired of dresses. I long for my trousers and loose tunics.

"Can't you make my excuses?" Orla draws the laces of my corset tight against my lower back. The bones pinch into my sides, and I wince. Wearing a corset is a special kind of torture. "Tell the king I'm ill."

"I cannot lie to him, my lady."

"It wouldn't be a lie. I do feel ill." My skin buzzes uncomfortably and my face is flushed, feverish. It happens sometimes when the thirst is too great. A droplet hits my tongue, and my mind empties, muscle memory taking over. Sip and swallow.

Clarity exists at the bottom of a bottle.

My maid huffs in exasperation, tying off the laces and turning me to face her. She tames my hair and cakes my face in colors until my sullen expression is forever frozen with the dried face paint. The gunk cracks around my eyes and mouth. I appreciate that she did not try to conceal my scar, merely evened out my skin tone. "If you hadn't drunk so much wine, you would not be in this predicament."

"If the Frost King hadn't forced me to marry him, I wouldn't have drunk so much wine." Probably.

She all but shoves me out the door. "Don't forget to smile."

My slippers whisper against the stone floor as I descend the stairs to the equally dim lower level. My ribs pinch with every inhale. Damn corset.

Wall sconces provide small, glowing pockets of light. It would help to know where I'm supposed to go. The king never mentioned it.

"Excuse me." I approach a man standing ramrod straight against the wall. "Which way—"

He points to a corridor on my right, but does not speak. The top of his skull—the area closest to the flame—shines transparent, whereas his lower torso, which is nearer to the dark, appears solid.

The doors in this hallway are all made of glass, but I can't see what lies inside them, for ice crystals coat their rounded edges. The stretch leads me to a set of massive double doors, open in invitation. Candlelight flickers in the gloom beyond.

The fabric of my dress hisses against my slippers as I cross the threshold. The room reminds me of a cave: low ceiling, cramped walls, windowless. Despite the dreary location, two men occupy the surprisingly elegant dining table. Crystal glasses reflect the candlelight and toss prisms of light onto the walls.

The Frost King glowers from his seat of power at the head of the table. An overcoat of lustrous black thread drapes his broad torso, and beneath, an equally black tunic is buttoned to his chin. No color. And no warmth.

His guest, on the other hand, is in direct contrast to him. The man's hair is a tumble of oaken curls, and as I cross the room, his clover eyes settle on me with a healthy amount of intrigue. A tunic of rough cloth the color of a growing forest presses against his lightly tanned skin. He's up and across the room, lithe body drawing my eye, taking my hand as if he has every right to. The way he moves reminds me of a dance.

My, but he is pretty. Thick lashes frame his crystalline eyes, and freckles dot the bridge of his straight nose like droplets of rain. I can't help but stare. His face is pleasing to me. Open.

"Lady Wren." A warm, cultured voice. "It's an honor."

This man is honored to meet me? He is polite, if nothing else. "Thank you." I expect an introduction, but it doesn't come. "And you are?"

"Most folk call me the Messenger." He still holds my hand. Nimble fingers rest lightly on mine, gentle as butterfly wings. "But to you, I am Zephyrus."

The man speaks as if he presumes I'm familiar with his identity. My wine-addled brain struggles to place it. He smells like moss.

"My brother," the king intones.

The Messenger. That would make him the West Wind, Bringer of Spring. No wonder he's so pleasant.

"Nice to meet you, Zephyrus." He is a few inches taller than me, although not nearly as tall as his brother.

"The pleasure is mine." An indulgent smile curves his mouth— the mouth of a man who looks as though he dearly loves to laugh. "When I heard Boreas found himself another wife, I did not expect her to be so lovely."

The Frost King scoffs.

My face warms, and my stomach sloshes uncomfortably. I've never been called lovely. Good enough to bed, but little else, what with my scarring. As for the king's response, I ignore it.

"Thank you." I'm not sure I believe this man, considering we just met, but it is more kindness than I've received from the king, and I find myself warming toward him. Bringer of Spring, indeed.

"The food grows cold." The king glares at us from his seat at the table, his words curdling.

I'm petty enough to make him wait, but Zephyrus offers his arm with a murmured, "May I?" Something passes between us, as though he understands my predicament.

The Frost King's attention sharpens as Zephyrus helps me to my seat before settling in the chair to my right. An entire table separates the king and I, and the distance is not enough. He sits perched at the edge of his high-backed, lacquered chair, body rigid. A strip of leather binds his hair in a tail so tightly not one strand hangs free.

A softness touches my surroundings at their edges. I've managed to regain some control over my faculties, but not much. My attention falls briefly to the table setting. Silver plates and bowls. Fresh flowers—I'm not sure where or how the servants managed to procure them—spring from squat vases, green vines creeping across the white tablecloth.

"So." Zephyrus lifts his wine glass. "Lady Wren."

With some effort, I manage to shift my attention to the king's brother. Looking at him is almost as nice as looking at the flowers. "Please, call me Wren." For I am many things, but I am no lady.

"Wren." Laughter brims in his melodious voice. "How are you finding the Deadlands?"

"About as pleasant as you find them, I imagine."

His eyes, how they dance. The West Wind is handsome, open, warm, affectionate. He draws me in quite helplessly. "And my brother?"

I take a sip from my own glass of wine. My stomach gurgles in protest, reminding me of everything I drank prior to entering this room. I ignore it. "That is assuming there is anything to like about him."

His chuckle echoes in the cavernous space. "Oh, I like you. I *really* like you."

The Frost King glowers at me as though I just admitted to a capital offense. If he can't bear the truth, he should leave. That would improve the dinner tremendously.

A line of servants files through a side door, bearing platters heaped with meats, cheeses, fruits, bread, and greens. The amount of food served to three people is absurd. They do not serve mere potatoes. It is a mountain of potatoes. Thick slabs of meat slathered in pats of butter. Baskets stuffed with brown dinner rolls that tumble onto the cloth when set down, knocked from their precarious positions. The bowl of gravy is so large a small animal could swim in it. Beside the plate piled with carrots, an entire roasted pig is displayed, the skin blackened to a crisp and dripping juice, an apple shoved into its mouth.

The smell of hot food makes my stomach twist queasily. Many nights I dreamed of such things, feasts and gluttony, the taste of fat melting across my tongue, the sweet bitterness of charred greens. I'd wake to a stomach so hollow it no longer cramped. It just was.

Zephyrus and the Frost King begin heaping food onto their plates. The former takes a knife, slices a piece of meat from the suckling pig. Saliva floods my mouth. There is enough food here to feed a family of four for weeks.

And then there is Edgewood. Tiny, forgotten Edgewood. Scant, starving Edgewood and its depleting population.

I push away my plate. I cannot eat, not when Elora hasn't the means to nourish herself.

The Frost King regards me as he would a mild pest before setting down his fork. "Is the food not to your liking?" His eyes are voids. His voice, a void. This place, a void.

I squint, but his wide-shouldered form still blurs. "I'm sure it's perfectly lovely food."

"Yet you refuse to eat."

"My people are starving."

"And?"

Zephyrus lifts his head in interest as I spew, "And it's your fault!"

The Frost King picks up his fork, spears a piece of cabbage, and brings it to his mouth. "Mortals live, and they die. I cannot control when their time ends. That is the way of the world, a cycle even older than I."

"You cannot control when their time ends," I manage thickly, "but you can certainly help it along."

"It is my nature."

"It is a choice."

Zephyrus' hand covers mine, and I sense something unspoken between us. *Calm*, he seems to say. *Be intentional with what fights you choose.*

I consider this. The food will go to waste either way. Better it fill my belly, nourish my body, sharpen my mind. All propelling me toward the Frost King's inevitable end.

I begin scooping food onto my plate when Zephyrus says, "So tell me about yourself."

"There's not much to tell." At the first bite, I almost moan. The carrots are decadent, slightly sweet, drenched in a spiced honey glaze.

"Oh, come now. I don't believe that."

An uncomfortable pause follows. Zephyrus watches me patiently. I'm not sure of the king's expression, but I sense his gaze on me as well. The truth is, no man has ever asked this of me. No one has ever cared to. And maybe, deep down, I wished they would.

"I . . . hunt. And read." Are my words slurring? I hope they're not slurring.

"Hunt?" He perks up at that. "Your weapon of choice?"

"The bow."

"Mm." Dancing eyes. "And what do you like to read?"

"Nothing in particular," I murmur, feeling suddenly faint. A bodice-ripping romance isn't proper dinner conversation, and I'd feel foolish were they to learn of my preference for stories of love and intimacy—two things I have never experienced before. Sex doesn't equate to intimacy. It's just doing what the body was created to do.

Zephyrus forks a strip of pork into his mouth. "And how have you been spending your time here so far?"

The question gives me pause. But—the truth, I suppose, is best. "Your brother tossed me into a dungeon."

The king's voice drones from a distance. "You lied to me."

I shove pork and potatoes into my mouth. My stomach finally settles now that I've decided to feed myself, and the wine keeps flowing. I continue to drink, damn the consequences. "It's not my fault—" I hiccup. "—you care so little you didn't notice I was a different person."

That he doesn't deny it stings. I'm not proud to admit it. Perhaps because no one aside from my sister has ever cared for me, and it is yet another reminder that I am nothing special in this world.

"You locked her in your dungeon? That's a new low, even for you," Zephyrus admonishes his brother.

The Frost King's fingers tighten on the stem of his wine glass. He doesn't respond.

Time lurches forward with every glass of wine. Zephyrus gorges himself. The Frost King picks at his plate. None of the foods touch, I notice foggily. Meat, vegetables, potatoes, bread. Four little islands atop the silver. At one point, the brothers dive into a heated, whispered discussion I'm not privy to.

When the last piece of bread on my plate is consumed and

my protruding stomach threatens to split the bones of my corset, I rise from my chair, leaning on the table for support. The room tilts dangerously.

Their conversation reaches an abrupt end.

"Excuse me," I mumble. My intention is to leave the room in a smooth rustle of skirts, with all the grace and poise of the sober, but my foot catches on the table leg, and I pitch forward, hitting the ground hard.

Quickened footsteps. Someone crouches by my side, one hand sliding to the small of my back. I'm overwhelmed by sensation, the smells of wet earth and fresh green, and a warm, soothing wind teasing the strands of hair glued to my sweaty skin. A second set of footsteps interrupts, heavier, more substantial. I lift my head in time to witness the Frost King's emotionless expression twist.

"Unhand her," he snaps, striding forward.

Zephyrus steps back, hands raised, gaze unflappable.

Large hands curve around my upper arms and pull me to my feet. Though the leather encasing his hands is cool, beneath lies the hidden warmth of his skin.

I don't think the Frost King knows how inebriated I am, because the moment he releases me, the ground rushes upward. He swears, catching me before I hit the ground. "You're drunk."

I pull away to slump against the wall. The cold stone is a relief against my sweating back. "Very."

Zephyrus says, "I would offer to help, but . . ."

"I can handle my wife, Brother."

His response manages to momentarily break through the fog. Of course he refers to me as if I'm his property, rather than a person with thoughts and beliefs and emotions.

The West Wind glances between us with obvious amusement. "I can see that, Boreas. Married to a woman who is repulsed by your touch. What else is new?" When he next smiles, I'm certain his teeth have grown points.

The king stiffens. Zephyrus released an arrow, and its aim was true. "You're dismissed, Zephyrus."

The West Wind bows low in my direction. "Wren, I hope we cross paths again during my stay." His soundless feet carry him from the dining room. With Zephyrus' absence, I'm reminded of how enormous the Frost King is, both in height and presence, that gaze probing too deeply.

"I'll see myself to my rooms," I state, pushing away from the wall. The overbalance sends me sideways. And with his brother gone, the king doesn't bother catching my fall. I crash into one of the chairs.

"Orla," he barks.

Running footsteps. "Yes, my lord?"

"Please escort my wife to her chambers. Be sure she makes it there in one piece."

# CHAPTER

## 7

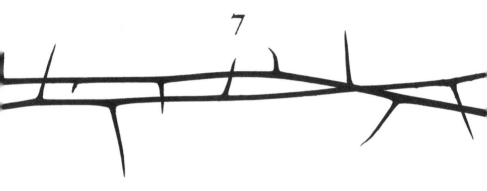

My first conscious thought upon waking is that I am dead.

My entire body throbs. Blood, pulsing sluggishly beneath the surface of my skin. A pounding in my head, again, again, again. My arm shakes as I reach up, eyes still closed, to touch my temple. The pounding persists. If I am not dead, then I am close to it. My mouth has the exact texture of chalk.

Slowly, I push myself upright, propping my back against the headboard. It's a mistake.

My stomach pitches violently. Bile laps at the back of my throat, and I have seconds to snatch a vase from the bedside table before the contents of last night's meal gush into its base. The rancid odor sends another wave of sickness through me. I retch until my stomach cramps before flopping back onto the pillows, the vase—now full of vomit—returned to its spot.

The thumping grows so loud that I can no longer ignore it, but it doesn't come from inside my head.

Someone is banging on the door.

Judging by the gray light to the east, it is not yet dawn. What kind of monster wakes someone up at this hour?

The Frost King? As soon as the thought forms, I banish the idea altogether. He wouldn't knock. He would barge in as if he had every right to. It can't be Orla, because she is too considerate to wake me in such a cruel manner.

The next knock sends a shockwave through the wall, toppling one of the paintings hanging above the fireplace.

"All right," I snap. "Give me a moment."

*Decent* is the best I can do, given the circumstances. Currently I wear a thin, white sleeping gown—something I do not remember changing into last night, but I will not think of that now. I slip on my robe, belt it at the waist, shuffle to the door, and yank it open.

Zephyrus waits on the other side.

His mouth curves playfully as he takes in my rumpled appearance and the smear of dried saliva on my cheek. The shoulder propped against the wall lends him a casual air, but the keenness to his gaze is anything but.

"Hello, Wren."

If I am the image of death, then he is life: green, animated, aglow with charm. Chestnut curls spring from his skull, interwoven with slender green shoots. Today he wears a gold tunic that hits mid-thigh, fitted breeches, and soft-soled boots, along with a fur-lined overcoat.

"What are you doing here?"

I've never seen a grown man pout, but then again, Zephyrus is no man. He is the West Wind. He can likely do whatever he wants. "I came to see how you were feeling this morning."

"By almost breaking down my door?" I snap with a dark scowl. It's far too early for this conversation. Or any conversation, for that matter.

Zephyrus scans my body lazily before his attention returns to my face, passing over my scar momentarily. My upper lip peels back in warning as I tighten the belt at my waist.

"If that's what it takes to wake you." He laughs and laughs. It sounds eerily like birdsong.

"What are you really doing here?"

"I've come to steal you away," he announces dramatically, tossing one hand in the air with flourish.

I'm reminded of last night's dinner. I may not trust the Frost King, but there is a reason he dislikes his brother. That, I cannot ignore. A god always has a motive, and the most dangerous are those I cannot see. "You know I can't pass through the Shade."

"Who said anything about the Shade?" There's a complicated emotion to his features I can't place. "Don't you want to escape outside for a few hours, away from this wretched place?" He glances around my room with obvious distaste. It is still quite dark, despite my removal of the curtains. Choked by opulence. "A woman needs the wind on her face as a flower needs sunlight."

When he puts it like that, he has a point. "That would be nice," I hear myself say slowly. Whatever averseness I feel about this meeting, it can't overshadow the truth, and the truth is I need to be outside, stretching my legs, distancing myself from my prison. "Let me change first."

"Do you need help?"

My skin prickles at his unexpected proposal. It is an effort to keep my tone level. "Did I request your help?"

The Messenger's eyes crinkle. "Oh dear," he whispers. "I have offended you."

He has not offended me. He has belittled me.

"You know, I think I've changed my mind." Stepping back, I begin to close the door.

Zephyrus inserts his foot against the jamb. "Have a laugh, Wren. It was nothing but harmless banter."

Ma always insisted Elora and I act polite toward those we don't know, but then I remember Ma is dead, and I am a woman grown, and this god dares test my boundaries as though it is a game, a harmless little game in which he has a laugh at my expense, and that is unacceptable.

Swinging open the door, I plant a palm against Zephyrus' chest, shove him back with all my strength. He trips over his feet in surprise. He is no longer laughing.

"Perhaps last night I gave the wrong impression." We stand nose to nose. His breath smells of sweet nectar. "Let me be clear. Do not toy with me. It will not end well for you."

The green of his eyes pales. "Are you threatening me?"

Foolish I may be, but I am who I am, and I won't apologize for it. "Interpret it how you will," I say, stepping back.

Zephyrus' mouth purses in reflection. Then he laughs gustily.

"Oh, Boreas will have his hands full with you." Once his chuckle dies down, he says, "I apologize for my behavior, Wren. You're absolutely right. I'd love to explore the grounds with you. As friends," he adds with a charming bow.

"Fine. One moment." The door slams shut in his face.

Though my stomach still feels queasy, it finally settles when I take a pull of the wineskin I've hidden in my dresser drawer. My hands ease their shaking. A craving soothed, for now.

Since we'll be outside, I don thick breeches and a tunic, two pairs of woolen socks, fur-lined boots in exactly my size, and my coat. Patchy and uneven it may be, but it's the warmest thing I own. One of my last ties to home. The coats I've been provided—soft white fox fur, plush mink—collect dust in the bureau.

Zephyrus pushes off the wall when I exit my room, my face washed, my teeth brushed. "Warm enough?"

"Yes. But don't you have a warmer coat? It's cold out."

"Bringer of Spring, remember?" He flicks a warm breeze toward me. "Helps keep the cold out, though my power isn't as strong in my brother's realm."

As he leads me down a side staircase, I ask, intrigued, "What is your realm like? Is there snow?"

"Snow." He shudders. "Snow does not fall in my realm, or it didn't." He sighs, and it is the first time I sense fatigue beneath those many layers of pleasantry. He's hidden it well. "When my brothers and I were banished, our powers were contained to our respective realms. Lately, however, things are changing. Plants are dying. The wildlife moves south as the weather grows harsh and chilled. Boreas' influence has begun to spread even farther and now threatens my realm."

"I'm sorry." Outside, we cross a side courtyard with snow-topped benches pushed against the curve of the outer wall. It may have once been a garden, for there are raised, empty beds and lingering tree skeletons. The stone is cracked underfoot. "Why does his power encroach on your lands?"

"Weakening control is my best guess. With what I've heard concerning the Shade, it does not surprise me, but I'm curious as to why it has not yet been addressed." He drags a hand through his curls, gripping them near the crown of his skull briefly. "I don't care for the reason. I want my lands cleansed of his hoarfrost. That is all. It's why I traveled all this way—to plead with him."

How very interesting. From what little I know of the Frost King, he is unlikely to grant Zephyrus that wish. But what is it Zephyrus knows of the Shade? Will it concern me? I want to question him, but I must take care revealing how much or how little I know until I'm more certain of his character, what risks he poses to me, if any.

The courtyard flows into an austere square with broken pillars. This is clearly not Zephyrus' first visit, if he is familiar with the layout of the citadel.

When we reach the gates, they open for us with nary an issue, and I walk right through, so pleased to have some semblance of freedom that I don't care about the repercussions. Even the snow can't dampen my uplifted mood.

Abruptly, Zephyrus states, "You favor the bow."

"Yes," I say with surprise. "How did you know?"

He chuckles at that. "You told me at dinner last night."

Now that he mentions it, I'm remembering a vague—extremely vague—recollection of the topic. Too slippery to grasp. "I don't remember much of last night, truthfully." As first impressions go, it wasn't the best. Not that I cared at the time. In hindsight, I should have never allowed myself to drink so much, but that's how it goes, generally. I'm not thinking about control or discipline or any of the other terms Elora has used in the past. I'm thinking of that far-away place I reach with just one more sip.

"I understand." He glances at me, then away. We veer from the road of trampled snow, vanishing into the surrounding forest. "And I don't blame you. Boreas would drive anyone to drink. Even if you hadn't mentioned the bow though, I would have known."

"How?" Snow dusts the hem of my coat, my breeches, my boots.

"Your hands." Light as a feather, he touches his gloved fingertips to mine. "Calloused, slender. A natural-born hunter."

The irony does not elude me. Here, I am but prey to a god. "Are you familiar with the bow?"

"My lady." It's as if the beauty of this immortal sharpens unexpectedly, like an intense beam of sunlight. "Am I not the Bringer of Spring? The bow was *made* for me."

One suddenly appears in hand, and I gasp. Proportionally, it is flawless. Smooth-grained wood carved with markings I cannot read. It is larger than what I'm used to, the string bearing a higher tension. My own bow remains in Edgewood, propped near my cottage's front door. I imagine it hasn't moved since I left. "May I?"

He passes it into my hands. Maple. The red-toned hardwood has a good snap, excellent flexibility. When I pluck the string, the air hums pleasantly.

"It's beautiful," I concede, returning it to him with reluctance. There is nothing like the feel of carved wood in my hand. Tangible weight, and a purpose. Without the need to hunt, I've felt untethered.

Zephyrus looks to me in consideration. "Would you like to try it?"

"Really?"

"Of course." He steers us east until we reach a large opening in the forest. The wind dries out my eyes, drawing tears from the corners. The cold is so absolute it steals my breath. "Why do you think I invited you?" He scans our surroundings. Light snowfall crusts the black branches of the trees at our backs. "See that boulder? Try to hit the stump at its base."

The stump is an easy shot. I'm almost offended. "What about that tree?" I say, pointing to the small, crooked shape farther in the distance.

Zephyrus shrugs. "If you wish." He passes me an arrow from the quiver that materialized at his back when his bow appeared. He uses goose feathers for the fletching, I'm pleased to note, like me.

With the string tightened to a higher tension, I had anticipated needing increased strength to draw the bow, but that's not the case. It's as if Zephyrus' weapon adjusts to my size and capabilities. The arrow pulls back, fluid as water. I release and hit the tree on the first try.

The West Wind nods, hands slipped into his pockets. "You are a fine shot."

The compliment pleases me.

We spend the morning shooting at various targets. It's the most fun I've had in ages. Zephyrus hits every mark, and he tells me stories about his home to the west, his childhood.

"I have a confession to make," he says at one point, trudging through the snow to pull one of his arrows free from a tree. He turns, his hair lightened to the color of wheat grass. The sun has climbed and now perches atop the sky's bowed peak. "I didn't invite you out here just to shoot."

"Oh?" He returns to my side, offering me the arrow. Though I fit it to the string, I don't draw.

"I came to ask for your help."

I'm so startled I nearly drop the bow. "My help?"

That fatigue has returned, and I'm offered an even deeper glimpse, another layer peeled back. At last, the gravity of the situation reveals itself. "My home is being destroyed by winter. It threatens my people, the peace I've worked tirelessly to maintain. I fear that unless something changes soon, I won't have a home to return to."

"And you can't talk to him about it?" I ask sympathetically.

A harsh, humorless laugh. "My brother formed his opinion of me a long time ago, and I do not think it will change." The green of his eyes has deadened. "But he might listen to you."

It's laughable how misguided he is. And yet, don't I understand how easily desperation can grow claws? How they dig and dig and dig? He seeks to save his home. Why should I not help him?

"I'll try," I say, "but I don't know how receptive he'll be to my request. I wasn't kidding when I said he threw me in a dungeon."

"I didn't think you were."

And I wonder if there might be more to the story. What exactly does Zephyrus know of the Frost King's past wives?

A breeze teases the ends of my hair, and I freeze. Woodsmoke.

"Wren? Hello?" Zephyrus waves a hand in front of my face. "Where did you go?"

"I thought I smelled a fire." At his quizzical expression, I explain, "The darkwalkers. They smell like a forge." The Frost King mentioned the forest disliking his presence. "We should head back." They generally feed in the evenings when they're most active, but not always.

He doesn't argue as we retrace our steps back toward the citadel.

"I have a question for you," I tell Zephyrus.

As we pick our way through the silent wood, Zephyrus brushes his fingertips along the long-dead trees and piles of tangled bramble. Green shoots sprout at the points of contact, then wither and blacken in the air. "Ask away."

I duck beneath some low-hanging branches. "Since you are the Bringer of Spring, would I be correct in assuming you're knowledgeable in the herbal arts?"

He glances sideways at me. "Yes."

I slow as we round a bend, thinking about how best to phrase the question without arousing suspicion. How easily the lies flow when you have nothing to lose. "I've been having difficulty sleeping since I arrived. Is there an herb that helps with deep sleep, do you know?"

There was little to do in the dungeon except think and plan. Killing the Frost King with a god-touched weapon is an excellent idea—in theory. But in order to accomplish that, it would need to occur at a moment of complete vulnerability.

A woman in my village dabbled in the herbal arts. With the right ingredients, one can brew a potion that stops one's heart for a day. A false death. But sleep, that small, quiet death, is what I need.

Zephyrus' gaze glows with a strange light. "There is a tonic I make from the petals of the poppy plant." He halts, and I stop as well. "I think we can help each other, Wren."

"What do you mean?" I ask, unable to keep the wariness, and the hope, from my tone.

"I mean I can give you what you want," he says, "in exchange for something I want. A trade of sorts."

Something in the way he says it has my back straightening, my chin lifting. He wants something, but it will not come free. "What is your price?"

He closes the distance between us. Flowers sprout from his footprints, bright pops of color that shrivel and disintegrate. It all happens in a matter of seconds.

"For you, dear sister-in-law? The price has already been paid."

It's a devious business, dealing with gods. "And what was the price?"

"Your company." Zephyrus graces me with the most charming of smiles, a dimple winking in one cheek.

Against my body's better judgment, my face warms, and I turn away with a mumbled, "Oh." For a moment, I thought the price would be something horrible, though it makes no sense at all.

"Well, that, and the favor I asked of you earlier."

Right. I suppose that's fair. "I'll speak to your brother. I can't promise he will listen, but I will try."

A clump of roses springs from where he touches the stripped bark of a tree. He plucks one of the scarlet blooms and passes it to me, his mouth touched by sudden somberness. "How soon do you need the tonic?"

Relief moves through me. This will work. It must. "As soon as possible."

"I'll see what I can do."

~

Later, after Zephyrus and I have parted ways with the promise to meet again soon, I return to my rooms. Warmth from the fire thaws my stiff, frozen cheeks. For the first time in days, I am smiling. Zephyrus and I may have begun the morning on uneven footing, but as the hours passed, I came to know this god who was curious and playful and sad.

"Where have you been?"

The deep command resonates at my back, and I whirl to find the Frost King occupying one of the chairs in the corner, glaring. Simmering firelight flames the side of his body nearest to the source of heat. He sits so rigidly it's easy to mistake him for a piece of furniture.

My good mood vanishes. Dashed like water onto hot embers. "I was taking a walk," I say, untying my coat to hang it on a hook near the fire. "Around the grounds." It's only half a lie.

That piercing scrutiny shifts from my face, though my relief is short-lived. "Where did you get that bow?"

I'm reminded of the weapon I carry, the color in my cheeks, the brightness of my eyes. After learning I'd left mine behind in Edgewood, Zephyrus gifted it to me. He insisted. "That is of no concern to you." Although I'm sure he already knows.

In one sinuous motion, the Frost King rises to his feet, and I brace myself against the onslaught of a budding storm. The black of his hair reminds me of raven feathers, for the colors alter with the flickering light, yellow and violet and green. His blue eyes narrow over his obnoxiously straight nose. "Zephyrus."

"He gave me some pointers on my form," I concede, moving to stoke the fire. "He, at least, doesn't despise my company."

"I don't want you spending time with him."

Iron poker in hand, I turn and stab the sooty tip into the rug beneath my feet. "And I care little of your opinion." Returning the poker to its hook, I move toward my bed, resting the bow and quiver of arrows on the mattress. "Why do you dislike him so much anyway?"

"The history between Zephyrus and I is of no concern to you."

Sounds like deflection to me.

"You want to know what I think?"

"Not especially."

It was a rhetorical question. "I think you're jealous," I say, crossing my arms as I appraise him.

His nostrils flare. I bite back a triumphant smile and dig deeper. There's so little to entertain me here, and sliding under the Frost King's skin holds a certain allure. "You're jealous because Zephyrus is likeable, approachable—"

"A trickster."

"You mean he has personality."

The king curls one hand over the back of his chair, fingers white with pressure. There must be something wrong with me for pushing him. I admit it. I want him to lose control.

But I can be civil. And Zephyrus and I made a deal, after all.

"Look," I say, moving toward him, "he's concerned. Your power is infiltrating his realm. So pull it back. Zephyrus can go home, and everyone is happy." Except me.

A great silence engulfs the space. It takes so long for him to respond I begin to question if he heard me at all. "Is that what he told you? Why he's traveled all this way?"

"Yes," I say slowly. And what does the king believe of Zephyrus' visit?

He says, in the most scathing tone yet, "I have never visited Zephyrus' realm. How am I to know if he speaks the truth?"

"I don't know. You're brothers. You're supposed to know these things." I grow tired of the king's mistrust. "Maybe consider visiting him."

"Let me rephrase. I have never visited Zephyrus' realm, and I have no desire to. If my power is corrupting his realm, he should consider strengthening his defenses."

I told Zephyrus his brother would not be receptive to me, and I was right. For now, I let the matter drop. Perhaps another time when the king is more open to discussion.

"If we're done here," I drawl, unknotting the ties at my wrists, laces trailing, "you can leave."

The Frost King stares at me. He does not move.

Well, he asked for it.

With a neat turn, I present to him my back and pull off my tunic, tossing it to the ground.

"What are you doing?" The words strike me with a combination of fury, confusion, and unease. It is that last emotion that snags my attention.

I glance over my shoulder. His focus bores into my upper back with all the intensity of a hailstorm. "I'm changing."

"Change behind the divider."

Normally I would, but knowing how uncomfortable it makes him, I decide to forgo that option. "This is my room," I state, facing him. "You're the unwanted guest. Don't like it? Leave." *Oh, please leave.*

Still glaring at me, though his gaze now rests on my throat and collarbones. My skin prickles oddly beneath his scrutiny. "I have something to discuss with you."

"Then discuss." With an impish smile, I untie my trousers and let them drop.

His gaze shies away, focusing on the blackening logs in the fireplace. There's no possible way this man hasn't seen a naked woman before. He's been married too many times to count. And I have *some* propriety. I still wear my underwear and breastband. "Your presence is required," he grits out.

"For what? Another excruciating dinner?" A never-ending supply of fresh tunics, breeches, dresses, stockings, and woolen socks stuffs my drawers and armoire. I'm in a black mood, so black it is. "I'll pass."

"It's not dinner." He clears his throat. Still looking pointedly elsewhere. "And you do not have a choice."

"I'm aware of what the word *required* means. But I'll say it again: I'll pass." Once I slip on my clean clothes, I dump the soiled ones in a basket that Orla collects every evening. The specter woman is too gentle for a place like this.

Now that I'm dressed, I've destroyed the only shield preventing the Frost King's approach. He strides to my side and takes my arm. "There is a reason I take a mortal woman as my bride every few decades," he says, those chilly blue eyes resting on me. "Today, we pay a visit to the Shade."

# CHAPTER 8

We share a mount. The Frost King sits with his arms curved around me, lightly gripping the reins of his equine-shaped darkwalker as the beast's agonizing plod rocks us from side to side. He doesn't trust me with my own mount. Perhaps he is smarter than I gave him credit for.

Our destination lies a full day's ride westward, across broken terrain and plunging valleys, the spread of the Deadlands' interior void of any and all life. Shades of white and gray land in hilly patches, interrupted by gleaming black trees. Every so often, I glimpse the bend of the glinting river. Mnemenos, I assume. While the Les circles the Deadlands, it doesn't pass through its center, though I've heard there are six rivers total within the realm, or so the stories claim. My hands tremble, so I tighten them around the saddle pommel. The Shade, that ravenous veil, awaits this journey's end. How much of my blood will be spilled?

It is midafternoon before my body's natural urges again make themselves known. "I have to piss."

I'm growing familiar with his silences. There is his *you're insufferable silence*. Different from his *I am king and you must obey* silence. I'm stumped by this silence. His *my wife is only a step above an animal* silence, perhaps. "You did so hours ago."

My fingers comb curiously through his mount's mane. It feels a bit like fog—weight without substance. Surprisingly, the beast doesn't seem to mind. Phaethon, he called it. "And now I have to go again."

From the way his chest slowly swells against my back, I sense his mounting irritation. He tugs the beast to a halt. "Make it quick."

After completing my business behind a tree, he helps me back into the saddle. The remainder of the day passes uneventfully. Clouds gather overhead, a heavy, slate gray. It smells sweet and musky, like an approaching storm.

"You know," I say, "this journey would pass a lot quicker if you attempted to make conversation."

The reins creak in the king's grip, leather on leather. "That is assuming there is something to discuss." Unruffled, composed. At this point, I would take his ire, however intense. Proof that he has the capacity to feel.

"You know what your problem is?"

"Hush."

"You think you can treat people—"

"Stop talking," he hisses, jerking his mount to a halt.

I'm suddenly aware of how rigidly the Frost King sits at my back. My skin prickles with new awareness. Not a breeze stirs the leafless, soot-colored branches, and that concerns me, for rarely is there lack of wind in the king's presence. The stillness has altered and deepened. It yawns like a mouth.

As I scan our surroundings, I reach for the bow hanging across my back. But it's not there. Zephyrus' gift hangs in my bedroom. Useless.

"Why does the forest dislike your presence?" I breathe as shadows blot in my periphery. Something is out there. Darkwalkers? I don't smell smoke, but then again, there is no wind to carry it.

"Is it not obvious?" His spear materializes in his right hand, and he angles it forward. "My power has killed the forest, corrupting the souls awaiting Judgment. They do not appreciate it."

One tense breath rolls into the next. My only weapon is a blade in my boot, but it will pass right through the spirits' amorphous forms unless it is dipped in blood. Without my satchel of salt, I'm defenseless. "Could you stop them, if needed?"

"Perhaps."

A twig snaps. My eyes cut in the direction of the sound.

He says lowly, "There are times when I am able to exert control over the darkwalkers, but their will has grown stronger of late."

The thought is utterly terrifying. Darkwalkers are highly intelligent, and their numbers seem to increase year after year. "How do you stop them?"

"You can't."

I scan our surroundings again. The forest is soundless, empty.

Eventually, the Frost King lowers his weapon. "They track us, but they won't attack in daylight. Sunlight weakens them." With a gentle nudge, he pushes our mount into a smooth trot. "We must hurry."

By the time the sun begins to set, my backside aches and my thighs twinge from the arduous ride. The land slopes into a gradual ascent. What trees remain fall away. Wind screams atop the bluff, hissing as it tangles ice-bitten fingers in my hair, and below, the world spreads flat and white.

Something inside me stills. "What is this?"

For below, something teems. A writhing mass, body upon body, the shape blurred behind the semi-opaque barrier that separates us. A horde of people has gathered, many hundreds, maybe even thousands. They blanket the landscape, trickle into the lower valley, huddle in unidentifiable shapes, their starved bodies swamped in thin cloth and ragged furs.

The air vibrates with their screams. They drive against the barrier in waves. They cannot pass through the Shade. Only the dead may do so, and only via the Les.

Yet they want in.

"Why are they trying to enter the Deadlands?"

A low, rough sound vibrates through the king's chest at my back. It reminds me of a growl. "The darkwalkers continue to escape into the Gray. The villagers blame me for the breach and seek to end my life, among other things."

I don't remember dismounting, but snow crunches beneath my boots. My muscles twinge as I lift my legs high and punch them through the thin layer of crust, trudging closer to the frozen Les. The Shade's eerie ripple spreads like cold through my veins. Its pulse is a heartbeat in my ears.

A mother with a young babe swaddled against her breast grapples at the barrier. It flows like dark water, shifting away from her touch.

Desperation ignites as her gaze meets mine. Now she is clawing at the wall. Now she is ramming into the blockade, again, again. Now she is screaming as her baby cries the feeblest of sounds, and she is pleading, she is wailing. *Monster! You monster!*

My stomach curdles into a hard, wrinkled pit. The men stab their knives and pitchforks and rusted swords against the wall, yet they bounce back so quickly they're torn from their hands. Here I stand with the Frost King as though we are a united front, and I feel close to vomiting, because it is the furthest thing from the truth. What must these people think of me?

"I'm sorry," I whisper. Their fists beat against the barrier, light flaring at the various points of contact. "I'm so sorry."

Snow shushes behind me, drawing my attention. The Frost King has dismounted and stands at my back, those dead eyes resting on the struggling townsfolk. I don't recognize anyone from Edgewood. These people must have traveled from the far-flung towns, the closest one lying fifty miles eastward. But he doesn't care. Their lives are of no concern to him.

"You have to help them." Two steps, and I'm before him. My hands curl into the front of his cloak.

He blinks at me in surprise. "Is that what you would have me do? Offer myself to those hungry for vengeance?"

A hoarse laugh claws free. "You cannot die. You said so yourself. And if you helped them, they wouldn't have a reason to kill you!"

For a moment, I think he might actually consider it. "No."

"Please." Snow seeps into my trousers, numbing my skin. "They are hungry and cold. You can do something."

His upper lip twitches, just once, like a nervous tic. "What would you have me do? I do not control the darkwalkers. They go where they wish."

"But they're escaping through the Shade somehow."

"Yes, and by giving your blood to the Shade, you are strengthening the barrier, closing the holes that have formed over time."

My mouth opens and closes dumbly. "What?"

Wrapping a hand around my upper arm, he hauls me closer. In his other hand, he holds a knife.

My pulse stutters before crashing head-first into the ground. "I thought you said you don't sacrifice your wives."

"I don't." The blatant frustration in his tone comes as a surprise. The Frost King toes an edge, though not one I'm aware of. He drags me nearer to the Shade despite my thrashing. The screams peak and die at my struggles, and I'm not sure if mine has joined the throng. The crowd jostles forward, a wave of skeletal hands and sagging flesh. My head spins. My gasps weaken. How much blood does he need? A drop? A bucketful? The line between life and death is thin.

"Take off your glove," he says.

The dark fabric ripples outward. It heaves and curls into itself, supple and warm and *alive*. My every pore recoils at the sight, that cruel, insidious sensation of a chilled finger drawn down my sweat-soaked spine. It will devour me. It will lap at my blood and slurp the marrow from my bones, drag every piece of my living flesh into its warped creation.

Elora. Think of Elora, her life, future, and happiness.

The Frost King stops an arm's length from the barrier. Since I've made no move to follow his order, he removes my glove for me, exposing my sweaty hand to the scouring air. His knifepoint digs into my palm, but it doesn't break skin. He looks to the horde of ill, down-trodden townsfolk congregating on the other side of the Shade before he begins to slice into me.

Faster than he can react, I twist, moving under his guard, and flip the knife from his hand to mine, whipping the blade so it kisses the base of his neck.

His mouth slackens with surprise. I bite back a grim smile. He is not the first to underestimate me.

"How bold of you. And how foolish." He appraises me without fear, but not without intrigue. "Will you kill me, then?" His voice softens and slows, curling around me with its beguiling threads.

I could do it. The dagger is his. God-touched.

Though I have my suspicions of the consequences of his death—destruction of the Shade, an end to winter, among other things—I do not know for certain that's what will happen. What if he dies, but the Shade remains? Or what if the Shade is destroyed, but the darkwalkers survive, able to roam the Gray freely? Until I am certain of the consequences, certain that I will be able to walk free of the Deadlands without obstacles, I need him alive.

Slowly, as if understanding it is no mortal weapon I hold, the Frost King lifts his hand. He bypasses the dagger hilt, instead resting his fingertips against my chin, drawing them up the curve of my face. My grip on the handle loosens at the unexpected touch.

He moves so quickly I can't track it. Clasping my wrist, he slices through the center of my palm. I hiss as my skin splits and blood wells. The murmuring crowd beyond the Shade dies as a whoosh roars in my ears.

"Mortal blood is necessary for the Shade's existence," he explains, as if he did not have a knife at his throat moments ago. "Any mortal blood will do, but the blood of a mortal bound in union to the king is far more potent. A willing donation is always stronger than reluctant giving."

That must be why he moved away from the practice of sacrifice. "But I'm not a willing participant." A small pool of scarlet gathers in the well of my palm. No, I'm definitely not willing.

"Choose," he says. "Your blood"—he tilts his head toward those trapped beyond the Shade—"or theirs."

Fury and helplessness twine into a choking amalgam. This is no choice. It is a poison I must swallow and be glad of: saving these people at the destruction of my own life. And yet, it is the price I paid switching places with Elora. What's done is done, yes? But for the first time since crossing into the Deadlands, I wonder if the price I paid was too high.

"Mine," I spit. Soon, this will not matter. I will be free of him. We will all, at long last, be free.

He deepens the incision. The blood flows hot and thick, trickling down my wrist. His grip unyielding, the king takes my hand and shoves it inside the barrier.

The darkness ignites. Red streaks in the cloth stretch to either side of me, gradually overtaking the darkness as it spreads far, traveling the length in its entirety. Suction around my wrist and fingers. A wet, hungry mouth. Dull pain shimmers up my arm. My scream cracks against the back of my clenched teeth. I can't pull free. The more blood it drags from my veins, the more opaque the Shade grows. And I ask myself why that is. Why the king needs my blood to strengthen the Shade, something of his own creation.

Unless his power is weakening.

The scarlet hue has burned away every piece of darkness. Then it snuffs out, the Shade one whole and continuous stretch that towers over me. It spits out my hand, the cut on my palm already scabbed over.

"Come, Wife." He sheathes the dagger at his waist. "It's time to depart."

The barrier, once thin as cloth, is now so dense I can't see the townsfolk beyond.

What have I done?

When I ram my shoulder against the substance, the darkness curls away, peels back. A glimpse—a frightened eye, grasping hands—before the darkness knits together, blocking my view of the other side.

What if I had refused to strengthen the Shade? If I had held out a little longer, could the townsfolk have crossed the weakened barrier? Would the Frost King's influence over the Gray have loosened?

Now I'll never know.

The Frost King begins towing me toward his mount, which stamps at the muddy snow and tosses its head impatiently.

"We can't leave them."

His fingers tighten around my upper arm as I attempt to jerk free. "Calm yourself, Wife."

I will not go quietly. I will not go at all.

"Think of the children," I cry, digging in my heels. "You can do something. You can call back winter. *Please*." My boots fling snow in all directions. I dig my heels in harder, but the ground remains frozen, the earth slick, my body weak compared to his immortal strength. No matter how I fight, I can't break free.

"Let her go."

The Frost King and I freeze.

A figure steps free of the shadows, snow dusting his wild curls.

The motion is so graceful there is no separation between god and earth. Something has changed in him. His eyes, perhaps. The green of new growth, of life, of spring. A color so rich in intensity I swear it bleeds out. Zephyrus is gone. Before me stands the West Wind, and he heralds a warning.

Bow drawn.

Arrow pointing at his brother's heart.

The wind breaks, a howling declaration, a scream of defiance as the North Wind's voice takes on an insidious, frightening edge, the hair sprouting along my arms. "You overstep, Zephyrus."

The West Wind treads lightly across the packed snow. Fresh pink buds bloom in his wake. "Let Wren go." His voice is different as well. Strange and ethereal.

The Frost King's grip around my arm loosens. His other hand shifts, sliding around the swell of my shoulder, moving to the knob at the apex of my spine. It then travels down, trailing over each raised vertebra, a slow, intentional touch, low, lower to the base of my spine where my backside curves outward. And that is where his hand comes to rest: at the small of my back.

The possessiveness of his touch elicits a shiver from me.

"My business is of no concern to you," he responds.

"Wren." Zephyrus ignores his brother. "Are you all right?"

"I'm fine."

Zephyrus appears out of place with his gold-stitched tunic, the burnished hue to his skin, the warm, laughing eyes. For this is the North Wind's land. It is he who passes Judgment onto souls. He who calls down the wrath of cold. He whose word is law. He who has become most intimate with death.

"What will you do, Zephyrus?" he asks softly. "Kill me?"

"I'm not here to kill you, Brother. I'm here to make you pay attention."

The bow string twangs. The arrow cuts clean and fleeting, a motion I can barely track with my mortal eyes. Thick, serpentine vines sprout from its tip and explode in every direction, tunneling belowground and wrapping around the blackened tree husks. The green swells inside its skins, growing engorged, leaves unfurling and buds bursting on the stems. A vine slithers toward me, curls gently around my wrist. Then the air ruptures and I'm tossed backward by a force so mammoth it feels as though the earth itself is heaving and breaking underfoot.

I hit a snowbank, sinking deep into soft cold. A shrieking flurry veils the land, and no light or sound or force may penetrate it. Yet there, standing like a pillar of gray at the heart of that white storm, the North Wind commands a power older than the earth, the celestial bodies. He calls down the breath of this world: the first of its life. To witness such power . . . I've never seen anything like it.

My skin hums from the crackle of its force. I can almost see the air take shape. Like two invisible hands guide its current and its bend. It splits and splits again, cutting itself into smaller and smaller fragments.

Something explodes to my right. I flatten myself against the ground as a branch whips overhead and plunges into the trunk of another tree, snapping it in half.

"Zephyrus!" roars the Frost King. "Zephyrus, enough!"

As I push to my knees, a gust batters my back, sending me flat on my face. It's becoming difficult to breathe.

Brother against brother, they rage. Two ageless gods unleashed: the Frost King, the Bringer of Spring. The air screams. A nearby boulder ruptures straight through. And unless I can find shelter, I will be the next thing to break.

I crawl toward the nearest tree, using its massive trunk to shield myself from the wind that tears and flays and shreds like teeth. My eyes water uncontrollably. Something cracks sharply, but the deluge is so thick I can't see what it is.

A vague, dim shape catches my attention then. Somehow, Zephyrus has made his way to the upper boughs of the trees, leaping from branch to branch as though the punishing gales are nothing but a minor breeze. Vines and leaves spring up from where his feet touch the stripped bark. Moments later, frost consumes the bits of green.

He leaps, and he is flying once more. The Frost King snaps his spear upward. Ice explodes from the tip, blasting shards of quicksilver toward Zephyrus, whose bow and arrow make a reappearance. Another arrow flies seconds before a wall of flowers and wood materializes to create a blockade around his body. The ice embeds itself into the barrier. Dropping his shield, Zephyrus engages in another flurry of attacks.

When there's a break in the gales, I haul myself to my feet, using the tree for support. Each footstep is a struggle. Pushing against the harshest, iciest, most ferocious wall of shifting air. Step by step, a stumble, a fall, another step, and again.

The king sends another blast of ice at Zephyrus, who evades, vanishing in a tangle of vines before materializing in a thicket of blackening flowers.

"You're going to destroy the whole forest!" My throat strains. The North Wind. The West Wind. Gods wearing the skins of men.

I clamp my hand around the Frost King's arm. His eyes snap to mine, the blue so dazzling it physically hurts to look at him, as though I stare into the sun. Something weakens in my chest. My fingers twitch against his sleeve, then tighten. He takes in the hand on his arm, and a frown shadows his mouth.

Movement draws my eye over his shoulder. A pair of vines rips up a tree by the roots. A rush of earth-scented wind catches the tree and flings it clear across the clearing.

The world slows, narrows. The trajectory is clear. The tree will crush my skull, fragment my bones. But the end will be swift. A small mercy.

My eyes close.

Peace.

One breath slides into two, then four, then seven, and I am still here, breathing, chilled to the bone.

My eyes open. The white heart of a storm surrounds me. I stand facing the Frost King's broad back. To my left lies the tree, the line it gouged into the snow as if having been flung to the side, sparing me a premature end.

The winds clash: warm and cold, life and death. Sound ruptures through the valley. The air trembles, and the ground, quaking deep in the earth's core.

They will destroy each other—and me—unless I give the Frost King what he wants. And what he wants is my compliance.

My stomach lurches as the ground shatters somewhere in the distance. Never have I bent a knee to a stronger force. Never. But my survival is a long game. It is not today. It is tomorrow and the next day and the next, a month from now, a year, ten. However long it takes to break free of these bonds. So I must not think of what I want, but of what I strive for. I must think of the road's distant end.

One of Zephyrus' vines lashes out, wrapping around the Frost

King's ankles faster than the eye can track, up to his calves, thighs, abdomen, chest. The plant disintegrates around his neck and the Frost King lunges, slashing his spear in a brutal, downward cut. Roots burst from the ground in retaliation and roll like great waves toward the North Wind, who does not bow, does not kneel, does not flinch, does not fade.

They never reach him. All at once, they drop to the snow-strewn earth, limp and twitching. The wind ceases.

All is quiet. All is still.

The snow clears to reveal Zephyrus partially encased in ice, his arms and legs frozen in an aggressive stance in preparation of attack. One pick of ice hovers at his neck.

And sinks in, slowly.

Blood trickles from the opening. Zephyrus bares his teeth, which have sharpened into points.

"Wait!" I stumble forward. The ice crawls over Zephyrus' chest. I'm imagining his heart slowing, the darkness that leaches into one's vision when the cold seeps into your bloodstream, when it is all you know, when it is eternity. "I'll come with you. Just let him go." Let him go, and he will live. I will have my sleep tonic. I will have my captor's death.

I will be free.

"Please . . . Boreas." I dare to rest my hand on his forearm. The muscle, sinuous and lean, twitches beneath my touch, but he doesn't pull away.

He growls, "This matter does not concern you, Wife."

"If the matter concerns my life, then yes, it does."

A tremor runs through him. He whispers, so faintly I almost miss it, "He has taken much from me. Why should I not return the favor?"

The rough, anguished tone strikes a chord in me, and I step closer without realizing it. They are brothers, and that bond is forever. Whatever wound exists between them, the flow cannot be staunched with revenge. "It doesn't have to come to this. You can choose to walk away."

"And turn my back so he can strike me unaware?" He murmurs too softly for his brother to overhear. But I hear him. And I hear the things he does not wish to say to me or anyone, whatever secrets he keeps.

He steps forward, breaking contact with me. A sharp gesture frees Zephyrus from the ice. "Leave," he booms, and the air screams its warning. "Leave my territory and do not return. Brother or not, I will kill you the next time the opportunity presents itself."

A brutal gust snaps me into the air and deposits me atop his darkwalker's back. Moments later, the Frost King settles behind me, and we tear out of the clearing as if death itself is at our heels.

# CHAPTER
## 9

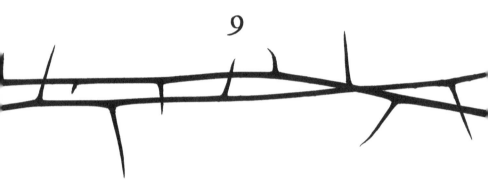

Three days have passed since I gave my blood to the Shade. In that time, I've slept little. My heart races at odd moments, and no amount of wine can dull that particular unease. I'm plagued by memories: dark, alarming things that press upon my eyes. I don't leave my room. I can't. If I am to be chained as an animal, then these walls offer the only sanctuary—distance from the king who reigns.

Instead of helping tear down the Shade, I fed it my blood. The blood of a mortal, intertwined with the Frost King's insidious power. Instead of killing the king, I helped him strengthen the barrier to his realm. Instead of ending people's suffering, I extended it. I failed them. I failed Edgewood, Elora most of all.

Inevitably, my thoughts turn toward Zephyrus. I imagine he's made himself scarce for the time being. If he traveled all this way, I doubt he'd return to his realm without trying to reach an understanding with his brother, a promise that winter will be lifted where it infringes on his territory. Anyway, we made a deal. He promised to investigate the sleep tonic. I do not think he would break that promise.

Rolling over in bed, I pinch my eyes shut so the darkness deepens and all I know is the void behind my eyelids.

The door opens after a brief knock. "My lady?"

I haven't the energy to reply, so I merely toss my arm over my eyes as a lamp flares, forcing back the dim that covers me like a cloak in winter.

Orla rushes to my side. "My lady, are you ill?" The back of her hand rests against my forehead, searching for fever.

"I'm fine, Orla." Sighing, I lower my arm, peering up at my maid. "What time is it?"

"It's nearly sundown. The king requests your presence at dinner."

So the Frost King has finally noticed my absence. It only took three days.

Pushing myself into a seated position, I pat down the strands of hair that stick up at odd angles. What must Orla think of me? "Please tell the king I decline his invitation." It sounds so much more accommodating than demanding he shove that meaningless request up his ass.

"My lady, I cannot do that. He insisted you wear this—" She plops a ridiculously frilly dress into my lap. "—and that you join him tonight."

The dress is lovely—as a sack. Pinching the fabric between my thumb and forefinger, I hold it against the light. It's hideous, and I'm being kind. I'm used to simpler cuts and long lines, plainer gowns. This billowing monstrosity bears layers upon layers of bile-colored fabric, enlarged, bulbous cap sleeves, and a collar that might very well strangle me should I manage to shove my head through.

"Orla," I say, my gaze cutting to hers so aggressively she stumbles backward. "I'm not wearing this. And I'm not attending dinner either." I toss the costume aside and snuggle into the pillows. There is little I desire save darkness and peace.

Snatching the dress with a surprising amount of frustration, my maid moves to drape it over a chair and returns, yanking on my arm. For a dead woman, she is surprisingly strong. "Get up, my lady. Now." Another yank brings me to the edge of the mattress, my upper torso hanging over the side. Her graying curls spring free of their tether. "At least attempt to make conversation."

My feet hook over the lip of the mattress as she tugs harder. Despite my morose mood, laughter tickles the back of my throat. "Orla."

"Someone has to watch out for you, my lady." Sweat dots her hairline, and she gives another great heave, her face reddening from exertion. "If you don't go, then he wins."

We both still.

*He wins.*

Dropping my hands, Orla steps back, head bowed. "I didn't mean . . ." Her voice trembles with the fear of having overstepped.

"It's all right." I gentle my tone. Orla did nothing wrong. She spoke the truth. She spoke from her heart. I am not one to punish courage, whatever form that might take.

Regardless, she is absolutely right. If I continue to cower in my rooms, the Frost King wins. And that is why I will attend dinner. On *my* terms.

Swinging my legs over the bed, I announce, "I will dine with the king."

Her face collapses in relief, and the flush gradually recedes from her skin, returning it to its semi-transparent hue. "Wonderful. I'll fill your bath—"

"I'm not taking a bath."

She halts on her way to the door. "But . . ." Her jaw unhinges. "You haven't bathed in days."

Yes, and if I smell atrocious, all the more reason to dine with husband dearest. If I can't fight him outright, I'll quietly rebel.

For the last three days, I've worn a loose tunic the color of a corpse and woolen trousers ripped at the knees. My hair holds the exact texture of a bird's nest. My breath absolutely reeks.

This man will regret calling me to heel like a damn dog.

"I'm going to wash my face," I all but sing, skipping behind the divider. Orla tosses the dress over the top, where it hangs. I ignore the offensive sight and lather the soothing lavender soap onto my hands above the small washing basin. My black mood peels from my flesh as, with every scrub against my oily skin, I'm washed anew.

When I emerge from behind the divider, wearing the same filthy attire, Orla moans in horror. "My lady, please don't." She shoves the dress into my arms, her expression stricken. "The dress. Wear the dress. It will look magnificent on you."

"Please don't fret, Orla." I rest my hands on her shoulders, give a comforting squeeze. "No harm will come to you, I promise. This is something I must do for myself."

"Could you not do it for yourself while wearing the dress?"

Oh, I do like this pluckier version of my maid. "No, I can't." Pulling her close for an apologetic embrace, I go to meet my fate.

I take the stairs two at a time, strangely eager for the evening. To add insult to the mix, I've draped my threadbare coat over my shoulders. It's a patched motley of animal skins. Come to think of it, I can't remember the last time it was washed. Dried blood coats the sleeves: the innards of butchered animals.

Upon entering the dining room, I brace myself for the ire that is sure to descend at my manner of dress, but the Frost King's chair is vacant. Darkness eats at the edges of the small circle of illumination cast by the candlesticks atop the table. It's so cold my breath spills white before me. Two men guard the doors, two servants stand against the walls, ready to refill a glass at a moment's notice, yet no one thinks to light a fire?

By some miracle, flint and steel rest atop the mantel, covered in centuries' worth of dust. The dry kindling catches, and when I add a few logs stacked off to the side of the grate, fire whooshes up and out, forcing me back a step. The sudden brightness stings my eyes. It's a beautiful sight.

"My lady." One of the servants shuffles forward, glancing at the licking flames nervously. "We're not allowed to use the fireplaces. The lord has forbidden it."

Of course he has. "Did you light the fire?"

"Well, no," she whispers, frowning.

"Then you have nothing to worry about." Already the heat licks at my skin, driving back the chill that is potent and undying. "Do you know when the king will arrive?"

"No, my lady."

Does he expect me to await his arrival before eating? Punish me for some unknowable slight? I wait for no one where hunger is concerned. "Can you show me to the kitchen, please?"

With obvious reluctance, the woman leads me through a side door, then a stairwell that descends belowground, pressed between walls of hardened permafrost, steam clumped like damp wool in the air.

The noise reaches me first. Voices call to one another behind a set of closed double doors, their green paint peeling under the humidity. Curious, I push open the right door and step inside the kitchen.

Wooden counters frame the perimeter of the large square room, nicked and burned and stained from countless knives or dings or spills. Cabinets painted a pale yellow—my brows lift in surprise at the sunny hue—are built into the walls. It smells divine. Garlic? A red sauce bubbles in a pan atop one of three woodfire stoves. One of the many apron-clad specters stirs it with a wooden spoon.

I'm remembering Orla remarking on her inability to enjoy the taste of food. If the kitchen staff have been sentenced to serve the Frost King, does food turn to ash in their mouths as well? Or has he revoked that punishment for them, since their palates are needed to ensure the food is well-seasoned?

Aside from the stoves, hefty barrels filled to the brim with various grains and roots occupy the space, as well as a large basin sink, where a tower of dirty dishes leans precariously. In the center of the chaos, a rotund, kind-looking man with a gray beard barks orders.

"Excuse me, are you the cook?"

His eyes widen as he turns. "Apologies, my lady. I did not see you."

"Call me Wren, please. And what is your name?"

The man plucks a towel from the counter, dries his hands. "Silas, my lady."

"Silas. I was wondering if you take requests for meals."

He glances at the fare currently bubbling or steaming in assorted pots and pans. "The food is almost done, but—"

"Not for dinner," I clarify. "Dessert."

His mouth works, and a squeak of air sounds from his throat. "Dessert." The workers pause in the middle of their tasks, the silence immediate in the wake of all that rattling and clanging.

"Yes." My eyes dart to the staff, who startle into motion again, stirring broth and whatnot. "Cake, to be specific."

"Cake?" More tentatively: "The lord requested this?"

"No, but it won't be a problem." I offer him an indulgent smile. "Cake is my favorite dessert and my husband wants to make sure I'm happy." And it's quite simple: cake makes me deliriously happy.

He tosses the towel aside, considering. "Well," he says, like he'd never thought of it that way before, "if the lord is amenable, then yes, my lady—"

I lift my eyebrows.

"Wren," he corrects. "I would be honored to bake a cake for you tonight. Is there a particular flavor you prefer?"

"Chocolate would be lovely." Start simple, start small. Beaming from ear to ear, I give a little curtsy and return upstairs to take my seat at the unoccupied dining room table. Moments later, dishes heaped with steaming food are served. I begin filling my plate with roasted sprouts, thick slices of soft bread that steam when broken open, whole quail, its skin crispy and smelling of rosemary, pillowy mounds of potatoes, and savory gravy that pours out rich and thick, among other things. I've barely eaten the last few days. Now I attack the food with a vengeance, pushing all thoughts of those starving across the Shade out of my head, including Elora. If I'm to help them, help her, I need to keep up my strength.

A full glass of wine awaits me. I take a sip. It feels like relief. It always feels like relief. Elora never understood. Time and again, I asked her if she would not cure someone who was ill, had the cure been in reach atop the table, red liquid in a clear glass. She never deigned to answer.

I'm halfway through my meal when the clear, precise gait of booted feet crosses into the dining room. My skin puckers in warning, cold tendrils of air licking the curve of my neck and sliding exploratory fingertips down my spine. My fingers twitch around my fork. I will them to settle.

With my back to the king, I'm blind to his approach. There is a distant recognition of his presence, however, those clipped heels echoing and dying in slow, sharp increments. Seconds later, he rounds the table, pinning me with the force of that otherworldly azure gaze.

My chin lifts despite the incessant hammering of my heart. The Frost King may be an absolute bastard, but he has impeccable taste in style. An overcoat of slate gray encases his wide shoulders and chest, bright silver buttons nestled like stars. Dark trim trousers showcase his long legs. The fire tosses wells of light and shade over his severe cheekbones, that sharp-edged jawline. The tips of his hair are damp, pulled into a low tail, suggesting he recently bathed.

He picks me apart slowly—my filthy attire, the oily lanks of hair, what is probably gravy smeared on my chin, a fat speck of pepper lodged between my teeth—and lingers on the wineglass clamped between my fingers. When his attention shifts to the roaring fire, his frown deepens.

I continue digging into my meal as if I'm not bothered by his presence in the slightest.

Eventually, the Frost King asks, "Did Orla bring you the dress?"

"Yes."

He stares at me as though I'm a simpleton. "And why aren't you wearing it?"

The king is no fool, but he is certainly succeeding at making me feel like one. I resent him for that.

I reply, offering him my sweetest smile, "I didn't want to."

The tic of his jaw reveals enough. He is not pleased. He expected my cooperation. And the fire . . . His gaze returns to the devouring flames. Another unforeseen surprise.

"You smell like a dead animal."

My mouth twitches. I manage to swallow down the absurd laughter, brought on by the bubbling, effervescent sensation warming my body. "And you wear the blood of innocents on your hands. What of it? Do not think to act like some noble lord when we both know there is nothing noble or lordly about you." Except the conquering part. He's done quite well with that.

The Frost King makes a sound of pure derision. "You are no lady."

I smile nastily. "If you wanted a lady, you should have married my sister."

"That was the intention."

With that, he sits, unfolds a napkin onto his lap, and begins filling his plate.

My lips pinch in displeasure. If he insists on being rude, I refuse to feel bad about my poor attire. This is my reality: married to a man whom I despise, and who despises me.

The Frost King is fastidious in his plating. He arranges everything in a circle. The foods do not touch. He digs a neat hollow in his potatoes where the gravy sits without spilling out. In fascination, I watch him slather butter onto a slice of warm bread. He smears the butter to the very edges. Like painting between the lines.

"You missed a spot."

His gaze snaps to mine. He has frozen mid-spread.

"The butter," I explain, pointing to the bread he holds. "You missed a spot."

The Frost King returns to his task, doing what he does best: ignoring me.

If I hadn't been watching him so closely, I would have missed it. The edge of his sleeve suddenly pulls back, revealing smudges of what appear to be moist soil on his wrist, a few blades of grass. I blink, but by then, the sleeve has slipped forward again. I frown. There is no fertile land in these parts, not for thousands of miles, across realms where the Frost King's power cannot penetrate. I must have imagined it.

And yet, we're served vegetables and fruits daily. There must be a garden nearby. It's the only explanation.

The Frost King moves on to his quail, cutting off small pieces, chewing slowly to savor the taste. I shovel greens into my mouth as though they might disappear.

"Why am I here," I ask mid-chew, "if you insist on ignoring me?"

His expression twists with borderline revulsion at the flash of mashed food caught in my mouth. "It's to keep an eye on you," he states, lips sealing cleanly over his fork and drawing a piece of roasted carrot between his teeth.

"Where would I go? I'm trapped here, remember?"

"I don't want you meeting with Zephyrus."

Ah. So his brother remains the issue. "You sent him away," I remind him. "I haven't seen him since."

He dips his chin, acknowledging my response. Then—more silence.

Since the king refuses to converse, I use the opportunity to study him. No detail is too insignificant. So far, I know very little about the man—god—I married. He is closed and aloof, distant and untouchable, prickly and inflexible. I've yet to see him smile. I've yet to hear his laugh. What will it take to thaw this man toward me? Somehow, I will need to earn his trust.

But he is also, I admit reluctantly, too pretty, though not feminine in the least. Whereas I resemble something the cat dragged in days ago, he is a shining jewel. Not a speck of dirt mars his image. His blue eyes, set beneath a level brow, have deepened in the low light, his pale skin luminous, smooth as porcelain. His bone structure contains an impossible symmetry. Truly, he bears every marking of perfection.

What a shame he has an intolerable personality.

As if sensing my gaze, those eyes lift to mine, and a current of shock runs through me as his focus shifts briefly to my scar, and the faintest line folds the skin between his black eyebrows. Does he wonder why I stare? Does he care?

One of the burning logs collapses, sending sparks dancing up the chimney. I finish off my drink, and a staff member appears to refill it for the umpteenth time. He watches me take another sip, gaze narrowed. My plate is nearly clean. I scrape up the last of the potato with my fork. There will be no wasted food from me.

*Scrape, scrape, scrape.*

His left eye begins to twitch.

I pop a piece of quail into my mouth and chew with gusto. I've changed my mind. This dinner isn't so bad. Why, if I focus on clearing my plate, I hardly notice the stilted atmosphere. It's as if we've been married for years rather than a week. Here we are, an unhappy couple, sick of the other's presence, wanting only peace of mind.

Elora would find herself right at home here. She lives for dresses, dinners, meaningless small talk. She would soften this man toward her. They would discuss the weather probably, or she would, a single-sided discussion, but the king would no doubt be enrapt with her kind nature. So I wonder. Maybe the lack of conversation isn't the king's fault. Maybe it's mine and I'm the worst dinner guest he's ever hosted.

*Scrape, scrape—*

The Frost King slams his fist onto the table. Plates and cutlery rattle. My wine glass topples, spilling red onto the white tablecloth. What a waste.

Calmly, I inquire, "Is something wrong?"

Leaning forward, he whips out, "You are purposefully doing everything in your power to irritate me." His voice has lost its chilly calculation. Now, a hint of fire thrums beneath. It's so rare a thing that I find my interest piqued, my attention focused fully on the man before me.

"Yes," I say, finally giving in to laughter. He recoils from the sight of half-chewed food in my mouth, a piece of which drops onto my soiled tunic. That only makes me laugh harder. Annoying the Frost King is the best entertainment I've had in months. "Is it working?"

He blinks. The lines around his mouth carve straight into his alabaster skin.

"I'm teasing you." I appraise him with slight concern. "You do know how to laugh, right?"

He spears another carrot in answer. It was a rhetorical question. Doubtful he knows how to laugh. What resides in those dead eyes but the promise of an early demise?

The basket of bread sits at my elbow. I'm hungry enough to inhale an entire loaf—indeed, I've eaten half already—but I grab two more pieces, set them on my plate, and ask with impressive courtesy, "Can you pass the butter?"

"You've already eaten two plates' worth of food," he points out.

"And now I'm having a third." When you have starved your whole life, you will never be satiated. As it is, my hunger extends far beyond my stomach. "Is that a problem?" There is enough food to feed an entire village twice over. I am barely making a dent.

The Frost King hands me the plate with stilted movements. He's so awkward it's painful to watch.

I slap a fat hunk of butter onto the bread before shoving it into my mouth. It is by far the best bread I've ever tasted, soft insides with a crusty shell. "So tell me about yourself. How do you spend your time?"

He examines me with what I believe is apprehension. Suspicious of some joke he believes is at play.

But it is no joke. The more I know of the enemy, the greater likelihood I will unearth a weakness of his. "Look, if I'm going to be stuck here until I die, don't you think it's best we learn about one another?"

"Why do you care to know me," he says, "when you've already passed judgment on my character?"

Absolutely, I have judged him. But he's judged me as well. Poor, wretched village scum, he sees. Weak, ugly mortal.

So where do we go from here?

"I don't know. Maybe you'll surprise me." Once I finish the first slice of bread, I move on to the second, sopping up the gravy pooling on my plate. The Frost King's upper lip curls as he watches me consume every available crumb. I smack my lips loudly, enjoying the shudder that moves through him.

After a time, he grinds out, "The Deadlands, as you know, are where the souls of those who have passed on arrive to await Judgment. I am responsible for serving their Judgment."

I know very little of the Deadlands' processes, but I do know that much. "How does that work?"

"Twice a month, on the full and new moons, I open my citadel to those awaiting Judgment. They are Judged based on the deeds of their past lives. Depending on the severity of those deeds, whether good or bad, they are sent to various resting places. It is my duty to fairly assess their life choices."

Interesting. I've not witnessed this process, but then again, I've yet to properly explore the citadel. I'd be interested to see how, exactly, the Frost King doles out punishment—or reward.

"And those souls that are doomed to live an eternity in punishment? Do you enjoy serving it to them?"

As soon as he polishes off his glass of water, a servant appears to refill it. "I'm not as horrible as you make me out to be," he says stiffly.

"Oh? You're saying you didn't steal me away from my home, lock me in a dungeon, threaten to chain me outside, force me to spill my blood for the Shade, all to strengthen your power?" Elbows perched on the table, I lean forward, peering beneath my eyelashes. "Please, tell me more."

He glowers down his flawlessly proportioned nose at me. "You chose to take your sister's place."

I wave his comment away. "Semantics."

"I do not lie."

"Then prove it. Name one thing you have done that serves someone other than yourself."

"There is little point. You would not believe me even if I told you."

He is not allowing me the chance.

I swipe one of the crispy quail legs and tear into the flesh, well aware I'm doing a poor job of coaxing him to lower his guard. His walls rise high. The stone is unbreakable.

"It's not just me, you know. You've wronged others as well. Forcing the staff into your service?" My hand clenches around my utensil. "Don't you see something wrong with that?"

"Is that what your maid told you? That I forced her, and all the staff, into service without reason?" He lifts his chin. "Perhaps you should have another conversation with her about the circumstances that led to her employment. And this time, demand the truth."

Straightening in my chair, I consider this new piece of information. I trust Orla, but the Frost King seems genuinely irked at hearing this. Could there be truth to his words? If that is so, why did Orla lie?

One of the servants emerges through the side door and sets a magnificent plated dessert onto the table with a small bow. "My lady."

The Frost King stares at the dessert. "What is this?"

"It's cake." And it's a sight to behold. Three layers coated in pillowy white icing with blue accents.

"I did not request cake," he says, lethally quiet.

Oh, he is not happy. That only serves to heighten my delight. "I did. Silas was happy enough to provide it." It's a shame to ruin such a beautiful work of art. He obviously put a lot of care into baking this for me, as evident by the intricate floral piping on the top and sides.

As I push away my dinner plate and tug the confection closer, the Frost King says, "Silas?"

"Your cook. You do know his name," I say, fork poised over the dessert as I lift my eyes to his, "don't you?"

"Of course I know his name." Terse.

I'm not entirely sure I believe him, but the sugary concoction drags my attention back to the matter at hand. Sinking the tines of my fork into the top layer of icing, I press down, severing the moist sponge to the bottom of the serving dish. The moment the chocolate cake touches my tongue, I am transported. The second bite is even richer than the first. I'm nearly a quarter of the way through when I remember my dinner companion, whose glare is so cold I would not be surprised to discover frostbite having manifested where his gaze touches me.

"Yes?" I say mid-chew.

That uncompromising focus lingers where I lick icing from my lower lip. "Are you going to consume that entire dessert on your own?"

"Well, I did ask Silas to bake it for me."

"You just ate three plates of food."

"Is it a slice you're asking for?" I might even give it to him.

"I don't like cake."

My forks clatters against the dish. "Who doesn't like cake?" I mean, really.

Grabbing a knife, I shave off the thinnest slice of cake possible—the width of a twig, if that—and place the miniscule bite on an empty plate. Rounding the table, I set it in front of him. The Frost King glowers at his meager portion. Then I return to my seat and proceed to inhale the rest of the cake myself.

Every smack of my lips makes him flinch in repulsion. Every smear of icing across my mouth, my chin, makes his jaw tighten from the disturbing display. I go one step further and groan as the sugary euphoria takes me far from this dreary room, this unbearable dinner companion. The king shudders, and I laugh, mashed, gummy food flashing between my teeth.

"You are an animal," he snarls.

Yes, and he has no idea what I'm capable of when cornered.

But I can be civil. In fact, it would be in my best interest, if only to coax out the information I need. Which, at the moment, is everything. "You have three brothers, yes?"

He nods stiffly. I wait, but he doesn't elaborate. "And their names are . . . ?"

"You've met Zephyrus." The name holds a bitter ring. "There is also Notus and Eurus."

"The South and East Winds."

Another shallow nod.

Pushing aside the empty dish, I fold my arms atop the table. A servant fills my wine glass to the brim, but I ignore it. This stifled reaction has revealed more emotion than any that has come before it. "You are not close with them."

"I have seen neither in centuries."

His fingers twitch against his glass. It is so small a thing. What bothers him? That he has not seen his brothers in hundreds of years, or that I am prying into his life?

"What are they like?" I ask, intrigued despite myself. The townsfolk know of the Four Winds, but the others in name only, for their influence does not touch the Gray. Zephyrus is the Bringer of Spring. The South Wind is said to reign over the hot desert winds. And the East Wind . . . Whatever power he controls, it must be immense.

He leans back to allow the servants to clear his place setting. "Eurus has a temper. Notus was always rather quiet."

"And they live in different realms?"

"Yes."

Places beyond the Gray. "Which brother is the eldest?"

"I am the eldest." There is an undercurrent of pride in his response.

Icing from the last bit of cake coats my lips. I wipe my mouth with my napkin, then ask, "Just out of curiosity, how old are you?" For he does not look a day over thirty. Not a single gray hair lightens his scalp.

The Frost King says, "I do not remember my birth, but I have been alive for many millennia. My mother is the dawn, my father the sky at dusk, the winds."

"*Millennia?*" I croak. Oh, mercy. My husband is ancient. "And your brothers are of a similar age?"

"Yes."

Ancient hearts, ancient winds. To him, I am a speck, a passing season. When I die, it is likely he will not even remember me. The thought doesn't sit well. "Have you ever visited them?"

"No," he growls.

Hm. Interesting reaction there. "Is there a reason?" Is he not allowed? But with Zephyrus here, able to cross into his brother's realm, that rule might not apply. The tales say the Anemoi were banished to the four corners of the world. What terrain have his brothers claimed as their homes? What towns have they ruined in their conquests?

He says, in a slightly colder tone, "Everything I need is right here." Simple. Yet I wonder, what is here for him? Because all I see is an empty house and a man who stands alone. "Now, if it's possible for you to stop talking for half a moment, I must ask a question of you."

Borderline insult aside, this is the first time the Frost King has shown an interest in me aside from the blood coursing through my veins. This should be good.

"Why are you not married?"

I startle so badly my fork rattles the side of the plate. Of all the questions to ask, that is the one he chooses? "But Husband," I grit out, "I am married."

"I mean why were you not married before. You are of marriageable age, are you not?"

"Yes," I snap. Twenty-three years of age, but I might as well carry the pox for my lack of suitors. People question if I am barren, if I house dark spirits within me, to have not secured a betrothed by this age.

Edgewood offers little prospects. Men do not want a headstrong woman. They want someone soft, someone to coddle. I do not fit into that mold. I never have. And I cannot trust that a man would not try to change me. I cannot trust that a man would not brush aside my needs. I cannot trust that a man would not turn away were I to let him in, let him see—me.

It is easier maintaining a physical relationship. The heart is never in danger of breaking.

But I only say, "I suppose I never met anyone I wanted to marry." It's not a lie.

That honed stare takes me in. "Not one person?"

My throat dips as I consider what to say and how much. He does not deserve anything, least of all my truths, but I give them to him anyway. "I would not make a very good wife. My sister, Elora, is the better choice."

Arms folded across his chest, he tilts his head, his full attention on me. I've absorbed him, at least momentarily. "Elaborate."

I trace the rim of my wine glass. "Elora is kind and nurturing. I am . . . not." Men find me too rough. And there is my scar to consider as well. I touch the edge of the raised skin, and the Frost King tracks my fingers with his gaze. I've made peace with it. I am not desirable in the eyes of men. So be it. My life was full when centered around Elora. Her need for me gave me purpose and strength and helped fill the void that has grown more pronounced in her absence.

I glance at the fire, but eventually my attention returns to the king's face, with its perfect, aggravating symmetry.

"How did you get your scar?" he asks.

I drop my hand. Normally I would punch whoever dared to ask such a personal question, but since I already despise the man sitting across from me and there's no possibility of that changing, I suppose I need not hide. "Darkwalker. One of my first hunting trips. I'm lucky though. It could have slashed my throat instead." My lips purse at his continued perusal. "It's rude to stare."

The Frost King turns away, his expression complicated. Too complicated to interpret. "Well," he says after a moment of silence. "At least you're not boring."

# CHAPTER
## 10

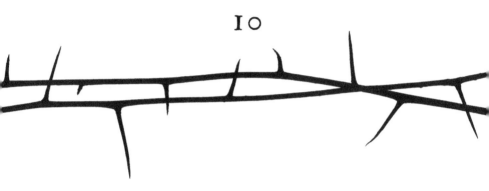

Two weeks I have been here, and I've yet to explore the citadel and its vast cold grounds. Grabbing my bow, quiver, and coat, I wander downstairs in search of a place to train. The fortress is so derelict no one would likely notice if I were to use an empty room for target practice. Dust and broken cobwebs glow silver in the wells of torchlight interspersed in the labyrinthine corridors. The shadows are large as cats, curling up in the corners with their wisped tails.

The south wing juts like a broken limb from the mammoth body of the citadel and contains large, gaping rooms lined with windows. They are the perfect size for gatherings, the chairs and tables and footstools all covered in white sheets. If there were gatherings once, when did they stop? And why?

As I exit one such room, I hear it: the meticulous footsteps of one who follows, who does not wish to be seen.

I continue on my way as if nothing is amiss. At times, the footsteps fade, yet always return. At the next bend, I sprint ahead, quiver slapping against my back. There—a curved, iron door tucked into the wall. Fumbling for the handle, I burst outside, veer left across one of the ice-encrusted courtyards to a walled pocket of open space, piles of swords and axes and arrows sprawled out in abandonment.

It's a practice court. Targets spaced at regular intervals are aligned next to what appears to be a small armory. Everything is overgrown with dead, knotted vines.

Crouching behind one of the targets near the wall, I lean back against the stones to brace myself, only nothing halts my motion. I fall backward through the wall until something soft and cold seeps into the back of my waistband. Snow. Quickly, I scramble upright, pushing aside the vines. It's a hole. And it leads to the outside— beyond the outer wall.

My heart thrums. It's not a way out of the Deadlands, but it's a start. A patch of blue sky after days of storms. Slotting that piece of information away, I nock an arrow to my bow and wait.

The man enters the practice yard moments later, gaze flitting from toppled rubble to darkened corner to collapsed roof. Then the fool turns his back on me. If I were a darkwalker, he'd be dead.

I tap the base of the target with my boot, rattling the structure. He whips around—to find an arrowhead inches from his face.

"Who are you?" I demand softly, voice steady, hands steady, weapon steady.

The man cannot die, seeing as he is already dead—at least, I don't think he can die again—but receiving an arrow to the face will certainly hurt. Thus, he remains wary as he retreats, hands raised.

"My name is Pallas, my lady. I am captain of my lord's guard."

A black tunic hits him at mid-thigh over clinging black breeches. Calf-high boots gleam with fresh polish. His semi-translucent form blends in with the toppled gray stone, the snow heaped in forgotten corners. His hair, secured with a strip of leather, fluctuates between light brown and fiery red. A trick of the light.

"Why are you following me?"

His attention never strays from the curl of my fingers around the bowstring, the arrow snug between. "My lord requested I keep an eye on you."

Wanted to make sure I wouldn't attempt to run, he means. There are hundreds of staff and guards moving throughout this crumbling fortress at any given moment. It's highly unlikely I'd be able to slip away unnoticed.

"Where does the king go during the day?" By the time I wake, he has already left the grounds, he and his darkwalker. No sighting until his return in the evenings. When I question him of his whereabouts over dinner, he states it's none of my business. I've overheard a few gossiping maidservants say they've spotted their lord returning coated in blood, his armor dented and smeared with remnants of battle. But I have not asked the king if this is true.

"I cannot say, my lady."

"Cannot? Or will not?"

He raises his chin. "Will not."

Such blind loyalty for someone who has no intention of ever releasing this man, or any of his staff, from service. "Look, I really don't want to shoot you, but since you've disrupted my morning, I'm not feeling particularly amicable. It's in your best interest to answer my question. Really."

When he doesn't respond, I shrug and drag the string back into a full draw. It vibrates with tension. "Last chance."

He glances between me and the bow, as though weighing the likelihood that I will keep my word. Whatever he spots in my face, well, that settles it.

"There has been unusual darkwalker activity the last few months. My lord is trying to find the source of this . . . change."

My attention sharpens in light of this information. A cold wind hisses through the cracks in the stone wall. "Unusual in what way?"

The captain crosses his arms, eyes narrowed. Sunlight streams through him in flat, narrow bands, brightening his outline and washing out the black hue of his garb. "Generally, the darkwalkers do not stray from the forest, but there have been multiple sightings of them near the citadel. It's almost as though . . ." He frowns, shakes his head.

*Almost as though the wards are losing strength*, is what he does not dare utter.

First the Shade. Now the wards. That's concerning, for a variety of reasons. But it supports my belief that the Frost King's power is weakening. "Would they enter the grounds, if given the chance?"

He takes me in, from my booted feet to my scarred face, and says, "My lord is doing all he can to ensure the citadel is secure. The darkwalkers have been under his rule for a long time. There is no need to fear this change in behavior."

Like I said: blind loyalty. "They may be under his rule, but they're not under his control." The darkwalkers wander wherever they wish to go. I haven't seen the king ever attempt to capture them or reverse the effects of the corruption.

Another long, searching look. "I think that's enough questions for today."

His generosity extends no further, is that it? "What a shame."

The arrow slices forward with unstoppable force, ending with the captain flat on his back, the arrow protruding from his right pectoral muscle.

Swinging my bow over my shoulder, I cross to his side and look down. "Tell the Frost King I don't need a chaperone. And don't follow me again."

The captain grits his teeth. I wonder how it works, the specters able to sustain wounds, yet unable to die. Will he need a healer? Not that it's any concern of mine. He reached his hand into a viper's nest. It's his own damn fault.

"You won't find a way out of the citadel," he growls, wrapping a shaking hand around the arrow shaft. Once he catches his breath, he gasps out, "You're wasting your time."

A fresh wave of fury seeps into my bloodstream. But I merely flick my hand toward him absently, striding from the practice court. I've already found a way out, and I'll take this secret to the grave. "So are you."

≈

My wanderings take me to the stables; the east wing; the parlor, dusty and abandoned; the second parlor; the kitchen, where I spend a good portion of the afternoon helping Silas cut vegetables; the courtyards, each more austere than the last. The day wanes, and I consider how I might successfully put an end to the North Wind's reign.

He's too guarded. A fortress shielded within a fortress, consumed by the deep silence of stone. I'm making little headway where trust is concerned. Evening meals remain stilted and pained, despite my best efforts to wheedle him into conversation. Everything he is, he holds tight to it, and at times I wonder what he fears would happen were he to loosen that fierce grip. What I might find.

Eventually, my thoughts circle back to Zephyrus, whom I haven't seen since the Frost King barred him from the citadel. If he seeks the poppy plant, could it possibly be somewhere nearby? If I found such a place, would I also find Zephyrus?

I go in search of Orla and find her arguing with another specter woman. She is slender, perhaps mid-thirties—the age in which she passed on—wearing large round glasses that magnify the majority of her narrow face. Small, opaque dots dust the bridge of her nose: freckles.

"I told you," Orla growls. "I told you over and over again. How difficult is it to remember a color?" She grasps one side of the basket the woman holds and yanks. "Give me the linens."

But the younger specter woman maintains her hold, near desperate as she pulls backs. "Wait. I can fix this. Please—"

Orla's fingers slip, and the basket snaps in the woman's direction, spilling out the contents.

The woman drops to her knees, hurriedly gathering the cloth while darting fearful glances in Orla's direction. "Sorry. So sorry . . ."

"Orla?"

My maid turns, spots me hovering a few yards away. Then she slumps against the wall and tips back her head, patting her neck with a square of white cloth. "Apologies, my lady. I've spent the last hour" —she lowers her voice— "trying to fix this one's mistakes."

I frown in puzzlement.

"Her name is Thyamine," she whispers into my ear, the words tinged with undeniable exasperation. "She drank the water of Mnemenos. Can't remember a thing most days."

Thyamine beams at the older woman, and Orla, being the kind, nurturing person she is, pats her atop the head. Thyamine seems like a sweet woman, if a bit foolish. If she knew drinking from Mnemenos would snatch her memories, why do it?

"Orla?" The woman glances at her superior with wide, beseeching eyes. "I'm sorry, what was I supposed to be doing?"

A vein throbs in Orla's temple. "Never mind that. I need you to find me the blue linens. Leave these here. I'll pick them up."

"Blue linens." Thyamine rises to her feet, pads down the hall until her form blurs, all the while chanting *blue linens* under her breath.

"Knowing her, she'll probably bring me back a basket of potatoes."

I am a horrible person to laugh at such a comment. Though it is rather humorous.

My maid's eyes twinkle, and she sighs as she begins picking up Thyamine's mess. Kneeling beside her, I lend a hand, tossing the white cloth into the basket. "I was wondering. Do they sell herbs in Neumovos?"

Orla pauses for half a heartbeat, cloth clutched in hand. "They do, my lady." She drops the bolt of fabric into the basket. "Why?"

"How far is the town from the citadel?"

Her head snaps in my direction. "My lady, the lord has forbidden you from leaving the grounds. And Neumovos—" The wrinkles around her eyes smooth, so tight and pressed is her disapproval. "You do not want to go there. It is not a good place for you."

She has no idea what I want. And she never will so long as there is hope of killing the king. "I can decide for myself what is good for me, what is not." I lock eyes with her until she lowers her gaze.

"Please," I whisper, covering her hand so she stops fiddling with the hem of her dress. "This is important. I would not ask this of you otherwise."

"And if I say no?"

Soft laughter fizzles in my chest. Quiet, skittish Orla, yet sometimes, bold, daring, dauntless. "And here I thought it might be fun. I had it all planned out, too. A daring escape from the citadel."

Her voice pitches high as she squeaks, "Daring escape?"

Indeed. "By any chance, do you have an extra servant's garb?"

# CHAPTER

## II

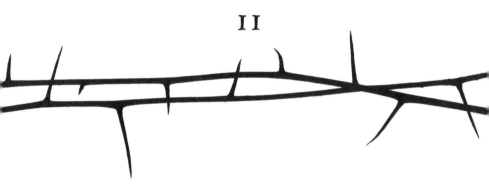

Ten miles from the citadel, the town of Neumovos sprouts from a forest clearing like fungi following a hard rain. It bears resemblance to Edgewood from this distance: mud cottages huddled in small clumps, a central square. Everything, from the empty goat pens to the hobbled wagons, is faded and surrounded by a tumbled stone wall.

The air hints at an approaching storm. Snow maybe, or hail. I take a sip from my flask. Orla puffs hard at my side, tugging her coat around her front with her mittened hands. "Nearly there, my lady," she gasps, sweat slithering down her temples. In the patches where sun streams, her body is all but invisible.

That's twice now I've escaped the confines of the citadel with the North Wind none the wiser. Disguised as a servant beneath my cloak, the parapet guards opened the gates under the belief that Orla and I were to replenish the grain stores, by order of the cook. Damn fools. It had been too easy.

As the trees fall away, I spot strange carvings on the barkless trunks. The pads of my gloved fingers trail the intricate swirls. I've never seen anything like them before.

"Protections, my lady." At my confusion, Orla adds, "From the darkwalkers."

My head snaps toward her. "But you're a specter." I did not think the darkwalkers posed a danger to them.

"The people living in Neumovos still retain some life. Enough that the darkwalkers feed on us, if given the chance."

The beasts must pose as much of a threat to the specters as to mortals then.

We step inside the protective ring of trees, and I hear it. Airy in timbre, the low tone rises and falls with hollow melancholy. "Is that . . . ?"

Orla's eyes glimmer with unshed tears. "My lady—"

"Music." I can't remember the last time I heard music. It softens what is hard inside me.

"It's not what you think." She sets her jaw, appearing pained. "When the flute sings, it represents someone having been sentenced to a life in Neumovos."

My footsteps falter. "Someone else has been forced into the king's service?"

She nods.

From the corner of my eye, I catch sight of a woman's incorporeal form moving swiftly through the trees.

"You're making a mistake!" she cries, stumbling over a tree root, fighting whatever invisible force drags her toward the town. "I had no choice! Please, you have to believe me!"

The woman vanishes between two buildings. Stillness hangs in the wake of her disappearance. The woman will continue a life that is only half present. To eat food but not experience its taste, to never know the peace of sleep again. A life of waiting. Beside me, Orla twists her hands together.

"Orla," I whisper. "Why are you bound in service to the king?" She tenses. "And this time, I would like the truth."

I need every piece. Every sliver, every fragment, every ugly, broken shard illuminated. Knowledge is my weapon. Knowledge is my power.

My maid murmurs, "I am sorry I gave you a false perception of my situation. I truly am. But I didn't want to disappoint you. You are strong and brave and there is much I admire about you." She turns, this middle-aged specter woman, with lowered eyes, head bowed meekly. "I said before that those who are sentenced to Neumovos have yet to fully pass on. What I should have said is that we are barred from passing on."

I've only known my maid for a number of weeks, but she has been kind to me. She is loyal and true. A friend, if I allow myself that luxury. "What do you mean?"

"Neumovos is where the lord sends those who have committed violent crimes in life. Our punishment is to serve him for an eternity. I've worked for the lord hundreds of years now. Most of us live at the citadel, but some remain here to farm or procure supplies he needs."

Violent crimes? That doesn't sound like Orla. A mayfly is more violent than this woman. "What did you do?"

"Please, my lady. I can't take more of your disappointment."

I'm not disappointed, but I let it go. For now. Although I realize I was unfair to the king at dinner the other night. It is his duty to Judge the dead, to determine who is worthy of an unburdened afterlife. If Orla did something terrible, then his actions would be justified, right?

The sound of the flute has almost faded. It is beautiful, even if it proclaims a morose end. "My mother would sing to me and my sister when we were young," I say, gesturing to continue our stroll. "She had a lovely voice."

Orla glances at me in question. "She is . . . gone?"

"Yes. My sister is all I have left." Already I struggle to remember the sound of Elora's voice. The longer I'm away from home, the more my memories fade. Soon, I fear they will disappear completely. "I switched places with her to keep her safe. The Frost King didn't realize what I had done until he removed my veil during the wedding ceremony." I take a breath. "I would give anything to see her again."

Orla's silence draws my attention. She peers through the trees, her footsteps light and nimble, the town coming into sharper focus as we near the surrounding stone wall.

Catching my maid's arm, I pull her to a halt. "None of the Frost King's wives has ever escaped the Deadlands, right?"

"It's difficult to say for certain." Nerves pitch her voice higher. Orla, as it turns out, is a terrible liar.

"What do you mean?"

She wets her lips. Still refusing to meet my eye.

"Orla," I warn.

"My lady!" Exasperated. "Why do you have to be so . . . ." She gestures to me. Her graying curls bounce with the motion. "You?"

I scoff. "Are you insulting me? You know what—" I lift a hand. "Doesn't matter. Tell me what you know about the king's wives. And about the doors." Because there is a connection. Something the king does not want me to learn.

We meander on, and soon reach the fringe of town. I'm not paying much attention to our surroundings as Orla says, "Only one of the king's previous wives has ever gone missing. Her name was Magdalena. She was quite beautiful, curious about the doors, like you. She spent most of her days exploring what lay beyond them. Then one evening, she didn't come down for dinner. We searched everywhere for her. She never left the grounds. Never once went outside. The staff believe one of the doors took her far away from this place. That's the last we heard of her."

The Frost King told me the doors did not lead beyond the Deadlands.

He lied.

Orla notices the fervent expression on my face. "My lady, you can't believe that story, can you?"

"Oh, but I do, Orla." Hastening my pace, I charge deeper into the village, a spring in my step. "I most certainly do."

"But there are thousands of doors!" she cries, lifting her skirts and dashing after me.

Then I'd best begin my search as soon as possible.

∽

A muddy brick road bisects the litter of shops and cottages with their peaked roofs groaning under the weight of snow, smoke drifting from the chimneys. The structures, faded and bleached from the sun, appear as apparitions, ghosts of what was once real. Sunlight pours *through* the buildings, the wagons, the townsfolk wandering the street. Everything is tinged by a washed-out pallor, lined by a gray, silvery hue.

Most people push wagons filled with crates. My eyebrows lift, then climb higher. "Are those chickens?" Upon a closer inspection, I discover there are, in fact, chickens in those crates. Live ones.

"You mentioned herbs, my lady. There is an apothecary down this way."

Halfway down the road, I sense a shift in the crowd. A honed focus, and many eyes falling against my back, the crown of my skull, my scar. They stare, but they do not approach.

I tug my hood forward to conceal my face. While I wear the outfit of a servant, people will have overheard Orla's use of my title. I'm not sure how welcoming they would be to learn I was the king's wife, considering he has doomed them to eternal servitude.

A set of stairs leads to a quaint shop with a bright yellow door that expels lavender-scented air when opened. Up the stairs we go. The wood flares beneath my boots, a brief revival of color and light. A little bell rings as we cross the threshold to the apothecary.

I drag in air as though starved. Lavender and—sage? Yes. Sage, the scent of Elora's hair.

I'm not sure where to look first. The color is so saturated it burns. Green. Green all around. The shop houses a myriad of flowering plants, climbing vines, shrubs bursting with fresh bulbs, various grasses, jars stuffed with clumps of herbs, everything from rosemary to thyme, and entire rows dedicated to the healing arts.

The floorboards creak beneath my weight as I step farther into the space. The air inside the shop is heavy with moisture, far warmer than the outside. After decades spent without color, my body does not know how to process the sudden change.

"How is this possible?" My whisper carries through the green-steeped quiet. Shelves nailed to the walls hold jars of salves, bowls of dried rose petals, and spices ground into fine dusts, black and orange and ochre and red. Fat wooden buckets have settled their bulk beneath the windows, long bunches of threshes bursting from their basins.

"The farms," Orla says, following me through the space. "It's how they acquire all of the food. As for the herbs, I'm not sure. I know Alba—she's the staff healer—purchases most of her supplies from this shop."

"Where are the farms?" It's not possible. Nothing grows in the Deadlands. The Frost King's power is far too strong for anything to thrive.

My maid wanders to a display of tins that hold dried tea leaves. "There are grounds west of here that are untouched by cold. That is where our men toil."

I'm able to steer my thoughts toward Orla rather than the mystery of the plants. "So not all of the Deadlands looks this . . . dead?"

She smiles at my choice of words. "I am forbidden to visit any places but Neumovos and the citadel, but yes, I have heard some parts are rather pleasant."

I'll believe it when I see it. For now, I peruse the vast array of tinctures and medicines for various ailments. Many of these are familiar. Our village herbalist was quite advanced in her studies. Blushwort for nausea. Smoked evergreen for aching joints. I sniff a container full of green paste, flinching at the whiff of decay. My eyes water as I promptly return the jar to its shelf.

A woman materializes to my left, her torso patched from the sunlight streaming through the square windows. Her height brings to mind striving oak. Her hair is flame. Deep wrinkles split her face into a mapped land, like rivers carved into clay. "May I help you?"

The leaves of the herb before me are soft to the touch, with branching veins. I lift the stem to my nose and inhale. Lemon and sugar.

"Where did you acquire this herb?" I ask, returning the clipping to its place among the bunch. "And the others?" Because I've never seen these plants before. As someone who spends the majority of my time hunting or foraging, I'm well versed in what plants can endure the frost. The answer is: very little.

The shopkeeper smiles, but the lines around her mouth reveal its strain. "They are traded from distant towns, those that exist beyond the Deadlands." She glances over my shoulder before watering one of the potted plants with the watering can she holds. "Do you seek something specific? If you are looking for a particular remedy, I might be able to acquire it. It would take a few weeks, but if you don't mind the wait . . ."

"I am, actually. I've heard there is a tonic made from the poppy flower that aids with sleep."

"If you're having trouble sleeping, my lady, I can put chamomile in your evening tea," Orla offers in concern.

"That's not necessary," I say quickly. "But thank you."

"Poppy." The woman frowns. "Yes, we sell such a tonic, but it is not in stock at the moment."

Voice lowered, I say, "I ask because I have a friend who is a talent with plants, but I have not seen him of late. Zephyrus."

Orla stiffens at my side. As I suspected, she disapproves of this developing relationship between me and the West Wind. Hopefully she will keep her opinion to herself.

The woman's fingers twitch around her watering can. The bands of light pouring in from the windows dim, and the woman's shape comes into sharper focus. "I apologize," she says. "It seems I was mistaken. We do not sell a tonic made from the poppy flower." She glances out the window where people have begun to gather. "Please let me know if there is anything else you need." She is perfectly polite. Kind, even.

And she lies.

Lowering my hood, I reveal my face, the flush in my cheeks where blood gathers and thrums hot beneath my chilled skin. The woman's eyes widen as she realizes I am not a specter. The North Wind's wife, a visitor in this shop.

"Zephyrus is my friend," I say. "He would be displeased to learn of your attempt to keep this information from me."

The shopkeeper opens her mouth. I lift a hand before she can reply.

"The Frost King will not hear of this exchange from me. From either of us," I add with a glance in Orla's direction.

Her mouth twitches, but eventually, she relents. "Zephyrus is due to return on the Day of Harvest."

The Day of Harvest is two weeks away. But I can wait.

With a gracious *thank you*, Orla and I exit the shop and descend the stairs to the road below. If I prioritize finding the door the king's past wife used to escape the Deadlands, it shouldn't take more than a few months to secure passage, bearing that I check a few hundred doors a day. After, all that will remain is taking the Frost King's life.

Prior to entering the shop, the road was rather stagnant. Now the area is full, bursting with people, but it is not a jovial affair. The back of my neck pricks as the many eyes track my progress. My hood shields my face, but I guess word spread of my arrival. Of course people would be curious.

And yet, I step quickly. My feet have barely touched the ground before they lift, carrying me nearer to the forest's seclusion. The bodies press in. I keep us moving.

"Orla." I reach for my maid's hand. "Something doesn't feel right."

"We're almost to the end of the road." She tugs her hood further over her head. She senses it as well.

Someone jostles me. It feels intentional. I don't stop, dragging Orla by strength alone, elbowing my way through. I've felt like prey far too many times in life to ignore the signs.

When a man bumps my side, I plant my hands on his chest and shove him back. "Keep your distance," I snarl. He sneers, then spits at my feet before the horde swallows him. The sentiment is enough to make my pulse climb.

Ahead, the crowd parts long enough to reveal the tree line. Nearly there.

" . . . king's wife . . ."

I glance around. Who said that?

Orla knocks against me. My fingers tighten around hers in silent comfort. The last thing I want to do is frighten her, but she is no fool. I imagine many of those sentenced to Neumovos believe themselves to have been Judged unfairly. And I am the king's wife, mortal and powerless.

The opening that appeared in the crowd, the one revealing our only means of escape, stitches up like a seam. Orla gasps. As though the townsfolk share one mind, they halt in the middle of the road and turn toward me.

All goes still for a heartbeat.

I'm squeezing Orla's fingers so tightly I feel her bones creak. "My lady," she whispers in horror.

The crowd surges, sweat and specter flesh lurching claw-like hands toward me. I lash out, trying to pull free long enough to grab my dagger. Something strikes the back of my skull, and my grip loosens from the hilt before I can draw the blade. "Down with her!" they cry. "Down with the queen!"

Orla vanishes, her hand slipping from mine, swallowed by the ravenous crowd.

"Stop!" A blow to my stomach punches a long, hissing breath from my lungs. "It's not . . . what you think."

Searing pain rips open my upper arm. My hand covers the hurt and pulls away coated in blood. Horror moves like paralysis through me. Someone stabbed me.

The next blow upsets my balance, and I'm falling. I'm slamming onto my back, people stomping on my hands and legs. A bone cracks. A howl wrenches free. Tears spring to my eyes, blurring my vision, and I scream as my head is jerked backward, scalp smarting as a chunk of hair rips away from the roots.

"Get up, my lady!"

Someone tugs on my arm. Orla. She stares down at me in bone-deep terror, sweat gleaming in the hollow of her throat. A woman attempts to knock Orla aside, but my maid whirls with far more aggression than I ever thought her capable of, and the woman tumbles back into the shifting mass. I manage to stumble to my feet, but then a fist plows into my stomach. Air explodes from my mouth as I'm thrown backward. Orla vanishes once more into the throng. Her terrified voice cuts off.

Too many people. They crush my limbs and tear at my clothes and pummel every part of my body they can reach. I fight like never before, scratching and ripping and tearing into them as they do me. They won't stop until I am dead, until they have properly punished the Frost King for ruining their lives. Don't they see? I am not the enemy. I am just like them, caged by a pitiless god whose only care is himself.

One man binds my arms from behind while a child scrabbles at my neck as if trying to reach my lifeblood. I slam my skull back as hard as I can. There's a crack, followed by a furious howl. The man's grip slackens, allowing me to shove him aside, where he's trampled. The current swells with aggression. The bodies pile atop me, and I'm dragged down.

The blows pound my body like chunks of hail. One strikes the back of my skull. A nerve pinches at my neck, ravaging the length of my spine. I retaliate, clawing at the townsfolk, biting when necessary. Yet for every hurt I inflict, I receive four more. The assaults land with violent ferocity. They want to kill me? I will not go quietly. With a crude shriek, I grab a woman's braid and punch her in the jaw. She goes down.

But it's not long until the crowd closes in. Every time I attempt to fight free, I'm slammed against the ground. Bootheels crush my fingers. I punch a man in the groin, and it feels incredibly satisfying to watch his legs fold, but a woman's open-palmed slap cracks against my ear, and I begin to weaken.

I did not think I would die today, at the hands of those who are just like me.

My vision flickers. Something small and dark rushes toward me. There's no time to turn away. The boot slams into my mouth, and agony ruptures across my face.

"Get back," a voice growls. It comes from my right . . . or is it my left? It sounds like Orla, but grittier and snarling, threatening violence.

"Back," cries the voice. "Back!"

The wet, dull thud of a blade cleaving flesh.

Screams spiderweb like cracks through glass. Blood clogs my throat, and I choke, spitting out the foul taste of iron and salt. Bodies jostle me left and right, a sudden rush bowling into my side. A scream cuts off, and then another. I can't see. I can't *see*, and as the world fades, so do the echoes of the last pounding feet until, at last, all is still.

"My lady? Oh, my lady." A whispered voice near my ear, wobbly and tear-stricken.

My body is awash in cold. When I try moving my right arm, pain sears near my elbow. My cheek presses into the cold, muddy ground. I am dizzy, but alive. Broken, but alive.

I bite the inside of my cheek as tears track hotly down my face. As if that matters. I'll likely be dead soon. The internal bleeding will finish me off.

Orla attempts to help me stand. I scream. Something is cleaving me in two, navel to sternum. My maid leaps backward, no longer touching me. I slump onto the ground, panting, blinking back yet more tears. Nausea rises. My stomach heaves, and vomit splatters onto the road. My head hangs, wet, stringy bile dripping from my open mouth.

"Go, Orla." I cough.

"I won't leave you." Her voice quavers.

Foolish, loyal woman. "And if they return?"

"Then they will return. Please. We must get you to safety."

Gently, she takes my arm. My locked muscles groan as, somehow, I manage to find my feet without fainting. A sharp pain shoots through my right leg when I rest my weight on it, but the adrenaline has dulled the worst of it.

"Orla." Blood pools from my split lip and tracks down my chin. "Did you . . ." *Save me?*

"Please, my lady. Hold on until we reach the citadel."

One step. Pain lances up my back.

Two steps. My knees wobble, and the world skews.

Progress is excruciating. My legs do not cooperate, my balance teetering this way and that. I'm thankful for Orla's arm around my waist—my only support. She is surprisingly sturdy for a woman so small.

"Orla." My feet shuffle against the wet snow. I'm forced to breathe out of my mouth since my nose is swollen—broken, no doubt. "I need rest." Even talking requires energy I don't have.

"We mustn't stop," she pants. How many miles has she carried me? How many miles remain? "We have to keep going."

Another step. I can't. I just can't. "Please."

"No," she snaps, adjusting my arm around her shoulder. Feet, legs, face, hands—all my extremities have turned numb. "You have to hold on for a while longer. I know you can do it."

Sweat coats my skin, and I'm shivering, frozen, so cold my veins have iced over. My teeth chatter uncontrollably. My joints ache with every stumble. But there is Orla, her plump body supporting mine as I trip and shuffle and trudge, foot after foot, in some nameless direction.

*Almost there, my lady.*

*Another few steps, you'll see.*

Color fades from sight, and all the world is shadow.

Orla's voice is all that guides me through the dark of unending agony. Her faith in me is puzzling. She says I am strong. She says I can hold on, but I don't know if I can.

"My lady." Orla taps my cheek, careful of the bruising. The skin stings momentarily. "Stay awake."

If only I could.

My weakened legs fold, and I slump against a nearby tree, slide down its trunk, and sprawl at the base. Another pulse of dulled pain carves through my right leg, near the ankle. My eyes flutter shut. No more. I can travel no more.

My heartbeat slows in the passing moments, the cold seeping through my coat, and sleep like a nefarious friend, coaxing me into that ageless oblivion.

My maid's ragged breathing reaches me. "You can't fall asleep."

"Orla," I whisper. One word, and I've exhausted myself. "I'm tired."

"I know, my lady." Her voice cracks. "I know you're tired." Her feet stamp out a furious rhythm of crunching snow. She has begun to pace, her footsteps fading, yet always returning, words muttered under her breath. " . . . don't know what to do. We're so far . . ." Then she begins to cry.

*Don't cry. Don't worry about me.* But my grasp on consciousness slips, and I'm free-falling.

"My lord, please! Lady Wren needs your help!" Her breath hitches, and she paces and paces. "Please help her. Please—"

The air stirs. It brushes the length of my arms, across my damp hairline, like the gentle prodding of curious fingers. Then the ground trembles. My ears ring with the sound of hooves, bright and vivid on the frozen earth.

The hoofbeats cease. Someone dismounts. Panic spikes through the dark place of which I sink. Is it someone from the town? Have they come to finish me off? I can't move, can't defend myself. Each breath feels like someone is gouging a jagged piece of metal into my chest.

"What happened?" The cold, emotionless tone can only belong to the Frost King.

"She was attacked, my lord!" Orla exclaims, near hysteria. *It's not your fault*, I wish to say. Without Orla's presence, I'm not sure I would have made it out of Neumovos alive. "The townspeople learned of who she was and they . . . they . . ." Her voice fades. The sound of her weeping drifts in and out.

"Why was she there? I gave an order. One order: she is not to leave the citadel."

"I'm so sorry. So, so sorry. It's my fault. She wanted to go and I couldn't say no and— Punish me as you see fit, but please don't let her die."

Footsteps. The bright, crisp scent of cedar nudges me closer to awareness. My eyes are so swollen I cannot see the Frost King's expression, though I sense his fury, so palpable is the emotion. My leg is broken. A few of my ribs, certainly. I tense in anticipation of his scorn.

Instead, there is this: gentleness.

Fingertips alight on my temple. They trace the bruising so carefully, mapping out each hurt. A profound, numbing cold radiates from the touch, and the throbbing alleviates. A soft sound of relief slips from my bruised throat.

"Come, Wife," he says, and gathers me into his arms.

The ground falls away, and I whimper as the movement sends another wave of crushing agony through my body. My fist lashes out against something solid. My struggles begin anew. Elora. Is she safe?

The arms tighten around me, and the king's voice, when he speaks, reminds me of my mother. "Shh," he says. "You are safe now."

Impossibly, I believe him. I'm placed atop a horse, I think. Moments later, the Frost King settles behind me. He tugs me against the front of his body where it is blessedly warm. My head lolls against his shoulder, my face tipped toward his neck.

That is the last thing I remember.

# CHAPTER

## 12

I lie in darkness, the curtains drawn, shadows draped like fabric across my eyes. My thoughts drift. They are dust, catching the light and fading. And slowly, slowly I remember.

Wet, packed earth against my back, frigid air prickling the exposed skin of my neck. The town noises clang to a high, discordant pitch, then momentarily cut off as pain shatters through my skull. It's dark in my memories. Searing heat boils through my leg, then a *snap*, sudden and cold. Through it all, there is Orla's voice—a thread leading me to salvation.

A tremor runs through my body. The softness of the mattress at my back reminds me I am safe, far from harm. The townsfolk of Neumovos tried to kill me. They failed.

Distancing myself from the memories, I focus on what is present. Namely, pain, however muted it might be. It feels as though my skin has been stripped, my bones scoured, all their innards scraped clean with a pick. My face is a tender, swollen mess, but I am alive.

I am alive.

Despite the discomfort, I manage to doze, albeit fitfully. When my skin rucks with the arrival of chill air, my eyes swing toward the door. Someone enters without knocking. A lamp flares, illuminating a face of punishing angles, breath gathering like a cloud before a stiff, unsmiling mouth.

A liquid gait brings the Frost King deeper into the room, the door shutting soundlessly at his back. Shadows trail the edge of the long robe he's thrown over his sleepwear. The king may have the emotional capacity of a twig, but I can't deny the grace of his movements.

He kneels before the fire, stirring the coals until they catch, adding logs atop them. Hair the color of deep night falls in unruly clumps against his shoulders, as though he's been running his fingers through it. I've never seen it free of its binding.

A log splits with a startling crack. He stokes the fire a second time, then moves to the window, peering out. He may be a pillar for how lifeless he stands.

To the best of my knowledge, the Frost King is unaware that I'm awake. For no other reason would he linger in my room. I'd think something would be different. A lack of stiffness to his features, maybe. It takes a moment, but I do notice the softening around his jaw. Light flames in the dip of his dark lashes.

Eventually, he leaves, yet returns to set something on my bedside table: a glass of water. So small a thing, really. But it's not the drink I need.

Something must alert him to my conscious state, because his gaze cuts to mine. The breath stills in my lungs, for there is a crack in the stone of his countenance, and the crack grows, spider-webbing into shallow veins, revealing glimpses of what lies beneath. There is rage, bright and smoldering at the edges. There is agitation in the flaring of his pupils. It makes him uncomfortable, being here. So why has he come?

We stare at one another. Husband and wife, yet strangers. Eventually, someone has to give.

Clearing my scratchy throat, I say, "I'd like a glass of wine, please." The *please* is merely to appease him.

His eyebrows snap together above his nose. "I brought you water." He gestures to the glass on the bedside table, fingers wrapped lovingly in black leather. Why he believes it necessary to wear gloves indoors, I have no idea.

"Yes, and I appreciate the gesture, but I really would like wine instead."

"It's after midnight. Why do you—"

"I just need it, all right?" My face burns with that rising unrest. There's no other way to make him understand. I need to drink like I need to eat, to sleep.

Another searching look. "All right," he growls. Moving to the door, he pokes his head outside to speak with whatever staff member is stationed in the hall. When he returns, bearing a cup of wine, I accept it with gratitude. Water is substance, water is life, but it won't cure the suffocation that hounds me. Only wine can do that.

"Thank you," I whisper, bringing the glass to my cracked lips, and sigh as the liquid warms me from the inside. "Nectar of the gods."

He inclines his chin. "Indeed."

I don't remember much from the attack, but I do remember one thing: the Frost King's low, soothing voice quieting my frayed nerves. He did not abandon me in my time of need. I'm not sure how to interpret his actions.

I take another sip before setting the glass aside. The weight of his gaze upon my throat slides through me, but when I shift my attention back to him, I find his eyes elsewhere.

"How did you know to come?" I ask, watching him closely for a reaction. He gives so little away—to anyone. "We were miles from the citadel. You could not have heard Orla calling you."

He hesitates. A rare thing, to see this uncertainty in him, and I feel a piece of myself lean toward the commonality we might share. "The Les," he mutters. "It passes near Neumovos. The spirits heard Orla's voice. They informed me of your location."

He does not look at me when he speaks. He watches the fire, he looks out the window, he studies the darkness clumped near the floorboards, he pins that unrelenting focus toward the door. For whatever reason, the Frost King cannot meet my eye.

My fingers uncurl from where they've clamped around the blankets and lift to touch my scarred cheek. I've lived with this unsightly display for eight years, and it is all anyone ever sees. Perhaps that is why.

I drop my hand. It doesn't matter anyway. "You're saying you speak to the dead."

"Their spirits. Who they were when breath flowed in their lungs."

Against all odds, he has whetted my curiosity. "I thought you only Judged them."

"Only in extreme circumstances do I speak to them outside of their Judgment."

And my attack must count as such. "So what's the difference between the spirits in the river and those who attend their Judgment?"

He eyes one of the chairs near the fireplace. What a grueling decision. Sit, and he has doomed himself to converse with his wife, of all people. I purse my lips and wait.

He sits. The chair itself is wonderfully comfortable, with deep, sinking cushions perfect for an afternoon of reading, yet the Frost King perches on the edge as though it were constructed of the hardest, toughest planks of wood. Did he have any social interaction before I arrived? I'm imagining him contained to his chambers, never venturing farther than his wing.

The king says, "The spirits immersed in the rivers are at an earlier phase of their passing. It is there they unravel who they were and come to terms with their deaths. A spirit can take as long as it needs in the Les. It is a safe place for them, free of Judgment. When they are ready to meet their final resting place, they attend their Judgment Day."

"What do these spirits have to say?"

"They are dead," he says stiffly. "Why should it matter what they say? It is their actions that show me who they were."

And just like that, my brief feelings of warmth toward the Frost

King vanish. I don't think I've ever met someone who so thoroughly infuriates me, and with so much ease.

I settle more comfortably against the pillows, my eyelids sinking half-closed. "Maybe it does not matter to you," I say, "as you will live forever, but I imagine it means something to them, to speak of their lives and their experiences."

He says tersely, hands curled over the arms of his chair, "My job is not to comfort them. They made their choices, and they died with those choices. So whatever guilt or regret they hold on to, comforting them is not my prerogative. My duty is to grant them allowance into the afterlife. To Judge how they will spend their eternities. Nothing more."

In eternity, time is meaningless. There is always another year, and another, and another. But with mortality, life is built brick by brick in the smallest of things. A lit candle. A woven blanket. Someone's hand pressing into yours, or a sweet perfume suffusing the room and teasing one's senses. The fear of death is very real. I would hate to think the North Wind would not attempt to offer comfort or compassion to those entering this new phase of life.

My soft sound of derision draws his ear—a slight head tilt. He still looks elsewhere. "What?"

"Nothing."

"It is not nothing, whatever it is."

It might as well be. "You are not interested in hearing what I have to say, so why should it matter what I think?"

There is a beat of silence. "And what if I am interested in hearing what you have to say?" He almost stumbles over the question. Almost.

And I'm surprised enough to answer him. "Is it so much to ask, extending a familiar hand to those who cross over? Had the situation been reversed, had you reached the end of your life and knew nothing of what lay beyond, wouldn't you want to be comforted?"

Briefly, his eyes flash to mine. His gaze is so piercing, so invasive, I feel as though I am but naked skin. Light and dark and the in-between. These are not the eyes of a man who feels nothing. These are the eyes of a man who has experienced immense pain.

And I wonder. Has the Frost King ever been comforted, or is it a completely foreign concept to him?

My previous anger banks to a low simmer. "You have been comforted," I whisper, "haven't you?"

He stands so violently the chair tips onto its side. His muscles contract as if he intends to dash from the room, yet his feet remain entrenched in the colorful rug covering the floor. "Tell me what happened at Neumovos."

Under normal circumstances, I would ignore his demands. But I am tired. I feel as though I have lived lifetimes between the fragile space of dusk and dawn. The sooner the Frost King leaves my company, the sooner I can sleep.

So I tell him. Some things, not all. I skip over the apothecary shop as though it never existed. The Frost King probes me for any untruth, but he does not know me. He has not bothered to converse with me at all except in situations that require it. So he does not see how easily I lie.

"This cannot stand," says the king when I have gone silent.

Something in his voice causes the hair along my arms to spike. "What will you do?"

His gaze is flat and cold. "I will repay them the same kindness they showed you, only I will make it so much worse."

I straighten against the headboard as my stomach drops. He will ensure their suffering is enduring. The thought feels worse than fear. Fear is a fleeting emotion. This feels like it adheres to my skin.

"You can't. It would only give them another reason to hate you, maybe even strike against you." As if I care about that. If he attacks Neumovos, I'll lose any chance of obtaining the tonic Zephyrus promised me.

"Strike against me?" His mouth curls. "They would do no such thing. I am their king."

"Loyalty is earned," I state. "It's not an obligation."

"They would have killed you," he hisses, upper lip peeling back to reveal his straight, white, even teeth.

I do not disagree. "They are afraid. They are suffering." As much as my body twinges with aches, I cannot blame them. If I were in their shoes, I would have done the same. We must live, and that means survival in all forms, often ugly ones.

The Frost King takes a step toward the window, the loose, soft trousers pooling over his feet. "You protect them, yet they would have disposed of you without a second thought."

My hands curl more firmly around the blankets. There is something here, something I can't put my finger on. "And this angers you, that they would harm me?"

"To harm you is to undermine my power. That is a slight I cannot ignore."

Each word drips contempt. My skin puckers with the violence lacing his statement, and I whisper, both dreading and desiring the answer, "What will you do?"

The Frost King's eyes blaze with the promise of devastation. "I will teach them not to touch what is mine."

A dark thrill runs through me. Here is the god of darkness and death, the devastating fist of winter. His words snap like bone and ring like metal forged. There is something alluring to his assuredness. He has lived millennia while I am but a gasping breath, dandelion fluff, ice beneath a summer sun. To stand in his path is to be cut down. The townsfolk must have known there would be consequences for their actions. How deep would their hatred of him have to run to override that caution?

*Mine.* That is what he called me. But it hadn't come from a desire of wanting to protect, as though defining me as a lover. He spoke of me like a possession, like that spear of his, or the silver plates, those perfect discs gracing his dinner table. Despite having never been claimed as such—mine—the sentiment holds no appeal. I am a person. My own person. I must have hit my head harder than I thought to react in such a way.

"Rest," he says, turning away. "You need it."

The Frost King reaches the door when I call, "Wait."

He stops, fingers resting against the curved handle.

"Why won't you look at me?" The scars at the corner of my mouth tug painfully. I've lived with this blemish long enough that it no longer defines me. But sometimes I am weak. Sometimes I am human. "Is it my face? You can't stand to look at it?"

The Frost King does not turn around as he says lowly, "There are many ugly things in this world, Wife. But I do not think you are one of them."

With those parting words, I'm left to the dark.

# CHAPTER
# 13

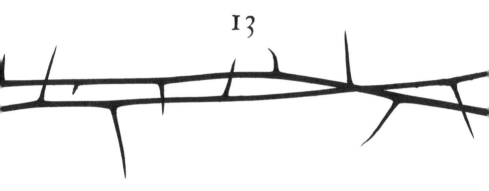

It takes time, but eventually, I do recover. Weeks of bedrest and quiet, many hours spent reading by the fire. My small sitting room houses a wall of shelves stuffed with books. I read them all. Never have so many stories been at my disposal. I escape to pirate-infested seas, dark caves burrowing to the center of the earth, cities that float on clouds, stately homes whose walls drip ivy. But there is a genre that is sorely lacking.

"Orla," I say to my maid one evening as she plumps the pillows behind my back. "Are there more books elsewhere in the citadel, by chance?" My current selection is a reread. It tells the tale of a man, a war hero, and his decade-long journey home after a ten-year war. His wife sits at home in Ithaca with their young son, weaving a burial shroud by day and unraveling her progress by night to keep the suitors at bay.

"Certainly. What do you prefer to read?"

I toss her a sidelong conspiratorial grin. "Do you really want to know?"

My maid blushes. "No?" She sounds unsure.

"Romance."

She sighs wistfully. "Love, my lady?"

"Sex, actually." Her eyes pop, and I chuckle. What can I say? I like my stories with copious amounts of sex. Especially when I'm getting none myself.

Love isn't made for people like me.

After a brief pondering, Orla says, "There might be some in the library. I can check tomorrow."

I sit up in surprise, and the mattress dips beneath my shifting weight. "There's a library?"

"Oh, yes. It's quite superb. The lord collects books from all over the world."

"Really."

She nods adamantly. "He dearly loves to read."

Hm. I suppose I never considered the possibility that the Frost King enjoyed any activity outside of his kingly duties. Namely, sentencing souls to a miserable eternity. How curious. How very, very curious. A small voice in my head questions what material he enjoys reading.

Before I can ask Orla where this library is, she grabs my dirty laundry and pulls the door shut behind her.

I take my meals in my rooms because, until my leg heals, I cannot walk down the stairs. Silas bakes me miniature cakes, and not even at my request. It's a sweet gesture. The healer, Alba, managed to set my nose, so at least I'm not left with a horribly crooked object on my face. Orla visits me thrice daily to tend the fire, serve my meals, and help me bathe. The Frost King never again darkens my doorway. Orla says he has been absent for many days now. Something stirs in the Deadlands. Dark, wild things.

The following week, when I'm strong enough to eat dinner downstairs, Orla informs me that the king is feeling unwell and has retired to his rooms. I'm certainly not crying over his absence, but after weeks spent in isolation, I was looking forward to some verbal sparring.

So I eat my meal alone, picking at my food. I miss Elora. I miss Edgewood. There is an absence in my life, has been for a long time, and the void continues to multiply. At this point, I'm not sure what to do. The Day of Harvest came and went, and I was unable to meet Zephyrus. I've yet to return to Neumovos. I've yet to kill the king.

There is but one saving grace: the doors, thousands upon thousands, lining every dusty, abandoned corridor of every wing on every floor. And if Orla's story is true, one of the Frost King's wives used them to escape this insufferable prison. My task stretches before me: secure a way out, so that when the Frost King is dead, I am able to flee.

In the days that follow, I turn my attention toward exploring what lies behind those doors. I divide everything by wing, and then by floor, inking a map of the citadel to keep track of the doors I've opened.

Door twenty-three: a charred field.

Door sixty-seven: a room constructed entirely out of dark wooden planking—floor, ceiling, walls. No windows. The only object inside the cramped interior is a deep armchair draped in scarlet cloth. For whatever reason, my entire body recoils in the presence of this chair, and I quickly return to the hallway, slamming the door shut behind me.

Door ninety-one: the base of a massive waterfall, the misted air colored by prisms of light.

Door one hundred and eight: the cracked marble of ancient ruins.

Another passage, doors and doors and doors, glass and mud and wood and cold, freezing iron curling into elegant shapes inside the frame. One doorway is covered in desiccated vines. Another is shaped like a triangle, curiously enough. But—nothing. Every realm behind the doors is completely contained. No matter how far I travel, at some point I hit the dark wall that is the Shade, which manages to manifest even inside the different lands.

Eventually, my wanderings lead me back to the center of the citadel, where the light is watery and the walls appear splintered in places. As I pass a nondescript wooden door, a male voice halts my forward motion.

"Please, my lord. I assure you my intentions were noble."

"Your intentions," a cool voice responds, sliding through the cracks in the wood, "were selfish, driven by fear and the greed of men."

"That's not true."

This must be where the king serves his Judgment. And it sounds as though Judgment is currently underway.

I press my ear to the door. The wood vibrates against my temple as the Frost King booms, "These are the facts. You walked into your brother's home while he slept. Stole the last of his—"

"If you would let me explain—"

"He's at it again."

I startle so hard my head slams against the door, and I reel backward, cupping my forehead where the skin stings. A blurred form takes shape as I blink away tears. It's the woman who drank from Mnemenos.

"Thyamine." She stands directly beneath one of the torches. I can see through her stomach to the wall at her back.

"My lady." The elegant curve of her neck flashes as she bends forward in a deep curtsy, and remains there until I grow uncomfortable.

"That's not necessary," I mutter, hauling her upright. "Is there something you need?"

Her eyes appear grossly magnified behind her glasses. "Yes." The smile softening her mouth begins to fade. "I remembered. I did this time. Orla requested something. I promised her, yet here I am. Thoughtless. Head empty." Her throat bobs. "A question, she asked. A request."

Sometimes, I wish I were a better person. Patience was always Elora's virtue. Never mine. "Well, when you think of it, let me know."

With my focus returned to the conversation behind the door, I all but forget about Thyamine until she gasps. "I remember. Orla asked me what you desire to wear this evening: a dress, green or blue?"

I suspect Orla sent Thyamine on this meaningless errand to keep her mind occupied, but I reply, "Blue is perfectly fine, thank you." The specter woman, with her big eyes and wish to please, smiles at me adoringly. She really is quite harmless.

Her gaze shifts to the door. The deep timbre of the Frost King's voice carries, the words lost due to distance. "Sometimes it saddens me, seeing what he has become. But I suppose his behavior is understandable, after all he's lost."

My awareness flashes to attention, and I face her fully. "What do you mean?"

Thyamine gives a slow blink. "Sorry?"

"What you just said. About the Frost King's behavior."

"What did I say, my lady?"

I sigh—deeply, tiredly—into my hands. Why I thought conversing with a woman who can barely remember her own name was a good idea, I'll never know. "Doesn't matter. It's fine." It's not fine. "Tell Orla I want to wear a blue dress, all right?"

"A dress?"

My mouth curls. Thyamine flinches at the sight, then turns and darts down the hall. Smart woman. At least I can return to my eavesdropping.

"On this day, your Judgment stands: Neumovos."

A keening wail lifts the hair on the back of my neck. There's a crash, and my fingers leap against the metal door handle, then tighten, pressing down. Locked. Sounds of struggle reach me—a body falling, slamming into hard stone. Rustling fabric. The click of bootheels. I'm imagining the king descending a set of shallow stairs, his hands caught behind his back, nose angled upward, mouth haughty. Does he grace a throne atop a dais?

"Please escort this man from the building."

"Please, *please*, my lord." The wail breaks and crumbles. "I beg of you to reconsider. My father was dying. I did not have a choice—"

"There is always a choice." His response whips out, effectively silencing the man's hysterics. "Be happy I am not sending you to the Chasm," he intones, and I wonder what horror the place might be.

"I'm sorry. I'm so sorry—"

I can listen no longer. Pushing away from the door, I steel my spine and continue down the corridor, hands clenched at my sides.

What a complete ass. Absolutely no compassion. No empathy. A heart of ice, as the stories claim. How much can the Frost King know of the souls who pass through the Shade? Their deeds? Their fortunes and misfortunes, lies and mistakes? Does he know them on an emotional level? Can he explain, with complete confidence, the reasons behind their actions, the needs people shield from others like acceptance, love, or fear?

None of my business. None of my damn business.

It's late afternoon. Sunset is still a few hours off. I've enough time to investigate a few more doors before I need to change for dinner.

The door in front of me is painted a lustrous black. Two white masks mark the foreground, one frowning, one smiling, with bright, colorful brushstrokes on the cheeks and brows. As soon as I touch the knob, I hear murmuring through the door. I push it open, excited for the prospect of people on the other side.

There *are* people on the other side.

I stand at the end of a narrow, cobblestoned road that sits snug between two rows of buildings. Colorful, buttoned-up storefronts are crowned in elegant plaster molding, having donned their sunny yellow attire, the shuttered windows painted pink in contrast. Men wearing tidy bowties and top hats stride arm in arm with women draped in pearls and silk, their white heeled shoes clicking musically against the stone.

The clop of hooves draws my attention to a horse-drawn carriage at the end of the lane. Laughter burbles in the small alleyways, tumbles from the open windows with their pretty flowers spilling from the window boxes. Gaggles of women drift from shop to shop, peering into windows, carting bags of purchased goods. Their wide-brimmed hats are nearly as complicated as the patterns decorating their open parasols, which twirl while resting upon their shoulders. It is sunny and warm. It smells of summer: salt and hot stone.

The door at my back lies open, revealing the dank hallway of the citadel. I shut it with a soft snick, taking care to remember the vivid green paint and white shutters of the building, the cheerful peaked roof for my eventual return.

The walkway flows into a tidy square with adorable wrought iron benches, a circular fountain splashing in its center. The crowd has thinned. The sun bakes the cobblestones underfoot and etches shadows that fall eastward.

No one appears to be in any rush. They have the leisure to wander, to be present. A woman reads on a bench. Two men play a game of dice. A girl and her mother fly a kite. Yet another group of women perch on the lip of the fountain, chattering about . . . I can't tell. I'll need to get closer.

The woman speaking wears her silver hair in an elegant coil atop her head. "Of course not, Lyra. I asked for rubies. Not that my husband ever remembers my preference for jewelry."

A brunet with long ringlets and a lavender, cap-sleeved gown says, "He got you sapphires, didn't he."

She shakes her head. "Emeralds. Fat, garish emeralds. As if I'd bear that humiliation."

"How odious!" a ginger-haired woman squawks.

My facial muscles twitch in amusement.

"Gerard didn't understand when I explained to him that emeralds wash out my coloring. So then I—"

I'm smiling as I wander past their huddle. It's a relief to know good things exist somewhere, and that I can have this day. That I can return whenever I wish to experience it again.

On the other side of the square, people gather around a small cart to purchase whatever goods are being sold. Upon closer inspection, I see they are miniature pies. They are baked a crisped brown, with beautiful lattice tops, elegant in their simplicity. The smell of baked flour and sugar teases through me. The menu reads: blueberry, lemon, cranberry. My stomach grumbles. How long have I been wandering?

"Hello," I say to the baker, an elderly man wearing an apron. "How much for the pies?" Not that I have coin, but . . .

The baker sets aside two lemon pies and one blueberry, then wraps them in brown paper and ties them off with twine.

"Hello?" I wave a hand in front of his face. "Sir?"

He pulls a handful of coins from a pocket in his apron, drops them into a bowl with other gold and copper pieces. That's when I notice my hand, the one reaching toward him. It's transparent.

The man can't see me. No one, I realize, can see me, hear me. It is as though I've become a ghost.

The excitement I felt at believing I might be able to socialize with people who had lives, freedom, choice, sours into disappointment. The doors may offer me a glimpse into other lives, but that's all it will ever be—a glimpse.

A low, sonorous clang reverberates through the square. I glance up, flinching from the intense sunlight. A large bell tower rings thrice. The group of women at the fountain stand and hurry toward a set of open doors to my right, as do a vast majority of those in the square. Out of curiosity, I follow them.

The doors lead to a small antechamber, which extends to another set of double doors. Beyond, a vaulted ceiling swells into the shape of a dome and sits flush atop curved walls with filigreed columns. The echoing space knocks the sound of the crowd's footsteps from wall to ceiling and back as I descend the sloped walkway intersecting rows upon rows of cushioned seating, all constructed in a gradual decline that eventually hits the curved front wall of a stage.

It's a theater.

Stopping in the middle of the walkway, a hand resting atop the soft, deeply red cushioned back of one of the chairs, I study the room in greater detail. Despite the expanse, it feels intimate somehow. Gold drapes—the same firelight warmth as the stage curtains—spill from unseen alcoves above, like melted gold poured from urns.

I've never been to a theater. I'm only aware of their existence from the books I've read. And so I wonder.

I glance around the space. Patrons begin to take their seats. Within minutes, the theater is almost full. The lamps dim save those illuminating the stage. A few seats remain vacant.

It's probably foolish, but I squeeze through one of the rows to a middle seat, then settle in.

The silence takes on a focused quality, as though the air itself tightens around me. My heart leaps, for the curtains part, whirring softly to expose the set that awaits behind its velveteen shield. A man steps onto the stage, and it begins.

I'm not sure how long the performance lasts. There is a king. A revolt. A god chained to a rock. And so the tale goes. It feels as though no time has passed before the curtains close, the lamps brighten, and a feeling of wakefulness passes through me, gentle as a sun rising on a cold morning. The audience stirs as well.

Slowly, I make my way back to the town square with the rest of the patrons, the shop-lined street, the door, the gloom-shrouded corridor, the chill of the citadel. I'm so preoccupied by the performance I accidentally run into something as I turn a corner. Or rather, someone.

The Frost King, his black cloak buttoned all the way to his neck, takes me in.

It's been weeks since I've seen him. He must still be recovering from whatever illness plagued him days ago, for his skin is gray with fatigue. We spend an uncomfortably long time watching one another in silence. I have my own reasons for skulking about. But what of him?

"You weren't at dinner," he says.

"What time is it?"

"Near midnight."

I was gone that long? I didn't think it was more than a few hours. "I got sidetracked. There was a door. And there was this town, this theater. I've never been to a theater before—"

The king studies me blankly.

And he likely doesn't care.

Turning heel, I take two steps before I'm drawn up short by an unexpected question.

"What play was performed?"

When facing him, I find genuine interest in his expression. A normal interaction between husband and wife. It's unanticipated, yes, but . . . not entirely unwanted. I feel such deep loneliness here that there have been times when I've wished for conversation from anyone, even the king.

"I'm not sure. It was about a god chained to a rock. He gave humans the gift of fire, and for that, he was punished. And at the end, he foresaw that he would be saved." I glance up. For whatever reason, I feel as though the king might lift his hand, cup my jaw and cheek. "But he wasn't saved. The end came: lightning and wind."

A little furrow mars the smooth plane of his forehead. His eyebrows are dark, bold, with a slight arch. "He is not saved—yet. But there will come a day when a man with divine blood frees him from his bonds."

"How can you know?" I ask, searching his face. "It's just a story."

"Do stories not reveal some underlying truth?"

I nod, stepping away to give myself space. Standing so near him, I'm not sure whether I want to step closer or take my blade and end him. But he's right. Is that not why I read? To be taken elsewhere, and to learn truths about myself.

"So you've seen that play before?"

He inclines his head. The way he studies me now is not how he studied me weeks ago. As if he no longer searches for reasons to turn me away, but instead looks for reasons that would cause him to stay, to extend this conversation. "There was a theater where I lived prior to my banishment. I attended when I could." He glances down the hall. No one is there. "I enjoy stories. I enjoy coming to know characters and their journeys, the choices they make."

This might be the most honest thing I've heard from him. Something personal. That he has chosen to share it with me, I feel oddly satisfied.

And of course, I have to ruin it. "So it's true. You know how to enjoy yourself, when not dooming people to eternal suffering."

The Frost King narrows his blue eyes at me. A question, though he does not speak it aloud.

"I overheard your Judgment," I explain.

"Then you know it was fair."

"How could it be fair if you did not hear the man's reasoning for his choice?"

His upper lip twitches. The hair on my arms lifts from the intensity of his focus. "I do not need to know his reasoning. I Judge souls by their actions. That is all."

The narrow-minded words of a narrow-minded god. "What did the man do? What was so terrible that you sentenced him to Neumovos?" And will I see this man's face around the citadel, now that he is forced to serve the king?

"He stole coin from his brother, who was not able to purchase medicine when his wife grew sick the following week. The illness took her quickly. She was dead three nights later."

His explanation gives me pause. An unfortunate mistake, to be certain. "His actions weren't intentional. He couldn't have known his brother's wife would take ill. Didn't he say his father was dying?"

"So he is justified in saving his father at the cost of his sister-in-law's life?"

"Of course not," I snap. "But someone's reasoning is a good indicator of *who* they are—their heart."

"I cannot concern myself with people's hearts. Otherwise, no one would ever be Judged in a timely manner. It could take years to dissect people's motives."

"What is a few years when you can live forever?"

He shakes his head. "I did not come here for a debate. I simply wanted to see that you had not collapsed in a wine-induced coma. Now that I have my answer, I will take my leave." His eyes flit across my face. "Good night."

I incline my head. I figure it's better than flicking a dagger into his eye. "And you as well."

~

Hours later, I still cannot sleep.

The moon is absent tonight, leaving a scar against the night sky. As I lie in my comfortable bed with its ridiculous amount of pillows, I grab the paperback romance novel from the bedside table and open it to the chapter where I left off. It tells the story of a woman who dresses as a man and boards a ship heading for distant lands. She begins to fall in love with the captain of the ship, who remains ignorant of her sex. Until she saves his life from a sea monster, that is. Now they dance around their attraction to one another, and it is my absolute favorite part.

Tension.

The pirate is a rogue, with a mouth quick to smile and enough charisma to win over an enemy fleet. And the Frost King is . . . the opposite of that.

It is clear the rogue cares for, maybe even loves, the heroine. Oh sure, he can speak the most romantic declarations, but the truth lies in the subtleties of his actions.

A thread of longing wends through me. I hate it. The weakness, how cruel the emotion is, but most of all, I hate—

My head snaps up as a hissing sound draws my attention to the door. "Hello?"

No response.

I wait a few moments, ears keen. Must have been the fire I heard.

I flip a page, returning to my reading for a time. When the sound comes again, I tense, my every sense heightened. "Orla?" But again, no answer. It was not the fire. This time I am sure of it.

A shadow moves in the crack beneath the door. Setting the book on my nightstand, I slide from beneath the blankets and approach the door with caution, moving quietly. Gripping the handle, I press my ear to the cool wood.

At first, nothing. Just the drugging pulse of blood in my eardrums, the wind moaning beyond the windowpanes. But then a low, rattling hiss sounds, emanating from deep in the chest. One, two, three heartbeats later, and I smell it. Smoke.

Every pore, every hair, every sliver of awareness narrows on the reek I would recognize anywhere.

Backing away slowly, I let my mind unspool, but only for a moment. One fleeting, harried moment before I reel it back in, regain control of my faculties. If the darkwalker has breached the citadel wards, no one is safe. My salt satchel is empty. The closest salt replenishment is in the kitchen—two levels below.

My attention catches on my bow and quiver, however, and I snatch them up, grabbing an arrow and digging its point into my palm. Blood wells, coating the iron point. The copper scent will attract any darkwalker in the vicinity, but the salt from my blood is all that stands between me and a fate worse than death.

Nocking the arrow, I point it at the door. Is there only one beast, or do more stalk the grounds? Where are the guards? Where is the Frost King? Wouldn't he know if the protections failed, or has something happened to him? My pulse careens, but my hand remains steady.

A rumble vibrates the air. I prepare myself for the moment the wood will splinter and cave inward. Massive paws tipped in black nails click as the creature paces beyond my door, then moves off. If the darkwalker finds someone in the citadel, if it's Orla—I have to bring it down.

Bounding for the door, I swing it open in time to spot its bowed, spindly legs disappearing around the corner at the end of the corridor. On silent feet I track it, hurrying after the shadowy impression of its hulking mass. I need it to face me. Only then will I be able to strike it through the heart, or whatever remains of that organ. It is the only way to kill a darkwalker, aside from cutting off its head.

I'm running flat out, but it's still too fast for me to catch. At the next turn, I slow. One of the doors on my right stands ajar, its face a collective patchwork of colored glass.

Pushing into the room, I stop short. A sound like music fills the air. Light, airy twittering and trilling tones of every pitch sparkle, while low, somber warbles punctuate a bass countermelody. And there, so faint I'm not sure if I imagine it, the clear call of a wren, the songbird after which I'd been named.

The aviary is a single great hall shaped like the moon when full, and every inch of the colossal space is filled to the rafters with various species of bird. The floor is bare, nothing to interrupt my view of the walls. No windows or doors, nothing that could allow the darkwalker to escape. Sunlight beams through an opening in the domed, filigreed ceiling far, far above.

It's not here. Only birdsong.

Turning back, I race down the hallway. The dim corridor stretches into deeper darkness. If it didn't enter the room, then it would have continued onward. I keep to the wide, main corridor, turn left, and stop.

Four men block my way forward. Cracked pillars hewn from dulled, dust-coated ebony flank this passage, and in the distance, I spot places where the ground has ruptured, as though the earth gave a great heave, leaving ruin in its wake. Shadow veils what lies beyond the first few doors.

The forbidden north wing.

"Where is it?" I demand, gasping hard. "Where did it go?" Sweat slithers down my face despite the chilly air.

There is a silence. They stare at me warily, at my drawn weapon, my partial state of dress, and I wonder if I am going mad. I saw the darkwalker. I smelled the hot, iron-coated odor of a belching forge. It was real. How could they not see it?

The tallest of the guards says, voice level, "Where is what, my lady?"

"The darkwalker."

A brief, wordless exchange between the specter men. "My lady," says one kindly, his semi-transparent fingers tightening around the hilt of his sheathed sword, "there are no darkwalkers in the citadel. My lord has warded it against them."

"Then you'll be interested to learn the wards have been breached, because I just saw one. Did it come this way? Did you see it?" Darkwalkers are known for their ability to merge into dark places unseen, essentially rendering themselves invisible, but I had hoped there was enough light from the wall sconces to prevent that from happening.

They don't look concerned. They barely look awake, as it is.

"My lady," says the tall man again. "It is late. Perhaps you were dreaming?"

"Is there a problem?"

I startle at the rolling smoothness of the Frost King's voice, whirl around to watch him stride from the gloomy corridor I just emerged from. He takes in my nocked arrow, the blood dripping from my palm, my legs bare beneath my short nightgown, which he lingers on.

"There's a darkwalker," I puff, lowering my weapon, "somewhere in the citadel."

It's as though his expression becomes a blade upon a whetting stone, honing into an edge in the passing moments. "Are you certain?"

"Yes. I smelled it from my room. It ran down this corridor, but I lost track of it."

He believes me. But he also doubts me. "The wards are impenetrable. Nothing may enter the gates or cross over the wall unless I will it—"

"Stop." Sharp and a little mean. I've not the patience to attempt otherwise. "Just . . . stop. I don't need you to tell me what you believe or what is. I need you to *listen*." At this moment, it is the smallest, most important thing. To hear me. To not cast me aside. "Can you do that?"

Holding himself stiffly, he says, "I'm trying—"

"Try harder."

The Frost King looks to my hand, white-knuckled around the curved wood of the bow. Not for the first time, I sense that he sees much, despite saying little.

"All right," he concedes, the polish lacquered onto his voice as though to provide an extra layer, to return it to its smooth texture. "I will have my men investigate. For your own safety, do not leave your room for the rest of the night. I will send Orla once it is clear."

At least he is taking my word seriously. With a terse nod, I begin my trek back to my rooms. To my surprise, he falls into step beside me. "What are you doing?"

"Accompanying you back to your chambers."

My blood is quite valuable to him, I suppose. It needs to be protected.

We walk the halls in silence. Was it only hours before that I'd returned from the theater? For a time, my conversation with the king had been almost pleasant—until I'd ruined it.

When we reach my quarters, I stride ahead with a muttered, "Thank you."

"Wife."

I grind my teeth. That term. But I spare him a glance over my shoulder. "What?"

His blue eyes flicker with an emotion beyond my comprehension. But he only says, "Make sure to lock your door."

# CHAPTER 14

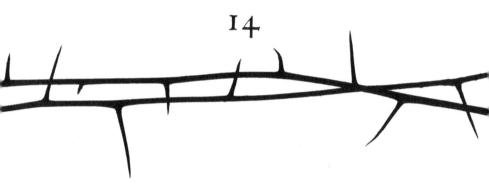

Late one morning, as I'm sitting at my window, stitching up a hole in my tunic, I spot movement from the landscape below.

A dark figure, blurred by distance, stumbles from the line of trees surrounding the outer wall. My spine snaps straight, but—no. It's not a darkwalker. The figure walks upright on two legs. A man, I believe. He makes slow progress, trudging through deep, new-fallen snow. He falls, picks himself up. Falls again, and lies there long enough for alarm to stricken me, yet somehow manages to push to his feet. Once he reaches the gates, he stops, swaying. His coat—if the tattered fabric hanging off his shoulders can be called that—flaps at his back. One of his arms hangs limp.

The sewing lies forgotten in my lap. The man is wounded, that much is clear. Where did he come from? How far did he travel in order to reach the citadel?

The man lifts his uninjured arm in a pleading gesture. He's

asking for entry. A healer, food, shelter. Any and all of those things. I expect the guards to open the gates. Instead, there's a shout. The man jerks suddenly and I gasp as he falls to his knees and collapses face-first into the snow.

Leaning forward, I press my nose against the icy glass for a closer look. The sight is unmistakable. An arrow sprouts from his shoulder.

They shot him.

My throat prickles with impending rage. So this is how the king answers a cry for help.

A chilling calm blankets me as I rise to my feet and set aside my sewing. Snatching up my bow and quiver, I hurry downstairs, fling open one of the side doors, and cross the courtyard in eating strides. My heart howls. My skin flushes with crawling heat, and I feel neither wind nor cold. In my fury, I forgot to grab my coat.

"Open the gates!" I scream, leaping over a crack in the paving stones. The snow is shoveled daily inside the wall, leaving the entrance clear.

One of the guards atop the wall calls, "We are forbidden to open the gates, my lady. Those are the lord's orders."

My arrow is nocked, the string fully drawn before he finishes his sentence. Had I less restraint, it would already be buried in his eye. A man bleeds out on the other side of this wall. That is no laughing matter.

"As your queen," I say, voice ringing with disdain, "I gave you an order. You *will* open the gates, men, or the king will hear of your disobedience." There is a pause. "Now!"

Silence.

The gate's teeth tumble then, unlocking the clanking mechanism. The hinges shriek.

Nestled in the snow, a body. Chapped skin and ragged cloth.

I rush to the man's side, then tense. He's not a specter. There is no transparency to his skin, no blurriness to his edges. The man is human, flesh and blood.

Impossible.

He is alive by the skin of his teeth. His chest rises and falls in shallow spurts. Ice encrusts his nostrils, the corners of his eyes. His cheeks are wind-chapped, pink with irritation. Blackened skin patches large areas of his unprotected hands and face. It even wreaths his neck. I'm no stranger to frostbite. I nearly lost two of my fingers from exposure years ago. This man must have traveled days to get here. Splotchy blood darkens his clothes, suggesting he's bleeding from multiple lacerations.

Calmly, I push to my feet, though my stomach clenches. "You three." I point to a group of guards that has come to investigate. "Carry this man to the infirmary. And make haste."

Despite their bewilderment at seeing another mortal in the Deadlands, they scramble to obey, hauling him by the arms and legs up the stairs, down the hall to the eastern wing. I have vague recollections of the infirmary in those early days following my attack.

Alba, the healer, gasps at her newest patient. "Set him on the bed," she barks, rounding her work table. The specter woman is as plump as the full moon, with kind eyes that have hardened in the wake of injury.

The man's filth and blood stain the white sheets. The infirmary consists of five freshly-made cots, a table cluttered with jars of salve and herbs, and a fire that I quickly stoke to life.

"Out," she demands. The guards make themselves scarce.

"How can I help?" The man's pallor resembles that of a corpse.

A wheezing sound, like breath whistling through a collapsed lung, stirs the air.

Alba passes me a knife. "Strip him of his clothes and cover him in blankets. We'll need to warm his body, but slowly, otherwise his heart might stop. I'll heat some water." She stares down at him in puzzlement. "He's alive. Really alive. Like . . ." Her gaze drifts to mine before she snaps into action.

With detached, utilitarian movements, I peel the man down to his skin. The sight is ghastly: deep puncture wounds across his abdomen, scored thighs seeping blood. Quickly, I heap blankets atop his body. Alba piles more wood onto the fire. She touches the man's forehead every so often, nodding to herself. "He is warming." Then her attention shifts to the arrow sprouting from his shoulder.

"That arrow is from our men," she says, lightly touching the fletching.

"Yes."

Her gaze latches onto mine, questioning.

"The guards shot him because he wouldn't leave when they ordered him to."

Alba's mask of calm breaks beneath her disgust. "Brutes. A life is a life. I do not see the difference."

Neither do I.

She sighs, ladling boiling water from the pot into a small bowl. "Hold him down. If he wakes while I attempt to remove the arrow, it could drive the head deeper."

I haven't the arm strength to restrain a fully grown man, so I lay across his chest, using my body weight to secure him.

The man has lost a lot of blood. There's no guarantee he will survive the night. He is young, too young to leave this life. How on earth did he manage to cross the Shade? How is he not in his specter form?

Blood pours from the opening as Alba pulls the arrowhead free. She applies pressure with a cloth to staunch the flow, then proceeds to clean the wound, stitching his skin shut.

I'm helping bandage the area when a cold wind slides down my spine, prickling my skin.

"What is this?" The hiss slithers from the doorway like the rasp of a sword sliding free of its sheath.

My pulse accelerates despite my outward calm. Girding myself for the battle ahead, I slowly straighten, sending the healer a wordless glance not to worry. His quarrel is with me.

The Frost King's form blackens the doorway. His hair hangs loose and tangled and so much wilder than I've ever seen it. The pale hue of his skin is completely colorless, save two pink stripes across his cut-glass cheekbones and the rich flush of his full mouth. He may be carved from marble for how still he is. With him, he carries the reek of death.

Blood coats the hem of his tunic, and scores mar his metal breastplate. His spear is nowhere in sight, but that makes him no less terrifying. And indeed, he is terrifying. Grit streaks his face, collecting in the folds around his eyes, in the creases of his neck. Fury claps across his countenance like a thundercloud.

"Hello, Husband." Striding to the king's side, I take his hand. "Let's talk."

He digs in his heels. I jerk him forward, and he follows me into the hall, growling under his breath like a damn animal.

Once the door shuts, giving us privacy, he pulls free. "My guards informed me you've sheltered a man from the outside. Is this true?"

"It's true." I plant my hands on my hips. "What of it?"

"Do you realize what you have done?"

"Saved someone's life?"

His nostrils flare. Every pore in my body attempts to recoil from his nearness. He is too close, this predator.

He says, "You have invited the enemy into my home."

The words give me pause. In the short time I have known my husband, I've learned something: to him, everyone is an enemy.

"Why do you say this man is an enemy?"

"Have you looked at his eyes?"

"No. I was too busy trying to prevent him from bleeding out." As well, his eyes are closed.

Cruel laughter coils in the space between our bodies. "Of course not," he says, as though he expected my oversight.

My spine snaps upright at the affront. He has some nerve. "I will tell you what I saw. A man, wounded and lost, who came to your citadel for help. Instead, he was shot." Every word expels in a single, diamond-pointed moment of rage. "You do not kill an unarmed man."

"He is not unarmed. And he is no longer a man."

For whatever reason, I swallow down my argument. The wounded man carried no weapons. But is there perhaps a weapon I cannot see? "I could not have his death on my conscience. So I acted. I do not regret it." Too many things die in the Gray. I could not allow one more to meet that fate.

His blue eyes flicker like a cold flame. It is another moment longer before he replies, "You had no authority to make this decision without my consent."

"I have all the authority," I cry, poking his chest hard with a finger. He rubs at the spot in bewilderment. "I'm not just a coat to hang on a rack and forget about. I am your wife. I live here, I eat here,

I sleep here. So yes, if I decide to save this man, I will, and you can do nothing about it."

"You don't know who this man is," he growls, infiltrating my personal space. My back hits the wall. The scent of cedar enfolds me, dizzying and clean beneath the heavy iron-salt odor clinging to his torn uniform. "He could have come here with the intention to kill me, or you. It could be a trap." That baleful glare rests heavy as stone upon me.

Oh, of all the ridiculous things I've heard, this tops it. "I suppose you're right. With all the blood he's lost, why, I would expect him to leap up any moment and stab you in the heart." That cold, unfeeling heart, which I will pierce soon enough.

The Frost King stops. A small line indents the skin between his black eyebrows. "You mock me."

"Of course I mock you!" I cry through disbelieving laughter. "Even if he came here to kill you, I doubt he'll succeed now. He is barely hanging on to life as it is!"

"That is beside the point," he tosses back. "If one person has managed to breach the Shade, who will be next? A force grows, one that I'm not sure I can fight for much longer."

"Say what you will," I retort, "but I will never turn my back on someone in need, even you."

The last part slips out unintentionally.

The Frost King opens his mouth. Then, as if my words finally sink in, closes it. Did I mean what I said? Absolutely not. Honestly, I'm baffled as to how I could utter that sentiment.

An awkward silence descends.

Then I realize what he said moments before. "Wait, that man breached the Shade? I thought only the dead can cross into the Deadlands."

He rubs a gloved hand over his jaw, smearing more dirt. "That is true, were the Shade intact."

"What?"

He leads me back into the infirmary. Alba has run off somewhere, which is probably for the best. Striding to the wounded man's side, he pulls back one of the patient's eyelids, and I gasp. The eye—pupil, iris, sclera—is entirely black.

"But—"

"See this?" He gestures to what I had believed to be frostbite, but upon closer inspection, I notice the blackened areas are located *beneath* the skin. And they are not still. They appear alive, twitching and curling into amorphous shapes.

My gut tightens at the wrongness of it all. "It looks like he's turning into a darkwalker."

"That is exactly what's happening."

I can't pull my attention away from those shadows. It's wrong. It's wrong, wrong, wrong. "I thought it was frostbite. I didn't know what he was." A darker patch blooms beneath the man's chin, then fades. "What will you do with him?"

"He must be killed. I will tell Alba to give him nightshade. It is a poison, but it will not pain him."

It's more than I expected from him.

I ask, "Any news on the darkwalker?" Three days have passed since I chased its form through the labyrinthine veins of this place.

Orla entered my room the following morning with the news that it had not been found, had it existed at all, but that the investigation would remain ongoing.

"No," he states. "None." He pinches the top of his nose, eyes squeezed shut.

"Has a breach occurred before?"

"The protections are the strongest in my power. Nothing enters without my knowledge. Nothing."

Yet something had.

My attention lowers to the nasty gash across his left forearm, the tunic ripped. He doesn't seem to notice the amount of blood seeping out. "You're hurt."

"I'll live."

He will. And yet I find myself saying, "It could become infected. I can clean it for you." I don't know where these words come from. As far as I'm concerned, the wound can fester. He cannot die, but he can suffer. He can feel pain. And yet, he came for me at a time of grave peril, when I might have died from the hurts sustained by his subjects, and I have not been able to forget it. "It won't take long."

He shifts his weight. And just like that, I've made the Frost King uncomfortable. "This won't grant you favors, Wife."

As if I want any favors from him. Brushing past him, I call over my shoulder, "This way." Just as I know the sun rises easterly, I know he will follow. The king can deny it all he likes, but he is curious of me. And some small, twisted part of me is curious of him, too.

I gesture to an empty cot. "Sit."

He sits.

The pot of water is still hot, so I ladle some into a bowl, grab a cloth, and pull up a stool.

He stiffens when I tug his arm for a closer look, but he doesn't attempt to pull away. He holds himself so tensely I'm reminded of a coiling asp. "What happened?" The skin beneath my fingertips is warm, dry.

He watches me push up the sleeve. He has a strong, solid wrist, and black, crinkly hair covers his forearm. "The townsfolk managed to break through the Shade. The barrier weakens. It needs your blood."

My head snaps up, taking him in. "So soon?" Why does the king's power weaken? Why does it fade? Questions I've yet to answer.

I swallow at the knowledge that I'll have to return to that horrible, hungry barrier. "Why isn't your skin healing like it did when I . . ."

"Stabbed me?"

Right. "Yes."

"I'm not sure." As he speaks, I clean his wound. "It is possible their weapons contain some type of power that nullifies my body's healing abilities."

I had no idea such things existed. "Where would they get such weapons?"

"That is a question I have yet to answer."

I return to my task in silence. Our knees touch, and the heat radiating from his body surges against me like waves lapping ashore. His shoulders stretch the fabric of his tunic, soiled and bloody as it is. He smells of man.

"You are too soft," he murmurs, watching my hands in careful study as I wrap the cloth around his forearm. His expression has thawed, if I'm not mistaken.

I'm probably mistaken.

"There is no softness in me." It is the only way to ensure my survival. A soft heart will not provide food. A soft heart may allow weakness to infiltrate. What kind of provider would I be if I allowed those vulnerable pieces to cloud my judgment?

It turns out people do not want a soft heart. So I hardened mine.

"You believe there is not, but your actions prove otherwise."

The king is wrong, but I don't bother arguing with him. "You speak as though this theoretical softness is a bad thing."

"It is, if you want to protect yourself from harm."

"And how would I do that?" I counter. "By isolating myself from the rest of the world?"

Always, that stubborn silence, and yet . . .

"Is that what you think? That my isolation is purposeful?"

I don't know what to think. He has given me no answers. "Not everyone seeks to harm others." I cut the end of the cloth and begin tying it off. The crackling fire warms my back. The Frost King's broad torso warms my front. *Who hurt you?* I wonder. *Why do you harbor so much mistrust?*

"You cannot know a man's heart." He gestures to the unconscious patient. "Who is to say you didn't doom this man to a worse fate?"

I've experienced terrible things in life. I have lost and I have grieved. I have struggled and toiled, and still I choose to look for the light, even when the immortal before me knows only darkness. "And if it had been you?" I challenge. "Should I have left you to die?"

Clearly, he doesn't know what to make of my query, because he reminds me, voice ripe with frustration, "I cannot die."

Our eyes lock and hold. A knock sounds at the door.

"Enter," intones the Frost King.

"My lord." A soldier takes us in and quickly averts his gaze. "Another hole has appeared in the Shade to the north. What are your orders?"

The king rises to his feet. If the Shade is weakening, might it fall all at once? Does that mean I could return to Edgewood?

"Send another unit to the west. I will deal with the breach in the north. Come, Wife."

"My name is Wren." As I move to dump the bloody water out the window, I mutter, "And you're welcome."

# CHAPTER 15

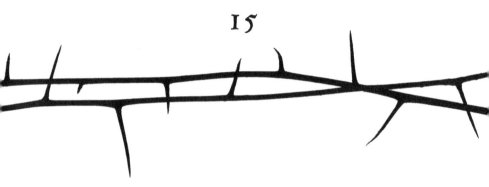

We make haste, racing on a black steed through the white land. Pressed forward over the saddle, the Frost King at my back, we move to the sound of thunder.

Something terrible awaits me at the Shade. There will be blood. I'm sure of it. The only question is how much. How many dead? And could those deaths have been prevented?

The darkwalker, Phaethon, weaves a broken path. The land rises steadily, uprooted trees piling up the higher we climb, casualties of avalanches, the hammering gales. Snow retreats in the presence of the exposed rock faces.

"Tell me what to expect," I cry, ducking my face against the scoring wind. My cheeks chafe and tears stream from my eyes. Whatever lies in wait, I must prepare myself.

His chest brushes my back as the darkwalker leaps over a fallen tree, clearing it easily. Its shadows reform as four legs once it hits the ground. "Mortals flood my lands as we speak. The rest of my force will arrive shortly. They have the authority to kill on sight."

He steers us slightly northwest. A frozen creek glimmers in the depression between two hills like a vein of poured, molten silver, but then we are past, we are climbing higher, and the momentary brightness vanishes behind the rising terrain. "Prepare for the worst."

The tree line lies ahead, and then we are through. The land spreads without interruption. The shadowy undulation of the Shade, the curved band of the Les. Weeks ago, all was pristine. Now the barrier has ripped open like cloth, its edges fluttering.

It is impossible to prepare. The violence hits without warning, and only in that moment do I learn whether I can absorb it, whether I will stand or kneel.

Metal screams upon parting the frosty air. The darkwalker streams into a weightless gallop, snow and mud flinging from its hooves, and the song of war rolls over me, snagging on the edge of fear.

Bodies litter the ground. The Frost King's soldiers beat back the swarming townsfolk, whose weathered boots and thin clothes appear to be patched to their emaciated bodies. Some can barely lift a weapon.

But that doesn't stop the desperate from spilling through by the hundreds. Desperate for change, for vengeance. Upon catching sight of the Frost King, they surge toward us, and I gasp, clutching the powerful arm that bands around my waist without realizing it.

The first villager reaches us. The Frost King swings his spear in an arc that spews blood. The man falls, but another takes his place.

And another.

And another.

It's a killing field. The snow runs dark and muddy, punched through by bootprints. The corpses rise like hills. I've never seen so many casualties in one place before. The horror is so great my body, as if sensing the extent of this tragedy, shuts down, and I feel nothing. *Prepare for the worst*, he said. I could never have fathomed something like this.

The townsfolk remain human, but only for so long. It's as though their forced entry into the Deadlands has corrupted them. They were not welcomed here. It was not their time. Their bodies remain mortal, but their eyes . . . black. Even their flesh begins to wither.

"You will need to feed the Shade your blood," shouts the Frost King, knocking an arrow aside with his spear. Ice shards fly from the tip, and the screams pitch, dozens of them, as ice meets skin and slices deep. "It's the only way to halt their intrusion."

The king directs his mount expertly using only his knees. The carved head of his spear shimmers with crackling power. The blood-drenched metal of his breastplate rests coldly against my back, chilling me through the fabric. Men, women, even children, raise ineffective weapons against a god: pieces of boards with nails, ropes, broom handles and pails.

And they fall, and they fall, and they fall.

Bodies tossed in snow.

Bodies buried in mud.

Pieces of bodies. Carnage. I'm paralyzed by the sight. People just like me.

"My men and I will push them back," he grunts, narrowly avoiding a knife to the leg. "They are untrained. It shouldn't be difficult."

Desperation can compensate for lack of formal training. Back in

Edgewood, raiders would strike on occasion, as those starving years passed. Most of the townsfolk couldn't tell one end of a sword from another, but we managed to hold our own.

His arm tightens around me. "Keep your seat." Then he cries, "To me!"

A unit of soldiers breaks away from the fighting to swarm us. They lock into formation, flanking the king as he pushes forward, driving through the throng like a wedge to pinch out a narrow path. The Frost King was right. The townsfolk are untrained. Everywhere I look, someone dies. A sword to the chest or belly split open. A few brave souls latch onto my legs, and the memory of Neumovos, of hands on flesh, my body crushed into the road, ignites fear in me. I scream and kick one in the face. The Frost King blasts the rest backward with a wall of wind.

"Make for the Shade," he growls in my ear. Two hands at my waist, and he lifts me clear of the saddle, setting me on the ground.

He cuts a swath through the thickest of the fighting, using his winds to drive back the interlopers. I'm leaping over bodies and climbing over missing appendages. Bloodshed hangs like a miasma over the sloped field. Someone slashes at me with a sword. I duck and drive my dagger into their belly. Dead.

I cannot trust the Frost King.

I cannot trust the villagers.

The only person I can trust is myself.

A bow has fallen to the ground, its owner having reached his demise. I snag it, then rip out an arrow embedded in a dead man's eye. My throat tightens. *Focus.* The wood in my hand, the bow's graceful curve. In seconds, the arrow is nocked. If this is my only means of protection, then so be it.

The king's army shifts to staunch the outpouring from a new tear in the Shade. The townsfolk stumble, fall, are trampled. And at last, I witness what happens to those who cross into the Deadlands before their time.

Their bodies morph. Shadows drift like a fog from their skin, and their eyes shutter completely, pupils swelling like growths. Their hands crimp and their fingers grow claws.

Darkwalkers.

My blood ices over. Darkness eats at the boundaries of their skin. Curved, protruding spines and a loping gait. Jaws so large they can unhinge, swallowing a fully grown man whole.

Pain shreds open my back and I scream, whirling around to release the arrow blindly. It hits a man half-shifted square in the eye. His head snaps backward. The pain is so great my hand spasms and the bow slips from my grip.

Beyond, the Shade pulses like a dark heart.

I lurch forward. Stop the influx of people into the Deadlands. Stop the darkwalkers from multiplying. The king fights a group of three in my periphery. Phaethon rears, clipping a darkwalker in the head. It goes down long enough for one of the soldiers to sever the head from its body.

Less than an arm span separates me from my destination. The Frost King assured me my blood would strengthen the barrier for a few years. It's barely been six weeks. For whatever reason, it failed.

"Do it," bellows the Frost King, and I swear fear fractures his voice. "Do it now!"

His eyes meet mine across the field. Another swing, another life. This is a long game. My captor will not die on this day, nor tomorrow, nor the next. I cannot squander my chance to kill him, cannot sacrifice my plan in a moment of eager revenge. And anyway, my dagger is not god-touched. The time will come. Soon.

Pain blooms bright beneath the knife's edge as I slice through the healed scar from the last encounter. Blood slides down my wrist, darkening the snow at my feet. I thought strengthening the Shade doomed these people to death. But if mortals are crossing into the Deadlands, turning into darkwalkers, and then escaping back into the Gray, this will help break that cycle.

My blood hits the Shade and swirls red among the black. The darkening power crawls across the holes, knitting them together like neat seams, until my reflection stares back at me: a wide-eyed woman who has failed her own people. Even if this helps stop the cycle of darkwalker creation, it is not a solution. I am sickened by my own powerlessness. Nothing I've done has been enough. And I wonder if I am enough to complete this task or if I am too weak. If someone braver, cleverer, might succeed.

Once the Shade is fortified, the battle does not last. The king's army puts an end to the remaining darkwalkers, though some manage to escape into the trees.

"Well done." The Frost King has reined in his beast against my side. He gazes down at me with approval—a first from him. "In a moment of uncertainty, you remained loyal."

I trudge a few paces toward the tree line. Truly, he thinks I am loyal to him?

"Wife."

"Give me space," I growl.

I lean against a tree for support. The trunk is rough and cold against my shoulder. My shredded back throbs, but the pain grounds me.

Somehow, I need to find Zephyrus.

A shout snaps my eyes open. Hoofbeats. Before I can process what is happening, an arm bands around my waist, scooping me up and depositing me atop a specter horse. The man's smell reaches me: copper and salt, the reek of battle. But it's not Boreas. No, Boreas is standing paces away, his eyes wild as he watches the man, my captor, dig his heels into the horse's sides. We spring through the trees and disappear.

I glance down. A dark, clawed hand curves at my waist with iron strength, and I scream, trying to tear free as the horse careens through dense wood, carrying me deeper into the Deadlands.

The Frost King's roar shakes the snow loose from the trees.

Hell hath no fury like a spurned god.

# CHAPTER
# 16

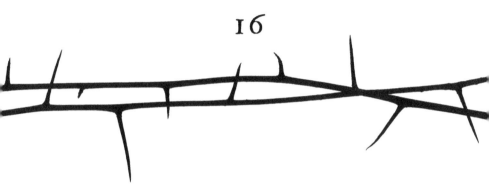

Fear—it is all I know. A man on the cusp of mutation at my back, his clawed, shadowy hand curling tightly around my waist, the promise of a fate beyond death, beyond what is natural in the cycle of life.

I fight. There is no other option. Multiple times, I attempt to toss myself from the saddle, but the arm banded around me is immoveable. No matter how I tear my nails into his forearm, it doesn't break skin.

The chase takes us east, then north. Scaling mountains and plunging into valleys, the forest strangely eerie. We do not slow, but always push forward. The specter horse, bearing the weight of an extra rider, breathes heavily as the man directs it down a snake of a path, which curves treacherously against a sheer rock face. Sweat coats the animal's flanks and steam puffs from its foam-lathered mouth. I could kick him for abusing the animal this way, even if it is technically dead.

The horse picks its way across the crumbling ledge, pebbles scattering beneath its hooves. Despite telling myself not to look, I peer into the long drop below. Far, far into that abyss is a thick gathering of shadow. I cannot see what lies at the bottom.

"You're making a mistake," I spit. My fingers clutch the front of the saddle as the horse stumbles. I squeeze my eyes shut.

"Quiet."

After an indeterminate amount of time, the clatter of rocks ceases, and I crack open my eyes. We're beyond the ledge, heading into a shallow descent of forest. The sun winks like an overly large eye.

"Take me back," I demand.

We pick up speed, soaring over a frozen streambed, and I lurch forward at the landing. "No."

"Then leave me." I gasp as we barrel toward a tree. Only a last-second twist saves us. "When the North Wind is through with you, you'll wish you were dead."

A wisp of darkness coils around my neck, stroking like a lover's caress. "The North Wind will attempt nothing." The man's voice is guttural, as though impeded by the bulk of teeth crowding his mouth. "Not when I have his wife."

"You don't understand. He doesn't care about me. He cares that you have stood against him." And he will do whatever it takes to get me back, for I am his prize, his precious tool. No method is too perverse.

The man isn't listening. Too blinded by foolish hope. Too overcome by greed. He has carved himself a path that can only lead to one thing, and it is certainly not everlasting life.

Pressed between the earth and the flat gray sky, we surge forward, the horse galloping to the opposite side of the snowy clearing. And then we're across, diving back into the finger-bone branches of the deepest wilds of the Deadlands. The wind picks up. A cold, wet flurry overtakes us, stealing the world from sight. Yet the man doesn't slow. If anything, he pushes his horse faster. Relief hits me like a strike to the throat as the wind howls with such unbridled strength it threatens to tear me from the saddle. The king is gaining ground.

The trees shake with agitation. The air crackles and snaps against my skin. It is growing, flourishing, mutating, rotting, dying. The snowfall becomes a deluge, and a massive shudder quakes the earth. Like some long-dead leviathan, awakening in the deep.

An enormous protrusion of ice bursts from the ground a few lengths ahead. The animal screams, rearing, as the snow melts and refreezes as a layer of ice. Hooves scrabble against the sleek surface. The man, cursing, jerks at the reins to regain control, but when the horse rears a second time, I'm tossed from the saddle. The ground punches into my back, crippling my lungs.

My ears ring. The air keens and swells, and the snow, a deep, impenetrable flurry, buries my legs in the time it takes me to sit up. Flakes cling to my eyelashes and coat the edges of my mouth.

Wind. It blasts through the clearing, rips trees from their roots, flicks them like twigs in every direction. No part of the land is spared—except me.

The man screams.

My head snaps to the side. He kneels on the ground, shaking, hands black and clawed, eyes all pupil. Because he can't stand, I realize. A shard of ice as thick as my forearm has ruptured from the earth, puncturing one of his thighs. He bends forward, whimpering as blood streams down his mutilated leg, steaming as it hits the snow.

The darkness deepens.

From out of the shadows, two clouds of steam appear, as though from exhaled breath. And two obsidian eyes.

What steps from the gloom can only be described as a nightmare. All this time, Phaethon has taken an equine shape, but now the darkwalker's form is decidedly more wild, similar to those that prowl Edgewood. It lurches forward on four bowed legs. Its shoulders sit crookedly, the back slopes downward, and the spine curves like a pointed ridge. Its long, skinny tail lashes back and forth, forked at the end. Lastly, the teeth: jagged, blade-like, dripping shadow thick as blood.

The Frost King sits astride its back, the head of his spear pointed at the small, cowering man. He dismounts with grace. His gaze flits to me, a brief head-to-toe assessment, before it returns to my captor. A slow, purposeful tread brings him closer, and the temperature plummets with the motion. This isn't cold. This is the absence of warmth. Clouds roil above, and the wind, the *wind*. It burrows beneath my skin and chills me so completely I momentarily cease to breathe.

"Please," the man blubbers, his plea a high whine. "Have mercy."

Another step forward. "Mercy." Blue eyes glow within that perfect, bloodless face wreathed in shadow. "The gods offered no mercy for me."

"I didn't know. Please my lord, I didn't know she was your wife!"

"You lie." He raises his spear, the tip digging into the man's narrow chest where, through his ripped tunic, I see that darkness creeping toward his neck. Changing him.

As the man bows forward, accepting his fate, my stomach pitches sickeningly. It's not his fault. I mean, it is his fault, but . . . when you have nothing, you make poor choices. You become crazed, obsessed by the idea that something could improve your life. Corruption warps the mind, devolves it to that of an animal. Maybe even a darkwalker.

The king draws back his arm. The air hisses, snow dampening my eyelashes. I rush forward, planting myself directly in the spear's path as power explodes forward.

Horror and fear widen the king's eyes as he realizes I stand between him and his prey, the ice already erupting toward me.

The deadly shards melt into harmless water, which splashes the front of my clothes.

His lips are pressed white. "Wife," he hisses. "Get out of the way."

"Spare him." The man cowers behind me, weeping nonsense pleas under his breath. "He didn't know what he was doing."

"He knew exactly what he was doing. He is a man. You are a woman, a prize he thought to take from me." He looms over me, forcing my head back, darkness rising like steam from his skin.

"All right," I say, lifting my hands, palms out. "Maybe he did. But consider that it was the choice of the darkwalker, not him."

The man makes a sound of assent before collapsing back into a sobbing mess.

The Frost King moves so fast my mortal eyes can't track it. A blink, and the man lies dead at my feet, a piece of ice sprouting from his throat.

"Are you hurt?" Before I can answer, he pats my body down.

Touching me—voluntarily, I might add. That has never happened before. I'm not deluding myself into thinking he cares for me. I'm valuable. A tool, nothing more.

When he brushes my back, I flinch away, hissing in pain. He goes still.

"Darkwalker." My gaze shies from the intensity of his own. "From the battle."

His right hand grazes the curve of my shoulder. Light, gloved fingertips. Gentle, even. "May I see?"

Wordlessly, I turn, presenting him what I imagine is a horribly shredded sight. He examines me, not speaking. "How bad is it?"

"You will need to see Alba when we return. The wounds are many, but they aren't deep."

"Will it scar?"

This silence stretches longer than the last. Perhaps he is thinking of the other scar I bear. "It shouldn't. I will have her use the strongest salves at her disposal."

It really shouldn't matter, but . . . I am grateful.

"Thank you." I glance again at the dead man. Or rather, the half man, half darkwalker.

The Frost King murmurs, "He wasn't one of the mortals who infiltrated. He was one of mine. See his skin?" He points to an area near the exposed collarbone. It's subtle, but there is a certain level of transparency there. "He worked the grounds. For the last three days he did not appear for work. I wondered where he had gone."

He whistles for Phaethon. The darkwalker, having returned to its equine form, trots over in streaming tendrils of night. The king mounts before offering me a hand. After some hesitation, I take it.

Strong, calloused fingers curl around mine, and the strength of his arm pulls me into the saddle.

I don't want to ask, but I have to know. "What now?"

His fingers twitch as they curl around the reins. "Now, we pay a visit to Neumovos."

~

We arrive at the village covered in blood and filth, signs of the dead coating our clothes and clinging to our hair. Despite the freezing temperature, sweat slicks my skin beneath the heavy coat I wear. The Frost King's arm bands around my waist, tucking me against his front, as though to keep me close. His wrath beats like the sun on my back.

Phaethon slinks from the forest's shadowed edge. The village streets are empty. The square is empty. The darkened windows, shuttered like gaps in a mouth full of teeth. Snow piles atop the thatched rooftops.

Hooves ring against stone.

*Clop.*

*Clop.*

*Clop.*

The Frost King holds his spear in his left hand, the reins in his right. His armor creaks. The corded arm pressed across my stomach tightens.

"What will you do?" I whisper, swiping my tongue across my chapped lips.

His response stirs the hair at the crown of my head. "I've yet to decide. If one of my staff turned on me, there is the likelihood that

others have as well. And if they are slowly turning into darkwalkers
. . ."

Then there is a problem.

The king nudges Phaethon onward, and we trot down the main road. In the corner of my eye, I spot movement—a window curtain swaying into place, as if someone had momentarily peered out at us.

My teeth chatter. When I last visited Neumovos, it ended with my shattered body abandoned at the end of the lane. Deep inside me, my organs harden, my muscles screaming with unbearable tightness.

"You're safe," the Frost King murmurs, and I release a slow exhale.

"People of Neumovos," he calls, deep voice booming. "You have one hour to gather in the village square, or your lives are forfeit to the Chasm."

He's threatened others with that punishment before, during the Judgment I overheard. Aside from a breeze blending the soft snowfall, the smattering covering the gray stones, nothing stirs.

Phaethon, as if sensing its rider's frustration, prances beneath us. The Frost King growls. "People of Neumovos," he cries. "Answer your king!"

Ice blasts one of the doors to splinters. Screams erupt from inside.

I go cold all over. A family of four stumbles out onto the street, huddled in their threadbare coats. Afternoon sunlight streams through their terrified faces.

The square fills within minutes. The king dismounts, his impressive height and presence dwarfing those who gather. "People of Neumovos," he intones. "Do you know why I have called you here?"

The crowd shifts like ripples moving through a still pool. No one dares speak.

"You have presumed to mutiny against me," he says flatly. "You have threatened the peace of the Deadlands, and thus, the balance I have worked tirelessly to achieve. You have spurned your king."

Each word falls like a sharp stone. His fury compounds, and the townsfolk flinch back. My hands tighten around the reins.

"This evening, one of your own attempted to kidnap my wife, who was nearly beaten to death only a few weeks prior. Only by her request did I not return and raze this place to the ground. Only by her request did I not withdraw my Judgment, and banish you to the pits of the Chasm." A few gasps ring free. "But this time, I do not know how far my leniency will extend."

Someone whimpers as he lifts the spear higher. The sight makes my teeth grind together. Just because one person from Neumovos was corrupted, doesn't mean that corruption has spread through the entire town. The Frost King is too strong, too gorged on power. What can I, a mortal woman, do to sway him?

What is it he wants?

Someone from the crowd calls, "It wasn't us, my lord. We swear it!"

The king sneers. "As you would have me believe."

"We know who you speak of," one man says, pushing forward. "His name was Oliver. Over the last few weeks, he began to . . . change." The man lowers his gaze uncomfortably. "His eyes turned black." There is a pause before he continues. "We don't know how or why he changed, my lord. We only know he was not the man he once was."

Against my better judgment, I say to the Frost King from atop his beast, "Maybe you should listen to them." Because I do not see these people capable of mutiny. How would they acquire weapons? They haven't any industry. This is a dying town, same as all the rest.

"You would have me believe only one of you has betrayed me?" Quiet. "That there are not others who will make attempts on my life?" The crowd stirs. "Tell me why I should not tear this town to rubble," he cries, eyes flooding with a terrifying light. "Tell me why I should not punish those who have scorned my trust, who work with those mortals attempting to cross into the Deadlands before their time. Tell me why I should not send you to the dark of the Chasm."

He swings his spear, the carved head blasting a frozen wind at the nearest structure. It ruptures into raining pieces. The screams rise as dust settles over the square. He points the spear at another building down the street, naught but a sagging porch and leaning walls, someone's washed-out, humble home, and draws back his arm.

"Stop." I hurry to dismount and grab his arm. "You've made your point."

Slowly, his gaze drops to mine. In the back of my mind, a whispered word: *peril*. Every part of me screams to cower, to make myself small and helpless and unthreatening, but I beat the sensation back.

"My point will not be made until this town is flattened," he seethes, "and those who betrayed me punished."

"And then what?" I retort, gesturing to the frightened huddle of people surrounding us. "Who will protect your precious citadel? Who will cook your meals? Who will dress you, guard your gates, exercise your horses?" His eyes flicker, evidence that he had not considered these things in his moment of rage. "You need these people. You need this town."

"I need," he says, "no one."

He believes he needs no one. But I don't think that's actually true. "Do you honestly think this town is working with the people attacking the Shade? Look around. They have nothing." For he has already taken anything of value, their autonomy most of all.

"Please, my lord." A woman with chapped, peeling cheeks falls forward onto her knees, prostrating herself. "Have mercy." She begins to cry. "We swear we did not break our vow against you. The spirits have been growing hungry of late. It might be them. Their corruption, spreading."

"I think you know they had no involvement in the attack," I say, low and even. "I think you're just looking for someone to blame."

The Frost King makes a sound of frustration before a skinny, elderly fellow shuffles forward. His cane trembles in his hand, old joints bulging at the knuckles. His coat is in tatters. "My lord, if I may be so bold, we will be celebrating Midwinter Eve at the end of the week. There will be food and music and . . . and dancing." His gaze briefly darts to me. "We would be honored if you and your wife would join us. Let us show you we mean no ill will toward you. Let us make amends for the pain we have caused your wife. A clean slate, if you will."

Just as the Frost King opens his mouth, I latch my hand around his arm, stopping him. "We appreciate the gesture," I say to the man. "And we accept."

# CHAPTER
## 17

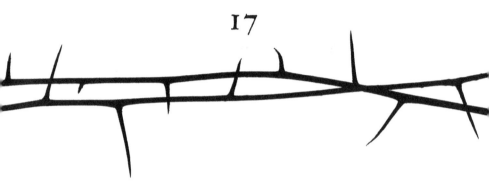

"You look lovely, my lady."

Turning away from the mirror, I offer Orla a tight smile as she nudges the door shut to my chambers and sets a basket of clean clothes at the foot of my bed. "It's not much."

"Nonsense." Gently, she turns me back to the mirror and stands beside me. "It is more than enough."

Wearing a dress was never the plan. Had it been up to me, I'd don my trousers and a tunic, my old fur coat, my sturdy boots. Simple and unobtrusive. Except Orla insisted I wear a dress. Actually, she threatened to skin me alive if I wore *those rags*, as she so scathingly put it. Hence, the dress.

Wool dyed the color of a cool midnight sky brightens my warm brown skin. The garment itself is simple in shape, with a tight-fitting bodice shaped by the cinched corset atop the fabric, and a loose skirt that skims my hips and hits my ankles.

Long sleeves offer protection from the chill air. The bodice is a thing to behold, a mapping of swirling, silver thread that thins once it hits the skirt. The same shimmery silver lines the sloping collar. Soft, worn boots peek from beneath the hem.

Tonight, the Frost King and I will attend the Midwinter Eve festival.

Orla spent the last three days fabricating this dress in preparation for the evening. Many hours of measuring, cutting, draping, sewing, pricking me with needles, and *for the love of the gods, stand still!* She and two other maidservants scrubbed my skin until it glowed—once Alba healed my back, that is—then wrangled my thick dark hair into a single braid, silver ribbon woven among the plaits. They plucked at wayward hairs, bemoaned my bitten nails and blistered feet, darkened my eyes with kohl and paints.

Orla was right. The woman in the mirror is lovely.

She is also a stranger.

No dirt smears my cheeks. No blood cakes the space beneath my fingernails. Were it not for the scar, why, I'd think I was looking at Elora.

Sweat slicks my palms, which I wipe on the front of my dress. Nerves. They've gotten worse throughout the evening. This is more Elora's realm, the dancing and preening, but she is not here. Maybe though, if I play my cards right, the king will allow me the chance to visit her soon. Just for a night.

I'm not concerned the Frost King will retaliate against Neumovos. As rigid as he is, he possesses an unexpected degree of honor, eked out by that refreshing candor. I'm more concerned that he and I are attending this festival as husband and wife, which means I'll be spending many hours in his company when I can barely get through the day without snapping at him or tossing out some underhanded insult. I'm aware of it. I *know* why I act the way I do. My understanding of the king is limited. And that frustrates me to no end.

"Let's tighten you up a bit." Orla gives an experimental tug on the corset lacings in the back.

"It's already as tight as it can go."

"Nonsense. A few more pulls will make a world of difference." So she pulls.

And pulls.

And pulls.

"What kind of devil-worshipper created this instrument of torture?" I grunt. Color begins to drain from my lips the harder she yanks on the laces.

"Suck in, my lady."

"I'm already sucking in," I grit out. The corset binds my torso so tightly it's rearranging my internal organs.

"Just one—" Pull. "More—" Pull. "Yank."

I wheeze as my ribs pinch and my stomach tucks in somewhere near my sternum. "Mercy, woman."

"There." Satisfied that she has permanently cut off circulation in my body, Orla steps back to admire her handiwork. Miracles upon miracles, I now have an even tinier waist, even if she had to cut it out of me. Indeed, I've never eaten so well for such a long period of time. Thus, I've put on weight since my arrival.

So long as I keep an eye on the amount of food I consume, I probably won't faint. As for my companion, we'll eat, bicker, and leave. All the things I do best. And if there's cake, even better.

"Thank you," I whisper, pulling my maid into an embrace. "For everything. You've been a true friend to me since I arrived." A friend, and in many ways, a mother, too. "I appreciate all that you've done, Orla." And I haven't told her nearly enough.

She pats me on the shoulder before pulling away, a sheen to her eyes. "Nonsense. You deserve it." Her round face glows with happiness. "Enjoy the evening, my lady."

Grabbing my coat—one of the nice, fur ones from the armoire, since it's a special occasion—I make my way downstairs to the enormous entrance hall. Around and around, the staircase spirals through the gaping space, step after step after step. The air cools in my descent to the first level, where every fireplace sits empty, their hearths cold. I'm growing sick of the dim, the lack of light.

A dry, hollow wind greets me the moment I step outside. My heels click against the gray stones as I cross the courtyard, heading for the stableyard, my blood running hot and my pulse unsteady for reasons I cannot name.

The stable smells of hay, and glows in the golden light cast by the lanterns hanging along the posts. Phaethon's stall is located in the back, around a bend. Boreas, busy saddling the beast, turns upon hearing my approach.

Midwinter Eve is a time when, traditionally, villagers gather to herald the arrival of spring. Dressing in one's best is expected. The Frost King is dressed for entertainment, as I am. The dark fabric of his knee-length cloak looks soft to the touch. It parts over a light gray tunic, a similar color to the ribbon around my waist. Elaborate silver threading rings his collar. Trousers the color of charcoal encase his long legs, those bunched, powerful thighs. His curling black hair is pulled back, but a few strands have managed to unravel from their strangulating hold.

"You look . . . nice." The words slip from my mouth clumsily, a blurt.

The Frost King frowns. He expected a slap on the hand and received a scratch behind the ears instead. Cool, uncooperative blue eyes drag from the tips of my boots to the wisps of dark brown hair that have escaped my braid to gently frame my face. It is almost his usual detached expression. Almost—but not quite. This stiff awkwardness is new, rooted in feeling out of place.

"Are you ready?" he demands.

The twinge of hurt hits unexpectedly. I'm not sure what angers me more: that a small, insecure part of me cares enough of his opinion to hope he'd return the compliment, or that I allowed myself to believe tonight could be different from our previous intolerable interactions. I'm trying to make an effort. The least he could do is attempt the same. "Figures," I mutter.

His gaze thins. "If you have thoughts, speak them."

"It's not important."

"Another lie."

My chest sears with bright, choking anger. Fine. He asked for it. "You could stand to compliment me just this once. I am your wife, after all."

He looks at me as if I'd suggested he strip naked. "Compliment?"

"Yes, compliment. You could say, *You look nice in that dress*. Or, *That color complements your skin tone*." Not that I actually think he'll say something nice . . . though I suppose a part of me yearns for kindness, even in the form of empty words.

Phaethon stamps its foreleg as Boreas finishes tightening the girth and straightens awkwardly. He looks painfully uncomfortable, which in turn makes me uncomfortable. Have I done something to offend him? Aside from existing, that is.

My cheeks warm from his lack of response. "Never mind." Why do I even bother?

Despite his offer to help me into the saddle, I choose to mount myself. Once my skirts are situated, he settles behind me, chest to back, his hips notched to mine, those powerful thighs compressing the outside of my legs. Every place we touch sears through my clothing. It does not soothe. It makes me feel as though I stand in the heart of a fire.

With a snap of the reins, we trot across the stableyard, through the open gates that boom shut at our backs, a current of air tossing the snow piled on the ground. Then there is this: inked sky, white earth, blackened trees, the world.

My fur coat provides adequate warmth, though the Frost King's body heat combats even the harshest chill. Time plods in excruciating increments. I lose track of how many trees we pass, each more skeletal than the last. I'm surprised we don't make haste. The sooner we arrive, the sooner we can leave.

"Do your people celebrate Midwinter Eve?"

We've been traveling in silence for so long that the Frost King's voice startles me out of my half-doze. I tip sideways in the saddle, but he catches me around the waist and resettles me at his front. His arm rests heavily around my middle. It's warm, so I let it be. "Sorry. What were you saying?"

"Do your people celebrate Midwinter Eve?"

"We do." Gray and bleak are the days, but on this night there is fire, there is laughter, there is hope, dangerous and elusive. My earliest Midwinter memories involve my parents, blurred and faded as they are, and for that, I cherish them. "It is the day when—"

"—the veil between the mortal and immortal realms is at its thinnest."

I frown in surprise. "Yes." The clear, star-dusted sky winks in patches through the branched canopy. "How do you know that?"

Although I cannot see his expression, I sense his bemusement. "Our worlds may be different, but many of our beliefs overlap. Where I come from, we call it the Crossing."

I wonder, suddenly, if that is how he became trapped here—if he was sent one Midwinter Eve across the veil, unable to return. If he harbors resentment for this day in particular because of that.

I say, "It's also the day when we appeal to the West Wind, so that he will bring growth to our lands in the coming months."

The king broods in silence. Right. He abhors everything related to his brother.

"I'm surprised the people of Neumovos celebrate it," I go on, desperate to press out the quiet, "considering it's . . . well . . ."

"Something that celebrates my demise?"

"Yes," I reply with an impertinent little grin, "though I was not going to put it so delicately."

The Frost King snorts. His chin brushes the side of my head as he shifts in the saddle, tucking our hips closer. "They were alive once, too. They retain their beliefs, their methods of worship, even in death. Who am I to demand what they can and can't believe?"

"How positively egalitarian of you."

We arrive at Neumovos shortly afterward. Phaethon passes through the protective ring of rune-carved trees, no different than passing safely through the circle of salt that encloses Edgewood.

Tonight, the moon is but an ice-shard crescent, a final vestige of light before the new moon. From this distance, laughter reaches me, and music.

Taking the reins from the Frost King, I pull Phaethon to a halt and dismount smoothly, brushing the dirt from my skirts.

The king blinks down at me. "What are you doing?"

"We'll walk from here."

"Walk?" He looks as though I've asked him to cut off his arm.

"Yes," I snap in exasperation. "Otherwise, you'll intimidate everyone by arriving on your creepy darkwalker horse and ruin the celebration before it's even started." I glance at Phaethon, and the spirit huffs as though irked. "No offense."

"They are not my equals."

And the conversation was so pleasant, too. "They eat and sleep and dream and grieve, same as you."

"But I cannot die."

"Not by mortal means, no."

His gaze sharpens on mine. Have I given too much away? "Just for tonight," I say, "can you pretend mortals are not the vermin you make us out to be?"

"I do not think you are vermin."

"Then what do you think?"

He does not respond as he dismounts and nudges the beast to wander. I've always believed his aloofness to stem from stubbornness, a purposeful choice, a method of punishment. Now I wonder if I've been wrong, and maybe he's unused to people asking his opinion. Maybe he doesn't know how to communicate his thoughts.

Without a backwards glance, I march down the torch-lined road, in desperate need of a drink, and possibly cake, but only if the bones of this strangulating corset will allow me to ingest anything. The Frost King follows at my heels. If I didn't know better, I'd guess that large crowds make him uneasy.

As soon as we're spotted, the lively, unruly energy dissipates like smoke on the wind.

The entire town is squished into the tiny square. Suspicion, wariness, mistrust—all turns the air potent and thick. Torches flicker around the square's perimeter. There must be a few hundred people present. The women wear long dresses and boots, the men stitched coats and shirts and trousers, forms blurred in the shifting light. Scarfs. Hats. I was under the impression the specters did not feel cold, but apparently they do. Young children cling to their mothers' skirts. Dogs search the ground for scraps.

No one speaks. The people stare, and all is dead.

The Frost King crowds against my side. "Say something," he mutters.

"Mm." I consider the request for about two seconds. "No, I don't think I will." It's about time someone other than me experienced this small humiliation. I pat his arm with absolutely no sympathy. "Good luck."

He stands stiff as a pole. It's rather comical. Oh, how I love the taste of petty revenge.

"People of Neumovos," he says, far more somberly than anyone should speak at a celebration. Then he stops, as if he's unsure how to continue.

Someone in the audience coughs.

"Where I come from, Midwinter Eve marks the day my brothers and I allied with the new gods to overthrow our ancestors, who rained flame upon us all. It is a night of dissent, a night of betrayal, a night of death."

My teeth grind together as a murmur disperses through the gathering. He's scaring them. Sadly, he isn't doing it on purpose either. He's just completely clueless as to his effect on others.

"Is this a celebration," I hiss, grabbing his arm, "or a funeral?" Behind me, the audience shifts, plainly uncomfortable with all this talk of death. I mean, really. "I'll finish this. And put that away," I snap, gesturing to the spear.

He seems more grateful than irritated. The weapon vanishes as I call out, "I will keep this brief, as I suspect most of you will want to return to your festivities. First, my husband and I—" I don't even choke on the term. "—thank you for inviting us to share this evening with you. It is my hope that tonight marks the start of a new partnership between us."

The Frost King utters an oath under his breath. I ignore him.

"Eat, drink, be merry. Let us focus on what brings us joy: family and friends, warmth, a roof over our heads." I raise my arms and cry, "Happy Midwinter Eve!"

The crowd echoes, "Happy Midwinter Eve!"

The tension breaks, the drumming begins, and all is jubilant. The townsfolk congregate in the center of the square, their semi-transparent bodies beginning to sway. Someone whoops, and it's as though lightning strikes, sparking currents of energy through the shifting mass. The delighted squeal of a child carries to me.

While I'll never understand Boreas' disdain toward humans, it must have taken a lot for him to set those views aside, if only for one night. He watches the festivities with an expression bordering on loathing, though he always appears distasteful, so I can't say there's a difference.

My attention continues to wander. I spot the ceremonial fire almost immediately. At some point this evening, people will line up to leap over the flames, which is supposed to symbolize the end of the cold season. The drumming hits its frenzied peak. My feet yearn to tap and scuff their way through a jig, but I know better than to expect the Frost King to ask me to dance.

With his attention turned elsewhere, I slip into the boisterous display, pushing to the opposite edge of the square where the musicians gather. In addition to the drums—animal skins secured to hollow gourds—there is also a violin that warbles slightly flat, an alto flute carved from wood, and another stringed instrument that produces an obnoxious twang when plucked.

The musicians grin at the sight of me, and I grin back, clapping as the beat picks up. But as the moments pass, they turn from me, choosing to engage a group of specters nearby, and the pleasure dims. I am here, but I am not truly part of their world, am I? I'm not a specter. I am Wren of Edgewood, a mortal woman and the North Wind's bride, someone who does not belong.

Still, I thank the musicians for their contribution as that familiar dryness tightens my throat.

Where is the wine?

After a bit of meandering, I find a man wearing a particularly endearing top hat filling cups of wine from a barrel. When he catches sight of me, he fumbles the cup.

"My lady," he stutters. "I didn't realize . . . who you were." He licks his lips and hurries to refill my cup. His hat tips crookedly atop his head. "Apologies, my lady."

"Call me Wren," I say, accepting the drink with thanks.

"My Lady Wren."

Close enough.

More wandering. The damn corset pinches like mad. I stumble across a small group gathering around an older man, who holds a bow. My fingertips itch to brush the wood, for it has been long since I've touched a bow this beautiful. The deep curves and mesmerizing length showcase the full range of carving expertise. "It's a lovely bow," I say. "Do you hunt?"

The man glances over my shoulder. Searching for the Frost King, is my assumption. It's been nearly an hour since I last saw him. "Not for many years now," he replies warily as the rest of the group looks on.

"May I?"

The man hesitates, his hands shaking with nerves. "Of course." Once I set down my wine, the bow passes into my hands. It's practically weightless, yet the wood is strong and supple, as it should be.

"My bow is not this nice," I state. The one I left at Edgewood, not the one Zephyrus gifted me.

"You hunt, my lady?" This from a boy on the cusp of manhood, his chin tufted with scraggly hair.

"I do."

Someone passes me an arrow and gestures to the target hanging from the boughs of a nearby tree. The swaying bullseye glares at me like a fiery eye. There has never been a mark I couldn't hit. Not for many seasons, at least. I want these people to understand I am on their side. I don't want them fearing me because of my association with the king.

"Shall we settle this with a bet?" I shout with sudden inspiration.

A great cry breaks over me. The men wave their fists and stamp their feet. The women join in, shoving aside their husbands and brothers and sons for a closer look.

"What'll it be? Behind my back? One-handed?" I've done all those things and more. Following my parents' deaths, I would practice in the clearing behind our cottage. Long hours standing in knee-deep snow, the bowstring blistering my fingers. Every painful failure pushed me closer to the perfect shot, another day with food in my stomach.

"Switch hands!" an old woman cries.

"Upside-down!" calls another.

I'm laughing. For the first time in many months, I feel free. "Tell me, and I will do it!"

"Eyes closed."

My head snaps sideways at the low command, even as my pulse escalates. No sign of him. Did my addled mind imagine his voice? Then the crowd parts, much of their earlier fear forgotten in the copious amounts of wine they've consumed, and the Frost King materializes at my side as though having peeled away from the shadows. There he stands, a pillar of darkness. A long, cool column with truculent blue eyes. He is, and forever will be, otherworldly.

His gaze locks onto mine. Another step closer and his shadow, cast by the wavering torchlight, falls over me.

"Unless," he whispers for my ears alone, "that lies beyond your capabilities?"

My blood sings, catching fire in my veins. This must be how a god feels, I think, knowing he cannot fail.

I take in the immortal who is my husband. He searches my face, seeking what, I cannot say. Every so often, the wind tosses that pine-sharp winter scent to me. I step closer, toe to toe, and he makes a soft sound of surprise, although it might be my imagination.

Conversation drops away. Every pair of eyes rests on the Frost King and me.

"You're in my way," I tell him.

His lips thin. With a brief nod, he steps aside, allowing me a view of the target, though I'm continually aware of his presence at my back, heat from how near he stands. I refocus on my task. Eyes closed. I've never attempted it before, but I'm ready. Anything to win this town over.

Drawing back the arrow, I sink into pure sensation. The string pulled taut. The brush of my first knuckle against my jaw—an anchor. My heart slows and my eyelids flutter shut.

My senses sharpen with the guttering of my sight. The wind gusts from the west, an eerie, stretched-thin sound like a hollow whistle. Strong enough to push my arrow off course. I compensate by angling slightly left. There is the bow, cool wood beneath my hand. There is the arrow, its carved stone head, and the goose feathers fletched. There is the target somewhere beyond sight. And me. There is me.

Inhale.

Exhale.

Release.

A cheer splits the quiet.

I'm smiling as I open my eyes. Another whoop of delight, and the spark catches and grows, leaping from person to person until the cheers reach a new level of intensity. The arrow quivers in the center of the target.

Beside me, the king studies my hands on the weapon.

"Well?" I quip, turning toward him. "Speak." If he is to inform me of my shortcomings, I will have something to say as well.

"You're a decent shot," he says as the crowd disperses.

I return the bow to its owner with heartfelt thanks, then pick up my wine. "And that surprises you."

"It may have, once."

"But not anymore."

"No." His voice softens. "Not anymore."

I'm almost positive that's a compliment.

Almost.

The tension radiating from the Frost King's body feels palpable. A taste in my mouth. Breath on my face. A long, unbroken stretch of time passes. I focus on the dancing couples, how jovial and carefree everyone is. At some point, Boreas speaks, but I'm too distracted to hear what it is he says. "Sorry?"

"I asked if you would like a glass of water?"

I'm so dumbfounded I make a choking sound in an attempt to breathe. "A glass of water?"

The strain between us spikes, reaching an unseen peak. I squint down at my glass of wine—empty, now. The king glares at me as though this awkward exchange is my fault when I have done nothing but stand here.

"Yes," I say, slowly and with much curiosity. "I would like another drink. Not water though. Wine." Then I add, because it seems like the right thing to say, "Thank you."

His expression hardens. He is . . . reluctant?

After another glance at my wine glass, he moves off to search for drinks while I retreat to the edge of the square to observe the celebration from a distance. The low, sonorous drumbeat thuds through the soles of my boots, that ancient heartbeat of the earth. A push and a pull. A quickening tempo. There is power on this night. Even the air has changed. It tastes alive. The townsfolk, their ghostly forms, gyrate and shimmy.

But one cloaked figure moves separately from the rest. Something about the elegant movement draws my eye in familiarity. As the figure's back is to me, I'm unable to see a face, but the figure is obviously a man, for he wears breeches and his back stretches the fabric of his cloak. I step forward. I'm positive I've seen him before.

Then the man turns, and moonlight splashes pale across his face, catching the gold flecks in his curls. Our eyes meet across the square.

He winks.

I'm pushing forward, knocking aside elbows and sidestepping children running underfoot. There is only one person I've met with eyes like leaves of green, and a devilish streak to match.

By the time I reach the place where Zephyrus stood, he's gone. Either the crowd has swallowed him, or he was never here to begin with.

"Something wrong?"

I startle as the king materializes by my side, offering me a glass of wine. I accept it, still reeling from what I saw. Or rather, what I think I saw. "No," I say quickly. "Nothing." I take a sip. A sweet, subtle flavor coats my tongue, reminiscent of cherries. Then I frown. There is barely any liquid in the glass. "Did you drink some of my wine?"

"No, but you've been drinking a lot this evening," he says with those eyes that see all. "I'd suggest reducing your consumption. Or switching to water."

My face grows hot. It feels like he's talking down to me. "I'll drink what I like, Husband." Water won't get me through the evening, it won't get me through the week, it won't get me through life. I've accepted this shameful truth. "You needn't worry."

The king observes me carefully, as though seeking an answer to a question he does not voice aloud. For whatever reason, a pit forms in my stomach.

"What is it you once called it? Nectar of the gods?"

The glass is halfway to my mouth when I pause, my lips touching the rim. "Yes," I say slowly, because I did not realize he remembered that.

Another long, probing look. What is up with him? "Does that offer extend to banished gods?"

"I suppose." His throat works as he swallows his drink. My treacherous gaze rests on the flexing muscles there. "You're in a good mood," I say. "Plotting murder?"

"I could ask the same of you."

Why do I suspect he's currently rummaging through my mind, overturning every stone, scrutinizing every word we've exchanged? And why am I not more concerned? Is it lack of propriety? Maybe I'm so confident I'll succeed at my task I don't view him as a threat. *That* way of thinking concerns me. The Frost King is nothing if not threatening.

I say, inspecting him over the rim of my glass, "I'm feeling remarkably less murderous this evening." Another pinch to my corset. "Is the festival as terrible as you thought it would be?"

"No." Then his mouth flattens. "It is . . ." A hesitation. He looks at me, then away. ". . . difficult for me to interact with others. I am not used to it."

His admittance doesn't go unnoticed. I recall the forbidden

north wing of the citadel, his order not to enter. What does he hide? What does he fear? If I were to know these things, I'd have a better understanding of this man.

"You *are* awful at making conversation," I agree, because I am nothing if not helpful.

Normally, I would stop there, and that would be that, yet his expression pinches in unhappiness. I have prodded what is obviously a bruise. An intentional jab. Perhaps I could be kinder toward him, just for tonight.

"It doesn't have to be difficult," I say. "Conversation, I mean. You can start with asking someone a question about themselves. It helps both parties reach new insight about the other person."

He stares at me. "Like what?"

"Anything. And if that fails, you can comment on the weather."

He tips his head back to survey the black, star-studded basin overhead. Returns his gaze to me. Still nothing.

"You could ask me to dance."

Another blurt, uglier, more difficult to ignore. My face burns with a crawling heat. Why did I say that? Lightheadedness. This damn corset cutting off my air supply. I don't want to dance with the Frost King—I think.

He is frowning. "That is assuming I want to dance."

His response tosses cold water into my face. I'm grateful for it. A reminder that I have no interest in interacting with my husband for longer than is necessary. If he will not dance with me, then I will find enjoyment elsewhere.

Plenty of men gather at the perimeter of the square. Many are attractive, too. I approach the one nearest to my left. He has kind brown eyes and a mouth soft enough to spout poetry. No need to ask when my intention is clear. Taking his hand, I drag him amidst the swaying couples, and as he scoops me up, swinging me around by the waist, my laughter bursts free.

Once my feet return to earth, I lift my skirts. The crowd cheers me on, and my dancing partner chuckles. Faster and faster and faster, the musicians propel the tune to its feverish conclusion. The man is tireless, nimble feet and flashing hands, an appealing, laughing mouth. My surroundings blur into shadow and light. My lungs strain against the bones of my corset. Again, my partner and I come together. He's laughing. I'm laughing. We are a perfect pair.

At the next turn, however, the man stops.

The Frost King stands before us.

I gaze up at him, panting, my heart not quite steady. His throat dips, and then those long, leather-clad fingers curl around mine as he says, "Dance with me."

# CHAPTER 18

Man and woman, mortal and god, we stare at one another, bound as one by duty, obligation, and deceit.

"Husband."

The Frost King's eyes darken. Nudging my lower back, he forces me a step closer, the distance between us reduced to the barest wisp of air. "Wife."

My breasts brush his chest on the inhale. My corset pinches ferociously. I hold his gaze steadily despite my sudden desire to flee, fast and far.

"People are staring," I mutter, lips stiff.

His mouth dips to my ear. Warm, fluttering air teases the shell, sensitizing the skin. My body goes taut. *The wine*, I think dazedly. The wine is to blame. "Then let's give them something to stare at."

I jerk my head back, searching his face. "Who are you?" I hiss.

"What have you done with the Frost King?" Because the dark god who rules the Deadlands would not wish to draw attention to himself. He prefers the shadows, the solitude.

"I'm right here," he says, holding my gaze. "Dance," he goads me, and my foolish, stubborn pride cannot ignore the challenge.

Our hands lift, press together, palm to palm. His left hand smooths up my back, then drops, settling against the curve above my backside. My left hand rests over the unyielding muscle of his shoulder. He draws me into a sweeping arc through the square, forcing the crowd into retreat. For a man who moves with such grace, his nimble feet come as no surprise, as though the wind itself gives aid to his motions.

Ma taught Elora and I to dance at a young age. Waltz, sarabande, allemande—I know them all. The dance shifts to the triple meter of a waltz, and I'm already lightening my tread to accommodate the change in rhythm, as is he.

He has perfect form. A polished veneer. It pushes me to give my all. *One*-two-three, *one*-two-three.

What madness is this, that I desire to look into the face of the man who wronged me? There is a small freckle near his right ear. His lower lip is fuller than the upper one. When the Frost King catches my eye, I glance away, feeling as though he's caught me doing something wicked.

On the next round of twirls, my head begins to spin. I am perched on a cliff's edge, and the drop sings the most beguiling melody.

"Slow down," I manage breathlessly.

"Why?" He peers down at me, and I struggle to remember my train of thought. How is it I am both repulsed and compelled by him? What spell has he cast over me?

"Because," I grit out, purposefully overextending one of my steps so he stumbles, "you're making me dizzy."

His heel smashes the toes of my right foot. "You're saying you can't keep up?"

"You did that on purpose."

His eyes, they dance and they dance. The Frost King is thoroughly enjoying my struggle. "I have no idea what you're talking about."

He spins me, and I nearly topple sideways as the toes of my boot catch on one of the cracks in the stone. But the hand at my waist stabilizes me. Yet another spin. I'm breathless. Reeling. Without realizing it, I grab the front of his cloak to keep my balance. The fabric, warmed from his body, scrunches in my clammy fist. "Damn it, slow down."

"I warned you about the wine." He directs us across the square, yet slows at my request. The crowd parts and knits closed at our backs.

"You should know by now how little I take your opinion into consideration."

He huffs. I'm not quite convinced it's laughter, but it does suggest humor on his part. "I'm well aware." The hand at my back slides to my hip and settles there, shaping the curve created by this blasted corset—the cause for my lack of air. "If you have to vomit," he remarks blandly, "please do not do so on my boots."

I doubt I'd survive that humiliation.

My thoughts eddy out. Beyond the square, people begin leaping across the ceremonial fire. Two years. That is how long it's been since I last danced. Edgewood had gathered to celebrate a birth, and the men and women dressed in their finest. Elora had a partner for every dance—multiple suitors over the course of the evening. A few brave souls asked for my hand, but never for more than one movement. Now I dance with the king, but it is a choice he made, a choice I made. For once, we are on equal ground. And for perhaps the first time since being taken captive, I am content.

"You dance well." It takes something from me to admit it.

His mouth twitches. I find myself awaiting the moment a smile breaks free, but it never does. Too much self-control. "And this surprises you."

"Yes." He spins me out before luring me back to his side, and I go willingly, too ensnared by the motion to understand my guard has lowered.

"There were many celebrations such as this one back in my homeland. The City of Gods, it is named. Wine was always flowing. My brothers and I were loved, worshipped, adored. It was a happy life, if not an empty one."

The bitterness in his tone reveals some deeper emotion. "Why was it empty?"

He stares at a point over my shoulder, though does not appear to see anything at all. "People love you for what you can give them," he says. "Had I or my brothers not controlled the changing seasons, would people have still chosen us?"

I'm so completely blindsided by his insight that I lose track of the steps. It takes a moment to regain my footing. I understand exactly what he means. "Something changed, didn't it."

We still circle the square, but our movements have slowed. I want to ask him more about his life—I'm nothing if not curious—but I'm familiar enough with the king's moods to recognize when I can push him, and when I can't.

"Our family reigned over all, but over time, they grew fatted on power. The city began to descend into madness. The gold-dusted roads lost their luster. There came a god who sparked lightning at his fingertips, and he had a vision. A ten-year war broke out, and at the end, my family, my parents and grandparents, were overthrown, imprisoned. It was my belief that my brothers and I would be welcome in this new regime. After all, we helped defeat the corrupt, our predecessors. Helped this new lightning god seat himself into power. Instead, we were banished. Forbidden to return to our homeland."

My knowledge surrounding the Anemoi's banishment is limited. Supposedly, each brother was sent to a different corner of the realm, and the territories do not overlap. Zephyrus' concern of the North Wind's infiltrating power, however, returns to me briefly.

"Help me understand. You sought to overthrow your parents . . . because your *parents* were corrupt?"

"They were destroying my home."

"Yet because of your actions, you're never to see it again, so what does it matter?"

He meets my droll tone with a clipped response. "The machinations of the gods are complex. You wouldn't understand."

"I understand you threw away everything for power. Now you have no family and no home." Harsh, but true. It doesn't seem worth it to me. What is the allure of an immortal life when one's days are empty?

The king glances at me before looking elsewhere. Perhaps he cannot face this truth. "Without power," he says lowly, "I have nothing."

What can power give you? It can't care for you when you've taken ill. It can't make one laugh. It is a rigid, cold thing, affectionless and barren. It does not give. It only takes.

The torchlight grows dim, wavering in a sudden gust of wind.

"I would like to ask you something," he states, the words halting. He spins me out, twirls me back into his embrace. The press of his palm against my lower spine sears through the fabric of my dress.

My hand uncurls from his shoulder, shifting to press over his heart, which beats steadily. "So ask."

He stares at the hand on his chest. "Why did you switch places with your sister?"

Has he pondered this question all this time? "Does it matter?" I ask, because it is easier than saying, *Why do you care?* "Because I love her. Because she deserves a better life. A free life."

"And you don't?"

My mouth opens, then shuts after further consideration. Just as the gods are complex, so too is a woman's heart. He wouldn't understand. "It doesn't matter what I do or do not deserve. She would not have survived you." This I know. Elora hasn't the backbone to stand against cruelty.

"Very few people survive me."

"I did."

"Yes," he replies slowly, as if conceding a point. More twirling. "You miss her."

I begin to grow lightheaded. How much does he see of me, truly? Family is not a topic I care to discuss, considering our circumstances. But as the dance continues, my body grows heavy. My breathing shallows, as though crushed beneath my toppled defenses. "Yes."

"I'm sorry." His thumb indents the curve of my spine.

His apology shouldn't matter. Words are nothing but pressure and air, after all, yet they hold a surprising amount of weight. "Let's not say things we don't mean, Husband."

"You are the liar, Wife, not I."

Yes, and I have been lying to myself this entire evening. As if we can dance and converse and find common ground, forgetting my circumstances, who I am married to: my captor.

"Excuse me," I say, pulling away.

Solitude awaits me at the edge of the grounds, just inside the mark-carved trees, where snow heaps against the roots, the music distant. Sweat beads on my upper lip, which I wipe away with a shaky hand. I'm not sure what has come over me, only that I'm not feeling especially combative tonight. And what about Boreas' apology? It sounded genuine. I did not think he cared about my well-being.

I take a short walk around the perimeter of the town, moving slowly so the dizziness doesn't worsen. My corset squeezes my abdomen to the point of pain. I try loosening the laces, but after all the wine I've consumed, my fingers only manage to tangle in the fabric.

The Frost King finds me leaning against a post near the ceremonial fire. "A storm approaches," he says. "We'll stay here for the night."

His voice sounds thin and far-off, despite him standing within an arm's length of me. "Accommodations?" Many of the townsfolk begin to disperse, returning to their homes, their forms wavering as they cross through patches of torchlight and shade.

He leads me down the road to a lone cottage perched on a hill with a thatched roof, the front door painted blue, pale as a robin's egg. The inside is small but clean, with a fire crackling in the grate and a partition separating the bathing area from the rest of the space. Someone must have given up their home to accommodate us for the evening. As such, there is only one bed.

*There is only one bed.*

It is all I see. The wooden frame bears a tiny, *tiny* mattress stuffed with straw, which is covered with a colorful quilt.

The Frost King begins to cross the threshold when I snag his arm. "Wait." The command wheezes out of me. "Let's . . . Can't we stay somewhere else?"

"Why?"

If I tell him it's because there is one bed, he will scoff at me. I'm acting ridiculous. We are, after all, husband and wife. And yet the marriage was never consummated.

"It smells weird."

He considers me in puzzlement. I can't imagine he could read me so easily, as we haven't spent much time together outside of meals. Though admittedly, I'm able to read him more readily as the weeks pass.

"Are you all right?" he asks. His fingers hover over my face, but he doesn't touch me.

Now that he mentions it, I feel close to passing out. "I think I'm going to faint."

Alarm flares in his eyes.

"My corset . . . is strangling me. You need to take it off." I cling to the doorframe, fingertips biting into the rough surface. "From the back. Hurry," I gasp. My lips begin to tingle from lack of air, and darkness slides through my vision. I clutch the wood paneling tighter.

"Damn laces," he growls behind me. He tugs at them to no avail.

"Cut it off me." I slump forward. My knees wobble. "The corset," I snap when his fingers still. "Cut it off me!"

Gripping my arms, the Frost King spins me around and rests my back against the outside of the cottage beneath the roof overhang. His dagger glints. He makes a deep score down the front, slicing through the ribbing, and then my visions blackens.

"Wife. Wren!"

I must be dreaming, because it sounds like the king is frightened.

With an enormous effort, I manage to pry my eyelids open. Boreas' face hovers inches from mine. I'm lying partially across his lap where he kneels on the porch, his arms supporting my upper torso. I frown. "I fainted?"

"Yes."

Wonderful. Brushing aside his hands, I push to a standing position. At least the vise around my body is gone.

He holds up the remains of my corset and asks, "What is this?"

I snort. "An instrument of torture." Snatching the corset, I toss it into the snow with satisfaction. May it forever rot into the earth. "I still think we should return to the citadel." Because the bigger issue is the single bed that squats inside like an ugly toad.

"Even gods must sleep." And with that, he tugs me into the cottage and shuts the door.

The sound of the lock tumbling makes my pulse flutter. One bed for two people who cannot stand the sight of each other. The gods must hate me. But no matter. This is yet another obstacle, and I've tackled plenty of those since my arrival at the Deadlands. If I'm to survive this night, I must regain control of this situation.

Striding toward the bed with far more confidence than I feel, I toss a pillow at his face, which he catches. "You can sleep on the floor." I cross my arms over my chest for good measure, lest he thinks I bluff.

The Frost King lowers the pillow, appraising me with what I believe is amusement. That cannot be. Humor isn't a concept that exists for him. I'm not even sure his mouth knows how to smile. "There's room enough for two."

There is not. The bed is as narrow as they come. "Like I said," I repeat slowly, because my tongue has swollen to the size of a watermelon, "you can sleep on the floor."

"We are married, Wife. It should not be difficult to share a bed. It is expected."

"I don't care." I'm not ready, especially with the confusion between body and mind. I do not like Boreas. My body, however, suggests otherwise. "The fire will keep you warm enough." Anyway, it's not as if he can die from hypothermia. He can't die, the bastard.

His lack of reply is suspect, but I think little of it as I begin turning down the bed. What kind of game is this, to share a mattress this tiny? And now I'm wondering how I'd ever survive the night pressed against him.

My skin warms from a slow, duplicitous flush.

Fabric rustles, and the sound pricks at my skin in recognition. There's a muffled thump, like cloth hitting the floor. I freeze, my hands gripping one of the pillows. He wouldn't dare.

Slowly, I turn around.

"What are you doing?" I shriek.

Boreas pauses in the middle of shedding his clothing. His cloak and tunic lay discarded on the ground.

Firelight renders the contouring of his torso in gold. Sleek, pale skin clings to a body of cut, rippling muscle. His shoulders are wide, his waist solid. The leanness of his upper arms shifts fluidly. My eyes drift lower. A smattering of black hair dusts the area between his nipples, trails to his navel, and disappears beneath the loosened waistband of his trousers.

I've seen my fair share of chests and abdomens. I've bedded more men than I can count, but not in recent months. The Frost King is an entirely different breed of male virility.

He says, "Preparing for bed." As though this were obvious.

Somehow, I manage to tear my attention away from the expanse of his chest. It is offensively perfect. "You can prepare for bed without removing your clothes." The ties at his waistband hang loose, the fabric resting uncomfortably low on his hips.

"I do not sleep in clothes."

Did I really need to know that the Frost King sleeps in nothing but his skin?

Turning from him, I resume plumping the pillows. My palms slap the fabric aggressively. "You're still sleeping on the floor."

"So you are free to ogle me, but I cannot share a bed with you?"

My cheeks grow hot. My mouth can't remember how to work properly. It takes three attempts before I'm able to speak. "I wasn't ogling you. I was . . ."

"Ogling," he finishes, sounding pleased. I don't think the Frost King has ever sounded pleased before.

I will deny this ogling until my last breath.

"I'm not sleeping on the floor," he continues. "If anyone is sleeping on the floor, it's you. You're young. I'm many millennia old. I have back pain."

"You do not have back pain!" I cry, whirling around. If he has back pain, then I'm a snail.

Except I notice the shape of his mouth, its subtle upward curve. "Did you just make a joke?"

He stares at me, and I expect the smile to disappear, but it doesn't. It looks completely out of place, this soft thing shaped by so severe a man.

"We share the bed." In this, he is firm. It's in his stance, the crossed arms, the braced legs, the unyielding ridge of his jaw. The stance of a man who is letting his wants be known.

"Have some decency," I squawk with mounting desperation. "You wouldn't want to make your own wife uncomfortable, would you? Not when she is frightened and—and shy and . . ."

Boreas snorts. "I believe we are referring to different people. For I did not think my wife was afraid of anything."

His words give me pause. Flattery, or truth? I tell myself I will not be swayed, but the possibility of this immortal seeing me as fearless is appealing. Gods, how twisted am I? "Fine," I say. "Just . . . keep your trousers on."

Boreas nods his agreement. As he turns to stoke the fire, however, I catch sight of his naked back. My heart stills.

The pale smoothness is interrupted by ropes of heavy scarring, welts that drip and smear down his spine like hot candlewax, slightly pinkened in the firelight. It is old, tough skin. A puckered mass like mountains carved into earth.

As if sensing my gaze, the Frost King stiffens.

Whipping around, I fluff the pillows to busy my hands. But I sense his attention on me, the space between my shoulder blades, the curve of my neck, lower. Hot saliva floods my mouth. I feel ill.

With their advanced healing abilities, I was under the impression gods did not suffer or bear scars, but I was wrong. The ruin of his back is evidence enough.

Someone hurt him. I do not know why this upsets me.

His bootheels clip the floorboards. Warmth at my back, and then he is past me, vanishing behind the washroom divider.

While the Frost King bathes, I kick off my shoes and climb into bed fully clothed. I reek of wine and sweat. Maybe the stench will keep him at arm's length.

Water splashes. Soapy hands scrubbing against skin. That I can hear the sounds of what I consider to be a private affair feels too intimate for words.

Sometime later, the Frost King rounds the divider, torso bare, having peeled away his boots and socks, yet redressed in his trousers. He's combed his hair. The tips of the black strands curl around his neck. After an uneasy pause, he climbs onto his side of the bed. The mattress dips beneath his weight, and I tense.

"You can rest easy, Wife. I'm not going to touch you."

His tone suggests he has little desire to, which shouldn't bother me, but his words sting. "My name is Wren."

"I'm aware."

"Why call me *wife*, then?"

He shifts onto his side so we face one another. "I could ask you the same question."

"When have I ever called you wife?"

"You know what I mean."

I have spoken his name exactly once, and it was one time too many. So long as he is the North Wind, the Frost King, he remains my enemy.

I say, "Aren't you going to remove your gloves?"

After a moment of hesitation, he does. I'm not sure what I expected. His hands look perfectly normal. After placing them on the bedside table, he shifts over an inch. I retreat an inch. He does so again, and again, until I'm perched on the sagging edge of the mattress, clawing at the bedframe to stop myself from dropping onto the floor. Flickering light brightens the slope of his shoulder, the dip of his taut waist above where the blanket pools. With him so near, the fire is all but obsolete. Heat pours from his skin.

"You can offer me a little more room," I growl. "I'm falling off the bed."

"Perhaps if you didn't act like I had an incurable disease, you would not be so uncomfortable." But he shifts back, conceding the mattress as though it is territory relinquished in conquest.

I tug the quilt around my body, tucking it in on all sides so no air can infiltrate. "You keep to your side of the bed," I mumble, focusing on my meager blanket defense, "and I'll keep to mine. Touch me, and I'll stab you." My dagger awaits use in my arm sheath.

He watches me through a slitted gaze. "And if you touch me?"

A slow heat crawls up my chest and down my back. As if that would ever happen. "I won't."

The Frost King watches me struggle with the quilt, his blue eyes too sharp. "As you wish . . . Wren."

# CHAPTER 19

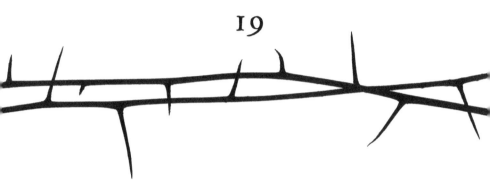

For the first time in recent memory, I wake warm.

I'm so unused to the sensation that I do not immediately open my eyes. True warmth, that feeling of flushed skin and loosened joints, has eluded me for years. A fire, while decent at combating the chill, eventually dies without tending. A coat, even a fur one, is full of holes, openings for the hands and head, allowing an icy wind to infiltrate.

Drifting in this half-state of wakefulness, I become vaguely aware of a distant sound, a low, even drumming. My eyebrows twitch. Something heavy weighs down my waist, a press of heat. It smells of cedar.

*Cedar.* It can't be, but . . . I glance down, squinting against the sunlight spilling into the room. The object pressed to my waist is an arm. Not my arm. A man's arm, with curling dark hair, defined muscle, the wrist thick and solid. And it's not pressed against my waist. It's wrapped around me from behind, fingertips shoved into the space between my dress-clad body and the mattress, like a noose.

The Frost King is dead to the world.

He didn't keep to his side of the bed. He rolled over to *my* side, invaded *my* personal space. And now I'm stuck, my back curved against his chest. If I'm the one wrapped in his arms, then clearly he reached for me in the middle of the night.

My teeth grit as he shifts against me. "Boreas."

His exhalation ruffles my hair. The sensation raises gooseflesh on my skin.

It's been too long since I've been intimate with a man. Oh, the irony. I would laugh were I not so breathless from our intertwined position, and that snaps me awake, the reminder of who shares my bed.

"Boreas."

Not even a twitch. It seems the North Wind is not a morning person. For whatever reason, this amuses me. The king, always so collected, so proper, would rather sleep in.

When I attempt to slide free of his embrace, his arm tightens across my stomach. One of his sturdy thighs is slotted between mine, my chilled feet pressed against the hot skin of his calf. He's completely boneless. My fidgeting only succeeds in pressing our bodies flush together. "Boreas!" I snap, my face warming.

Then something long and hard nestles against my backside, and my eyes pop wide. Taut, vibrating energy clamps my muscles. They tighten to the point of snapping, then loosen all at once, tension melting away. My poor, sex-starved body doesn't care whose arms I've found myself in. All it knows is the solidity at my back, breath against my neck from where Boreas has buried his face in my hair. And then—oh, gods—his hips give a slow roll that sends heat spilling through my core, and I all but leap out of my skin. With a dramatic cry, I claw free of his embrace, toppling from the bed and slamming my elbows against the hard floor.

The Frost King hurries around the side of the bed, spear in hand. Mussed hair and a bleary gaze give him a recently tumbled look, though there was no tumbling to be had last night. Definitely not. His trousers hang so low on his hips it's positively indecent. "What happened?" He speaks in a low, husky rasp.

I turn my head away, blowing out a strange, airless breath. "Nothing." Why am I suddenly affected by his touch and presence? The Frost King's beauty is riveting, sure, but he has the personality of a pustule. I loathe the man.

Right?

"I told you to stay on your side of the bed." Curt.

I sense his uncertainty, which in turn makes me feel unbalanced. "You said you were cold."

"I did not!" I cry, leaping to my feet. Because if what he says is true, I would remember it.

He shrugs, completely unfazed by my dramatic display. "I have little reason to lie." Something in his gaze sharpens as it rests on me, and my heart skips a beat. "The first time you asked me to move closer, I reminded you of your boundaries."

If there is a first time, then I must have asked more than once. I don't want to know. I have to know. "What was my response?"

"You said you didn't care."

Then I must have been delirious. Borderline hypothermic. "You should have respected my initial request."

"You are my wife. If you were cold, then it was my duty to make you comfortable."

That's . . . unexpectedly sweet of him. I wish I could blame the wine for my confusing thoughts, but I woke up without a headache. My tongue, however, has that unmistakable papery texture. I will need a drink once we return to the citadel. The need is not yet dire.

"Then—" I close my mouth and swallow. Brush wrinkles from my dress. "Thank you."

If I'm not mistaken, his mouth shapes a faint upward curve.

Enough of this. Rushing around him, I grab my coat and shrug it on. It gives me some semblance of security. "I'm going for a walk."

The smile vanishes. "Wait." He rounds the bed as I reach the door.

"If you're going to tell me to stay here," I say, my hand clutching the knob with nervous energy, "don't bother."

He searches my face. "When you last walked through Neumovos, you were beaten to within an inch of your life."

His voice, normally smooth as glass, ripples with an undercurrent of fury. He stares at me so intensely my eyes drop to his chest for a reprieve. His unfairly chiseled chest.

"They would not dare do so again," I respond quietly. "Not with you here."

Focus far too keen for my liking, he says, "We leave within the hour."

"I'll meet you in the square." Hopefully what I'm looking for won't take long to find. "And put some clothes on," I quip.

I'm not freed until the door closes behind me, severing his gaze from sight.

~

If I were the West Wind, where would I hide?

The woods come to mind first. Multiple trails lead from the village to the forest. Leaving town means leaving the protective circle of rune-carved trees, but it is morning, and the darkwalkers only swarm when it is deep night. I choose a trail at random and follow its curving path until the thatched homes disappear from view. I cannot be long. Otherwise, the king will come looking for me.

The trees are but brittle, blackened bones, branches like stiffened fingers that clack in the barest huff of wind. The sky's backdrop—blue and pure—is a cruel contrast. After about a mile, I reach a clearing patched with snow, large snowdrifts swathing the bases of the trees.

"Wren, you look as lovely as ever."

My pulse surges against my skin like a breaking wave, but I force myself to turn around slowly, as though I'm not startled by the West Wind's sudden presence. "Zephyrus."

"The one and only." His pointed teeth flash like the fiend he is, and his green eyes sparkle with the game he always seems to be playing.

"I've been looking for you," I tell him.

"I know." He sighs dramatically and props a slim shoulder against a tree. He wears his usual greens: a heavy, woolen tunic, brown leather boots sitting snug around his calves, and breeches that cling to his sleek thighs. Zephyrus and Boreas could not be more different. The mess of curls tangled with leaves and vines suggests Zephyrus does everything in his power to extend himself, whereas Boreas straps himself down with ruthless precision. "Jeline, the woman who owns the apothecary, told me you stopped by."

"Oh?" I find it interesting that he knew this, yet didn't seek me out. "Is that all she said?"

"Yes. Why?"

"Did she tell you I was beaten to within an inch of my life?"

The smile falls. "She did." I've never seen him look so grave. "I'm sorry to hear what happened. My brother . . ."

"Your brother what?"

"They attacked you because you are tied to him. Because he sentenced them to an eternity of servitude, and they are angry, rightfully so. He should have known better than to send you here."

I seriously doubt the king thought these people would attack me, considering their subordinacy. And he didn't send me. I chose to visit myself, despite Orla's warnings. "Boreas is the one who saved me."

"You were innocent," he goes on. "A victim."

I'm not sure what to think. Zephyrus and I aren't friends, but I thought we were at least friendly. Something about this meeting makes my hair stand on end. He is a god who, along with his three brothers, participated in a coup against their parents, their bloodline. And now he is here, weaving threads and setting traps. Above all, he seeks power. I must never forget that.

"Where have you been?" I ask. "I looked for you after . . ." *Your fight with Boreas.*

His lips thin. "Oh, here and there. I heal quickly. Anyway, it's not the first time Boreas has threatened to kill me." He's clearly amused by the notion of fratricide.

"I spoke to him about your concerns," I say, "but he wasn't receptive to them." What was it he'd said? *If my power is corrupting his realm, he should consider strengthening his own defenses.*

"That does not surprise me. It was worth the attempt, anyway."

He shrugs. "But I assume you're not here for my tales of brotherly woe." At this, he steps closer, the scent of mist and damp earth overriding the snow and cold. He pulls something from his pocket, holding it flat in his palm.

I swallow, staring at the small vial of clear liquid: the answer to my freedom. It has always felt like a dream, to return home, but now that dream is tangible. It holds shape and weight. "You got it."

His fingers brush mine as he passes the tonic into my hand. There, his touch lingers, resting against the fleshy curve of my palm. "It's not what you wanted, but it's the best I could do. This tonic is made from the valerian root, but it's not nearly potent enough to put him to sleep."

We both freeze at the same time.

*Him.*

I never told Zephyrus the real reason I needed the tonic. I claimed I was having difficulty sleeping. Insomnia. Boreas was never mentioned.

Dread thickens inside me. He knows. How did he find out, and what am I going to do now that my plan is no longer secret? If he tells someone, everything I'd hoped for will be ruined.

"Wren." Zephyrus speaks in a soothing tone. "I'm not going to tell anyone. I swear I'm not. What you're doing is admirable. Think of everyone you'll save. Many of Boreas' past wives tried to end his life, but you're the first one whom I believe can succeed."

It shouldn't matter that Zephyrus shows no remorse for wanting his brother's death, but it does. And it makes no sense, considering I'm the one who's going to end the Frost King's life one way or another.

So many things could go wrong. An internal voice screams that it's ruined, all of it. But I neutralize my expression so Zephyrus can't see how upset I am over this.

My fingers curl around the small glass vial. "If it won't put him to sleep, then how—" *How am I supposed to kill him?*

"If you want guaranteed slumber, you'll need the flowers of the poppy plant. Unfortunately, the vendor I usually buy from has gone missing. I can get you the flowers, but I won't be able to do it alone." He gives me an expectant look.

I don't ask why he would need my presence, even though it is a bit odd. But if I can't get the proper draught, I'll never be able to leave. "What do I have to do?"

"There's a cave where the light from neither sun nor moon penetrates. Within this cave grows the Garden of Slumber, tended by . . . well, technically he is a distant relative of mine, but to you, he is Sleep. His powers are strong, very strong. I will need assistance in gathering the flowers, on the chance that I succumb to Sleep's influence."

"Wouldn't I be in danger as well?" I'm assuming this very powerful being is a god.

"Normally, yes, but seeing as you are in the Deadlands, rather than the realm of the living, Sleep's powers are muted for you. You might fight some drowsiness, but it shouldn't be enough to pull you under completely. His powers are most potent to other immortals. A form of defense, if you will, so that we are unable to strike against one another with our full strength."

Zephyrus takes one of my hands in both of his. His fingers are far more slender than Boreas', elegant and refined. "Wren." That's all he says. My name, paired with a soft, almost pained, smile. "I wouldn't ask this of you unless it was the only option. If you decide it's too dangerous, I understand, but the poppy flower is the strongest of Sleep's plants. Anything less might not work."

"I understand." My chest twinges. This is the right decision. It has to be.

"Don't feel bad," he says, as though sensing my distress. "So long as winter subsists, our world dies."

It's true. Only the North Wind's death will bring about life.

"Wren?" The king calls from nearby, his voice carried on the wind.

Zephyrus tightens his grip on my hand before I can pull away. "I'm barred from the fortress. Can you find a way to meet me a mile north, near Mnemenos?"

The River of Forgetting. I vaguely recall its location. "When?"

"Tomorrow. No, wait." He tilts his head. "Three days from now. Dawn. I'll wait for you."

Boreas calls my name again.

"Do not let him cow you," Zephyrus whispers urgently. "Remember who you are. Remember what he has taken from you—and from the world." With that, he releases me, but the ghost of his bruising touch lingers long after he is gone.

# CHAPTER

## 20

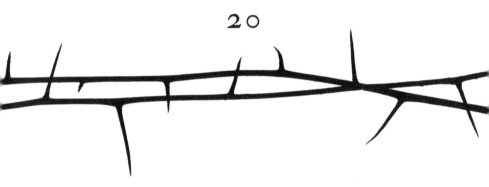

It is cold enough to crawl beneath my skin and leave marks. Little wind, but frost forms wherever the air touches, clumped at the corners of my eyes, coating my nostrils in white that cracks with every exhale. Wrapped in my furs, I'm protected well enough, but my lungs and belly grow chilly with my breath, absorbing the cold that is eternal.

Zephyrus has yet to arrive. I slipped out the door before Orla could wake me for breakfast. My dear husband will have to eat on his own, though I'm not certain he will even attend. Three days have passed since we returned from Neumovos, and I've yet to see him. Orla claims he has been feeling poorly, and thus keeps to his rooms.

Something doesn't sit right. The king cannot die. He cannot fall ill. Why lie? What is it he hides from me?

A twig snaps to my right. When Zephyrus emerges from

the thicket a heartbeat later, my shoulders relax. He must have purposefully alerted me to his presence, since he is usually silent.

He beams upon sighting me, white teeth against golden skin. His coat clings to his lithe frame. "Wren. You look lovely this morning."

My face warms from the praise. "I was wondering if you would show."

"You doubted me?" He pokes out his lower lip, but his green eyes twinkle. "How could I treat my sister-in-law so poorly? Come. We haven't time to waste."

"About that . . ." I tug on his sleeve to draw his attention back to me. "I'm not alone."

"I beg your pardon?"

Soft, delicate footsteps. Thyamine steps into the small clearing, the eerie transparency of her form allowing her to blend easily into her surroundings. Her round glasses sit askew on her pert nose.

Something hardens in Zephyrus' eyes, and he faces me with a raised eyebrow. "Is there a particular reason why you've brought company?"

"My lady?" Thyamine minces her way to my side, breathless from the hike. "You— Oh." Upon catching sight of Zephyrus, her jaw slackens. Her nose scrunches in concentration, as though she attempts to place his features. It is futile. Moments after leaving the citadel, she asked me what my name was. The poor woman is hopeless. "Who are you?"

"Thyamine, this is Zephyrus." No need to inform her he is the North Wind's brother, since he has technically been banned from the Deadlands. Not that she'll remember that detail anyway. "I'm helping him with a favor."

I mutter to Zephyrus, "She found me while I was trying to get away. I didn't have much of a choice. It was either invite her, or risk the guards spotting me."

"This isn't going to be an issue, is it?" he asks. "Because there can be no distractions once we reach the cave."

"She promised she would listen to my instructions. Right, Thyamine?"

"Yes, my lady." Another glance at Zephyrus. "What were your instructions again?"

The West Wind doesn't appear pleased by the additional companion, but he shrugs and gestures us to follow him.

"How did you manage to leave the citadel without anyone noticing?" he asks in curiosity.

"There's a hole in the outer wall of one of the practice courts," I say, picking my way over a tree root that's pushed through the snow. For whatever reason, it's far wetter today, as if the air has warmed, though I know I must be imagining it. "I don't think anyone's noticed it because it's covered in vines."

He tosses a grin in my direction, one that reveals his sharpened canines. "Clever girl."

Mnemenos' glassy surface slithers into a wide depression walled in by sheer rock. The farther we travel, chasing the river to its end, the taller the trees stretch, and the sky dims, slipping into obscurity. I've never traveled this far from the citadel. Aside from Neumovos, of course. I'm a skilled enough tracker to read the terrain, despite its unfamiliarity. We've been climbing steadily in altitude over the past hour.

"There is something you must know, Wren, before we reach the cave of Sleep." A light, graceful leap over a fallen tree, and he lands soundlessly on the other side while I clamber over the trunk. Thyamine merely flows through it, a childlike curiosity to her expression as she takes in our surroundings.

He turns to me then, face grave. "When you fall asleep in the realm of the living, it is but a brief visitation to Sleep's dominion. Should you succumb to Sleep's power in the Deadlands, however, there's a chance you might not wake." His mouth pinches. "Ever."

What is worse: the surprise, or the lack of it? Deep down, did I expect such a thing?

"You said the god's power would be muted for me," I remind him, fighting the queasiness slithering through my stomach. The God of Death, and the God of Small Death. I had not thought of their realms overlapping, but they must, if they share the Deadlands.

"It will be, but you must still remain vigilant."

How lovely for him to inform me of this when we're halfway to our destination. "You're making it very hard for me to trust you," I snap. "Why didn't you tell me this before?"

At least he appears properly contrite, though it is still no excuse. "Would you have agreed to it, were that the case?"

After some consideration, yes, I probably would have. Because I'm desperate. Because there is no other choice. Now it feels as if I've been led astray, despite sharing the same goal.

"I'm sorry, but what are we doing here again?"

I turn to Thyamine, who squints at me as though I stand in a thick fog, and only a distant sun might banish it. She is properly confused, and I cannot blame her. I'm beginning to wonder if this outing was a mistake.

As if sensing my discontent, Zephyrus comes forward, brushing snow from my coat, all smiles and reassurance. "Here is the plan. I will invite myself into my cousin's humble abode. While I distract him, you find the garden and take the poppy flowers. A handful is enough. It shouldn't take more than an hour."

As much as I want to call this off, we might not have another chance. I need that tonic. "How will I find the garden? And how am I supposed to see? You said there's no light inside."

"Here." He passes me a round glass orb the size of my fist that emits a pale, rosy light. It warms my palm through my glove like the smallest of suns.

Thyamine leans toward the light so it shines through her glasses. She gives a slow blink with her magnified eyes. "What is that?"

"That," says Zephyrus, "is called a roselight." He taps the glass with a fingernail, and the pink shimmers with an iridescent glow. "In my realm, roses are harvested for their petals. The liquid is extracted and altered to a substance of pure light." He sounds proud of this accomplishment. It is quite the marvel. "Now, the garden is located in the cave's center, which you'll find by following the river until you reach an opening in the ceiling." He searches my gaze for a long moment. "All right?"

We've made it this far. And what is life without a little risk? If we manage to get the poppy flowers, that's one step closer to my freedom, and I want my freedom more than anything.

I nod, chin lifted. Thyamine says, "Are we going on a trip, my lady?"

"We are." I pat her hand comfortingly, poor thing. "But you'll need to be quiet the rest of the way. Can you do that?"

"Why do I need to be quiet?"

"Because otherwise Sleep will learn we're nearby, and we won't be able to finish our mission."

The specter woman nods eagerly. "Yes. I think I can do that. I enjoy sleep, though I never dream. Or I never remember the dreams." Her face folds into an expression of extreme perplexity.

Zephyrus mutters something about insanity before striding ahead. Another half-mile passes before the river splits. One branch continues onward, while the other curves eastward. Thyamine gasps, and I, too, experience a similar disbelief, mystification at the two massive arches before us.

They are, quite simply, gargantuan. Thrice the height of the surrounding trees, I have to tilt back my head to get a proper look at them. The arches are wide enough for twenty, thirty men to walk abreast beneath, and frame each branch of Mnemenos separately, like individual doorways. I'm not sure of the material they're carved from. One glows with a white luster. The other, equally pale, is flattened in color, without radiance.

"What are those?" I approach the flowing river in curiosity, careful to maintain a healthy distance from the treacherous bank.

"The gates of ivory and horn," Zephyrus answers. "Dreams pass beneath them, and Mnemenos carries them to the mortal realm."

He gestures to the eastbound branch, where the smooth, lustrous arch curves overhead, shimmering as though polished. "True dreams pass beneath the gate of horn. False dreams, those meant to deceive"—he gestures to its dulled twin—"pass beneath the gate of ivory."

A closer glance reveals wisps of faded yellow light amidst the water.

"Do you dream, my lady?"

I smile at Thyamine's question, although it doesn't reach my eyes. Passivity. That is what a dream is. I choose to act rather than to dream, for to act is to move forward, and to dream is to stand still. Do I dream? Yes. Doesn't everyone? But I cannot let dreams cloud my reality.

"Sometimes," I say.

"What do you dream of?"

I sense Zephyrus listening nearby. I dream of what Elora dreams of, though I've never mentioned my own wish to find love and safety, a home with a man. I don't need those things, of course. But it would be nice, I think.

Thyamine awaits my answer. I only pat her on the arm and say, "It matters not."

After passing the gates of ivory and horn, it doesn't take long before Zephyrus lifts a hand, signaling us to stop. Thyamine bumps into my back with a soft, "Oh."

Beyond the bend, I spot the wide and flattened cave, the river pushing through its mouth. It's part of a much larger structure, one that is carved from the cliff itself. A massive edifice not unlike the Frost King's citadel. Smoothed towers and over-reaching rooms.

I state, wondering if I'm seeing things correctly, "You said Sleep dwells in a cave."

"Technically, it is a cave." He snorts. "Terribly morose. I, for one, will never understand how Sleep and his brother, Death, have not gone mad from it." At my questioning glance, he elaborates, "The darkness."

Indeed, a shroud encompasses the cave, hiding the majority of it from sight.

"This moment forward," he says, "there can be no sound. Sleep must not sense your presence." He pins the specter woman with a glittering, green-eyed glare. "Wren, you're with me. Your maid will have to stay behind. Keep the roselight off until I've successfully distracted him." He taps the orb, and the light fades. "As long as you remain awake, Sleep will not sense you. Once inside, follow the river until you reach the garden."

How many times, exactly, has Zephyrus visited this cave? Enough to know what to expect. Enough to concern me. Enough to settle me, too.

I nod in agreement, then begin trailing him across the smooth, raised rocks spilling toward the frozen bank of Mnemenos. He leaps across the slick, ice-coated stones gracefully, landing on the balls of his feet, before springing farther out.

"Wait, my lady." Thyamine is not a particularly strong woman, so the fierceness of her grip around my arm is surprising. Her breathing shallows as she stares straight ahead, watching Zephyrus' form blur as he pushes through the dark that thickens around the cave. "I don't think you should go. Something tells me this is a bad idea."

"I already know this is a bad idea." I try prying her fingers free, but they tighten painfully.

"It's something else. Something—" She breaks off with a sound of frustration. Her eyes sheen. "If only I could remember."

A gentle pat to her hand, and miraculously, her fingers loosen around my arm. The skin stings from the sudden flare of blood, of recirculation. "It's all right. Zephyrus warned me about the dangers in coming here. I must do this. I must return to my sister, my life at Edgewood."

"But you have a life here." Her expression is so sweetly confused.

"It's a life, but it's not *my* life." As her confusion deepens, I shake my head. It's pointless to explain, considering she will not remember this conversation tomorrow. "What I mean is, I didn't choose it."

Thyamine again glances in Zephyrus' direction. He's stopped near the mouth of the cave and waves to me. "But what about the Midwinter Eve festival?"

"What about it?"

"My lord said he enjoyed himself. He said he thought you enjoyed yourself, too."

Though I raise my hand in answer to Zephyrus, mentally, my thoughts veer toward this information. I did enjoy myself, but I didn't think the king had noticed. I'd believed him to be immune to it. "When did he say that?"

"Yesterday, my lady. You smiled. He said that, too."

And he is far too observant for my liking. Going forward, I will need to have more care of the things I say around him, my reactions.

But . . . he noticed my smile.

"You'll be safe here," I tell the specter woman. "Just stay put and keep watch for anything that might appear."

"Darkwalkers, my lady?"

I sincerely hope no darkwalkers lurk in the vicinity.

"Keep low, and keep quiet." I squeeze her shoulder and dart the remaining length separating me from where Zephyrus stands. The glass containing the roselight pulses softly in my grip. Into that ageless, primordial dark where Sleep dwells. Zephyrus' hand in mine guides me to where I need to go.

Moments later, we stop. There is a knock, and I hear the rush of the river to my right. Not even the vivid blue hue of the water can penetrate this lightless place.

The sound of an opening door. Still, that gulf of endless night.

"Cousin!" Zephyrus' warm greeting rings out. I can't see his smile, but I can imagine it, a hungry white grin beneath those laughing clover eyes.

"To what do I owe the pleasure, Zephyrus?" The voice is so resonant my ears vibrate. Sleep, the deity who owns half of mortals' lives.

"Can't a god visit family? You know I missed you, S."

A moment of silence. "I told you not to call me that."

"Yes, well, my memory is not as good as it once was. Can I come in? I'd rather discuss things where I can *see*, you know." He squeezes my hand. We are about to move.

"This better be quick." Shuffling footsteps, as though Sleep has stepped back to allow Zephyrus to enter. I trail him quietly, taking care to lift my feet so I don't trip over any cracks or wayward rocks.

"I always preferred you over your brother, you know."

Sleep rumbles, "I will be sure to tell him that."

The door shuts, and sweat springs to my armpits. I imagine that is the only exit, and without light, who knows if I will find it again.

Zephyrus lets go of my hand, his voice growing faint as he draws his distant cousin into another part of the cave. The splashing water drowns out additional sound. I wait until Zephyrus' voice fades completely before lifting the roselight in the dark—only to realize I have no idea how to make it glow.

"Um . . . light?"

Not even a flicker. I strain my ears to make sure I'm still alone, though I swear the darkness seems to mute sound as well.

"Please?"

The glass warms in my palm. And then it is aglow, emanating a soft pink light. Lifting my hand, I allow the roselight to brighten the surrounding area, my eyes slowly adjusting to the illumination.

This is no cave. This is a stronghold, a manor hewn from the black, glittering quartz of the mountain. It is a place of dark beauty. Here, night sings like the nightingale.

Mnemenos curves through the rock in a flat ebony band. Around me are great, pointed arches cut from the walls, tunnels leading into distant depths. Zephyrus said to follow the river, so that is what I do, keeping the roselight lifted high so it reveals the way. Every so often, a drop of water pings somewhere beyond sight and echoes in shallow waves of sound. The blackness squeezes the frail pink hue, trying to snuff it out. I quicken my footsteps. The sooner I find the garden, the sooner I can leave.

After an indeterminable amount of time, I notice the darkness shifting ahead of me. Another step forward. Now the blackness lifts. Now there is gray—light.

It pours from a hole in the cavern ceiling to reveal a myriad of plants growing in rich soil. The red poppies flash like small, licking tongues, hungry mouths with dark centers. The flowers sway in a nonexistent breeze. The air, strangely enough, is warmer here, as though the Frost King's power doesn't completely penetrate Sleep's abode. The deeper the plants sit in the cave, the thicker the veil shielding them from view.

Zephyrus, with his fluid nature and soundless tread, is the perfect candidate—perhaps the only candidate—with the capability to steal Sleep's treasured blooms. But that task has now fallen to me.

Light footsteps bring me to the plot's edge. While the poppies with their scarlet crowns are the most plentiful in the moonlight, the space holds other sleep-inducing plants and herbs. I spot chamomile, lavender. Crouching, I pick a handful of poppies and tuck them into my pocket.

The air seems to thicken, pushing against my limbs as though curious of the intruder. My ears prick in a silence that suddenly feels so much more alive as, from out of the darkness, a voice trembles in the walls.

"Who dares pick from the Garden of Slumber?"

# CHAPTER
## 21

The roselight blinks out like a dying star. I shake the orb as shudders pulse through the rock, closer, closer, spaced apart like footsteps. Nothing. The light does not revive itself.

Blackness blooms before my eyes. Despite holding my hand in front of my face, I can't see it. And the longer I am without light, the greater my panic multiplies, spinning out of control. What happened to Zephyrus? How am I supposed to navigate these tunnels without light?

Again, I give the glass a furious shake. "Light," I whisper. "*Please.*" It remains stubbornly dark.

My hands tremble. I tighten my grip on the roselight as though it is an anchor. If the light will not work, then I will find another way out of here. My sight may be masked, but I still have sound, smell, and touch to help guide me.

Sleep speaks again, and it is like the essence of the world, before darkness, before time. "Why do you touch that which does not belong to you?"

It sounds as if Sleep approaches from behind. The dark is confusing enough without sound involved. I could be wrong. Maybe additional doorways or tunnels exist beyond the garden.

But I don't stand around to find out. I stumble in the direction of the wall—away from the river. Mnemenos, whose touch brings forgetfulness. With my hand braced against the cave wall, and the river to my left, I retrace my steps.

Progress is slow. With my vision veiled, I have to lift my feet higher than I normally would so as to avoid tripping on cracks in the ground. Then there is the increasing drowsiness, my mind drifting in this dark womb. *Zephyrus*, I think. I must find Zephyrus.

As I travel farther from the garden, the murk gradually begins to lift. My roselight flickers. I push my legs faster. Soon, the pink light blooms, forcing the black into retreat. Mnemenos races swiftly to my left, leading me back to the cave entrance. The smooth hewn archways and halls are but fleeting shapes and curves in the pink glow.

In the end, I need not find Zephyrus, because he finds me first. As soon as I reenter the large entrance chamber, I trip over something on the ground. The West Wind, unconscious. I crouch at his side and tap his cheek, ears keen for the god's approach, but all I hear is the hiss of the river. When I pull back one of his eyelids, I see his eyes have rolled into the back of his head. He's out cold.

"Zephyrus." I shake him hard. His head flops to the side. It's no good. Even slapping him across the face fails me.

So that's it then. Zephyrus has succumbed to Sleep's power, and I'm likely not far behind.

The urge to laugh squeezes my lungs so fiercely only the reminder that I now stand alone in Sleep's dwelling grinds the urge to dust. My options are limited: save myself or drag Zephyrus to safety. I won't abandon him, but when I attempt to move his body, he barely budges. My strength has been drained.

Something stirs in the long black throat of the cave.

My fingers tingle inside my gloves where they grasp for Zephyrus' sleeve, and for whatever reason, I can't concentrate long enough to grip the fabric. It continually slips through my fingers. The tingling sensation spreads up my arms, chest, and face. A hard exhale punches out of me. I can't catch my breath.

"Zephyrus."

*Rest*, the air croons. A deep, restorative rest in a dark mouth surrounded by red petals. Bloody things, growing things.

Sleep slides across my consciousness, and the world fades into obscurity.

～

I drift for a time, and I dream. Nonsensical things, mostly. But then I am swimming, pushing from the silt bottom of a river whose current carves into the earthen ground. Light ripples in the distance, drawing me nearer to the surface. My lungs swell with air, my eyes fly open, and the blackness seeps into my vision, cloaking all sight.

Pebbles dig into my lower spine where I lie on the ground. I am awake, yet I feel as though I still dream.

Am I dreaming?

"My lady?" The whisper tickles my ear.

Not a dream then. Thyamine's voice, but I can't see her. Can't see anything.

"Where am I? What happened?" My struggles increase as I become aware of my arms and legs bound together. Why is it so dark?

*Sleep.*

This is his cave, his domain. He must be somewhere nearby, and if I folded to his power once, it could happen again.

Pink, shining light blazes forth, and I squint against the intensity. Thyamine rises over me, the roselight flickering in her transparent hand, her lips all but nonexistent, so forcefully are they pressed together. Wide, terror-stricken eyes peer at me like pale moons behind her glasses. She presses a finger to my lips to signal my quiet. Gradually, I fall still, though my breath hisses between my clenched teeth.

"Please, my lady. You mustn't speak." She glances over her shoulder watchfully.

Bit by bit, the roar in my head dissolves, and I strain for any sound—the river, footsteps, clattering pebbles. It's silent as Thyamine sets down the roselight and begins to pick at the knots binding my wrists and ankles.

"When you didn't return," she says in a fretful tone, "I grew worried. You told me to stay put, I know. I'm sorry I disobeyed."

"No, you did the right thing." To think if she hadn't come after me . . . What would have happened? Was this to be my new prison? Would the Frost King have even noticed my absence?

She shudders. "I found you collapsed on the ground. I tried to wake you, but Sleep came. I ran. Hid. He dragged you away, but I followed. I couldn't let him take you."

I've never been more grateful that Thyamine refused to follow instructions. "Where's Zephyrus?"

"I don't know. I didn't see him with you."

It's possible the god separated us. Highly probable, even. Zephyrus deceived him. What punishment would he receive?

"He's probably not far," I whisper, rubbing the chafed skin of my wrists and ankles once the rope slides free. Blood pulses through the cold, stiff appendages so viciously they sting. When I check my pockets for the poppies, however, I find them empty. My stomach drops. Sleep must have taken them from me.

It's disheartening, but I can't worry about that now. Our safety comes first. "We need to find Zephyrus before Sleep returns."

"Should we split up, my lady? It will cover more ground."

It's actually a smart idea. First the rescue, now this. I think I may have underestimated her. "I would say yes, but I don't want either of us getting lost, unable to find the other. Stay close."

Thyamine's spectral outline glows white in the dim. The tunnel narrows and widens and twists back on itself, yet before long, we reach a wide room, empty save for Mnemenos rushing through the rock. The chamber branches into two halls, their entrances carved with symbols atop their great archways. Thyamine gestures to the left, so we go left, guided by the warm, colored roselight. The passage circles back to the previous chamber. The right tunnel leads us to a dead end.

"Let's go back to where you found me. We'll try another direction."

More dead ends and crisscrossing paths eventually lead us to the place where Zephyrus is being kept: a barred cell, one of many lining this particular tunnel. I lift the roselight higher so its glow brightens the carved interior. His arms and legs aren't bound. Perhaps the sleep-inducing plants have a greater effect on him? I can feel sleep tickling the edge of my consciousness, but as long as I focus on the task at hand, I can stave off the urge to close my eyes.

I whisper through the bars, "Zephyrus."

He doesn't wake. I assumed as much.

"My lady, if I may?" And Thyamine steps forward, a glowing hand pressed to the lock. It thunks open, much to my astonishment.

The specter woman explains, "Since the dead are under the lord's rule, Sleep's influence cannot touch us. This includes any object brushed by his power."

I will have to remember that.

Pulling open the cell door, I hurry to Zephyrus' side. If I were of a gentler nature, I'd lightly tap his cheek to wake him. But there's no time for gentleness. Thyamine gasps as I stab him in the center of his palm with a sharp rock, drawing blood.

The West Wind lurches into an upright position, teeth bared before I slap my hand over his mouth, muffling the sound.

"Hush. It's me." His fingers dig into the tendons on the underside of my wrist, and tears spring to my eyes from the pain. I gouge the rock deeper into his palm with a growled, "Let go."

His hand slackens. He blinks once, slowly. "Wren?" The word is muffled.

"We haven't much time. Can you stand?"

Three heartbeats pass before he nods, releasing me.

"I don't know how to get out of here," I say. Mnemenos could direct us, but I strayed from the river at some point. No longer can I hear the burbling current.

Zephyrus squeezes his eyes shut, rubs at a spot on his forehead. "Shit. He knew. Somehow he could sense you near the garden. And then he spoke a word of power, and I went under." He sighs. "I know the way out. I'm still dizzy though, so I'll need help."

Looping my arm around the god's lithe waist, I help support his weight as we shuffle back to the entrance, Thyamine on our trail. And there is Mnemenos, leading the way back.

"Nearly there," Zephyrus murmurs.

A rumble of power rattles my bones, my teeth.

My head snaps around. The tunnel appears to constrict, and a flash of light reveals the walls are not rock, as I had imagined, but woven with every color of plant, flower, and grass that spills from the ceiling.

*Wait for me*, sings the dark.

My heart slows and my limbs stutter, for that voice is my salvation, my eternal rest. I begin to turn, drawn by the promise of refuge, everlasting night.

Zephyrus pinches my side. "Block it out," he barks. The sleep is gone from his voice. He comes alive, half dragging me toward the glow of the entrance, a faint outline around the door.

*Zephyrus.* A slow croon. *Why do you flee?*

"Faster," gasps the West Wind.

The air thickens with a haze, yet we push forward, quickening our footsteps. But a shadowy substance drips from above, blotting out our escape.

"We're not going to make it," Thyamine whimpers.

A dart of pain lances down my back from the effort of supporting Zephyrus' weight. I can't stand against a god. Neither can Thyamine. Only a god can stand against a god.

"You have powers," I snap to Zephyrus. "Use them!"

Something honed and lethal narrows his gaze. Pushing away from me, he says, "Get to the entrance. I'll catch up."

He doesn't have to tell me twice. Thyamine and I scramble to safety as stone cracks from the force of an otherworldly scream. A glance over my shoulder showcases Zephyrus with his bow, the arrow glowing a deeply saturated green. He shoots, and the arrow hits a bulked, shadowy figure. A roar shakes the cave.

The West Wind sends a warm breeze at my heels, lifting me far ahead, out of reach of the primordial god's wrath. We burst from the mouth of the cave and follow Mnemenos' serpentine form south, where the Deadlands shallow out.

Behind me, Zephyrus pants, "We're safe. He won't emerge from his cave in the daylight."

My knees hit the ground. Sweat slithers down my temples to sink between my lips. My hands are empty.

"I didn't get the poppies," I whisper. We came all this way. A waste. That was to be our only chance, and we will not be able to enter Sleep's domain a second time, now that he is aware of what we seek. "I'm sorry. I put them in my pocket, but they were gone when I woke."

Zephyrus shakes his head. The strain around his mouth deepens. "It's not your fault. I should have been more careful around Sleep. I underestimated him."

What now? Without the poppies, Zephyrus will be unable to make the sleeping draught. We can't move forward. We can't return to the cave. It's possible he could obtain the poppies via other means, but it's no guarantee.

"My lady?" Thyamine's stocking-clad legs enter my line of sight.

I glance upward. Opening her hand, she reveals the crushed red petals of the poppy flowers, her smile wide and buoyant.

The relief is so monumental I know my knees would have given out had they not already done so. It wasn't all for naught. "How . . . ?"

"I saw Sleep take them from your pocket. I picked more flowers from the garden before going to search for you."

I'm honestly speechless. "You did it, Thyamine. Thank you." Never again would I think her to be incompetent.

"Yes, thank you." Zephyrus plucks the petals from her palm and tucks them into his coat pocket. "It will take a few weeks to make the tonic," he says. "Once it's complete, I'll find you, and together, we'll put an end to this winter."

# CHAPTER

## 22

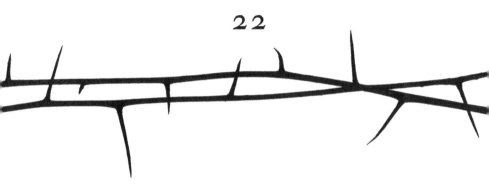

Nine hundred and forty-eight doors.

The south wing contains nine hundred and forty-eight doors, and I've explored them all.

Three weeks I've spent searching, mapping, questioning, *hoping*. I've swam in warm lagoons with clear waters. I've visited towns of splendor, with colorful scarves and flags hanging from strings crisscrossed between buildings. I've spent evenings perched atop mountains, the stars as my witness. I've returned to the cobblestoned city streets to visit the theater not once, but thrice. And yet, no door has led me from the Deadlands. Freedom, as usual, eludes me.

"Patience," I mutter, loosening my grip around the document I carry.

The four wings converge in the very center of the citadel, a perpendicular crossroads where I now stand. A few soldiers guard the north wing, but I ignore them as I cross to the east wing, unfolding the document and setting it on the ground before me.

The map began as a single sheet of parchment, simple charcoal sketches of the doors from a bird's eye view. It is now so large I have to spread it flat on the floor. In addition to the drawings, it contains notes, descriptions of where the doors lead, and a numbering system. Since I'm starting on a new corridor, I attach a blank piece of parchment to the collective drawing and begin sketching the unexplored doors surrounding me. Thirty doors on each side of the hallway, plus one at the end, for a total of sixty-one.

Yet another long day ahead of me, but it is early yet. Folding back the map and returning it to my coat pocket, I begin with the door at the end of the hall. With a hard push against the ornately carved handle, the door opens, and I step inside.

Something flutters in my heart. The door snicks shut, enfolding me in utter quiet.

It's a library.

A place to sit. A place to read, to rest. A place to think, a place to learn, a place to go inside oneself. Long ago, when the realm was still known as the Green, there was talk of great cities whose libraries housed vast repositories of knowledge, open to anyone who visited.

This library houses three stories of bookshelves that flow around the room's curving walls. It's a fluid architectural wonder, no angles, only curves. Wheeled ladders offer height assistance in accessing the taller shelves, and to my right, a spiral staircase vanishes one level above.

Moving across the central chamber, I take in the fire blazing in the hearth, the cushioned armchairs, the lit oil lamps gilding the book spines. Rugs cloak the floor—wood, not stone. Warm, inviting, cozy. It feels familiar, though I've never stepped foot in this library in my life.

Planting myself at the end of one row, I begin browsing the collection. There's a decent mystery selection, as well as adventure novels. A man marooned on an island. A goddess who's stolen into the underworld, poor thing.

The next book is small and slender, able to fit into the palm of my hand. It tells the tale of a boy lost at sea, his return journey home. An inscription written in flowing calligraphy marks the inside of the cover.

*To my beloved Calais. May you always find your way.*

And then I spot the spine of a book I'm quite familiar with. *The Complete Guide to Elk Hunting.* A faded red cover with gold-stamped lettering. I don't feel entirely grounded as I slide the volume from its slot on the shelf and flip to the title page, taking in the small pencil marking in the top right corner. Four letters. *Wren.*

My mind goes blank. How is this possible? This book should be at Edgewood, tucked onto the bookshelf near the fireplace, right where I left it. Unless the king has since returned to the Gray and .. . grabbed my books to bring them here?

The idea is so absurd I snort. The Frost King does not cross into the Gray except to choose his bride. Finding my book here is merely a strange—very strange—coincidence.

The citadel's enchantments work in unexplainable ways, so I don't question the oddity as, book in hand, I settle into one of the plush armchairs near a window overlooking a tiered garden. I'm so engrossed by the story that I don't immediately notice the sound of the opening door, nor do I hear the approaching footsteps.

"Wife."

I startle so hard the book whacks my nose. "Shit." My head swivels toward the center of the room where Boreas stands, hands tucked into the pockets of his black breeches. A violet tunic cascades down his front, slightly rumpled. No gloves today. "Are you trying to stop my heart? And I told you, it's Wren." He moves toward one of the shelves in my periphery. "What are you doing here?"

"I live here."

Smart mouth. "I meant Orla mentioned you weren't feeling well this morning." A continuing oddity of which I've found no explanation.

"I've since recovered."

Right.

As the king places a hand across the book spines, he says, "I was wondering when you would find this place. Orla mentioned you like reading."

What else has she mentioned to him, I wonder? "I would have found it much faster had you volunteered to show me." There I go again, flinging my responses as though they are sharpened knives. With some effort, I manage to tamp down my prickly nature. "Do you know where each of these doors leads to?"

"I would hope so," he says, "considering I built this citadel, and everything in it."

Wait, he created these doors? All this time I thought they preceded his reign. "Why are there so many?"

He drops his eyes, turns away from the shelf. It feels like a self-conscious gesture. "Sometimes I desire to see other realms, places beyond the Deadlands."

"Oh," I say, because it's the last thing I ever thought I'd hear from his mouth. An admittance, that some part of himself feels the walls pressing in.

"Do you like it?" At my look of confusion, he elaborates, "The library."

Leaning down, I pick up my book, set it on my lap. "I do. My mother taught me and my sister how to read, but there were few books in our house growing up." What little money our parents had wasn't spent on the written word. "Orla said you collect books from other lands."

"I do, when I can get away." He selects a scroll bound with twine. "Ancient kingdoms, dead languages, the fringe of society. I like knowing their stories. I . . ." He speaks haltingly. " . . . want to understand where people come from and why they make the choices they do." He returns the scroll, briefly disappears down another row between the shelves, and returns holding a great tome the size of my head. "This is one of my favorites." He sets it atop the table beside my chair.

I quirk my brow at it. Whatever the title is, it's written in a completely different language. "What is it?"

"The complete history of the sea privateers."

"Pirates?" I settle back into the chair, smirking. "I would never have guessed you were interested in such things."

His mouth twitches. "When you live forever, sometimes the only mystery left is knowledge yet to be acquired. Did you know that pirates have a complex governing system within their ship ranks? The captains were elected by popular vote, and could be removed from the position if their performance suffered."

"I didn't, but I read a book recently about pirates. Well, about a woman who fell in love with a pirate," I amend, my face warming.

He nods, wanders over to the window that overlooks the raised flowerbeds, the tidy, manicured lawn. I'm not sure where this library exists, but I've decided it's my favorite room in the citadel, if only for the view. "You know something of my literary tastes, but I admit, I know nothing of yours."

My stupid heart leaps at that. I mentally kick it in some forgotten corner and gesture to the book I hold. "This is one of my favorites. Would you like to hear a passage?"

He turns, hands clasped behind his back, notes the slip-cover, the outline of an elk stitched on the front. "A hunting manual?"

That is what he would assume. I don't bother correcting him. "Yes," I say with an innocent smile. "It's quite stimulating."

He surprises me by settling in the chair beside mine, ankles crossed, blue gaze level. If I were to shift my foot a few inches to the right, our shoes would touch.

"As the bedroom door shut," I murmur, "the woman turned toward her lover. Wide shoulders, a deep chest, and flinty gray eyes. She inhaled, taking the musk of his skin into her lungs. He stepped closer. His large hands curved over her backside, and her ripe mouth softened, parting for his tongue."

The Frost King has gone still. He shifts toward me in his chair. "That's not a hunting manual."

Well, what do you know? It's not.

Long ago, I wrapped the slip-cover of a local hunting manual over the naked hardcover of this erotic romance novel so Elora wouldn't be inclined to pick it up. Wait until he hears chapter twenty. It's positively filthy.

"The kiss deepened over time. The man's tongue flirted with hers, prodding the soft recesses of her mouth. Her sex throbbed in anticipation of their coupling. She could all but feel his length stretching her—"

"Stop." The demand cuts viciously.

I slowly drag my eyes up to his. They flare with bright, cutting emotion, the blue so vivid they shine like newborn stars.

Turning the page, I go on, fighting a grin. "As she pressed closer, her hand slipped into the waistband of his breeches, and her fingers curled around his jutting cock—"

The book is ripped from my grip.

The Frost King stands over me, book in hand, color suffusing the pale skin of his cheeks. His chest stutters on the next inhale as my gaze drifts south, drawn unexplainably to the front of his breeches.

He's hard.

Every thought eddies from my head. His erection is unmistakable. It strains against the soft fabric, a well-endowed ridge, and my belly twists in sudden response.

My head snaps up. Our eyes lock. He is now that much nearer, the heat from his powerful, rippling thighs hitting me in waves.

With some effort, I glance away from the evidence of his desire. "Ah . . ."

"Look at me."

I can't. For when I do, I'll remember waking in the shadowed curve of his body, warm and secure. I'll remember the network of interlocking scars marring the beautiful skin of his broad back. I'll remember—

Two callous-roughened fingertips catch the edge of my jaw, directing it toward him. He flips to a page further along in the book. And then he begins to speak.

"The man tilted back his lover's head, baring her neck to him," he growls in a low rasp. "He thought fleetingly of where this would lead: his bed. The wet heat of his mouth explored the elegant curve of her nape, the mounds of her breasts." Boreas' eyes flick to mine, as if to check that I am still listening. "Lower."

To my horror, I feel heat scorching my skin, crawling across my cheeks, through my chest. Something about the shape of the words in Boreas' mouth rattles my mental state.

"He tossed her onto the mattress and spread her legs." There's a pause, during which the king licks his lips, before he goes on. "Her sex, pink and swollen, glistened from where he stood above her, inexplicably aroused."

Parchment hisses as he turns another page.

"The man's own desire hardened in him. The sweet scent of his lover's perfume teased his senses, and he locked his knees to remain standing, for he had the wish to kneel before her, draw her sex into his mouth—"

My nipples peak at the juxtaposition of the words *sex* and *mouth* spoken in the North Wind's smooth, deep voice.

"—and play with her wet folds."

My breath quickens. By the gods, I must be halfway to insanity. I clench my legs tighter together, but another pulse of pleasure darts through me. And there the Frost King stands, unruffled, placid as a frozen pond. All this time, I've positioned the pieces on the gameboard, but he rearranged them when my back was turned.

With slow, ambling footfalls, he rounds my chair, halting behind me. "He would begin slowly. Soft brushes with the flat of his tongue, which would glide so smoothly through her slick. As the heat built, he'd increase the pressure, yet skirt the bud that ached." His chin brushes my ear, and a stream of warm breath tickles my skin. "When she began to writhe for more, he'd press her hips down with his hands and suckle the engorged flesh—"

My core clenches painfully. My skin tightens with unbearable heat. The combination of his rumbling voice, the warmth of his pine-scented breath, has become my undoing.

Suddenly, wet heat slides down my bare neck, and a moan flies out of my mouth. My eyes pop wide. His tongue. He's licking my skin and—

I'm out of the chair, across the room, darting through the open door and down the hall, running, not looking back, not daring to look back. Up the stairs to the third level, turn right, and again. Hauling open the door to my quarters, I lunge inside, slam the door, and manage to lock it moments before my knees fold and I collapse onto the floor.

~

I keep to my rooms for the remainder of the day. I don't want to chance running into Boreas after . . . well. I'm still processing it.

I skip dinner, though Orla is kind enough to bring me something from the kitchen. I'm in the middle of reading by the fire when she enters, bearing a tray, and sets it on the table beside me. She turns to leave when I say, "Will you tell me why you were sentenced to Neumovos?"

The specter woman stills, one hand reaching for the door handle. I want to know, but not enough to push. If she isn't comfortable opening up to me just yet, she is free to walk.

But Orla pivots to face me. Her expression folds inward, the skin of her face wobbling around her jowls. "The choice I made . . . I am not proud of it. But if I were to do it all over again, I would not do anything differently."

I wait.

"I killed my husband. Stuck him in the chest with a butcher knife."

It is the last thing I expect to hear, but I keep my face calm, no evidence of my distress in wondering what, exactly, would drive sweet Orla to violence. "Why?"

"Does it matter?"

"Of course it matters. It will always matter." Then I understand. "He never asked you why you did it, did he? The king?" Because the North Wind doesn't care about people's motivations. In his mind, a choice is a choice. The reasons behind it are irrelevant.

Orla's chest rises and falls. She clenches her hands, then relaxes them. "My husband abused me, my lady. Left bruises in the places where people couldn't see. Twice, he raped me."

Revulsion rises like gorge in my throat. But the rage . . . the rage is so much worse. My maid is the gentlest of creatures. Only a monster could dare harm her. "I am so sorry, Orla." It's not as if the words mean anything, but I feel helpless otherwise. What's done is done. Her reality is the same for many women. Some I knew. Some were my friends, once.

She shrugs sadly. "You are treated so poorly for so long you start to believe those actions toward you are justified."

"No," I growl. "Abuse is never justified. Never. And it wasn't your fault."

A brief, meek nod. "I know that now, despite my punishment." She goes on, "No one in my village knew it was I who had killed him. Everyone thought he'd crossed the wrong man. He was not yet thirty. I was only eighteen." She unfolds the napkin atop my tray, removes the domed, silver covering. Normally I would complete the task myself, but I imagine she needs to move, to escape that feeling of standing still. "I never remarried, but I lived a long life. Longer than it would have been had my husband survived."

Setting my book aside, I ask, "Do you know where your husband was sent when he died?"

"I do not know, my lady. I've considered asking the lord, but I've never had the courage to do so."

I imagine if the Frost King gave her an answer she wasn't satisfied with, it had the potential to haunt her. Only the blackest depths of the Chasm would suffice.

Orla clears her throat. "It's not so bad serving the lord. I am free in ways I never was in life. The people here are my friends." She falls quiet. "If that's all, I must be returning to the dining room." Turning, she heads for the door.

"Thank you," I whisper to her retreating back, "for telling me. For trusting me with your story."

I hear the tentative smile in her voice when she responds, "Thank you for asking."

❦

When the sky is wine-dark, I set my book aside and climb into bed. The intention is to sleep, of course. The day was long. Yet my skin feels flushed and particularly sensitive when brushing against the blankets. The curve of my neck prickles, as though in memory of Boreas' mouth.

Kicking off the blankets, I rummage through my dresser where I've hidden my flask and take a long pull, then another. My head hangs, hands trembling. One last sip. No—two. Two sips, and then I stuff it back among the fabric and return to bed. I'd hoped the wine would help settle my nerves, but it doesn't. All night, I toss and turn, and then it is morning, rosy-fingered dawn perched on the cusp of the world.

My limbs vibrate with untapped energy. I need to do something. Were I at Edgewood, I'd hike or complete target practice in the backyard, or seek out a warm body. I'm not allowed beyond the grounds. I've exhausted my interest in exploring the doors today. The only bodies that exist in the Deadlands are dead. But there *is* the practice court.

The citadel still sleeps as I slip out the door dressed in fitted trousers and a long-sleeved tunic, warm winter coat fending off the worst of the cold. Bow in hand, quiver thumping against my back, I cross the open courtyard to the walled area where the targets await. Nock, draw, release, I fall into the rhythm of the hunt.

A layer of sweat sheens my skin when the sound of footsteps draws my attention to the training yard entrance. It is there the Frost King stands, halted by my presence in the middle of the walkway, his spear in hand.

Lowering my bow, I tip my head in acknowledgement. "Good morning." Composed, though my stomach twists nervously, my gaze flicking to his mouth.

He crosses into the walled area. "Good morning." Equally composed. He notes the arrow-decorated targets. "I wasn't aware you used this court."

"I don't. Or I haven't, until now." A quick assessment is all I allow myself to give him. It gives me pause. "What's wrong?" Bruises darken the skin beneath his eyes, which have dulled. His pupils sit flush against the thin rings of blue surrounding them.

He rubs a hand across his jaw in a rare show of frustration. "There is another tear in the Shade."

I'm surprised he decided to divulge the reason for his lack of sleep. "Again?" I rest my bow against the ground.

"It's contained for now, but I might need your assistance if it grows worse. More darkwalkers appear by the week. They are multiplying at a concerning rate."

"Is that all you know how to do? Spill blood?" It is a low blow. I'm unsatisfied by his flinch.

"I am a god," he says for the umpteenth time. "War is our native language."

Perhaps he has grown so desensitized he has forgotten that violence is a choice. "Maybe if you helped people," I say, "they would not attempt to enter the Deadlands. If you lifted your influence from the Gray, let the land warm itself—"

"We've discussed this."

"We have not. I come to you with concerns. You either ignore them or brush them aside. I'd hardly call that a discussion."

The quiet speaks so much louder than words. He says, "I am never going to change."

I am aware of who he is. I do not expect him to change. All I ask is that he see me, hear me. Sometimes I think he does, in rare moments when he lowers his guard. "I do not ask you to be anyone other than yourself. I ask that you consider opening your mind. That is all."

"In what way?" He speaks gruffly, as though the question brings him discomfort.

"Are you mocking me?"

"No." He frowns. Shifts his hands on the haft of his weapon. "You once said asking questions helps you better understand someone. So I would like to know."

It takes a moment for his words to process. When they do, I feel like I've been struck in the stomach. "And you want to better understand me?"

Do his cheeks redden, or is that my imagination? "Not exactly."

"Ha!" I poke his chest. "I knew you were mocking me."

"I'm not mocking you." His terse reply is infused with an unusual amount of exasperation. Hm. Maybe he isn't mocking me. That he wants to better understand me isn't an entirely unwelcome notion.

I step back, needing space. But mostly I need air that does not taste and smell like pine. "The court is large enough for two," I say. "We can work on our respective exercises, if you don't mind the company."

"Thank you." He watches my retreat, then turns and stalks toward a bench.

I leave him to his training while I focus on hitting targets. For every ten bullseyes, I miss one. Not good enough. Not nearly good enough when that eleventh shot could mean my death. Ripping the arrows from the wooden targets, I turn and catch a glimpse of Boreas across the court.

Tall, muscled, broad. The pale skin of his torso gleams like dew under sun as he spins through a set of intense exercises, slashing and dodging with the spear he holds. Sweat slithers down every raw-boned facet of his face. Stripped to his breeches, hair pulled into a knot, he moves like air, or water, or a combination of the two. A deadly, whirring cyclone of precise cuts and jabs.

That man is my husband.

In all my years, never have I seen a more perfect form. A smattering of dark hair runs down his flat, ridged abdomen. His back ripples with strength. His arms . . . I swallow. My, but his arms are remarkable, beautifully corded, lean, in perfect proportion. Muscle flexes in a captivating display of prowess.

Once he completes the current set of patterns, the Frost King lowers his spear, glancing over at me, as if he's been aware of my prolonged ogling. The shock of his blue eyes on mine is enough to send me forward. Always face an opponent or problem head-on.

"I would ask your permission to visit my sister." I stop a few feet away, forcing my attention to stray no lower than his chin. A bead of sweat slithers down his temple, which he wipes clear with his forearm.

"The answer is no."

The Frost King controls the Shade. Without his permission, I will be unable to pass into the Gray. And I need this more than I need to breathe. "Why?"

His fingers twitch around the spear haft. The point, carved of crude stone, looks sharp enough to impale someone through the spine. "The forest is overrun by darkwalkers. It's not safe."

"Don't use the darkwalkers as an excuse. You say no because, were I to leave, that's one less person under your control."

His face darkens.

"I've been here two months and I have no idea what state Elora is in, whether she is sick or well." Midwinter Eve planted the idea to visit her, and now I've come to demand he heed my request.

"The answer remains."

Not that I am at all surprised, but . . . fine. Time for a different approach. "Why don't we settle this with a bet?"

Those slitted eyes flicker. Maybe he knows of my intended strategy. And maybe he doesn't.

"Unless," I add, needling him, "you're afraid to lose?"

If I were not so certain the king disliked my presence, I might almost think he were amused.

"What are the terms?" he asks in that low, smooth tone.

"If I win, you have to let me visit my sister—alone."

The king considers me carefully, as though searching for deception. His chest swells. The movement draws my eye to that gleaming torso. It's unfair how beautiful he is. When I exercise, I look like a waterlogged corpse. "And if I win?"

"You won't." I'll ensure it. Nothing will keep me from Elora. Nothing.

He huffs, and his spear disappears into the ether. "If I win, I want something in return."

"You already have my blood. What more could you want?"

"Dinner. At the time and place of my choosing."

I stare at him in confusion. "But we already eat dinner every night together." A vast improvement to our earlier meals, dinner now consists of silence that is no longer awkward, and even occasional conversation.

"That is my request."

I shrug. "Fine." An easy request to fulfill, should I lose. Which I won't.

Moving to the weapons hanging on the wall, the Frost King chooses an enormous bow of pale cedar wood, along with arrows fletched in goose feathers. I have never seen Boreas use a bow. He holds his spear as if it is an extension of himself. The bow, not so much.

We position ourselves across from the target. "You first," I say. "Three attempts each. The person whose arrow hits nearest to the center of the bullseye wins."

The Frost King draws. The muscles of his arm bulge as he fights the tension in the bow. He appears to be hewn from stone, an inflexible pillar. The temperature must not bother him. His skin is not pricked with cold.

The arrow hits the edge of the red mark. Decent, but not good enough.

I'm already drawing my bow. On the exhale, I release. My arrow hits nearer to the center, slightly inside the bullseye. Closer than the Frost King's.

"Adequate."

My gaze cuts to his, and narrows. The edges of his mouth soften. Not quite a smile, but close enough.

His second arrow lands even nearer to the mark, just bypassing mine. And now it is a game, because he makes a sound of deep satisfaction. My pulse climbs, rising to meet the challenge. I nock, draw, release. My second arrow lands a hairsbreadth off-center.

"Close," he murmurs with what I believe is approval.

But not close enough.

The king prepares his final shot. Yet instead of looking at the target, he looks at me. A study of continuous tension as he searches my face. I lick my lips, drawing his focus there. With his gaze locked on my mouth, I feel the undeniable urge to lean closer. The back of my neck burns in memory of his tongue there. "Second thoughts?" I whisper.

And he breathes, "Never."

His arrow lands dead-center, quivering from the force of impact. He has hit the target's heart.

"A worthy attempt," he says, "but I'm afraid that concludes the competition." The Frost King slides me a pitying look before leaning his bow against a nearby bench. He thinks he's won.

This is not how it will end.

One arrow remains. I draw it from the quiver, brush my fingertips over the fletching. Who am I? Wren of Edgewood. Provider, sister, survivor. My world narrows to the arrow protruding from the target's center, and a feeling of rightness moves through me. My breath unspools. *Now*, I think, and release.

The bowstring twangs. The arrow screams and arcs like a falling star, splintering through the middle of the existing arrow shaft, the head buried so deeply in the target it has disappeared from view.

# CHAPTER

## 23

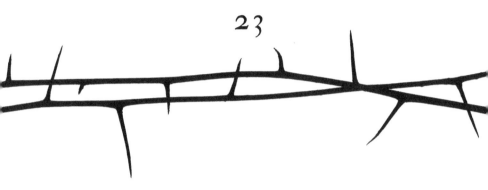

"You will take Phaethon."

We stand in one of the stables, the Frost King and I. The lamps have been extinguished, for it is a bright, cloudless day, the doors open to the sun. A good omen.

Phaethon, the fiend, arches his long, smoky neck over the stall, sniffing my trousers for possible treats. It turns out the darkwalker is, in fact, male. I shove the brute's head away, unwilling to admit that he might have a personality. "I will walk." I'm still not entirely convinced his beloved darkwalker doesn't serve as his eyes in his absence.

The king tightens his fingers around the reins, creaking leather squeezed in his gloved hand. His eyes are so dark they appear black, no distinction between pupil and iris. He looked at me much the same days ago in the library, his arousal evident. I didn't know what to do about it then. I still don't.

"You ride Phaethon, or you don't go at all. Your choice."

Choice? That's hilarious. "Fine." My chin juts forward. Without the Frost King's approval, I am barred from crossing the Shade into the Gray. And I need this. Like air.

He opens the stall and walks Phaethon into the open. I never noticed before, but the beast's coal-dark coat is the exact shade as the king's hair. "You will return by sundown." Clipped.

"I am spending the night."

He opens his mouth in retaliation, but my hand flies up, cutting him off. "I stay the night," I repeat, no room for negotiation. "I haven't seen my sister in months. I will return tomorrow morning." Damn his controlling tendencies.

Boreas looks like he's spent the last few hours sucking on a lemon. However— "Tomorrow morning," he relents.

He lifts me into the saddle, though I'm more than capable of mounting myself. The king warned me of the consequences, should I overstay my welcome at Edgewood: my town's blood to feed the Shade. It's a threat I take seriously. Until that stone-cold heart of his ceases to beat, I will be on my best behavior.

He leads Phaethon to the gates, those strange, shadowy hooves clopping. Once there, he passes me the reins, but doesn't let go when our hands meet. "Tomorrow morning," he repeats, gaze boring into mine.

I nod. "You have my word."

The gate mechanisms lurch into motion: enormous cogs; heavy, clunking teeth. The hinges groan. As soon as the opening is wide enough, I dig my heels into the darkwalker's sides.

We spring forward into wind and cold. My eyes water and burn, and as I push the creature harder, he rises to meet my challenge, tossing his head and weaving through the woodland, leaping over fallen trees and frozen, glinting creeks.

Miles and miles into the deep stillness we go. When the river comes into view, I slow the beast to a walk, then dismount at the bank. This would be Mnemenos, which eventually flows into the Les. So long as I don't touch the water, I'll retain my memories, my sense of self.

The boat is frozen in the same place as when I first arrived. A smooth, glassy sheet. Although, upon closer inspection, I notice the river is not as smooth as I first perceived. Faint hairline cracks interrupt the unbroken flow, and in some places, darker patches mar the ice, signaling weaker areas that have begun to melt.

"You don't have to wait for me," I tell Phaethon.

His cavernous eyes lock onto mine. Then he tosses his head and vanishes into the trees.

Once I clamber into the vessel and settle on the bench, the ice melts and the river's current carries me downstream.

The journey takes the day. White foam froths over smooth, protruding stones, and water beats the curved hull. I cling to the sides of the boat because I cannot swim. There was never a need to learn, with the river frozen year-round. Ahead, the Shade looms. It grows and spreads and slides coolly over my skin as I pass through. When I open my eyes, I am no longer in the Deadlands. I have returned to the Gray at last.

The boat deposits me at a bend in the river, which freezes solid as soon as I disembark. I have spent the better part of my life exploring these backwoods, so I'm familiar with my location in relation to

Edgewood. With darkness approaching, I make haste, heading south, tromping through dense, new-fallen snow.

Night trickles in from the east, the west glowing red as the last of the sun's rays slip beyond sight. I am going home, for however brief a time. Home, where my heart lies. It feels as though my entire body leans forward, straining toward what awaits beyond the trees, and soon I'm running, crashing through dead brush, leaping over the salt barrier enveloping the town, darting through the deserted square.

The cottage comes into view, perched atop its little hill. "Elora!" I'm so overcome with happiness I do not immediately notice the signs. "Elora, I'm home!"

The snow deepens leading to the front door. White ladens the peaked roof. Hand on knob, I stumble across the threshold, expecting to be greeted by a fire, my sister's sweet face as she knits one of her beloved woolen hats.

Instead, there is this: a vacant space, a cold hearth, and an overturned chair.

I move farther inside without bothering to shut the door. The air is tinged with dust, as though it has been locked up for many months. The cottage bears signs of abandonment and disuse.

"Elora?" Another tentative step. The floorboards creak beneath my weight. The hair on my body sprouts upward in growing alarm as I move toward the bed. Bare mattress, no blankets. I pull open the bureau drawers: empty. The kitchen pantry: empty. The extra stores: empty. It all sits empty.

I am no stranger to death. It has cloaked Edgewood for most of my life. A home only sits empty when there is no longer someone to occupy the space.

My legs weaken, then fold, knees slamming against the floor.

Something snaps inside me. A clean, quiet break. Elora is my heart and my joy. She cannot be gone.

For how long? Who, or what, took her from me? The elk meat I left should have lasted her for months. She would not have starved. Is it possible someone stole from her? It doesn't happen often, but as the years pass, desperation grows. With no food and no means to hunt, she would have wasted away slowly.

My mind begins to crumble over this knowledge.

"Wren?"

I flinch at the voice. It's familiar, as is every piece of this town, yet I've spent enough time in isolation that its owner doesn't immediately come to mind.

Dazed, I turn. Miss Millie stands in the doorway, her furred hood encrusted with ice. A haggard face, bones protruding beneath limpid, watery eyes. Shock in the blown, wide-eyed gaze. It feels as though I've been gone years, not months. She is thinner. A ghost.

"How long?" I whisper brokenly. My shaking intensifies. "How long has she been gone?"

"Gone?" Miss Millie stares at me in bewilderment. "Elora isn't gone. She's married now. She and her husband live across town."

"Married?" Which means . . . "She's alive?"

"Of course she's alive." Cautiously, Miss Millie hobbles toward me. A limp—that's new. Her hand hovers over my arm, but she doesn't touch me, as if afraid I've been corrupted in some manner. "We did not expect you to return. It's wonderful to see you, Wren." She smiles, but the skin around her eyes remains smooth. It is the kind of smile you offer out of politeness and obligation, nothing more. She doesn't trust me. I was taken as the North Wind's sacrifice, yet here I am, very much alive.

She asks into the silence, "Where is the Frost King?"

For whatever reason, her suspicion prods my irritation to life. "You need not worry. He's not here. I was granted permission to visit."

"He let you go?" Shocked.

"For a brief time, yes. Where is Elora?"

A hesitation.

"Miss Millie," I repeat, iron in my voice. "Where is Elora?"

The woman caves. "Come." She gestures me out the door. "I'll take you to her."

We arrive at a sturdy cottage nearest to the edge of the encroaching forest. Snow is piled so high it covers the front windows. It must have stormed recently.

Smoke puffs from the crooked chimney, and the smell of burning wood takes me back to childhood, curled against Elora near the fire, my stomach cramping from hunger, and exhaustion blanketing every sight and sound. Miss Millie knocks. My pulse surges in an emotion that is not unlike fear.

The door opens, and there she is. Elora: lovely, soft, obedient. Even after months away, she still rivals the sun.

Shock fractures her expression. That tender mouth gapes like a fish out of water. Her arms hang slack at her sides, but she stumbles forward a step, lifts her hand as if to touch me, question if I am an apparition. "Wren?" The hoarse sound of my name given shape is the best thing I've heard in months.

My airway swells. It's difficult to swallow. "Elora." I look at her, at a thinner, fading version of myself, her worn gray dress bagging around her frame. It's not right.

I enfold her in my arms. She's so slight—too slight. A sob cracks the air, and I'm not sure who breaks first. It doesn't matter. We're together, for however short a time. I tell myself it's enough.

"I thought—" Elora pulls away, strands of hair hanging like strips of sodden wool around her face. Moonlight gleams against the dampness coating her cheeks. "I thought you—"

"I know." I tuck a lock of hair behind her ear. "I did, too."

Elora denies me her face, gazing out at the frozen landscape with a troubled expression. Miss Millie has made herself scarce. I'm not sure if I'd prefer her presence, for the air is changing, shaping itself around Elora's thoughts. Like armor.

"How?" she whispers.

*How are you here?*

*How are you alive?*

I'm unable to answer, for the next question is far, far worse.

"Why?"

One word, spoken as a curse. She stares me straight in the face, but I do not recognize her. Elora, sweet Elora, never allows those harder emotions to weigh her down. But she has changed since our parting. Or perhaps I have. Her eyes glint like a blade, and I find myself retreating a step, lest I prick myself on its point.

"Why am I here?" I ask. My previous joy is gone. Vanished. "I wanted to visit you—"

"You left me," she hisses, and I flinch. One of her small hands curls around the doorframe, her dirt-encrusted fingernails bitten down to the quick. "You . . . you drugged me and left and when I woke, you were gone. I thought you had *died*. I thought—"

"Elora."

"No!" She smacks her palm against the wood. I fall silent, my spine rigid. Elora never raises her voice. Never.

And suddenly, I am someplace I have never been.

To be cast in this villainous light, to be marked as the cause of my sister's pain, fury, and resentment . . . that I did not expect.

What *did* I expect? For Elora to welcome me back into my old life. For her to have remained familiar, unchanged. My absence, what she considers a betrayal, has hardened her. Anger I can understand. But the way she looks at me now, as though she does not know me, after I came all this way—

I thought of her. Every day. I never stopped trying to return to her.

A long stream of air escapes my nostrils. I draw myself taller. If she's displeased, then we'll talk. I'll explain everything. We have time now, as we didn't the day the Frost King arrived at Edgewood.

"I'd like to explain. I've missed you."

"It's a little late for that, Wren. You should have told me what you were planning. Do you know how it felt waking to an empty house, learning my only sister had left with the Frost King as his sacrifice?"

"Frightened," I whisper. Alone. Furious, obviously. "There was no time for goodbyes. I did what I thought was best."

"For whom?"

Is that an actual question? "For you. Do you think I would have let him take you?" I manage, my molars clenching so hard my jaw twinges.

"You did not give me a choice."

"You're saying you would have rather I did nothing? You're saying you would have rather been sacrificed, tortured?"

"You are alive enough," she says.

A pit forms in my stomach at the direction of this conversation.

I did not know the Frost King would spare my life when I left Edgewood. I was fully prepared to die so that Elora could live. "Help me understand. You're saying you would have rather I died, so that my deception wouldn't have been for naught?"

"No, of course not." She crosses her thin arms, that rosebud mouth pinched.

"Then what are you saying?"

"I'm saying," she growls, "you always had to play the hero. It's what you do."

My ire rises to meet hers. "I was trying to protect you."

"It was selfish!"

The word falls like a scythe across my neck. My lungs shrivel, and the pit in my stomach amasses, my unrest at last molting into turmoil, queasy disbelief. I glance toward the snow-blanketed landscape. It's fully dark. The air feels oily against my skin, warning me of the darkwalkers lurking beyond the salt barrier, far from the village lights. I came here expecting to stay the night. Now I wonder if I am even welcome. Me. Elora's own flesh and blood. My mind is paralyzed, pinned somewhere between denial and disbelief. And I wonder, who has changed?

"Elora?"

A man strides into view, placing a protective hand on Elora's hip. Shaw. I remember him as a boy with too many freckles and too little common sense, but he has grown into a man, powerfully built, with the thick shoulders of a bull and a neatly trimmed beard. He's a carpenter who does well for himself, last I heard. And now he is Elora's husband.

"Wren?" He blinks slowly. "You're back."

"Just for a short visit," I assure him with a tense smile.

It's so strange, seeing this. Seeing Elora standing in a house that is not ours, with a man I know little of, and the snow and the cold at my back, because I've yet to be invited inside. They would have hosted a wedding, the entire town participating in the festivities. Elora would have been the loveliest bride. She'd dreamed of gold ribbons in her hair.

Was it a mistake, coming here? Does Elora not see everything I did was for her, so that she may live, and continue to live, and die in old age?

*Selfish.* My throat burns with approaching tears. Only by sheer will do I stomp them into submission. What else was selfish? Spending days, sometimes weeks, away to hunt so she would have food in her belly.

What else?

Spending extra coin on fabric to make her a new dress because her old one developed too many holes, while I've only two shirts and two pairs of trousers and one dress.

What else?

Missing countless parties to chop wood, repair the roof while she danced and danced and danced.

I never wanted to be parted from her. I made the difficult decision. *Me*, not her. I always made the difficult decisions, always placed her comfort over my struggles, her happiness over my pain. In the process, I convinced myself my needs didn't matter. That I wasn't worthy of such things.

But I wonder if she would have done the same, were our roles reversed. Would she have sacrificed herself in order to save me from the Frost King? Would she have put my needs, dreams, future before her own?

Truth has such prickly edges. Deep in my heart, I know the answer.

She wouldn't have.

If I were at the citadel, Boreas and I would be sharing a meal. A quiet affair, tension simmering in the background as I debated how best to aggravate him. Oddly enough, I miss the interaction. Better ugly honesty than a pretty lie.

Shaw glances between me and his wife, brow furrowed. Perhaps wondering why I've yet to be welcomed inside.

A crack runs through my heart as I step back. If this is her choice, then I must respect that. But damn if I let her see how this hurts. "I was just leaving."

Turning, I begin descending the stairs when Elora calls out, "Wait."

I halt on the bottom step.

"Come inside," she says. A long, uncertain pause. "Have dinner with us."

Since I cannot see Elora's expression, I'm forced to interpret the inflection of her voice. Fury, sadness, reluctance. My intention was never to hurt her. But for her to claim my actions were selfish, I'm not sure I can forgive that so easily.

With a final glance at the darkened landscape, I climb the stairs and enter my sister's new home.

∾

I had thought, with complete certainty, that nothing could be more unbearable than sharing dinner with the Frost King.

This is worse.

There is such a thing as agonized silence. No one speaks. The utensils clatter against the cracked clay dishware. We sit at a beautiful oaken table that Shaw built himself, in addition to the four chairs surrounding it. Though we share this dinner, we are not together. Elora and Shaw sit on one side of the table, and I sit on the other. My sister focuses on cutting into her hare. The meat is stringy, for there is little fat on the animal. I've grown accustomed to the rich foods served in the citadel, and I must be a truly horrible person to turn my nose up at what they offer, considering I once survived on such fare. Shaw chews on a potato. I sip from my wooden cup.

"This is a lovely meal," I offer.

Elora clears her throat, nods her head in appreciation.

Thankfully, Shaw attempts conversation. He speaks of their wedding, how happy a day it was. I ask how they fell in love. Supposedly, he began helping Elora around the house, fixing broken cabinets and chopping wood, and over time, they developed feelings for one another. To think, if I hadn't left, Elora would not have found someone to share her life with. Perhaps my departure was for the best.

"I'm happy for you," I say, attempting a smile. Because if I don't smile, I will cry, and I can't have that. "Truly."

Elora watches me gulp my wine over the rim of her cup. She sets it down, then shares a glance with Shaw. "There is news, Wren."

"Oh?" My pulse throbs in my temples. How much longer is acceptable before I can excuse myself?

"We're expecting."

The piece of meat in my mouth melts into an ashen lump. I choke and force myself to swallow. The only sound is the wind, its mournful wail as the cottage walls shake, and my soft, almost inaudible, stuttering breath.

My sister is going to be a mother.

"That's . . ." My fingers tremble around my fork. Too many emotions fight for attention. Elora always wanted a family, yet this came sooner than I expected. First she is married. Now she is pregnant. And I . . . I am trapped in a loveless marriage with a man who cannot stand my company, unaware of my motive to kill him. My airway closes with the realization that I have been replaced. Elora cares for Shaw, not I. Our cottage and life have been abandoned.

It takes a truly valiant effort to soften my features. This is Elora's day. I will never have what she does, but it's not her fault. I made my choice, and I have to live with it. "That's wonderful, Elora. You must be thrilled."

She picks at the cloth napkin in her lap, eyes downcast. "Yes."

I will be an aunt, but I will not be present to offer my support. She has Shaw, the town. She will be taken care of. It's what I always wanted for her. "Have you chosen a name?"

"Micah if it's a boy," Shaw says, squeezing Elora's hand atop the table. "And Iliana if it's a girl."

Iliana was our mother's name.

"They are wonderful names." I lift my cup to my mouth, only to realize it is empty. Elora stares as I refill it, but doesn't say anything. It matters not. Her disappointed gaze says enough.

I've resigned myself to a meal completed in silence when Elora says, "Wren, how are you still alive? I thought the Frost King sacrificed those he took."

I'd almost given up hope of Elora inquiring about my life. Better late than never. "He did sacrifice the women he took captive, but that stopped decades ago."

"So you're his prisoner?"

"Actually . . ." Here we go. "I married him."

"*What?*" She lurches upright in her chair, horrified. "Tell me that's not true."

That old shame rises in me, singeing the skin of my face.

"Wren." The word lashes out. "How can you marry that man? He is the one responsible for our misfortune!"

"You think I don't know that? I didn't have a choice."

She bows her head, properly abashed.

"It's not all bad," I say in a softer tone. "I'm left alone most days. I have free rein of the grounds." As long as I stay inside the walls. "And he is not as cruel as I first believed." Strange, how I find myself wanting to defend him from my sister, when he is an immortal who took me from my home.

"He let you visit Edgewood?"

"Yes."

"He isn't afraid you'll run away?"

I'm not sure why I lie. To look less like a failure? To stand against the pity on their faces? "He trusts me."

Elora's eyes widen. "Oh. That's . . . that's good."

"What is he like?" Shaw asks. Like the majority of Edgewood, he's curious of the North Wind. Curious—and terrified.

"He's . . . cold." Or maybe cold is the wrong word. *Remote* is a more apt description of his character. I've learned his stiff formality derives from his desire to remain separate. He struggles to connect with others. He is not sure how to navigate relationships. Not for the first time, I wonder why that is.

"Well," Elora says, "he *is* the Frost King. Unless he has another name?"

"Boreas." It's strange to think of him as such. A man rather than a myth. Flesh and blood. The word feels pleasant in my mouth, a sound of rolling curves.

"Boreas," says Elora.

I expect her to ask more questions about my life. How I spend my time, if I've made any friends. What it's like in the Deadlands. But Elora returns to her meal, signaling the end of conversation.

And that's that.

# CHAPTER

## 24

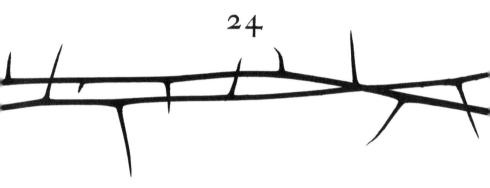

It is hours past midnight by the time I return to the frozen Les. The temperature has plummeted since the sun's disappearance. My coat provides adequate warmth, yet I barely notice it, barely notice the seepage of black shadows in my periphery. I pass through the land like smoke, frail and drifting. My thoughts circle without end.

Once I settle into the boat, the ice melts, and the current pulls me back through the Shade, all the way to where Phaethon awaits. He greets me upon my arrival, and I hurriedly climb into the saddle, my stiff fingers curling white-knuckled around the reins. He doesn't fuss. Merely turns to make his way through the Deadlands while I huddle in the saddle, wondering how everything went wrong.

I left Elora with little more than a lukewarm farewell. A wave, a pained smile, and I was gone. It was clear I had overstayed my welcome, if I had ever been welcome in the first place.

My chest pains me. My stomach sloshes with wine, my mind fogged, lethargic. The air is cold, but my sister's judgment was far colder, and I hadn't the means to defend myself against it. The ache worsens as the land rises and falls. It does not relent.

Eventually, I reach the entrance gates to the citadel. Iron barbs spear into the darkness: a warning to stay clear.

"State your name and purpose," a guard calls from the gatehouse.

Keeping one hand on the reins, I lower my hood.

It's so quiet I catch the sound of the man scrambling to an upright position. "My lady," he stutters. "My lord said you would not return until tomorrow."

"Open the gates, please."

"Yes, my lady. I'll inform my lord of your return."

"That won't be necessary," I call harshly. It's been a long, arduous night, and my heart feels as though it is full of stones. The last person I want to interact with at the moment is the king. My defenses are too weak. "I'll inform him of my return." Lies, but they don't need to know that.

"Yes, my lady."

The gate opens to allow me entry. Phaethon plods through, his head hanging low. His shadowy hooves clop against the stone courtyard. Upon reaching the stables, I dismount and lead him inside, taking time to remove his saddle and bridle in the wavering light of the lamp hanging from the post. I've unsaddled many a horse in my life, so I don't have to think while doing it. I don't *want* to think.

The darkwalker butts his snout against my shoulder in affection. I didn't think a corrupted spirit could ever be affectionate, but it seems I was wrong. I rub the soft nose, watching in fascination as the shadows ebb and flow, lapping at my hand like waves. "You are not such a brutish beast," I whisper to him, those black eyes taking me in with a surprising amount of intelligence.

A bucket of grooming brushes hangs on the stall door. How curious. Does a darkwalker need grooming? I choose a curry brush and begin moving it in a circular motion across the shadowy hide. Normally this would lift dander and dirt while distributing the oils throughout the coat, but I question its usefulness on a creature without hair. He appears to enjoy the motion however, his head lowered in contentment, so I continue, gradually moving toward his flank as my internal tumult quiets.

I'm nearly finished when the scent of cedar reaches me. I do not make my awareness of the Frost King known, not at first. I continue brushing Phaethon as if nothing is amiss. I'm curious of what the king will do, why he is at the stables. Yet moments pass, and still he does not speak.

"Are you going to stand there all night?" I demand.

His bootheels click in the stillness. I tuck my face near the darkwalker's cheek and continue to brush. Surprisingly, I notice a difference to the beast's shadows. They now shine with luminosity.

"How did you know it was me?"

My shoulders slowly relax. The Frost King's presence is not entirely unwelcome after my disastrous visit to Edgewood. At least I know what to expect with him. I am on stable ground, strangely enough. "Your smell."

"My smell?" He is near enough that his voice, piqued with interest, resonates against my back.

"Has no one ever told you that you smell of winter?"

There is a pause. I can almost feel his mind examining my words, turning them this way and that in a careful study. "What does winter smell like to you?"

It smells of sharp things. Something the body reacts to physically. I know the exact scent of an approaching storm. The crackling air and a cold so invasive you're certain it will kill you. Similarly, winter has a complex, layered scent. It borders on yearning, or perhaps nostalgia. Something you wish you could remember, but cannot. That is what the Frost King's smell reminds me of.

"Cedar," I tell him. Phaethon snorts against my neck. "There's a cedar tree in Edgewood that blooms when it's time for you to take a bride. Apparently, the trees are said to symbolize resiliency and strength."

"I have heard that," he says, rounding the other side of the stall where light pools.

A cloak hangs off his powerful frame, parted across the chest, revealing loose trousers and a long sleepshirt. Any sign of his usual strapped-down attire is absent. Without taking his gaze from me, he selects a dandy brush to remove the dirt I've brought to the surface of Phaethon's coat—though there is no dirt to speak of. "I thought you were staying the night."

We draw the brushes down the spirit's stomach in tandem. The open stable doors welcome the night sounds, a deep, moaning wind and creaking branches. He expects an answer, but I'm not ready to talk about it.

"Why do you brush Phaethon if he is in spirit form?" I ask. "He hasn't any hair."

"He was a horse once, but he turned to shadow when I was banished to this realm."

"Will he always remain a darkwalker?"

I sense his caution despite there being no outward sign of it. "I'm not sure. The first few decades, he remained in horse form, but over time, his soul grew corrupted. I assume, unless he returns to the City of Gods, that he will remain a darkwalker." Boreas stares at me, taking in my glassy-eyed gaze, the brushing having been forgotten. "He likes you."

"What's there not to like?"

His eyebrows hitch upward, as if conceding that point. He tosses his dandy brush into the bucket and says, "I want to show you something."

My intention was to return to my rooms, but I'm no closer to sleep than I was hours ago. Whatever it is he wishes to show me, it will help divert my attention from Elora. "All right." I return the curry brush to the bucket.

As it turns out, there are a few places I overlooked in my investigation of the grounds, because the Frost King stops at a door tucked into one of the corridors I failed to notice previously. "I could have sworn this door wasn't here before."

"You're correct," he says, pushing it open. "It's visible only to a select few."

Darkness blankets my vision—a swallowing mouth that sucks the Frost King across the threshold. After a moment's hesitation, I follow him down a set of damp stone steps that spiral deeper into the subterranean warren. At the bottom, a tunnel leads to a second set of stairs, which we ascend, higher and higher, winding around a fat, stone pillar. At the top, we reach a wooden door. The Frost King pushes it open, and my gasp shatters the surrounding quiet.

Green.

The color is so painfully vivid I shy away from the sight. It smells of the earth, like damp loam and decay, and it is blessedly warm. The chill against my skin begins to thaw.

It's a greenhouse.

A glass-encased chamber with a double vaulted ceiling, twin peaks like mountains drawing the glass to points above, encapsulates an area twice the size of Edgewood's town square. Moonlight pours through the geometric panes, dousing the area in shades of white and silver. There are trees—beautiful, sweeping, towering trees clumped like school children—and thick vines, and flowering plants tucked into pots, carpeting various tables and shelves, spilling across the ground. Everything clambers for space, leaving the narrowest path squeezing through the lush green beyond.

In wonder, I move toward a rose bush in full bloom. The flowers, fat as my palm, release a sugary scent. Red, pink, yellow, white. I'm staring into tints and hues I have never before seen.

My feet wander the moonlit path, and before long, the door disappears behind the density of interlocking leaves.

"Lilies," I say, dumbstruck. Pretty white flowers shaped like trumpets. Water burbles to my right. A shallow creek winks playfully at me as it flows across the rocky bottom of the bed. Ferns congregate on the banks, unfurling their long, crenated tongues to catch the moonlight that drips like candlewax.

"Are these . . . ?"

"Blackberries," the king says from behind.

Blackberries. Imagine that. Lightly, I trace the dark, bumpy skin of the fruit growing from the bush. It's not real. It can't be real. The land is naught but brittle, frozen wood, yet here lies a glass-encased heart, warm and beating and green.

"How is this possible?" I ask breathlessly.

Reaching over my shoulder, Boreas picks one of the berries and offers it to me. The juice stains his fingertips violet.

My eyes lift to his. A new intensity enters his gaze. An offering. But will I accept the gift?

*This means nothing*, I tell myself, even as I pluck the berry from his grasp and slip it between my lips. Sweetness explodes across my tongue. My throat tightens. It tastes like all the good things I've never had a chance to experience.

The Frost King grabs a small metal can and begins watering the plants. "My power works in two ways. I can call down winter and the winds, but I can banish them as well. I've set limits so they cannot cross into this space."

Two heartbeats later, the berry turns to flavorless paste in my mouth. Whatever amiable emotions I began to feel toward the king vanish, and I turn my back on him. I know he has the ability to banish this eternal winter. I know the face the Frost King wears. I know his heart, or lack of it. I know he cares for no one. Power is his comfort. Power is his shield. Power is his obsession.

The greenhouse did well enough to lure me into a feeling of false security, but now I see what the glass walls truly are: a prison.

"You are angry." He sounds puzzled.

"And you continually state the obvious."

Striding down the path, I walk until I lose sight of him. My solitude doesn't last. He trails me while I wander under the pretense of exploring the greenhouse, when I am really trying to put as much distance between us as possible. I pass a multitude of flowers, fruits I cannot identify, chasing the new smells, the spill of creeping groundcover brushing my ankles. The moon hits the glass just so, and the light all but sings. A pretty pocket of tranquility, yet no one is able to access it. The Frost King hides it away like the disgraceful secret it is.

At the curve ahead, the king appears, blocking my path, his arms crossed. "Why are you angry with me?"

"Have you ever considered what the world would be like if you got rid of winter altogether?"

The silence alters. It takes a new shape that loses its edge, a softening on the inside. "It will not change my mind," he says, "but I would like to know your perspective on the matter."

His eyes are not nearly as emotionless as I expected. That he is willing to listen to me speaks louder than any previous action.

"You are a god. As such, you have always been in a position of power. Even here, banished by your people, you reign over all. Whether eternal winter is your intention or not, you decide who lives and who dies."

Dropping his arms, he strides toward me, drawn by curiosity, compelled perhaps, as I am, by an unexplainable pull. "You think me cold and narrow-minded."

That sounds about right. "Yes."

"I think you brash and reckless."

I shrug, letting the sting of his thoughts slide down my back. "You're entitled to your opinion."

"I did not ask to be a god. I was born immortal, granted strength and power. It is all I know."

"No," I correct him. "It is all you *allow* yourself to know."

His lips part in retaliation, but by then, I'm moving past him. The trail eventually splits. I go right, crossing a small footbridge arching over the trickling creek.

"If I must suffer," the Frost King calls to my back, "then others must suffer, too."

A god speaks of suffering. How quaint.

I'm so disgusted by his lack of self-awareness that I consider strangling him with one of these vines. He can't die, but at the very least, I will be rid of this lashing emotion, this turmoil that refuses to abate in his presence, only mutates into something frightening and unrecognizable. A black, eroding thing.

Whirling around, I bare my teeth and spit, "You, Boreas, are the most selfish, narrow-minded, heartless god I've ever had the misfortune of meeting, much less marrying! You speak of suffering, yet food piles your table like mountains, your clothes are made of the thickest furs, you live in a fortress able to house thousands, and disease cannot ruin your body." I step toward him. He retreats, knocking against one of the hanging plants. "You are not burdened by your life."

His nostrils flare with impatience. It is a victory. The more cracks in his armor, the more human he appears. I seek what lies beneath that hardened exterior. I seek the truth. Maybe then we would not be so different, he and I. "Think what you will of me—"

"I do."

"—but know that a mortal's suffering ends with death. A god's suffering is forever."

I'm reminded of the scars coiling up his back. Is that what he refers to? Might he have other scars, internal, like my own? I've glimpsed pain in him, however fleeting. "Tell me," I demand. "Tell me how you have suffered." So that I may not loathe the sight of my husband day in and day out.

"I have suffered," he says, "more than you could ever imagine. But my suffering is not what pains you. It is not what dims your spirit." His throat dips with his swallow. "Will you tell me what happened at your village?"

I'm not sure what's more shocking: that he recognizes my pain, or that he seeks to remedy it. "Why do you even care?" I whisper. My well-being is irrelevant to him. So long as I am alive, he can use my blood to fortify the Shade. His tool sharpened at will.

"You are my wife," he says, as if that is all the explanation needed. He picks a rose from a nearby bush, passes it into my hand. "Tell me."

I want to tell him. I don't want to tell him. I want to be alone. I want company—any company, even his. He utters a command, yet it is phrased as a question. It is for that reason alone I reveal this dark, rotted seed that has rooted inside me.

"My sister is married now. Our home sits empty." Although I did not attend the wedding, I imagine Elora would have been a lovely bride. She would have worn our mother's wedding dress, with the beaded sleeves and sweetheart neckline. An elegant dress for an elegant woman. "She invited me to dinner with her husband, Shaw." A sweet, sugary scent rises to my nostrils, and I realize I have crushed the flower in my hand. The mangled red petals float to the ground.

Boreas frowns at the discarded flower. He looks like he might say something, but he gifts me silence so that I may continue my story.

"Shaw is a good man. Dependable. Loyal and doting. I sat at their dinner table and did not know the woman sitting across from me. I thought Elora would be happy to see me, but she wasn't."

There is nothing I would not do for my sister. Always, I sought to make her feel safe and loved. I built the walls of our lives, the roof, the door. Does Elora not realize every sacrifice I ever made was for her?

"Why wasn't she happy to see you?"

A deep, fortifying breath. "The night you came to Edgewood, I promised I wouldn't leave her. But I broke that promise when I gave her a sleeping draught, took her place without her knowledge. She was angry with me. She said . . ."

No. I cannot, will not, say it. Not in front of him.

"What did she say?" Gently.

I feel my will crumbling. And I wonder if it would be so terrible if I stopped trying to patch the holes. If I let the pieces fall. If I am brave enough for that.

"She was cruel." Barbs meant to wound, and they did. "She said my actions were selfish."

"And that hurt you," he says, as if he understands, but how could he possibly understand when he does not know me?

I'm reaching unaware for another flower, the petals colored like muted sunlight. "All my life I have cared for Elora. I made sure there was food on the table. I sewed her coats and dresses. I kept our cottage warm, ensured there was always firewood. Sometimes I was forced to travel hundreds of miles just to fell an animal." And to act as though my actions meant nothing? It feels like servitude.

The nearby creek bubbles and gurgles and sings. When the Frost King speaks, his voice is soft. "I do not think what you did was selfish. Rather, I believe it was self*less*."

My gaze cuts to his in surprise. His expression lacks the remoteness I've come to expect, but it is definitely guarded. At least I'm not the only one uncomfortable with this conversation.

"Thank you," I say stiffly. And I mean it. I do.

He glances at me, then away. "People do not always say what they mean. It is possible your sister misses your presence."

As possible as it is for a tree to birth a pig. Elora's sentiment toward me was plain. "No, I'm certain she does not. She said more. The selfish comment wasn't even the worst of it."

"You don't have to continue. Not if it will cause you pain."

The flower is still caught in my hand, its velvety texture pleasant beneath the pads of my fingers. He regards me calmly. He sounded honest. Of course, that is exactly why I don't believe him. "We may not like one another," I say tartly, "but you do not have to be cruel about it." I'd prefer the Frost King's callous nature instead of this false compassion.

His eyebrows creep slowly upward. "You think I lie?"

I did. Now I am unsure.

"Why would I seek to cause you pain?"

Because that is what he has been doing—unintentionally or otherwise—my entire life? What is it he wants to know? Weaknesses to exploit? Mistrust is my only armor. If I am to let that go, if I am to believe the king asks because he desires to know my deepest, most hidden thoughts, I do not know what that means. If I cannot read him, I have lost ground. If I am unsure, I have weakened my stance.

One step brings him closer. The leaves stamp shadows onto his skin. The planes of his cheekbones flow into that angular jaw and full mouth. When the vines stir at my back, I gasp at the sensation of one trailing down my spine in a teasing touch, curling lightly around my wrist like a bracelet. I look down. It's covered in tiny white flowers with pale, sunny centers.

"How are you doing this? I thought only Zephyrus could control plants."

"You are correct. I am merely bending the air around the vine." His eyelids drift closed, slitting the blue gaze beneath. "You have not answered my question."

We are having a conversation, my husband and I, and there is little animosity between us. It is not so bad, I think.

"Elora's life is full," I whisper, pained. "She doesn't need me anymore." And I do not know who I am if I'm not caring for someone. If I'm not needed, am I obsolete? If I'm not needed, what reason has she, or anyone for that matter, to choose me?

The Frost King considers this, head tilted. It's a relief to find no judgment in his gaze. "How do you know she doesn't need you?" He reaches toward me, and I stiffen, thinking he might do something rash like touch my face. But his hand passes over my shoulder, and when it retreats, a blue flower is all but swallowed by his fingers.

Another step toward me. "How do you know she doesn't need you?" he presses, voice deepening.

My skin tingles from his proximity. It's the chill he carries with him, I tell myself. Nothing more. "Because she didn't tell me."

"Just because someone does not say it aloud," says the king, "does not mean that person doesn't need you."

Does he speak of my sister? Or does he speak of someone else?

"It doesn't matter." My tongue darts out to wet my lips. He stands too close for comfort but I haven't the courage to shove him back. "Elora has the life she wants, and I'm . . . alone."

It is done. Finally, at last, I have spoken aloud this fear, yet I feel no better for it. I've only revealed yet another weakness.

"You have Orla," he points out. "And Zephyrus," he adds, though reluctantly. "Silas, the cook."

A knot of emotion lodges in my throat. "It's not that." If only it were that easy.

Something sharpens in his gaze, as if he reaches an understanding. "Then what is it?"

Maybe I want to free myself from this shame. Maybe I want to make *some* connection with the man who is my husband, regardless of my feelings toward him. Whatever the reason, I don't hold back.

"I am alone in here," I say, pressing a hand to my heart.

The creases around Boreas' eyes smooth with unexpected solemnity. I wince. I can't believe I dumped that emotional baggage onto him. He does not care. And I am a fool.

Except the king doesn't leave. Rather, he lowers his head, and my hand lifts to rest over his heart. To push him back, I tell myself, even as my fingers curl into the front of his bedclothes, the fabric warmed from his body. His palm—wide, calloused—shapes the curve of my hip before slipping to my back, and my pulse rises, it leaps upward and climbs.

"Please," he whispers. His scent floods my senses, crisp and clean.

My tongue refuses to cooperate. My heart careens toward an unknown destination. The space between our bodies shrinks to nothing. His thighs brush mine, the hand on my lower spine hot as a brand. "Please . . . what?"

"Please don't stab me for this."

That is the last I see of his eyes, for the Frost King closes the distance, fitting his mouth seamlessly to mine.

His lips are dry, yet warm. He parts my mouth with the barest pressure, but it goes no further than that. His very breath is cool, and floods my mouth like the iciest of breezes.

The kiss doesn't last more than a few heartbeats. When he pulls away, my head is spinning.

The king has nearly reached the greenhouse door before I realize he has moved.

"Wait."

His footsteps slow and come to a standstill. My knees wobble. I cling to the back of a chair so I don't collapse. "Why did you kiss me?"

Boreas turns his head so that I'm given a view of his face in profile. "I, too, know what it's like to be alone." His eyes lift, the blue so pure and unguarded I feel as though I am seeing him for the first time. "Maybe we can be alone together."

# CHAPTER

## 25

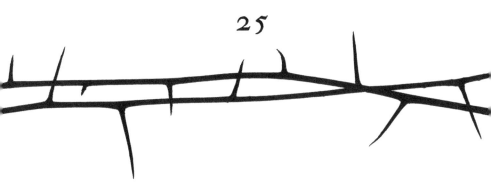

*Maybe we can be alone together.*

It's all I've been able to think about the last three days. The memory lingers like a cloud of hot air. It sits inside me, circulating through, until it coats my tongue: his taste, potent and sweet and divine.

I've spent all afternoon exploring the citadel. Thirty-two doors in the east wing, adding those discoveries to my growing map. My explorations led me here, to the gaping interior of a stone cathedral, the columns like ribs, the vaulted ceiling full of one's breath. Long, rectangular stained glass windows brighten the lamplit interior, and rows of worn benches bisected by a long pathway fill the space. At the end stands the altar, stone draped in cloth, a circular window placed at its back, its jeweled tones rivaling the sun.

Perched on one of the benches, I close my eyes, let the distant echoing hymns drift through my mind as I reexamine every gesture, every glance we've exchanged since that night. Every so often, my fingers graze my lower lip. Something happened in that greenhouse. Something that felt terrifyingly like a truth. I've kissed plenty of men. What Boreas and I shared could hardly be considered a kiss, but it shook me down to the soles of my feet.

I didn't think the Frost King was capable of compassion. To comfort me, a mortal and his wife, whom he has shown time and again he does not care for. Something is changing in him. Softening.

I'm not sure of my way forward. It would be so much easier to hate him if he blasted me with that damn ice spear. With the poppy plant in Zephyrus' possession, I'll soon have the tonic, the means to end my suffering. I only wonder if that unchanging path, and my own, are still one and the same or if they are beginning to diverge.

Pushing to my feet, I retrace my steps back to the hallway, shutting the door behind me. I search the citadel until I find Orla attacking the cobwebs in one of the large, unoccupied ballrooms. White sheets cover the multitude of tables and stacked chairs. Long, draping curtains veil the windows, shrouding the space. A shame, really. Were sunlight to stream through, it would make the most magnificent gathering space.

I wait until she descends the ladder. "Orla?"

A smear of dust darkens the bridge of her nose. She puffs her exertion, the other servants wiping dust from the fireplace mantels, the ceiling rafters. It seems pointless, since the room sits vacant. "Yes, my lady?"

"I was wondering—" The words catch behind my teeth. They need a little push. "Is there something Boreas enjoys doing? A preferred pastime, maybe?"

Orla, wiping her hands on her skirts, appraises me with an odd look. "Is there a specific reason, my lady?"

I'm not about to divulge the details of my calamitous visit to Edgewood, so I stick to a shallower truth. "He helped me the other day, and I would like to thank him somehow."

He did not judge me. He did not brush aside my fears. He did not abandon me. He chose to stay, and I am afraid of what it means.

Orla looks thoughtful. "The lord is partial to reading."

Reading. I knew this. And then I remember one chance meeting in particular, after I'd spent the evening wandering cobblestoned streets. Maybe I'll ask him if he would like to accompany me to the theater.

The idea takes hold. With a hurried *thank you*, I go in search of Boreas. Taking the stairs to the third level, I halt. The south wing entrance sits to my left. The north wing entrance sits to my right, an air of abandonment surrounding it.

No guards.

Boreas dispatched the majority of his force to the Shade in an attempt to stymie infiltration into the Deadlands. Today, there is no one to prevent entrance into this forbidden wing. One of the doors sits open a crack. I'm not in my right mind. I think of that kiss, and I wonder. Who is the North Wind? What scars does he bear that I cannot see?

Against my better judgment, I cross into the north wing. Resting my fingertips against the partially open door, I push. The hinges swing open soundlessly.

I'm greeted by pale yellow walls that may have once been sunny, but that now appear sickly in the gloom. The space is much smaller than I expected. Charcoal drawings hang from the walls, trees and stick figures and mountains. A large, stuffed bear sits in the corner, black button eyes staring vacantly. Curtains drawn. A frayed blue rug covers the floor.

It's a child's room, with a child's bed, blankets twisted atop the mattress as if someone recently left, though the air is stagnant and closed. Whoever slept in this room is gone and has been for a long time.

A bookshelf spans the length of one wall. Of course, I am drawn there first. I crack open one of the books. It's full of large, blocky letters paired with paintings of animals. I flip through another volume with pictures of whimsical clouds before returning it to its place and assessing the room with new eyes. Dust coats everything in a thick layer.

It never crossed my mind that Boreas could be a father. I associate parentage with love, affection, selflessness. He has never displayed those traits. But is it possible he might have, once? And as I stand here, surrounded by memories that are not mine, I wonder. Where is the child now? Where is the mother of this child?

My feet carry me to the other side of the room. At the foot of the bed sits a wooden chest. Inside lies a collection of seemingly random objects, but as I sort through them, my understanding of this abandoned room begins to clarify. A small box contains more drawings with various titles. *To Papa. Mama, Papa, and Me. Me and Papa. Mama and the Snow.* My heart beats unsteadily, for in some drawings, the man named Papa holds a spear. His hair is black, his eyes blue. They are dated over three hundred years ago.

Returning the drawings to their box, I shut the chest and turn away, my throat uncomfortably tight.

A stack of dusty books rests on the bedside table, as well as a piece of wood carved in the shape of a bird. The wood is cool against my skin, the object like a toy, perhaps, and fits perfectly in my hand.

"What are you doing here?"

The words slap my back like a stinging rain, and I whirl to find Boreas frozen in the doorway, his silhouette backlit by the hallway sconces. The flat rage in his eyes sends me back a step. "Boreas." My hip bumps the bedpost.

In three strides, he reaches me, snatching the figurine from my hand and, gently, returning it to the nightstand. The sight of his large fingers curved around the small object sends a wave of confusing sadness through me.

"Who said you could enter this room?" he hisses.

My attention swings back to his face. He takes another menacing step toward me, and it is like his arrival at Edgewood all over again: the pit in my stomach, the fear sweeping across my skin in chill bumps. The strength and breadth of his body cloaks mine. He could tear me in half so easily. "The guards—" My mouth is so dry it takes multiple attempts to croak out, "—said I could pass—"

Frost shrieks as it crawls from beneath his feet to coat the floor and walls. His glove-clad hands twitch at his sides. "There are no guards," he growls. "You lie. You always lie."

I mince sideways, slowly rounding the bed, not daring to shift my attention from the god whose eyes darken with unspeakable power. I don't think it's my imagination. No sign of those blue irises, only enlarged pupils that push against the white sclerae.

"You're right," I rush to say. "There weren't any guards, but I saw the door was open . . ."

"So you took it upon yourself to enter a space you had no business entering."

"No." My teeth chatter. "Well, yes, but it wasn't as though I was intentionally trying to upset you." *Hurt you.* For is not anger the bud, hurt and betrayal the roots? It is not fury in his eyes, not really. It is devastation. An overwhelming, fractured thing. "I didn't know," I gasp.

A rattle invades my chest as he takes another step forward. My legs knock into a table in my haste to put distance between us. The air slithers and stirs. Strands of hair float around my head as a breeze picks up, crackling with potent energy and a rage the likes I've never seen before.

The wind rises.

"Boreas." I flinch as a vase shatters. "Boreas, calm yourself!"

A gust tears through the room, tossing objects and pieces of furniture left and right. I duck to avoid a small projectile. The books fling from their shelves, ripped parchment, worn cloth.

A table splinters upon hitting the wall. The blankets covering the bed peel away like old skin. The room deteriorates piece by piece, and there the North Wind stands, in the eye of that squall.

"You have deceived me since the moment I took you from Edgewood," he booms. His voice is the air, and the air is thunder. "You have done everything in your power to weaken my resolve, to undermine my command, and I have granted you far more leniency than you deserve. But this is where it ends."

At the word *ends*, I grow cold. His face appears to be changing. My every breath screams at me to run, but terror has rooted my feet to the ground.

The first column collapses, a clean crack through the center. An ominous groan draws my attention upward. Fissures scatter through the ceiling, widening into rifts. All at once, a portion of the stone caves in a spitting rain of rock and dust, and I lunge to the side, the rock crushing the ground where I'd stood moments before.

My eyes are wet when they find the Frost King behind the thickening cloud of debris. "I'm sorry," I whisper. "I didn't think—"

"You never do." His coat flaps around him. The whites of his eyes at last succumb to shadow. "You think only of what you can gain, without thought for others."

It's not true. I think of everyone *but* myself, right?

Except he's right. I wanted to know what lay behind the door despite Boreas' insistence that I do not enter the north wing. I never, not once, took his wish into account. I never respected it because I didn't think he was worthy of that respect, and this realization has come too late.

"You think I don't know how deeply your loathing of me runs?" he growls gutturally. "You think I'm ignorant of the knives you carry, your desire to drive them into my skin until it splits into ribbons, drive them into my blackened heart?" An insidious laugh slithers from his mouth, between those sharp, dripping fangs.

"That's not it," I croak. "It was a mistake. It wasn't intentional—"

A feeble shriek flies from my mouth. His hands. The fingers lengthen, curl inward, and the gloves split apart as long, curved talons puncture through the fabric, revealing grotesque claws that ooze shadow. My eyes dart to his neck. The paleness of Boreas' skin is gone, overwhelmed by writhing black tendrils that crawl across his face.

Boreas is a darkwalker.

I scramble backward so fast I trip over my feet and go sprawling across the floor. His towering form hunches forward, spine and limbs rearranging themselves. It's not real, it's not real, it's not real—

He releases a roar that blasts outward with concussive force.

A wave of power slams me into the wall. My head cracks against stone. I crumple, my body so flooded with adrenaline it aches to move.

"Leave!" He blurs as the grime gathers into a spinning cloud, lacerating the walls with the coldest, harshest, most invasive wind.

Coughing on a lungful of dust, I lurch for the doorway. The wind plows into my back, pinning me against a column until I manage to claw free of its grip. It lashes at my heels as I flee down the corridor, taking the stairs two at a time. At the ground floor, I catch the staircase railing and use my momentum to swing myself into the entrance hall, which echoes with my crashing footsteps.

"My lady!"

Orla's shrill voice pierces my fear-addled mind. Can't stop. Adrenaline fires my blood, and I'm bursting through the front doors, boots slapping on stone.

The gate opens, and I am through, escaping straight into the snow-deadened woods surrounding the citadel. I flee as I have never fled before, and I pray to whatever gods remain that my life is not forfeit.

# CHAPTER
## 26

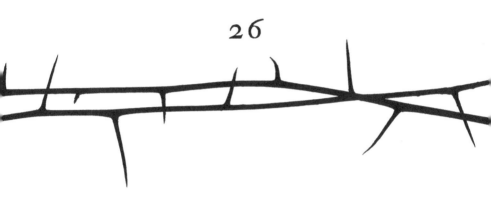

I am going to die.

For too long, I've avoided looking this truth in the eye. It is too frightening a thing. But there is something to be said about acceptance. The water rises—chest, neck, chin. Mouth, then throat, then lungs. It feels like weakness to give in, but fighting tires me. And so at last I inhale. The pain dulls and I drift and there is peace.

Except my body has mutinied against me. Since my harrowing flight from the citadel, the sun has risen and set five times. The sky has deepened, lightened, darkened again in quick succession.

The first two days were a blur. Deeper and deeper, I plunged into the forgotten wilds of the Deadlands with no destination in mind. The king demanded I go, and so I went, spurred by the fear of his reprisal, those blackening eyes and lengthening nails. At the time, I'd thought nothing of the freedom he'd given me. Free of his fortress, but not free of the Deadlands.

Sickness hit at the close of the second day.

It arrived as a tearing sensation through my stomach lining. My feet stumbled, and I hunched over, whimpering as pain flooded my every pore. I grew dizzy, no longer certain of the direction I had traveled from. A wavering, snow-heavy sight before me, and cold, terrible cold. By some miracle, I stumbled upon an abandoned burrow. It was there I collapsed, tucked beneath the overarching roots of a fallen tree, and where I remain days later.

A storm blew in on the third day. It pounded snow onto the earth and forced me to carve out a breathing hole. The temperature continued to drop with the approaching night. I could not move as time leaked out, could not even begin to separate reality from the fog.

It is now day five. An eternity, really. My throat sears. It craves the drink, but my hands are empty. Sweat coats me from head to toe, cooling my feverish skin. Every so often my stomach heaves and I retch, expelling nothing but watery bile from the small, very small amount of snow I've ingested. Eating snow lowers one's body temperature, but if I eat enough of it, it tastes like wine. Almost.

My thoughts circle listlessly. Cracked lips and a parched mouth, the rasp of my tongue felt inside my head. The agony runs so deep it melts my bones, rips open my nerves, as though some growth erupts beneath my skin. My heart beats like it is struggling to hold on.

I have no cloak, no gloves, no hood. I fled the citadel with only my dress and leggings, a thin layer of wool all that protects me from the most ruthless elements. It is my belief that only the fever raging through my body has kept me alive for this long.

It is so cold I've begun to feel warm.

So yes, I am going to die. Sleep will take me first. A slow death, but at least it won't hurt. Isn't that what I want? For this nightmare to end?

My eyes prick with tears, which immediately crystallize, pinching the skin of my eyelids. A dark shape wavers before me. The shape mutates, stretching open a black maw, folding itself forward so that I'm staring into two chipped holes in a face. The sight dissipates with my next blink.

Another tear in my abdomen. I hunch into a tighter ball with a frail cry. "Elora," I whisper.

But Elora is not here. She is far away, safe at home with her husband. I will not be able to say goodbye.

It is that thought, clean when all the rest are clouded, that shocks something inside me awake. I am as proud as they come, but am I so proud I would not return to the Frost King, begging for my life?

These are my lies:

Elora needs me.

The Frost King is my enemy.

Nothing can break me.

These are my truths:

Elora chose Shaw over me.

The Frost King is my husband.

I am already broken.

I think I've been broken for a long time. I've lived with this hole in my chest for so long I got used to it. I adapted because I hadn't a choice. Caring for Elora gave me purpose following the death of our parents. Any inkling of sadness, fear, unhappiness—I shoved it down, far into the dark. I told myself these feelings, my feelings, did not matter. Until I began to believe it.

And then the North Wind arrived at Edgewood and I decided my life did not matter. I made a decision then: sacrifice. Rash and foolish it may have been, but if I were to relive that moment, I believe I'd choose no differently.

I then vowed to kill the Frost King, put an end to my suffering, and return home to the life that awaited me. But over the months, something changed. I learned Boreas was not so rigid, or callous. As we spent time together, he offered me pieces of himself, and I accepted them with the sole intention of fashioning them into blades, sliding them into all the soft parts of his body. But he'd gifted me those pieces. And that changed things. It changed everything.

Fool that I am, I sank into that lull. I began to forget who and what he was. But he reminded me. Oh, he reminded me.

I feel like a complete idiot for not recognizing the signs. Boreas is a darkwalker. Probably the same darkwalker I sensed beyond my bedroom door that first month. The Frost King, too dangerous to let live, sent me away to die. And I went, because I had forgotten how to fight.

It shames me. I have always fought. I have never given in. Always, I have pushed through darkness and cold, toward a fire I cannot see. Why did I stop? Why did I continually make myself smaller, less than? Everyone dies. But not everyone has a choice as to how they will go.

If I am going to die, it will be on my terms. On my feet, not on my knees. And I would rather leave this world knowing I took the Frost King with me.

"Get up, Wren."

The voice is mine. The frigid air slips into my mouth and sears my teeth.

"Get up." The other choice is death, and I am not ready for that just yet.

My joints ache, and my wind-chafed skin twinges like a painful rash, but I manage to crawl from the burrow and push to my feet, using a fallen tree for support. After days spent curled in a ball, it hurts to stand.

Yet there's a fire in me. It pushes me into a stumble, then a walk, and I keep walking, retracing my steps, clambering over fallen trees and tracking the changes in elevation. I've been traveling west this entire trek, so it isn't difficult to return east. All I do is follow the rising sun.

I'm so delirious with cold that I don't immediately recognize the signs. The deep gouges in the otherwise pristine snow. Tree trunks splintered into twigs. And a change in the atmosphere, the air sharpening with an ash-like odor. A ripple in the realm, something beyond this world.

A frail, eerie wail startles me. I halt, glancing around, and notice how strong the reek of burning has become. Strong enough that I wonder if it's already too late.

Ordering my fatigued body into motion, I push eastward. The cry came from the south. After a few more wobbly paces, I stop, listening carefully for sounds of movement. It is close. It is coming.

No time. I scramble across the snow toward a hole in a tree and discover a dead animal inside the entrance. The decay chokes me. It's cold enough for snow, but some days the air has warmed unexpectedly. I hold my breath and crawl into the opening, eyes watering.

Eventually, the darkwalker heaves its grotesque body into view.

It's absolutely massive. The largest, ugliest, most horrendous thing I've ever seen. A gargantuan nightmare of long, spindly limbs; a block head; and misshapen shoulders. Wisps of shadows trail it like strips of torn fabric. I swallow around the knot of fear in my throat.

I have a dagger—a paltry butter knife in the face of death. Do I risk cutting into my skin to coat the blade in blood? It will attract any darkwalker within the vicinity, but salt is my only protection. Without it, the metal will slice right through the shadowy substance.

Breath held, I watch the creature snuffle around the base of the tree. It's picked up the scent of the decaying animal carcass. The bulk of its substantial frame lurches with every thunderous step. That abhorrent snout, crammed with broken teeth, pushes aside the snow. I press deeper into the tree's hollow. I have long since believed in the gods, but I pray now. If not for life, then a swift death.

And maybe they listen. Maybe my prayers are answered because after a few curious sniffs, the darkwalker trundles away. Only when the reek has cleared do I scramble free. And now I run. I don't stop.

By the time the citadel comes into view, it's dark. The turrets twist against the mountain, black on black. The wall rises in height as I near. It is a cold, unforgiving, and unwelcoming place. It has never, not once, felt like home.

Keeping to the shadows, I seek out the hole in the outer wall near the practice court and crawl through on hands and knees. From there, I backtrack to the northern courtyard. The Frost King's bedroom is the third window to the right in the north wing, third floor. Identifying his bedroom was one of the first tasks I'd given myself, and I managed to spot him in the window many weeks prior. As luck would have it, a dead tree slants against the wall of the citadel, and it is tall enough to allow me to reach the window.

The rotted crack at the base of the trunk serves as an adequate foothold. Reaching for one of the lower boughs, I haul myself onto the branch, climbing steadily upward. The shadows clumped against the wall shield me from the guards atop the wall, those completing their rounds below. Sweat springs to my skin, my lungs heave, but at least I am alive.

Searching out the next handhold, I scramble higher. My limbs tremble with fatigue. Up, up, until I'm balanced on the tallest branch, my face inches from the window. Moonlight shines onto the glass, tossing my reflection back at me.

I do not recognize this woman. Dark, crescent-shaped bruises rest beneath her bloodshot eyes. Her hair hangs in damp lanks, unbrushed and unwashed. The scar, however, is familiar: a savage mark upon her face, a reminder that the past is never truly gone.

I've always avoided my reflection. I've been ashamed of my appearance. I've felt lacking. As for this woman, vengeance has burned holes into her heart, reducing it to a shredded bit of cloth. She cannot go on living like this. *I* cannot go on living like this.

A gentle push against the pane of glass, and it swings open noiselessly. Overconfident prick that he is, Boreas wouldn't expect his wife to climb through the window with murder on her mind.

The king's quarters are thrice the size of mine, with multiple doorways leading to rooms beyond sight. No fire warms the hearth. Thick drapery conceals the windows, with only the barest sliver of moonlight squeezing through. The walls are not stone, as I have come to expect, but paneled in dark wood. An enormous bookcase extends across the entire southern wall.

The king himself is a dark shape atop his bed. He sleeps on his side, hair fanning black across the white pillows, the blanket pooling around his waist. The wide span of his back—pale skin and paler scars—all but glows. In sleep, he appears harmless enough. His breath itself sounds like the wind.

Steeling myself, I approach his bedside. In the blurred shadows, I can almost convince myself he is a man, mortal, were his face not forged to perfection. How many times have I imagined this situation? I hold the power at last, and I have come to set myself, my people, free.

His spear is nowhere in sight, but that is to be expected. His dagger, however, rests on the bedside table. The hilt cools my hot, sweaty palm. It is firm where I feel unstable.

In one seamless motion, I slide the weapon free of its sheath, the tip kissing the base of his throat.

His eyes snap open.

*Blue, blue, blue—*

It takes half a heartbeat for clarity to replace the sleep in his gaze. Surprise settles in the lines of his hauntingly beautiful mien, and it does not leave. "Wife," he murmurs.

My hand flinches. "Don't call me that."

His chin lifts a fraction as he searches my face. "But that is who you are. My wife." His skin glows with an incandescent sheen despite the lack of light. As usual, he keeps his reaction under careful guard, though the fold between his eyebrows reveals his puzzlement. "I thought I sent you away."

I lean into him, one of my knees pressed into the mattress for leverage. "It's going to take a little more than a bit of wind to stop me from completing my task."

"And that is?" Calm. Frighteningly calm. Since opening his eyes, he has yet to blink.

"I think you know."

A slight nod, as if conceding a point. "Killing me."

I bare my teeth as my stomach gives a warning lurch. I pray I do not retch. "Why do you look unsurprised?"

"That you have decided to kill me?" He inhales a slow, deep breath. "I knew you would make an attempt. You harbor much anger toward me. Eventually, it would take control."

"If you knew," I demand, "why didn't you stop me?"

The dark fringe of his eyelashes lowers to shield his gaze from mine. "You are here against your will. I have taken that choice from you, but I did not want to take away your autonomy."

My heart quickens its dulled beat. I shouldn't believe him, yet I do. He has little to lose in telling the truth. "Am I the first wife to attempt to kill you?"

"No. But you are the first one I believed might succeed."

I lean closer. He sucks in air through his mouth, as though drawing my exhale into his lungs. "You sent me away. Left me to die out in the cold. Killing you would be a mercy."

"I've told you before. I am a god—"

"You're no god," I hiss. "You're a darkwalker."

He stiffens. My knee slides closer to his thigh. I don't recall changing position, but now I hover atop him lengthwise.

"Do you deny it?"

He glances away. "No."

A bark of disbelieving laughter breaks free. "All this time you warned me not to venture beyond the gates, when a darkwalker occupied these halls. The king himself." Irony can be so cruel. "Does anyone know?"

"No." A pause before he goes on. "The transformation has been gradual. I've yet to reach the point of no return."

Doesn't matter. He lied. He put my life, the lives of his staff, people like Orla, in danger. He cannot live.

"I've put protective measures in place." An attempt to explain himself. "If I begin to lose control—"

"You think this is about you? It's never been about you. It's about me." Through my tightening airway, I hiss, "You took *everything* from me. My mother, my father, my sister. You have no idea the ways in which I've suffered by your hand. This will end. My suffering will end, the suffering of my people. I don't care if I have to kill you a thousand times for winter to finally break." I push the knife in deeper. Men I have killed. Never a god.

May his death be a symbol. Death to my grief. Death to my torment. Death to power. Death to the dark water that has closed over my head.

Yet I don't move.

"You have come this far," he says, strangely intense as the dagger point slices the vulnerable skin of his neck. A drop of blood slides down its curve, collecting in the hollow of his throat. "Why stop now?"

Indeed.

He presses forward so the dagger sinks in further. "Kill me."

My fingers tremble around the hilt, and I swallow. It should be simple. It should be an act of complete effortlessness. My stomach tenses in anticipation of the blade parting flesh. It is not murder. It is retribution. Restoration. The North Wind has no true heart to speak of, no love but his power. So why do I feel as though I'm making a mistake?

My eyes sting, and the pressure spreads through my skull. I have hardened every part of myself, but what if it does not work on him? He has seen the inner workings of my heart, things I have revealed to no one else. He did not turn away. I have not forgotten that.

"Kill me," Boreas demands. "Finish it."

Through my trembling, I grit, "I can't." Oh, how I hate that word.

He studies me warily. "Why not?"

"If I knew," I say, voice cracking, "do you think I would be in this position?" If I had known what lay behind that door in the north wing, I never would have opened it. Because there was pain in that room, tarnishing that empty bed, the dusty children's books. I tore open a wound and he suffered, and I should be glad, but I'm not and I haven't the slightest idea why.

Sobs tear from a deep, black place inside me. The bed shakes from the intensity of my trembling. "I hate you," I spit, the sound garbled and wretched, choked by my own shame. "I hate you so much. And I'm sorry." The rage fades. "I'm sorry about the room. I didn't know . . ."

My head hangs. Tears and sweat slide down my nose, spattering the Frost King's bare chest. Had I made this decision months ago, the blade would have punctured his heart. No remorse. But I waited. First I waited for the opportune moment. Then I waited because he began to treat me kindly. And now, at the moment of having to act, needing to act, I hesitate.

I've failed in carrying out this task. Does that make me weak? Has cowardice always lurked in my heart? Even if I kill the Frost King, my situation will not change. I am still trapped here, without a means to leave the Deadlands. I am still unbearably alone.

"I have nowhere to go." The words are hoarse, strained by confession. "I can't return to Edgewood." What is left for me there but the remnants of an old life?

If I do not belong in the Deadlands, if I do not belong in Edgewood, then where do I belong? Where is home for me?

"I know you told me to leave," I whisper.

He is so still his heart beats visibly against his sternum. He is a shadow against the darker backdrop of the room.

Boreas says, in a quiet way, "What do you need?"

My chin wobbles, because I did not realize how much I desired to hear those words. "I need—" The Frost King? No, I don't need him. I don't *want* him. I need comfort. I need compassion. I need patience and understanding. I need to know that someone in this world needs me, too. I know Boreas doesn't. It's a ridiculous notion. But he kissed me. He told me he was alone, like me. So is it so bad, to voice this to him? "I n-need . . ."

His hand envelopes mine, his skin rough, yet warm—the first true touch of compassion I've received in months. I cry harder, each sob choked, because I didn't realize how starved I've been. Of all the people to show kindness to me now—my husband, and the man I find I cannot kill.

My grip loosens around the weapon. Without removing his eyes from mine, Boreas slides the dagger free of my trembling fingers and tosses it onto the ground.

"Wren," he says. "You're safe now."

I'm too distraught to move. Everything has gone so wrong, but as his arms slip around me, gathering my body to his warm, solid chest, I settle. Thrashed in the fury of a storm, I find a sliver of calm.

The world drifts into sensation: hot skin against my cheek, the slow drag of his breath, the scrape of his calloused palms against my skin.

Then: softness at my back. I crack open my eyes. Boreas stands over me, tucking the blanket around my stiff, chilled body. I'm in my chambers, nestled in the panoply of pillows. The fire, having died to embers, etches his naked torso in burnished light.

Leaning forward, the king tucks a strand of hair behind my ear, frowning slightly. And that is the last I remember of this night.

# PART 2

# HOUSE OF DREAMS

# CHAPTER

## 27

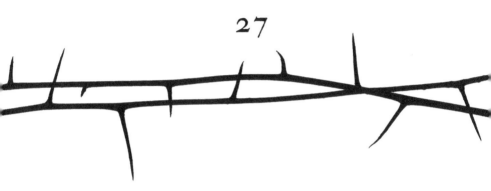

The morning greets me with a cold slap.

Intense sunlight pours through the windowpanes, banishing any lingering darkness. My head throbs as though someone hammers a fist against it, demanding to be let in.

I shift onto my side. Horrible decision, as it turns out. My stomach cramps with the intense pain of emptiness, and grit has clumped in the corners of my eyes. But it doesn't take long for the memories of last night to resurface. And when they do, I wish for nothing more than the dark forgetfulness of sleep.

What do I remember?

I remember the smooth grain of the carved wooden bird in my hand. I remember the crack of the first crumbling pillar. I remember, *You lie. You always lie.* I remember the blacks of Boreas' eyes, without iris or sclera. I remember a numbing cold, fatigue, shame, turmoil after realizing I'd misstepped. I remember running. Hiding. Dying. The craving for wine so acute it reduced me to some mindless animal, throat parched and belly empty. And then my return to the citadel, shining blade held to Boreas' throat. The drop of blood sliding down his neck.

And then—

*Wren.* His voice, deep and enticing, burrowing into the heart of me. *You're safe now.*

I had slipped into the Frost King's room in the dead of night to kill him, and he had *comforted* me.

Last night did not unfold how I imagined it would. Am I too weak to kill the one who has wronged me in so many ways? Too soft? Too . . . incompetent? For whatever reason, in that moment of truth, I was not able to slide the blade into my husband's heart.

A moment of weakness, that's all. I was guilt-ridden, exhausted. If I had been anything less than certain, I would not have been able to carry out the task, so of course I could not follow through. Having sowed the seeds of doubt, my surety wavered.

Even if I had managed to kill him, it wouldn't have mattered. I've yet to find the door leading from the Deadlands. And even if I did find an escape route . . . would I take it? If I am no longer welcome at Edgewood, where would I go? Whether I like it or not, this place is my only sanctuary.

My arms shake as I push myself into a seated position, the blankets falling to my waist. What on earth . . . ? My nightgown sticks to my chest, completely soaked through with dampness. Did I fall asleep in the tub fully dressed?

"My lady?" Orla knocks softly, then opens the door. She takes one look at me and gasps. "You're awake!" Beaming from ear to ear, she hurries to my bedside and takes one of my clammy hands in both of hers. "It is so good to see you well."

The sight of Orla's plump, familiar face never fails to soothe that which is uncertain. But her words confuse me. "It's only been a night."

She lifts her eyebrows. "It's been quite a bit longer than that. You've been asleep for a week, my lady."

"A *week*?" It's not possible.

Orla sobers. "You were very ill when you returned. The lord had Alba give you a tonic for deep sleep so your body could restore itself. You were not yourself."

That first frisson of panic itches at my skin. I pluck at my sweat-soaked nightgown, as if it will give me answers to the sense of trepidation wending through me. "Of course I wasn't myself. He kicked me out of the citadel. I nearly died from exposure. I was delirious with hypothermia."

My maid clasps her hands at her front, fiddling with her apron. She frowns in concern. "You talked in your sleep, my lady. Asked for wine, always wine. He told me not to give you any."

The blood turns to ice in my veins. Dropping my legs over the side of the bed, I shuffle toward the armoire across the room, yank open the doors, and dig through the pile of clothes at the bottom. I hid two wineskins here months ago, but I don't feel them anywhere. I grab the clothes, toss them onto the floor. The wine is gone.

Mounting alarm sends me in the direction of my dresser, the bottom drawer. The flask I keep stashed there is gone, too.

No matter how I try to level my breathing, it punches out of my chest in gasping exhalations. This can't be happening. Pushing to my feet, I stride toward the wall-to-wall bookshelves in my sitting room. Third row to the right, fourth shelf from the bottom. I drag every book off that shelf, dump them in a haphazard pile at my feet to reveal the space behind them. No wine. Only dust.

Dazed, I return the books to the shelf with a trembling hand. Will I have no relief from this thirst? "Orla." I stare at the engraved spines. "You didn't search through my belongings while I was ill, did you?"

"No, my lady."

My entire body threatens to deflate. I will steel into my spine. If my cache has been confiscated, then I will restore it, and this time, I will choose better hiding places. I've thousands of doors to choose from, after all.

I cross the room with every intention of doing exactly that when I catch sight of my reflection in the full-length mirror hanging from the wall. The view is so ghastly I physically recoil.

Puffy eyes, cracked lips, and a haggard complexion. Wonderful. My hands cup my chapped cheeks. The knee-length nightdress clings to my hunched frame.

Orla appears at my side. "Let's get you out of these wet clothes."

The wet nightgown: sweat. My cramping stomach: the effects of having purged every last drop from my body. Lightheadedness, fatigue, body aches. The craving digs hooks beneath my skin.

I'm lucid enough to understand why I was given a tonic, the blessed veil of sleep, to shield me from the worst of the withdrawal symptoms. The need to wet my tongue, however, has not abated.

As though I am five years old, my maid peels away the damp fabric from my skin and pulls a dry, clean tunic over my head, loose trousers up to my waist. To my horror, tears sting my eyes.

Orla pauses in tightening my waistband. "My lady."

"Orla, I told you to call me Wren."

"Yes, my lady."

I hate crying. As if I didn't purge enough last night. Or rather, last week. The past seven days do not exist for me.

"What if . . ." The words stick in my throat. "Orla, what if what you believed to be true wasn't actually true, and what if what wasn't true was true, or at least partly?" Am I even making sense? "And what if you made a mistake, a really big mistake, but you don't know how to fix it, or weren't sure it could even be fixed?"

She watches me intently, that natural kindness reaching out to envelope us both. She knows. Of course she does. "What happened between you and the lord?"

I say, with a surprising amount of calm, "I entered a room I shouldn't have. It was on the third level, in the north wing. A child's room."

Orla cannot hide her surprise. I have to know.

"Whose room did I enter?"

My maid plucks at her apron, a deep wrinkle folding her brow. "It's not my place to say, my lady."

"Please." I take both her hands in mine. "This is important, and I really don't want to throw you out the window."

Weeks ago, she would have refused, pulled away, exited through the door with the excuse of folding laundry. Now she moves to the bed, drawing the sheets tight across the mattress. The heaviest of sighs escapes her. "A long time ago, the lord was married."

I know this. After all, I am not the first of his wives.

"And . . . they had a son."

I assumed a child was involved. But to hear it aloud, that he *had* a son, a little boy, judging by the youth of the room, sends a wave of foreboding through me. Whatever story I am about to hear, it will not end happily. "What happened?"

Her fingers curl against the blankets. Then she attacks the bedding with a vengeance. "A horrible, *horrible* man took them away," she whispers roughly. "Stole the lord's wife and child."

Slowly, I round the bed so I can see Orla's face. She wears a stricken expression, and my chest pinches in response.

"They were taken captive," she continues, "across the mountains to the west, an area known for bandit attacks. They got caught in the crossfire, and the lord's wife and child were killed."

"When was this?"

"By my guess, I would say three centuries ago."

A time before the Gray, when all was green. But winter encroached, and stayed. And the Frost King would have been alone, locked away in this citadel, grieving those he'd loved and lost.

"Orla," I whisper. "What was Boreas' son's name?"

There is a pause. "Calais, my lady. His name was Calais."

∽

When midday hits, hunger pangs drive me downstairs to the dining room. The table is set for our typical overly elaborate meal, but the room itself is vacant, dark, and cold. I glance at the empty fireplace and consider lighting a fire, then think better of it. Best not to push the Frost King more than I already have.

So I sit. I dish food onto my silver plate, sausage and rice and bread and fruit. My stomach cramps after a few bites, but I force myself to eat half the meal. Generally, Boreas wanders in when he feels like it, so I've learned not to wait for him. Today, however, I watch the doorway for his imposing form. My heart pounds with a confusing mixture of anticipation and nerves, the conversation I shared with Orla lingering. Calais. Just a boy. Gone now.

"Excuse me," I say to a serving woman. "I noticed there isn't wine on the table. Is there a particular reason for that?"

"Unfortunately we are all out, my lady."

Right. My fingers tap against the tabletop. "Do you know if the king will be dining with me this afternoon?"

"He did not say, my lady." She sends me an apologetic glance before clearing the table.

I snatch his plate before she can collect it. Then I pile the remainder of the food on it—making sure the individual servings do not touch—and go in search of the Frost King. If he hasn't eaten lunch, then I imagine he is hungry.

He's not in his rooms. He's not in the library. He's not in the stables, or the practice yard. I wander the grounds for so long the food goes cold. And that is when I remember the greenhouse.

I take the stairs belowground, then climb the second staircase from the subterranean chamber. The door at the top stands open a crack. I push inside, step out into the bright day, the glimmer of light on glass. The table to my left supports many small pots of violets, in addition to a mint plant that seems out of place. There's a ladder leaning against one of the glass walls, and vines clamber up the rungs and slither toward the sharply sloped ceiling. Thick, steamy air coats the back of my throat as I inhale: damp loam, crushed pine, perfumed sugar, citrus.

I spot Boreas as I cross a narrow bridge arching over one of the babbling creeks. He's partially concealed by a rose bush and appears to be in the middle of replanting flowers.

He isn't aware of my presence.

He plunges his hands into the soil. The dark earth coats his wrists and forearms, clinging to the curling black hair, coating his leather gloves. Dirt sifts between his fingers, and patters into the large round pot. He wears a thin white tunic, the long sleeves hastily rolled up, and his hair hangs in a low tail, bits of leaves tangled in the strands.

Here, Boreas is humble. He is connected to the earth. He is, for once, at peace. That he completes this process with such care, devotion even, I feel drawn to him in new, unexplainable ways. Even with his back to me, I sense the intensity in him, on focusing wholly on this task, to hold nothing back. He works the earth like a laborer, not a god.

I'm almost sorry to interrupt his work, but I've been carrying around this plate of food for over an hour. There's a table to his right cluttered with gardening tools. Girding my stomach for whatever may befall me, I step forward and set down the plate.

The Frost King goes still. Slowly, he steps away from the pot and begins wiping the soil from his hands with a rag, his back to me. He speaks without turning around in that frigid tone, the one that puckers my skin and makes my heart race. "What are you doing here?"

I swallow, bringing moisture to my mouth, then straighten to my full height. "It's a peace offering," I say, refusing to be cowed into retreat.

A brief glance at the plate. "Is it poisoned?"

My mouth opens, then snaps shut. "If it were," I growl, "I daresay I wouldn't inform you about it."

His shoulders, naked skin visible through the damp fabric

sticking to the expanse of his back, jerk slightly, as though releasing a huff of air.

When he doesn't respond, I take a breath. I came here to make amends, but if he's uninterested, fine. "What did you do with my wine?"

He tilts his head. "Your wine?"

"The wine that was in my room."

"I believe that would be my wine."

"Am I not your wife?" I bite out. "Are we not equal partners in this sham of a union?" At this, he shifts his weight. He has yet to turn around. "That wine is just as much mine as it is yours, but regardless of who claims ownership over it, you had no right to go through my belongings. That's an invasion of privacy."

"You want to talk about invasion of privacy?" He sounds coldly amused.

Some of my ire settles at the reminder of what transpired last week. In an impressively level voice, I begin, "Look—"

"No." At last, Boreas turns. Takes me in from toe to scalp. A streak of dirt smudges the pale skin of his cheek, another smeared on the underside of his jaw. The dirt-coated cloth hangs from one hand. "Listen carefully, Wren, because I'm not going to repeat myself. From this moment on, there will be no more drinking. I've disposed of all the wine in the citadel. You will not find even a drop of it."

The panic I've tried to suppress since waking rises up and lashes through me. "I don't believe you. There's an entire cellar underground. Hundreds of bottles. Centuries of collecting. You wouldn't throw it away."

"It's gone. Every last drop drained." He does not flinch.

Then there can be only one explanation. He's trying to punish me. I will not accept it. "Have you considered the possibility that I drink because I was stolen from my home, forced to marry someone against my will?"

"You drank before ever arriving here, so what does that say about you?"

My lips tighten, compress into the thinnest, whitest line. He's right. I drank long before ever stepping foot into the Deadlands. It is my greatest need, my greatest shame. And yet, the craving lives on. "It's not that bad," I argue, though some of my urgency has depleted. "I can control my intake. It's not as though I spend the day drowning myself in oblivion."

"Only on the nights you're forced to dine with me, is that it?"

The first few instances, yes. Now I just . . . drink. My hand reaches for the glass before my mind is aware of it. A completely involuntary gesture.

"You don't understand." And neither did Elora.

"You're sick," Boreas rumbles, though not unkindly. "Don't you see how the drink ravages your body? You believe it gives you strength and clarity, but it weakens you, drop by drop. Wine is the liar. Wine is the thief."

I cross my arms over my stomach, fingers curling into the front of my tunic, strangling it. "I'm not . . ."

The moment he rests his palms on my shoulders, fingertips dimpling my shoulder blades, I have to bite the inside of my cheek to halt the flood of emotion. He touches me, and against my will, I weaken.

"Just one sip," I whisper. "One more. It will be the last time. I promise."

"Wren." Gently. "I can't let you do that. Whether you believe it or not, I'm trying to help you."

A sharp inhale drives the breath deeper into my lungs, and yet it feels like I'm suffocating.

He says, "The worst of your withdrawal symptoms have passed. I've spoken with Alba, and she's agreed to help you these next few months. There are ways to help manage the cravings."

"I do not have a choice in this?" Prickly words.

Boreas replies, without a hint of remorse, "No."

To be denied the one thing I cannot live without? I cannot accept this. I must accept this. He is convinced this will help me. I'm not sure I believe that.

"I used it sometimes," I whisper, "to cope. After my parents passed. It wasn't often. Every few weeks, maybe, when the grief became too much. Then I drank to pass the time. I drank to feel alive again. I drank because, if I did not, I was afraid I might float away." It gave me clarity. It cured me, pain and all. It cured all the parts of me that I hated.

The irony is, the more I drank, the more ashamed and guilty I felt over my destructive behavior, the lack of emotional stability I could offer Elora. It was the most awful feedback loop, and I wasn't able to break free of it.

Boreas clears his throat. "I never turned to the bottle, but there have been times when the temptation presented itself. I suppose isolating myself isn't the healthiest coping mechanism either."

He doesn't mention the reason for his isolation, but I know.

"It will be a difficult road. You're strong though." With that, he removes his hands from my shoulders, giving me space.

The ache in my throat and jaw does not relent. I don't especially agree with him, but . . . I suppose we will see just how strong in the coming weeks.

Pulling out a rickety chair from the table, I lower myself into it, then gather my courage. This is, after all, why I came. "I'm sorry. For everything. For . . . hurting you."

The knob in his throat dips, but he doesn't interrupt. He's listening.

"I didn't know about your son," I whisper, the words dying out. It takes every bit of strength to maintain eye contact. He deserves that much. "It wasn't my business. I should have respected your privacy. My actions were selfish and rude and completely unacceptable. I promise, it won't happen again."

The king takes his time wiping the remainder of the dirt from his palms. Then he tosses the cloth into a bucket with a slow exhale, looking out through the glass. "Orla told you."

"Please don't blame her. I threatened to toss her out the window if she didn't."

He shakes his head. *Toss her out the window*, he seems to say. *What else is new?* "You are uniquely persuasive when you want to be."

Do I detect a note of grudging admiration in his tone?

"Thank you for the apology." He does not look at me as he speaks, and I wish he would. It feels as though I ruined something when I'm not even sure what is damaged.

The silence widens and takes up space in the room. Enough time passes that I grow uncomfortable enough to fill it. "I know I said it before, but I really am sorry. Really. I'm absolutely appalled by my behavior and—"

I'm babbling. I never babble. It suggests a lack of control, and my only excuse is that the events that unfolded have completely altered my perspective on, well, a lot of things.

"Wren." His attention returns to my face and my emotional torrent dries up. He appears fatigued. I suppose that's my fault, too. "It's all right."

My heart grows heavy at that unanticipated kindness, for I expected so much worse. Maybe I am doubly wrong in assuming things of him when I do not know nearly half of what I thought I did.

That's when his attention returns to the plate of food I set on the table.

My face warms. "I thought you might be hungry. You weren't at lunch."

"That's kind of you." He studies the food suspiciously. Questioning my earlier claim, I imagine.

"I told you it's not poisoned. You will have to take my word for it, whatever you believe it to be worth." If I had wanted him dead, I would have finished the job when I had the chance. At some point, I will need to think about the road forward and what that means for me, but not now. I haven't the patience to sort through my tumultuous thoughts.

Coming to a decision, he slides into the unoccupied chair, picks up the fork, and passes a chunk of sausage into his mouth. His lips close around the tines, pulling the piece of meat free. When his gaze catches mine, I turn away. For whatever reason, I'm having difficulty breathing normally.

This particular area of the greenhouse hosts many blueberry bushes that have grown unruly in their plot of land. The fruits, tiny and sour, cling to the branches. In a few weeks they'll swell fat and round, perfect for harvest.

"I apologize as well," he says after a time, "for my actions the other day. I— Sometimes I lose control of my temper."

If losing his temper means shifting into a darkwalker, no wonder he always seems so emotionless. And I must be a wreck if I'm able to rationally process Boreas morphing into a darkwalker without going mad. Or maybe it's too late for me and I'm already mad.

"It's all right."

"It's not," he says simply. And I appreciate it, because it wasn't.

I expected the Frost King's anger. I did not expect an apology, nor his understanding.

Maybe that's why I mention my family.

"I understand what it means to lose someone you love," I murmur, studying him closely. This time does not feel like the others. There is an openness to the space, an ease to my breathing, and a strange lack of fear in divulging things so personal to me. "I lost my parents when I was only fifteen."

He spears another chunk of meat with his fork, and his eyes lift to mine. "Because of me."

Something in my voice must have given away that piece of information. "Yes," I say after a hesitation.

He stares at his plate. Sets down his fork. "I'm sorry."

Again, the apology is unforeseen. That wasn't the reason I told him. But I can't deny that the genuine remorse in his tone helps heal that wound.

I've been living in the past for so long I've forgotten what it's like to live in the present. I'm not here to punish him. That wasn't the point of this meeting. I'm just here. To comfort him, I think. And to comfort myself, too.

"I can sense your curiosity," he states. "You might as well ask."

And I think, *Darkwalker.*

"I didn't imagine the part where your hands turned into claws, did I?" It was a possibility, considering how delirious I'd been.

"No." The response reeks of bitterness.

My attention falls to his hands. Gloved. No sign of the shadows. Do the changes only occur in moments of intense emotional turmoil? "That's why you wear gloves, isn't it? To hide your claws?"

His mouth pinches. He nods.

"Can you take them off? I'd like to see."

He removes the gloves and tosses them onto the table. With the leather free of his skin, I'm able to study my husband's naked hands—something I've rarely done. The nails are pointed, but they look filed down. Shadows blot beneath his skin and retreat, like flashes of light. They don't appear nearly as monstrous as they did the other night.

"Those times Orla said you were sick—"

"I wasn't able to control the change." He sighs, taps his pointed nails on the table with light clicks. "Generally, I'm able to anticipate the transformation before it occurs, but some weeks are particularly difficult."

"Why? What provokes it?"

From the length of time it takes him to reply, I assume he discards multiple responses before answering my question. "Frustration. Exhaustion, both of the body and of the mind." Quieter: "Confusion."

And I wonder. Does his confusion bear the same roots as mine? I'm not brave enough to ask.

I absorb that information and store it someplace to examine later. "How long have you been this way?"

Briefly, he closes his eyes. His fingers go still. "The change began after my wife's and son's deaths. It's worsened over the last few decades."

My attention returns to the shadows beneath his skin. Occasionally a blemish seeps somewhere near his neck, then disappears. There must be something wrong with me, that I am not put off over the fact that my husband's spirit is turning corrupt. Looking at him dirtied from his gardening, sweaty and rumpled, he looks like he belongs here. Strapped down in his most restrictive clothing, he is the Frost King, but today, he is simply Boreas.

"Are you afraid of me?"

My eyes lock onto his and hold. I see it now. A window pried open, that soft, vulnerable interior on display. And I say, with complete honesty, "No more than I was before."

He nods after a time, sinking back into the chair. Beads of sweat dot his upper lip.

"Did you plant everything in the greenhouse?"

"Yes."

"It comforts you, being here. Planting things."

He glances down at his hands folded in front of him, the plate of food abandoned. "I've always been envious of Zephyrus' power. To bring life to something rather than death. This—" He touches one of the waxy leaves of a nearby plant. "—does not come easily to me."

"If you enjoy this—" I gesture to the surrounding greenery. "—why do you insist on prolonging winter? You could have plants everywhere, not just in the greenhouse."

"Why do you insist on returning home when it is clear your sister has never appreciated anything you've done for her?"

They sting, his words. That must mean they hold some truth. "But Husband," I growl through a manic smile, "we're talking about *you*."

"We were," he corrects.

"It's not that I believe she is unappreciative," I say.

"Has she ever thanked you?" he demands, lips flush with color. "Has she ever offered to help lighten your load?"

No matter how far back I go into my memories, I can't remember a time when she offered to do so. But those were the roles we fell into. And with my addiction worsening over the years, I began to weaponize my emotions—guilt, shame—against myself. Reasons why she shouldn't have to do more because I was already an emotional mess. "It wasn't her responsibility."

He slams a palm atop the table, startling me. The utensils clatter against the plate. "No. Her responsibility was to be a good sister. To care for you as you care for her. I can understand her willingness to let you carry that burden as children, but that is no excuse now. Your sister is an adult. She made the conscious choice to let you sacrifice your time and happiness."

My eyes well. Tears, this early in the morning? This is becoming a terrible habit. "I'm slowly coming to realize that, but she's the only family I have left."

The king pushes the plate aside, setting his elbows in its place. "And you still want to return to Edgewood?" he asks carefully.

"I don't know." And that is also the truth. Elora treated me so poorly. Unforgivably poorly. Some nights, I lie awake and wonder what it would be like to hit her, or worse. Hurt her the way she hurt me. If I cannot have the relationship we once shared, what is the point of returning?

Boreas says, "We hold fast to what is familiar. Fear often prevents us from stepping beyond that boundary."

The tips of my fingers brush the plate of food. I grab a huckleberry before courage fails me. "What can a god fear?" I ask him.

"Many things, as it turns out."

"Death?"

"No." He arches one black eyebrow. "Sorry to disappoint you."

"Then I guess it's a good thing I didn't kill you," I say in an attempt to lighten the mood.

His mouth thaws somewhat. "But you wanted to." He plucks a grape from the plate and chews thoughtfully. I eat the huckleberry. "Why didn't you? You had every chance."

And I didn't take it.

When the time came, I could not follow through. Something held me back.

"I have no idea," I say. "But . . . I don't think you're the villain people make you out to be." As I learn more about the North Wind, I see he bears many hurts, soft spots he's encased in hardened armor. We are not so different, he and I.

He selects a piece of cheese from the plate. Instead of bringing it to his mouth, however, he offers it to me, which I accept with surprise. He nudges the plate across the table so that we might share the meal.

"I think, given time, we could become friends," I say.

"Friends." The intensity of his stare takes me off guard. "That is what you want?"

What I want I can't have, or it no longer exists. My village, my sister, my family alive again. And yes, a part of me craves friendship in whatever form, even with an immortal, even with my captor. There is so little interaction in my day-to-day life. It's an entirely selfish desire.

"Yes, that is what I want."

"I've never had a friend," he admits.

I can't help it. I laugh.

"What?" He looks affronted, with those dark eyebrows slashing across his forehead. The Frost King is painfully lacking in social skills.

"Nothing." My laughter tapers off as he grabs another slice of cheese, grumbling under his breath. "That does not surprise me, is all."

The scowl has completely taken over his face. I snort and shove a handful of berries into my mouth. Together, we clear the plate of food.

The Frost King taps a finger against the table. Turns his head to stare out at the barren land below. "So what do friends do?"

He sounds like a nervous child. It's rather endearing. "They talk. Listen to one another. Spend time together."

"You're saying you'd willingly listen to me?" The creases around his eyes have deepened, and I realize he is laughing at me, in his own way.

I cross my arms. "I can try."

He looks uncomfortable by the idea, but— "Then I suppose I can try as well."

And that is how I leave him.

Not friends.

But perhaps no longer enemies.

# CHAPTER
# 28

Today marks the new moon: a masked sky, without illumination.

Judgment Day.

Boreas has already locked himself into the parlor. From sunup to sundown, the North Wind looks into the past lives of those who gather inside, ready to face their eternity. He has stated, very clearly, that he is not to be disturbed.

Raising a fist, I pound it against the entrance door. The crash echoes in the dim, cobweb-draped corridor of stone, and dies, leaving sputtering silence in its wake.

A low, chilling voice hisses, "Who dares interrupt me?"

The lock tumbles from within, and the door swings open. Sauntering inside, I circle around one of the stone pillars and toss the Frost King a grin, hip cocked. "That would be your wife."

He's speechless as I stride across the vast, pillar-lined space, acknowledging the newly dead awaiting their sentence. A long, threadbare rug connects the entrance to the dark stone throne atop which the king sits, sheathed in black—cloak, boots, gloves, breeches. Those pale, cut-knife cheekbones sharpen as his mouth folds into a shape of utter distaste. My grin widens. At least he's predictable.

Many of the specters bow as I pass, much to my surprise. Only when I've planted myself in the empty stone chair located to his left does Boreas quietly demand, "What are you doing here?"

"You're a smart man," I murmur in response, taking note of the room. Perhaps twenty specters await Judgment. A massive, candlelit chandelier hangs from the vaulted ceiling by a heavy chain—the only light in the shrouded interior. A surprising amount of artistry was put into the architecture of the space. The white plaster molding takes the shapes of serpents, owls, and cypress trees. "You figure it out."

"God," he corrects me. By now, it's a reflex.

The arm of the chair—cut with harsh angles—digs into my back. I shift to a more comfortable position, only to realize one does not exist. The seat of the throne—a smaller version of Boreas'—feels as if it has been fashioned from knives. "How can you stand sitting in this thing?"

"If you're uncomfortable, feel free to leave."

"Give me your cloak."

His attention darts to the awaiting specters, who quickly look elsewhere. "Why?"

"Just give it to me." I wiggle my fingers expectantly. It's not as though the cold affects him anyway. The only time I'm truly warm in this place is in my bedroom, the fire roaring.

With a few choice mutterings, he slides his arms from the sleeves, revealing a slate tunic edged in white, and hands me the balled-up cloak. That was easier than I thought it would be.

I stuff the heavy fabric against my back, protection from the sharp edge of the chair arm. Much better.

Seeing that he continues to glower at me, I gesture to his subjects. "Please continue."

As though deciding I won't interrupt further, he returns to his task. Since our amicable conversation a few days prior, we've settled into a tentative truce with each other. He has even begun to acknowledge me in the halls—and not even under threat.

In truth, I'm curious about the inner workings of his reign over the Deadlands. To these souls, he is a king. And I question how this king rules.

"State your name."

A rumpled man glances up from his kneeled position at the front of the line. "Adamo of Rockthorn, my lord."

"Adamo of Rockthorn." The king's eyes lose focus, and I startle as the air between him and the specter wavers. This is his power, to choose: you are worthy, you are not.

The rippling air clears, as do Boreas' eyes. He studies his subject for a time. The man cowers beneath that icy countenance. I take in the king's profile, how each slope and angle sits with complete rigidity. In the back of the line, the souls clump together, as if terrified of inviting the king's attention.

"Adamo of Rockthorn," he intones. "Husband, brother, father. You are survived by your wife and three children. Your mother. Your sister. You made your livelihood as a wool merchant. When you were five, you pushed your sister into a frozen pond, nearly drowning her.

When you were nine, you beat a village cur that dared to beg for scraps, and killed it."

My gasp is near inaudible, but the king briefly glances at me from the corner of his eye.

"Please, my lord." The man bows lower, and the tip of his nose brushes the frayed rug on which he kneels. "I understand I have made poor choices in life, but I was only a child—"

"When you were sixteen," Boreas continues, crushing the man's timidity beneath his larger presence, "you lured a girl from your village into the local barn and raped her. Again, at age seventeen, though a different victim. With each woman, you threatened to end her life if she breathed a word of the transgression to anyone."

The specter is almost completely transparent. He visibly trembles.

"Do you have the means to defend yourself against these actions?"

"It was a difficult time," he says in a breathless rush, "m-my lord. My father had recently passed on. I was angry, confused. I needed to feel in control."

"So you took the choice away from those women? Is that what you're saying?" There is a pause. "Look at me."

The man lifts his head. Tears glimmer on his washed-out cheeks. I am remembering the story of Orla's past, and the revulsion rises so thickly in my throat it blocks my airway. This man does not deserve my pity. Whatever punishment he receives, it will be just.

"Does your wife know how depraved your thoughts are? How, even after your marriage vows, you lured not one, but two women into the wood, and raped them?"

A cold sweat springs to the hollow of my throat. I could never have known the depth of this man's revolting actions. How could

I? The only thing I see is a man on his knees, suffering, terrified. I realize I have misjudged Boreas in more ways than one. I assumed he did not bother to Judge the dead fairly, did not pick through the details of the past, however minute.

"No, my lord," he gasps, trembling so hard he topples onto his side. "She is blinded by her love for me."

"You have erred," says the North Wind. "You have erred badly, and for a long time."

"Please, my lord. My children. I love my children."

"The love of a child is not enough. Do you understand that your actions have lasting consequences? You have inflicted wounds on these women that will outlive your death, that will crush their confidence and surety of the world." The chill in his tone crystallizes, and I swear I feel it scrape against my skin. "You are hereby sentenced to the Chasm for the raping of five women over the course of your lifetime, including your wife. On each new moon henceforth, you will be castrated, your appendage regrown until the next lunar cycle. May your suffering be eternal."

The wailing man vanishes, the space where he knelt empty. The tension ratchets higher the longer the quiet lasts. In my peripheral vision, I watch Boreas inhale, then slowly exhale. It weighs on him. This responsibility weighs on him.

"Next in line, please step forward."

A woman near the front steps aside to reveal a young boy, perhaps eight years of age. With her urging, he shuffles forward and goes to his knees. Poor thing. Dark hair that may have been black in life lies tangled atop his scalp, clumped with dirt.

"State your name."

"Nolan of Ashwing," he whispers hoarsely. "My lord."

The air shimmers as the Frost King delves into the boy's past. A few heartbeats later, he releases the tether. "Nolan of Ashwing. You are survived by your older sister and your parents. Is this correct?"

A slow, sullen nod. "I got sick, my lord. Mama said I would get better, but she had no coin for medicine."

The boy is so, so small, and frightened. Boreas softens in the presence of the child. A glimpse of who he might have been with his late wife and son.

"I see you pushed your sister down last year. She stole your toy, is that it?"

"I didn't mean to hurt her. Mama told me to apologize, and I did. I said she could play with my toys after that." The boy sniffles, and my heart squeezes. "Are you sending me to the bad place?"

The Frost King sits back in his chair, deep in study. A smile comes unbidden to his mouth. "No, Nolan, I am not sending you to the bad place. I'm sending you to a place with other children where you can play all day. You will always have enough to eat, and you will never get sick. There is a woman there who will take care of you. How does that sound?"

The boy lifts his watery gaze. "Will Mama be there?"

"Not for a long time, unfortunately. But you will have plenty to tell her when she arrives, whenever that may be."

The boy, reassured that he is not being punished, calms. Radiating from his chubby face is a peace the likes of which I've never seen. Complete trust in the North Wind's word.

Boreas raises a hand. There's a flash, and then the boy vanishes.

He does not immediately call the next specter forward, as though needing time to settle the complicated emotions flickering in his eyes.

Turning toward him in my chair, I murmur, "That was kind of you to soothe the boy." When he does not respond, I ask, "What does it feel like to look into someone's past?"

He stares straight ahead, unblinking. Those flickering emotions weave into greater complexity. "It feels like a wave crashing over me. I'm accosted by scenes and moments and bursts of sight and sound, the culmination of one's life, and it is my job to separate the threads, to look down the timeline from the beginning and move forward. It is easier with children. There is less weight for them to carry. Their motives are simple, driven by emotion rather than intellect. I think I have only sent a handful of children to Neumovos, but they were older."

"What about the Chasm?"

"No child has ever been sent to the Chasm."

I open my mouth to ask him additional questions when someone knocks on the entrance doors to the parlor.

Boreas goes still, those black gloved hands curling atop the arms of his throne.

The quiet falls like a death knell.

"Come in," I call.

The door creaks as it slowly, slowly opens. The specters turn to see who is foolish enough to interrupt the Frost King's Judgment.

"Over here, Thyamine." I wave to the maidservant, whose eyes appear massive behind her glasses. She scurries toward me bearing a small, covered plate. In the corner of my vision, Boreas' upper lip twitches, his eyebrows snapped so tightly together over his nose they appear as one unbroken line. It warrants merit that he does not snarl at her approach.

She curtsies, head bent low. "Lady Wren." Flicks a worried look at the bristling king. After passing over the plate, she scuttles off. Boreas continues to bore a hole in the side of my face with his narrowed stare.

I gesture toward the hall, his awaiting subjects. "Please continue."

"Is this going to be the last interruption, or can I expect another ridiculous display?"

"I guess that depends. What other ridiculous display did you have in mind?"

His face crinkles, but in the end, he deigns to respond with another question of his own. "What did she bring you?"

"Don't you have a Judgment to focus on?"

He glances at the line of curious specters. "It can wait."

Pleased surprise moves through me, that he would set aside his duty, if only for a few moments, considering I barged in here uninvited.

"Raspberry vanilla cake," I announce, plucking the round silver covering from the dish to reveal the perfect slice beneath. Mounds of gleaming white icing perch on the dessert's edge in a crenated trim.

My mouth waters as I snatch the fork resting beside the slice of cake. The tines sink smoothly through the moist confection. As I bring the morsel to my mouth and chew, a tiny helpless sound slips out. Silas never fails me. Every cake is absolute perfection. Boreas shifts in his seat, his nostrils flaring.

I offer him my fork, cheeks bulging. "Cake?" Which sounds more like, *Cek?* A few crumbs plop onto my lap. I glance down at the mess, then back at Boreas, who studies me with a quirked brow, his cold, cold eyes softened by a rare amusement. I'm still not convinced he dislikes cake. No one dislikes cake.

"Come on. One tiny little bite?" The fork encroaches in his personal space, and he leans away from it suspiciously. "Please?" My lips form a pout. "Friends share dessert, you know."

He stares at my mouth long enough for my cheeks to heat. I've never been one to retreat, so I maintain my position, even if I have the desire to wet my lips with my tongue, curious as to how his eyes might darken, deepen, were I to do so.

"If I take a bite," he asks, "will you remain quiet until this session is complete?"

"Yes." Maybe.

He shifts his focus to the slice of cake. A single bite awaiting consumption. The dip of his throat draws my eye, and his brief nod allows me the opportunity to bring the fork to his mouth.

His lips part and close around the tines, and as I pull back the utensil, the sweet slides free, trapped inside a mouth whose very breath is cool, but whose lips, in this moment, are softened, and warm.

"Good?"

He shrugs, chews. The curve of his mouth gives him away.

"You like it." I waggle the fork at him. "Admit it."

"I like nothing of the sort." But he gestures toward the plate, and I pass him the fork so he can scoop another bite into his mouth.

Clearing my throat, I lean back in my seat to face the parlor. The specters watch their god, whose word is law, whose Judgment is their eternity, consume half the dessert in only a few bites. I'm helpless to stop the smile spreading across my face.

The North Wind likes cake.

I knew it.

"Next in line, step forward." Boreas' voice, deep and ringing, fills the vast, echoing space.

A timid woman minces a few steps forward, her bent form weighed down by a thick shawl.

"State your—"

The king stiffens. He's on his feet, a sinuous motion so quick my mortal eyes can't follow, as the doors at the end of the parlor slam open with such force they're torn clean from their hinges.

They crash into the windows. Glass shatters in an explosion of glittering darkness, and sweeps into a tight, spiraling coil that gradually expands, forcing the specters back from the display.

The spear materializes in Boreas' hand, crackling with power. Ice erupts from the spearpoint, shooting toward the whirlwind colored like deepest night. The shards splinter, and their small fragments slice tears into the hazy substance that pushes farther into the room.

One by one, the specters begin to fall.

I clutch the arms of my chair, frozen. A woman tumbles to the ground with splayed limbs. Then a man, his braid whipping him in the cheek as he falls forward. The cold bites into my naked hands, my bared neck, as clouds develop against the curved beams of the ceiling. Snow begins to fall in sheets—a means of defense against the infiltration. The black force retreats slightly.

"What's happening?" My voice is lost to the wind, my eyes watering uncontrollably. "Darkwalkers?"

Beside me, Boreas grits his teeth. "No." He spits the word. "Just another distant relative."

He plants himself in front of me, and a cool substance slides across my skin. I peer around his shoulder, unable to tear my eyes away from the motionless, corpse-like specters, whose chests do not rise and fall, whose eyes, unseeing, might never blink again. The dead cannot die again. So what power have they succumbed to?

As quickly as it appeared, the blackness clears. "Who dares pick from the Garden of Slumber?"

And my heart ceases to beat.

Slowly, so slowly I'm not sure if I'm moving at all, I turn my head to the right. A massive figure stands backlit against the windows. He must be eight or nine feet tall, with shoulders so broad they remind me of mountains.

Again, I take in the specters' still forms. Their *sleeping* forms. For the man—god—standing before me, before the Frost King, is none other than Sleep.

That first encounter, he was but a voice in the void, pulsating senses, mind adrift. Now here he stands, an entity given shape. It is only his eyes, however, that I'm able to focus on. When I attempt to make sense of his face, the garments he wears, the image eludes me.

"Boreas," says the god who is Sleep.

After a moment, Boreas lowers his weapon and inclines his head. "It has been some time, cousin."

"Give or take a few centuries."

He takes in the unconscious specters, mouth pinching with displeasure. "You've interrupted a critical occasion for these souls. I do not appreciate the unannounced visit."

The dark, blurred shape shifts forward. "I know a thing or two about unannounced visits." Sleep's depthless gaze locks onto me where I stand partially shielded by Boreas. "I daresay your wife does as well."

The hair at my nape lifts as the surrounding atmosphere snaps with breathless cold. Boreas says, "You are acquainted with one another." It is not a question.

"To an extent."

The king doesn't remove his attention from his visitor as he asks me, "Does he speak plainly? Are you acquainted with Sleep?"

I'm given seconds to respond. Hesitate, and I dig my own grave. I can't lose Boreas' trust now, not when I've begun to feel the change between us, a mutual understanding, at times respect. Potential for more.

"Wren." It is both demand and inquiry, soft with denial. He doesn't believe his cousin, but he has not been given evidence to trust otherwise.

A selective truth will have to do.

"I have met Sleep," I say.

Boreas tenses. The very air, it seems, tenses. I've the unexplainable urge to look into the face that has been so distant, so remote toward me, but whose deeper emotions have begun to thaw. I fear what I might find. Disappointment? Anything less than acceptance would hurt.

Retreating a step, he moves to stand behind me, denying me his expression. "Explain."

A very, very fine line exists between truth and lie. I stole the poppy plant, but Zephyrus needed it to create the sleep tonic. I do not have to divulge every detail. Just enough to angle the light to my needs.

"I accompanied Zephyrus to Sleep's cave." Boreas is so still I wouldn't be surprised to learn he has turned to stone. At the time, I did not consider my actions a betrayal to my husband. So much has changed since then. "Your brother needed one of the plants for a special tonic. While Zephyrus distracted him, I took the herbs he needed."

The North Wind's gloved hand curves around my nape. The leather is cool against my flushed skin. "I told you to stay away from him," he growls through gritted teeth.

A shudder runs through me, and my hands visibly shake. I lock them together in an attempt to regain control of my body's response to his proximity. "And when have I ever listened to you?" The knot in my throat tightens. Somehow, I manage to swallow it down. "I was trying to help a friend."

He scoffs. "My brother is no friend to you."

My chest aches as the temperature plummets and the breath around my nostrils crystallizes. There is nothing more frightening than the North Wind's temper, black shadow sprouting from his skin.

"Control yourself," I hiss. "I'm sorry I went against your word, but you can't expect me to stay locked up in this place for the remainder of my life."

He steps around me. "We'll discuss this later, Wife."

*Wife.* I nearly slap him. "So it's back to that?" Worse than the regret is the knowledge that it's my own damn fault for getting myself into this mess.

He ignores me, turning to face this relative of his. "What is it you want, cousin?"

"I only want what was stolen from me to be returned." A weighted, expectant gaze.

Even if I wanted to return the flowers, I can't. They're in Zephyrus' possession. "I don't have them. Zephyrus does. I don't know where he went." All truths.

Sleep shifts his upper body in a gesture reminiscent of a shrug. "Then I require payment for the plants you stole."

Boreas goes deathly still beside me.

"How much?" I croak. I haven't coin. I've never had coin. Mayhap the king does?

A lick of laughter, raspy and full, sends a strange current through my body. "I'm not interested in your coin. I'm interested in your dreams."

I blink at the god stupidly. My dreams?

"You overstep," Boreas cuts in.

"Do I? Do you know how long it takes to grow one poppy flower?" He huffs at Boreas' lack of reply. Likely he already knew the king wouldn't be able to answer him. "Seven years. She picked three flowers for a combined loss of twenty-one growing years. I believe a dream, something she will no longer remember, is a fair price."

"What use have you for dreams? The dream world is not your realm. That is for the Dream Weaver to decide."

I hear the smile in Sleep's voice when he replies, "I have respected the boundaries we established long ago. I do not step foot beyond your high stone wall. I have not taken anything from your possession. That your wife was not aware of these limitations is due to your lack of foresight, not mine. She has overstepped, and I expect recompence for that which has been lost."

There is a pause. I'm convinced Boreas will strike his cousin down, if the pallor around his compressed lips is any indication. "What of my brother and his punishment?"

"I will deal with the West Wind, in time."

"Let him take it," I say to Boreas. "I don't care."

"No."

"What does it matter if he takes one of my dreams?"

"Because—" He speaks succinctly, all points. "—there is a difference between a dream that is ambient and a dream that is gifted. The Dream Weaver is allowed to enter your ambient dreams, but he has no control over them. He lacks access to the inner workings of your mind. A gifted dream is different." Boreas stares at his cousin in disgust. "In a gifted dream, the Dream Weaver can enter your mind and insert his influences over its development. The dream will no longer belong to you."

So? It's only a dream.

The king elaborates, "If that gifted dream acts as a doorway, there is the chance that the Dream Weaver's influence can bleed into your thoughts, potentially your actions. Who will you be if those do not belong to you?"

I'm suddenly grateful Boreas stepped in before I could be taken advantage of.

"While that is likely true," Sleep inputs, "it does not disregard the fact that I need something of equal value to the plants I lost."

A cool, calculating study from the king. "You owe a debt to the Dream Weaver, do you not? Take one of mine, and give it to your son. Let this issue be resolved."

The darkness throbs, and Sleep comes into sharper focus. There is a chin, firm and angled, and a bulbous nose. "You are serious?"

"You don't have to do that," I protest. Grabbing Boreas' arm, I wait until he looks down at me. "It's my punishment. Let me bear it."

"And you are mine to protect, so let me shield you from this."

My mouth parts, yet the sound travels no farther than my cinched throat. A heartbeat later, I ask, "Even though it's my fault?"

He brushes my chin with his thumb. "Even then."

He's descending the stairs before I realize he's gone. The click of his bootheels cuts the atmosphere into thin ribbons of lingering strain. He meets Sleep halfway across the parlor. I remain standing atop the dais, nerves creeping through me, and guilt, the animal that dogs my heels, that always manages to scent me out.

Had I not accompanied Zephyrus to Sleep's cave, the king wouldn't have found himself in this predicament. But I can't change the past. I must trust that Boreas knows what he's doing, the sacrifice he's making. A sacrifice for me. No one has ever gone such lengths to protect me before.

Two blurred shapes—hands?—lift and rest against the king's temples. The darkness encroaches, shielding them from view.

It takes no longer than a few moments before Sleep steps back. The shroud lifts.

"Now get out," Boreas clips.

With the god's departure, the specters awaken, sitting up and peering around the room in confusion. Boreas returns to his throne, a muscle pulsing in his jaw. I perch on the edge of my seat warily. "Will the Dream Weaver control your dreams now?"

He does not immediately respond, and I can't say I blame him, considering all the trouble I've caused. Boreas could have let me give up a dream as payment, but he took the fall instead. He shielded me against a potential threat. And he can never know that the poppy flowers I stole were used to create a tonic as a means to kill him.

I am a terrible person.

"The Dream Weaver," he murmurs, "is not privy to the dreams of the divine. Thus, his power does not affect us to the same extent as it does mortals. A dream of mine is a boon to him, but no, he will not be able to infiltrate my dreams or thoughts. He has a single dream whose power may be extracted for use of something else. I care not."

I don't think I entirely believe him about the lack of caring. "I'm sorry," I whisper. "Do you want me to go?"

"Did I say I wanted you to go?"

The specters shuffle into something resembling a line. The day is not yet over, and he still has souls to Judge. "No, but people often say the opposite of what they feel."

He gives me a long, searching look. "Not me."

My skin tightens; my cheeks warm. I think I already knew that. It's none of my business, but I ask, "What dream did you give him?"

Boreas leans back in his throne, a small smile curving his mouth. All he says is, "Pass the cake."

# CHAPTER
## 29

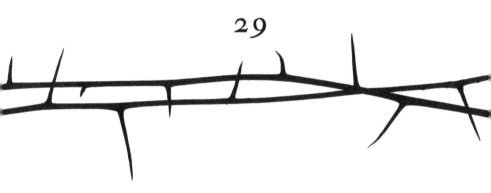

As has become habit, I wake before the sun. Beyond the window lies a bruised sky, the midnight hue gradually leaching to gray. Today, the sight of winter doesn't send me into resigned acceptance. The world is cold, but it is also beautiful, lovely, pure.

I have an idea.

Leaping from bed, I empty my bladder, lather up my lavender soap, wash my face, brush my teeth, and pull on the trousers and tunic Orla set out the night before. A few tugs of the comb through my hair allows me to braid it down my back. By the time I'm dressed and ready to greet the day, the sun has risen and tips the highest branches in shining gold.

The past week has been strange, awkward, as Boreas and I continued to navigate the growing pains of our developing relationship. Meals have been a pleasant affair, and no one is more surprised than I to learn the king is quite the conversationalist when the mood strikes. We've discussed everything from our childhoods, to dreams, to the mundane like preferred tea flavors or favorite time of day—I love the mornings, Boreas is partial to night. Once, I almost managed to make him laugh.

I'm on my way out the door when something atop my desk catches my eye. I frown, picking up a sealed envelope addressed to me in elegant script. Breaking the wax seal, I unfold the parchment and read.

*Wren, the tonic is ready. Please respond with a day and time to meet and leave your response in the opening near the courtyard wall.*

The sleep tonic. I would not have gone through the trouble of stealing from the Garden of Slumber if I didn't want this, but many weeks have passed since then, and I no longer feel certain of my path. My racing heart tells me I should deal with this later, when I don't feel so confused.

"Orla!" I call, shrugging on my winter coat and stuffing the note inside an inner pocket.

My maid bustles into the room. "Yes, my lady?"

"I'll need extra hands today. I want to clean the south ballroom from top to bottom. And I need to speak with Silas as well."

Her mouth opens, then clicks shut in confusion. "May I ask why?"

I toss her a grin on my way out the door. "I'm throwing a party."

~

My footsteps reverberate in the enormous, echoing expanse of the ballroom. It's a long, rectangular space shrouded in darkness and neglect. The air is so thick with dust I feel the particles coat the back of my throat. The north and south ends harbor massive stone fireplaces. Curtains cloak the entire western wall. Reviving this room will not be easy. I, however, am looking forward to the challenge.

But first, the curtains have to go.

"Orla."

My maid appears with two other maidservants, plus a young man dragging a ladder behind him.

"I'll need tools: a hammer, nails. And can you please light the fireplaces?" It's about time they're put to use.

The staff disperses. In minutes, the fireplaces are lit, gorging on piles of cut, dried wood. The man leans the ladder against one of the windows. I climb to the top and remove the curtain rod, tilting it toward the floor so the cloth slides free. The thump of the fabric hitting the floorboards is oddly satisfying, though the cloud of dust sends me into a coughing fit.

"My lady." Orla fidgets below, her gaze darting from the curtains to the now unblocked window. Bright, shimmering sunlight floods the space, so intense my eyes water. "Are you sure the lord won't mind this?"

"Positive." I descend the ladder and jump the last few rungs. Grabbing one end of the drapery, I drag the entire length toward the fireplace. Flames snap and lick the brick innards. I'm smiling as I heave the enormous lump of fabric into the grate and watch it burn.

"My lady!" A tortured moan chases Orla's outburst. Rapid footsteps sound at my back. "You . . . you can't *burn* the curtains!"

Too late. "They were a personal offense. They had to go."

Another broken sound. I dearly love Orla, even her anxious tendencies. Especially her anxious tendencies. With a few words of reassurance, I send her off to help in the kitchen.

It takes two hours to remove—and destroy—the curtains. Another hour to clean the cobwebs from the rafters. A fourth to remove three centuries' worth of dust caking the floor. A little soap, a lot of scrubbing, a bit of polish, and the wooden floorboards begin to shine.

Throughout the morning, I check in with Silas. Neumovos holds upward of five hundred people, but the kitchen has sufficient space, and he is looking forward to catering for a large crowd. Nothing too extravagant. I'm interested in more traditional fare. Elk, if it can be found. Perhaps a hearty stew.

An hour past noon, I'm busy hanging swaths of gauzy fabric atop one of the fireplace mantels when the doors at the end of the hall crash open, a howling, screaming wind lacerating the warm air and extinguishing the fire to smoke and the memory of light.

My lips purse in irritation.

The Frost King's bootheels clip against the newly polished floor, each footfall singular and precise. His presence is to be expected. I'd prepared for it all morning: what I might say, what he might say. In the end, I have a right to be here. I have a right to grow some happiness in my life.

"What is the meaning of this?" the king demands.

I continue draping the pale blue fabric until I'm pleased with the result. Whimsical and elegant, just as I imagined it to be. Only then do I turn to study Boreas. Clinging breeches and knee-high boots, a snow-dusted sable overcoat. Every round, golden button gleams, the collar parted to reveal the shadowed indentations of his collarbones. "You're going to have to be a little more specific, Husband."

He pivots, gesturing to the western wall, its many windows spared the insufferable weight of layered cloth. "What happened to the curtains?"

I step away to study my handiwork. The glass is so spotless my mind tricks me into thinking it's not there at all, just open-aired archways offering an unobstructed view of the western courtyard. A vast improvement to the previous gloom, as far as I'm concerned.

Turning away with a shrug, I reply, "I burned them."

His eyes bulge, dark eyebrows slashing above that mordacious blue gaze. "Burned them?"

"Yes." The smell of cedar teases my senses as I brush past him. "That's not going to be a problem, is it?"

He trails my heels, boots stomping so obnoxiously I'm grateful we cleaned the floor before his arrival, otherwise I'd be maneuvering through a haze of filth. "That is going to be a problem," he snarls. "You destroyed my property!"

"Yes, well—" Another shrug. "I suppose it's too late for that. And stop barking at me. You're scaring the servants."

The people in question currently huddle around one of the uncovered tables, hands tangled with ribbons, eyes shifting from me to the king and back in quiet unrest. He spares them a cursory glance before returning his furious gaze to me. "I'm not—"

"Yes," I snap, yanking another bolt of gauze from the pile in the corner, "you are. You're also in my way."

His nostrils flare, but he steps aside. I stride toward the second fireplace on the opposite side of the room. Absolutely no one is surprised when Boreas follows, still fuming.

"You are not to host anything without my permission," he whisper-hisses. He is near enough that I can feel the shimmer of his anger against my back. "I forbid you."

Short, startled laughter breaks free. Oh, he *is* funny. "Like I said, it's too late for that." I toss a wide, beaming smile at him over my shoulder. "Now hold this."

He stares at the fabric in his hands, as if confused as to how it has suddenly appeared in his possession. "Too late?" A vein throbs in his temple. "Explain!"

This man. "It's quite simple," I express in an unruffled manner as I drape one end of the blue gauze above the fireplace mantel so it matches the other in style. "There will be a celebration in three days' time. I extended an invitation to Neumovos in hopes of establishing an allyship between us." Stepping back, I study the hung decorations. The left end of the fabric needs to be a little higher, but I can't reach.

"Allyship?" he demands incredulously. "With Neumovos?"

"Boreas, can you adjust the fabric so it's centered?"

He frowns, but does as I ask. His coat stretches taut against his upper back as he lifts his arms to fiddle with the placement. In this light, the color of his hair is not true black, but rather blue and deeper violet. "They are not our allies, nor are they our equals."

"That's what you think."

"I am a god. I *know*. They were Judged to serve me. That is their punishment. They were foolish mortals—"

"As am I," I snap, for his blustering begins to grate on me. "It's time you stopped living in the past, Boreas. You can't live locked away in this citadel for the rest of your immortal life, because *I* refuse to live like that."

He stiffens, face turned partially away, and a pit takes shape in my stomach. Already he's striding toward the door, but I catch his arm, pulling him to a halt. "Wait." My fingers press into muscles frozen with rigidity, and I sigh. "I apologize. That was insensitive of me." I placed blame on him for something I don't understand, and that is because I've yet to form a clear image of the situation. I haven't demanded answers, in part because I hoped he would offer them freely.

Two heartbeats pass before he says, "An apology from you? Is the world ending?"

My fingernails bite into his wrist. "Prick," I mutter, and he snorts, tension bleeding from his frame. I'm relieved to have not ruined the moment completely.

He turns. I still hold his wrist. After a moment, I release him, vaguely aware of the staff decorating in the background.

Quietly, I ask, "Why do you hate mortals so much?"

Equally quiet, he responds, "The bandits."

Of course. "I'm sorry for your loss. I can't imagine how hard that must have been for you." I hesitate, then decide to push onward. It must be said, one way or another. "I know it's probably not what you want to hear, but not every human is like that. People might surprise you."

"Like you did?"

My lips quirk to the side. Lately I've been wondering how different my life might be if I accepted my circumstances. If I stopped fighting. I fight because it's all I know, but I'm tired. I'm tired and I'm hurting, but I think I might be healing, too. For without the bottle, my head is at last clear.

I'm not giving up. I'm just . . . putting this mission on pause, my need to return to Edgewood on pause. I'm choosing something different. For myself.

I step closer, for these words are for his ears only. "Maybe it's time to step away from the darkness. Time to step into the light."

He fears it, the light. I know he does. And why should he not? It is a powerful force of illumination.

The last time we stood this close, the glass, geometric walls of the greenhouse enclosed us. I revealed my insecurities and he did not judge me. He is trusting me to do the same.

"It is not so bad," I say lowly, "when you do not walk in the light alone."

Those blue irises thin as the black centers pool outward like dark water. The face of a cruel king, but he is not all hard edges. There are pieces of gentleness to him.

Something crashes in the kitchen. Clearing my throat, I step away to analyze his handiwork.

"The fabric is still crooked." Turning heel, I stride for the long table pushed against the eastern wall. It's not fleeing if I maintain a walking pace.

"Wren!"

Orla and Thyamine, who busy themselves making wreaths from the gathered dead branches, jump in fright.

The North Wind, a god whose existence spans many millennia, is throwing a tantrum.

I sigh, turning to face him. The amount of outward calm I display is impressive. "Yes?"

"I will not allow the people of Neumovos to infiltrate my home—"

"They are not infiltrating. They were invited." Still calm.

"Regardless, they are not welcome here. You'll have to send them back—"

His desperation grows evident in the sharp hand gestures he makes, which he's obviously not aware of. It's quite humorous. But also concerning. Because when Boreas does not feel in control, his powers tend to manifest in dangerous ways.

A stack of completed wreaths awaits hanging. Grabbing one off the top, I climb the ladder resting against the wall to hang it from one of the nails I hammered in earlier. Boreas stabilizes the ladder as I position the wreath. He's completely unaware that even as he attempts to thwart my plans, he gives aid.

"You are my wife," he continues, "and my word is law."

I bite the inside of my cheek so I won't dissolve into laughter. Truly, he's quite harmless. Like a kitten. "Well," I say once I've gathered myself, "today, you are *my* husband, and I'm in charge." Standing atop the ladder, I'm for once at a height advantage. It's a heady feeling. "I'm doing this. You can try to stop me, but you'll only make yourself miserable, because I promise I'll make you regret it. Now, hand me that hammer, or else."

His glower clashes with mine. He thinks I'll look away first. Doesn't he know me at all?

Eventually, Boreas passes me the hammer. And he does not complain for the remainder of the day.

~

Three days. It's not enough time to bring this crumbling, derelict citadel out of the shadows, but I've never shied from a challenge before. Once the ballroom is transformed, every span polished to a high shine, the space artfully arranged with tables, chairs, and draping fabric, I shift my focus to the dining room, the foyer, the east parlor, the west parlor. The Frost King observes the transformation of his home with borderline hostility, flipping between horror and rage. When given the opportunity, I rope him into a task or three, as I find it helps distract him from the change. The enormous spiral staircase is dusted, wiped down, the oaken banister wrapped in sheer fabric. A few last-minute touches, and it will be perfect.

Currently, Boreas hangs a tapestry I pulled out of storage in the entrance hall. The hammer thunks against something soft—his hand, I imagine. Spitting curses follow. He climbs down the ladder, growling expletives under his breath.

"Let me see," I say.

He cradles his hand against his chest with a wary look.

I sigh in exasperation. "I want to make sure nothing's broken."

"Who's to say you won't break my fingers further to prove a point?"

"You'll just have to trust me."

As soon as the words escape, I wish to call them back. It was a mistake, to say that. Boreas' eyes darken with troubling emotion.

*Trust me.*

A breeze nudges my back. Strangely enough, it is warm. It pushes me forward, into the king's towering body, and something heavy settles against the curve of my spine—his hand, pressed to my lower back.

"You can, you know," I whisper. "Trust me." It doesn't feel like a lie. Edgewood has grown distant over the passing days. Elora, too. Weeks have passed since I've seen Zephyrus. Regardless, I'm not sure I need the sleeping draught anymore.

The knob in his throat dips. "Wife—"

"Wren," I correct, though gently.

His thumb sweeps across the lower vertebrae of my spine, pressing into soft skin. "Wren. I don't do well with social interaction." He speaks barely above a whisper. I can't look away from his mouth.

"You talk to me just fine," I breathe.

He touches my chin, pushing it down so my lips part, teeth on display, the motion strange and mesmerizing, and the deliberate stroke up my back equally so. "You're different."

"Different how?"

The hand on my back slides low again, stopping shy of my backside. My skin prickles as heat carries through me, gathering in my pelvic region. If I were smarter, I'd put distance between us. But I've already established I'm mostly a fool when it comes to my husband.

"You are headstrong." Gruff, as though the very thought displeases him. He squeezes my waist, nudging me closer.

I snort. "You really know how to make a woman swoon, you know that?"

"It was a compliment."

"If you say so."

"Headstrong," he says, "fearless, and brave. I have never met another like you." His eyes burn with an intensity that frightens me, even as some broken piece of me, the one that does not view myself as worthy of such words, smooths over. "I have never met someone who challenges me to see what lies outside of my experience. Never met someone who so easily slides beneath my skin." He breathes in deeply, as if taking the scent of me into his lungs.

Headstrong. Perhaps it is a compliment after all. I will take it.

Clearing his throat, Boreas says, "Have you heard of Makarios?"

I shake my head. He's put a bit of space between us, and I tell myself that is a good thing. The tapestry is now forgotten.

"The Deadlands is a complex realm. Neumovos is but one facet to the whole of this place. There is also the Meadows. There, souls are sent if they've committed no crimes or completed no worthy deeds. It's a peaceful life, if a bit dull. Then there is the Chasm, where only the truly corrupt are sent, including my ancestors."

"It sounds absolutely lovely." As a tumor. "What is it? You've mentioned it before, but I'm not clear as to what it looks like."

"It is a void. An abyss. A crater in the earth." He drags his thumb and forefinger down the sides of his mouth. "Technically, it exists beneath the Deadlands. It is where gods and men receive their eternal punishment, should their actions doom them to such a fate."

"So why aren't you there? Didn't you help overthrow your parents?"

As the silence settles, I loosen my grip on the need to pressure him into a quicker response. I give him the space to think, because if our positions were switched and I was attempting to do something frightening like tear down one of the walls I'd erected around myself, I'd like to know I was safe in doing so.

"My brothers and I were spared," Boreas finally says, "because we helped the coup succeed. But the new gods did not trust us to remain loyal. So we were overpowered, and banished."

"And you were sent here?"

"We drew lots. I was the unlucky one to inherit the Deadlands." The quirk of his mouth draws my focus to the peaks of his upper lip.

"And Makarios? What's it like?" I ask, eager to learn more of this place.

"Makarios is a place that shouldn't belong here, and yet it manages to thrive. It's not something I can explain. It must be experienced." And now he hesitates, the breath contained to his chest. "I would like to show you that the Deadlands, while dark, also hold the greatest potential for light. And nothing shines brighter than Makarios."

# CHAPTER

## 30

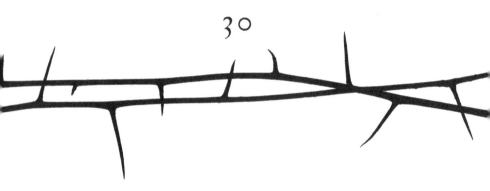

Makarios is a three-day ride from the citadel, but traveling via river only takes a few hours. Standing at the frozen bank of Mnemenos, Boreas melts the ice with a touch, and the arrow-shaped boat drifts from upstream to knock against the soil.

Bundled in my thick winter coat, I'm surprised to find my body sweating beneath the heavy layers.

"It feels warmer," I say. When I glance in Boreas' direction, I find a small notch between his eyebrows. "Do you feel it?"

"No."

Then I must be well and truly going mad. That, or I'm ill. Thinking back on the past few weeks, however, I'm positive the weather has begun to warm. The snow, trickling into slush. Another side-effect of the North Wind's weakening influence?

Once settled in the tiny vessel, the current carries us upstream, through rocky lowlands and austere plains. Eventually, we reach a split in the river, and Boreas touches the water. The current shifts, sending us to the right. Snow and rock dissolve into gray sand, and now I'm certain the air is warming. Enough to remove my coat without fear of frostbite.

Though my attention clings to the passing landscape, I remain aware of the king's gaze on my face, my neck. Mayhap he's curious of my reaction to everything. Gray sand becomes brown soil, then grass, then trees, plentiful and burgeoning, respiring the scent of wet earth following a hard rain.

My heartbeat isn't quite steady as we drift closer to what I imagined the Gray looked like centuries ago, when it was still known as the Green.

The little boat bumps against the river bank, and Boreas helps me ashore. Wet silt and mud suck at my boots. Beyond the bank lies a flawless impression of an untouched land.

"Makarios," he murmurs.

It is a far cry from Neumovos. In fact, this has to be the most beautiful place I've ever seen, the landscape so swollen with green I momentarily forget I stand amidst the Deadlands.

For whatever reason, winter has not touched this stretch of earth. Pressed between eastern and western horizons, the grassy fields roll in gentle undulations, bright pops of wildflowers sprinkled throughout. It is a dream, or a dream of a dream. The sky is a clean sweep, curved and blue, dappled by soft clouds that fade in the distance. The smells are sweeter, the colors brighter, and the air all but sings.

Taking my hand, Boreas draws me up one of the hills, down into its wide depression. The soft grass unfolds beneath our wandering feet. "This is where souls of divine origin, as well as virtuous men and women, are laid to rest. Those worthy of a peaceful life."

After a moment, he pulls his hand free. I'm almost sad to see it go. "How often does that happen?"

"Rarely. To be Judged worthy of this eternity is the highest of honors."

The hearts of mortals, of men, harbor great potential for wickedness. Only the select few are given this grace. My parents would not have been laid to rest here. The Meadows is a greater likelihood. No crimes committed, but no completion of worthy deeds. They were simple folk.

My footsteps make not a sound as I trail after Boreas. He walks slowly. An amble, really, as though he does not have a destination in mind and would rather use this time to meander.

The perimeter of the field is marked by cypress trees interspersed with white poplar, a canopy crowned by silvery leaves, slender trunks pale and splotched with darker bark. The grass-covered hills shallow out, and I glimpse glinting creeks in the dips and hollows. It's so peaceful I'm afraid to speak. This is a quiet that will remain undisturbed for all eternity.

A little farther on, the river peeps into view. A few specters crouch at its bank, filling buckets.

"The souls of Makarios spend their days doing whatever they see fit," says the king. "Here, it does not snow, storm, or rain. Here, they are untouched by sorrow. They have everything they need to build a life, but it is up to them to decide how they might live."

One of the men, dressed in simple clothes, cups the water in his hands and brings it to his mouth. I step forward in alarm. "He's drinking the water. Won't he lose his memories?"

"That river is not Mnemenos."

Oh. And then I remember the split in the waterway. "What river did we travel on?" This water is the deep, endless blue of a jewel. It winds forth, unhurried and appeased.

"It is not named. It originates in Makarios, up near the mountains." He points west, where the rocky earth serrates a patch of sky. "When it reaches the end of the Deadlands, it drops off, falling into mist."

"Do the inhabitants of Makarios retain their memories?"

"They do not," he says. "Over the years, I've found that remembrance often leads to rifts in the population. A breeding ground for jealousy, envy, greed. It is better to begin a new life with a blank slate."

"What about families? People who are related?"

"Families are an exception," he says. "If two or more people from the same family arrive at Makarios, they maintain their relations with one another. Most family members are elderly when they pass on, but that is not always the case. Occasionally, a parent might die young, or a child grows to old age. Memories of their former lives, however, are lost."

As much as I hate the thought of losing the memories of my current life, I think I agree with him. Life ends, just as it begins. I would not want anything holding me back from embracing who I could be in the afterlife. Starting anew.

We continue across the hilly ground until reaching the cool shade of the trees. Beyond, the souls gather in a large clearing within a circle of tents that butts against the fenced-in fields plowed for growing things.

They are dancing. Loose, flowing dresses for the women and trousers for the men, their transparent forms winking in and out as they pass through the light of the sun.

"They look happy," I say in surprise.

"They are happy."

I glance up at Boreas. He continues to watch the specters—many of them children—trade off partners. There is an ease to his features. Contentment.

"Come." He tugs me forward by the hand. "I'd like everyone to meet you."

And by everyone, he means *everyone*. Uncles and daughters and cousins and friends and family pets and neighbors. A woman with a face pressed by deep folds shuffles toward us. She reaches out, takes Boreas' hands in her own. "Quiet one." The words, more breath than substance, sound pleasing to my ears.

That he is letting someone enter his space is shocking enough, but to let her touch him? And without fear?

"This is my wife, Wren." He rests a hand on my shoulder. It grounds me. "It is her first visit to Makarios."

Wrinkles swallow the elder's smiling eyes, and she nods, releasing his hands to take mine. Faint warmth radiates from her grip. Rays of sunlight fall in wide bands through her plump body, the fabric of her dress simple and clean. How long has she been here? Decades? Centuries? What must it be like to wake every day and know no sadness or grief?

"Good girl," the woman announces. She pats my hand. "A good partner. Loyal and strong."

And how would she know that?

Boreas is drawn into a short discussion about the harvest, and I use the time to idly observe the festivities. After she leaves us, I turn to Boreas with newfound revelation. "They know you."

He peers down at me. "Of course they know me."

"No, I mean they *know* you." This level of familiarity is not established from a single meeting, Judgment served in the vast halls of his citadel. It comes from exposure over time. Frequent visits, if my assumption is correct. "How often do you visit Makarios?"

He accepts a flower garland from a young girl, who skips off to play with a group of children, yet turns from my gaze. Does he think I judge him for visiting these souls? I was under the impression that his interest in the dead ended once their Judgment was determined. Another thing I was wrong about.

"One of my duties as the North Wind is to visit the various parts of the Deadlands, to ensure they are in working order." He drapes the garland—blooming roses and iris—around my neck. "But I spend additional time in Makarios when I can. The people are kind, deserving of this life."

These souls don't view Boreas as a monster. He has granted them a place to sleep without worries, an opportunity to rise with the knowledge that a day has endless potential for all the good things.

"You're right." Never did I think those words could pass my lips, but things have changed. I've changed. "This place—it's beautiful." Not the physical location, though that is certainly magnificent, but what he has created here. A haven, safe from the encroaching cold.

He could have shown me Makarios at any point. But it wouldn't have made a difference. My mind would not have changed. I would have found a way to sully this place. I wasn't ready to accept the truth, and he knew that. Only now does he let me in, let me see.

And so we stand in the field where peace has bedded down, the spirits drifting hand-in-hand with one another, and I ask my husband a question I have long since wondered.

"What became of Orla's husband?"

The tips of his naked fingers brush the bark of a nearby tree, curved black talons scraping the rough texture. I'd like to view his hesitation as a step, however small. Evidence of the trust between us, that Boreas no longer feels the need to guard his words as carefully as his heart.

A corner of his mouth slides diagonally into his cheek. "I admit, I brought you here to show you that another side exists to the Deadlands."

*I brought you here to show you that another side exists to the Deadlands—and to me.*

Had he spoken those final three words, I would be inclined to agree. The North Wind is not a plane of ice, flat and uninspiring and of a single dimension. He is like the snowflakes he calls down, each multi-faceted, uniquely wrought.

"But I am afraid," he goes on, "that if I were to tell you what horrors Orla's husband currently suffers through, you will return to your previous perspective of the Deadlands, and of me."

"And what perspective would that be?"

"That the Deadlands, and everything in it, is abhorrent."

I believe at one point I did call Boreas a selfish, narrow-minded, heartless god. Although at the time, I thought that was the least of what he deserved.

Without being consciously aware of it, I shift nearer, my arm brushing his, the fabric of our sleeves clinging. "You told me you seek to make a fair assessment of a soul's choices. So I trust that however you sentenced her husband, it was justified."

He drops his hand from the tree, where it hangs at his side. Shadows coat his knuckles and wrists in swaths thick as paint.

"Orla was one of the earliest souls I sentenced to Neumovos. I Judged her based on the murder of her husband, but I looked no deeper than that. I didn't care to, and the fault was mine."

He takes a bracing breath. "It was my first wife, actually, who told me of what had led Orla to kill her husband."

"The one who threatened to castrate you?"

"Yes." His face softens, and my heart twinges with a sudden, unforeseen pain. I empathize with him, but that's not all, is it? The thought of Boreas harboring lingering feelings toward his late wife bristles in me. Pathetic and petty, that's me. "She learned what this man had done to Orla during their marriage." At this, his expression hardens, and the wrath flickering in his pupils is so potent I nearly take a step back. "I realized I had misjudged Orla. I did not complete my due diligence in learning the truth behind her actions." Boreas angles his body toward mine, and now my shoulder brushes his chest. "As for her husband, I sent him to the Chasm. For the beating, neglect, and raping of his wife, his punishment is to be ripped to shreds by wild dogs, day after day. As well, his fingernails are pried off with rusted nails, and regrown. His body starves, on the cusp of total collapse. The pain keeps him awake, never allowing him to sleep."

By the gods, it sounds horrid. But—deserved. Absolutely deserved.

I study him closely. Relieved to know he tried to set things right, but also concerned. The greater the responsibility, the heavier the weight. "Does it ever feel like a burden to you? You are the deciding voice of so many eternities."

A slow, solemn nod. "All the time. But Judging people's lives objectively isn't always possible." He nudges me with his shoulder, a lighthearted gesture, so unlike him. "You taught me that."

"You're saying you take my perspective into consideration?" I gesture wiping away an imaginary tear.

Boreas releases a sigh that can only belong to the long-suffering. "I rescind my thoughts."

"It's too late for that." Oh, I try fighting the smile, I really do. But my teeth make a brief appearance in the king's company.

He shakes his head, stares out at the peaceful field with its long stalks of swaying grass. I could very well let the conversation end there, but it doesn't seem right, considering how far we've come, that we can stand together in companionable silence without wanting to do the other harm.

"Thank you." My voice, a hoarse whisper, disintegrates like threads after too-frequent a washing.

He peers down at me. "For?"

"For what you did for Orla. And," I continue before courage can fail me, "for what I suspect you'd do for me."

❧

We depart Makarios mid-afternoon, when the air has warmed enough to wish for cotton garments as opposed to wool. The flower crown perched atop my head—a gift from the villagers—bears tiny white blossoms, and I pat my hair into place as Boreas and I drift down the river in peace, sitting side by side on the bench. This has never happened before. To sit, to empty the mind, to not think of the next step, every action a means to spring a trap.

I could learn to love it, I realize. Just . . . sitting. Breathing. Here, with him.

"There is one more place I'd like to show you." The low notes of his voice travel through where our arms press together, and I turn my head a fraction, catching his face in the fringe of my vision, that strong nose, which he always insists on glaring down at me. Can't say I haven't done the same.

"A king, a banished god, and . . . benevolent guide?" My mouth quirks playfully.

"Are you interested? I think you'd like it." His smile climbs all the way to his eyes, creasing the skin there. For once, Boreas is completely relaxed. It feels earned. "They serve cake."

Why didn't he say so? "Lead the way."

Back at the citadel, Boreas directs me to the north wing. His guards part to let us pass. Aside from entering his son's room, I've yet to explore this part of the fortress.

At the end of the hall, we turn right. The structure falls into further disrepair, a dilapidated cavern shrouded in neglect. Not a home, not now, but might it have been, once? Might it one day be again?

Tapestries and curtains hang in tatters on the walls, and the stone floor is a broken mess, slabs of gray rock peaked and uneven, overgrown with old, twisting roots. The doors lining these halls are nothing but pieces of wood or metal hanging before holes in the walls, leading nowhere.

As we round the next corner, I'm met with the largest tapestry yet, slender threads woven into an image of four men standing atop a cliff, the world behind flooded with golden light.

The Anemoi.

I recognize Boreas, the spear he carries, his long black cloak. There is Zephyrus with his bow, the tumble of curls. The third brother carries a sleek curved sword. He is the shortest of the four, yet his chest and arms strain with muscle, his deep brown skin agleam in the fiery sun. Notus, the South Wind, if I were to guess.

That leaves the last figure: Eurus, the East Wind. But the only depiction is a tall, cloaked man with broad shoulders, his face wreathed by the shadowy opening of his hood.

"There isn't much family resemblance," I state. Boreas is pale-skinned. Zephyrus, golden and sun-kissed. Black eyes and black hair for Notus. I'm deeply curious of what Eurus looks like beneath the cowl.

Boreas says nothing. What does he see when he looks upon the faces of his siblings? I suppose I might never know.

He pivots and continues down the hall. I hurry to catch up with him, leaping over broken furniture and crippled pillars of stone. The walls are pocked with holes as though having been torn open by two hands in a fit of unchecked rage.

"Some months are more difficult than others." He won't look at me. "It's harder to control the change as time goes on."

Clearly. "Why do you think your soul is turning corrupt?"

"If I knew, do you think I would be in this situation?"

I rein in the lashing retort rising to coat my tongue. Fire cannot contest fire. Only water, gentle and healing, may dampen the rage that climbs and climbs. "I may not have a corrupted soul, but I understand darkness. I understand that as long as you blame yourself for past mistakes, you'll never move forward."

His gait quickens. From between his teeth, he pushes out, "I'm not sure what you mean by that."

Does he not? "You blame yourself for the deaths of your wife and child," I state, chasing after him. Fragmented doors flicker past. "Tell me I'm wrong."

That he does not speak reveals enough. I did not lie. I understand plenty. Enough to realize that Boreas and I are, in many ways, a reflection of the other. I'm not sure how I didn't see it sooner.

His hand cuts the air, pain etched in every line on his face. "I have suffered and I have grieved, but I have not forgotten. I don't know if I will ever be able to forget."

"Maybe the problem isn't forgetting," I say, pulling him to a standstill. "Maybe the problem is you haven't forgiven yourself for something you had absolutely no control over."

We stand chest to chest, my head tilted back so I can gaze into his face fully. He grinds out, "It was my duty to protect my wife and child, and I failed."

"Was it your duty to protect them, or to love them?"

A muscle pulses in his cheek. "Both."

I nod at that. Shelter and provide and defend. This, too, I understand. "Is this to be your life then? Trapping yourself in this blame, to never find reprieve from the weight of your guilt?" Quieter, I ask, "Can't a god earn forgiveness, even a banished one?"

I'm not sure how long, exactly, we stare at one another. But I feel like I'm falling. Or I've been falling, and my only wish is to continue this drop because my heart is soaring. It's been given wings.

The North Wind asks, "Am I worthy of such a thing?"

"I don't know," I counter. "Are you?"

"No." He speaks with the conviction of one who has asked himself this question before. "I am not."

My heart breaks for him. This isn't right. How can he think so little of himself? How can I think so little of myself? "And what if I think you are?" I challenge. "What then?"

The king takes a strand of my hair, then tucks it behind my ear, the tips of his fingers brushing its sensitive shell. His touch shifts to the curve of my jaw, and he hesitates. But he continues up to my cheek, and coasts along my scarring, and I fight the need to bow my head beneath the caress, a wave of gooseflesh pebbling my skin. "You are," he says, "not what I expected."

And now we tread untrodden ground. A road whose path is full of ruts, and I stare down the stretch before me, wondering if a broken ankle would be worth it. I remind him, "You wanted to show me something?"

Boreas nods, steps back. A little twist in my stomach but . . . it's for the best.

He leads me to a gold-wrought door at the end of the hall, sunlight pouring through the panes of glass from within. He turns the knob. "Welcome," he says, "to the City of Gods."

# CHAPTER

## 31

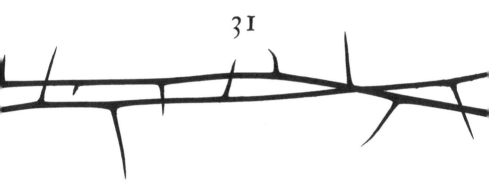

Gold and light and marble columns. Flat rooftops and airy courtyards and filigreed molding. Fountains and the musk of pressed olives. Climbing wisteria and summer on the breeze. In other words: perfection.

Boreas and I stand on the threshold looking out at a spherical plaza marked by an incredibly elaborate fountain. Gauzy curtains flap from open windows of teetering, multi-storied buildings. Plant-filled alcoves pocket the space between the balconies, from which hang cloth colored the white of snow and the blue of the deepest sea. Damp spray sends prisms of colored light fluttering across the ground, which is fashioned from pure, hammered gold. The air feels strange. There is a presence here I cannot detect.

Sensing Boreas' gaze on me, I say in wonder, "This is where you grew up."

He surveys our view for a time. "Technically, I grew up outside the city limits." He points to a spot far beyond the rooftops, nestled among the mountainous region surrounding the city proper. The columned edifice, constructed from moon-white stone, appears to be a temple of some sort. "But my family would visit the city on occasion."

Boreas as a child. I'm imagining him splashing in the fountains or playing marbles in the streets. It's an odd thought, considering the North Wind is, firstly, many millennia old, and secondly, not a figure who inspires childhood nostalgia. "Do you miss it?"

The fountain burbles gladly. He watches the arc of the falling water, and again glances at that mountain temple. "It has been many years since I've returned." He shuts the door at our backs and begins unbuttoning his coat. Indeed, it is far warmer here. I quickly follow his example and lay my coat alongside his on an empty bench. "But it is hard to miss a place where you are no longer welcome."

Took the words right out of my mouth.

I fall into step beside him as we take a side street leading away from the plaza, a path of uneven white stones. A few people pass us by. Gods and goddesses, rather. They don't notice our presence. "Can anyone see us?"

"No." It is a word coated in bitterness, vile and acerbic. "My name—as well as my brothers'—was struck from the books following our banishment. We no longer exist to the gods. As a mortal, however, you haven't the power to manifest in this city. They may sense something in passing, but you are so far beneath them your physical presence doesn't register."

It's strangely comforting, in a vain, pretentious way.

Boreas gestures me down an avenue lined with open-air market stands and wheeled carts. I move through it eagerly. It's a pleasure to sift through the bustle of life in a new place. The divine act as both vendors and patrons, moving about from stall to table to wagon to investigate wares: wooden buckets of the sweetest, ripest apricots; bushels of freshly picked flowers; furniture; marble sculptures shaped as nude men and women—"The divine are notoriously narcissistic," Boreas mutters—caged birds; various textiles; leather sandals; tomes and scrolls. For a city ruled by the divine, the market is surprisingly . . . humble.

As we meander through the throng, Boreas explains the importance of agriculture to his society, the offerings gods prefer at their altars, the various methods of worship. I haven't prayed in a long time, haven't left offerings for any god, not when I believe them to have abandoned my people.

One of the vendors catches my eye near the end of the road. He's positioned his stand in the shade of two columns at his back, wide stone steps leading to a temple on his right. He sells wine—bottles of it. At the moment, he's deep in conversation with a goddess wearing a long, flowing dress, an owl perched on her shoulder.

Though none of the patrons notice our presence, the owl turns its head, peers at me unblinkingly over the folded wings across its back. The vendor's yellow hair glints where it curls over his naked shoulders. He laughs with abandon, and the sound pours out as he offers a cup of wine to the goddess.

"That would be the Vintner," Boreas mutters darkly. "If he's not participating in some debauched revelry, he's sticking his cock in a willing body. Drunken fool."

I turn away from the unintentional sting of his insult. The king wasn't referring to me, but he might as well have been. I have found myself in that very same position more times than I can count. I shouldn't care. I shouldn't give a damn what Boreas thinks of me—

The king stops me with a hand on my arm. Grips it gently, then tugs me to face him. Every line imprinted in his flawless countenance reveals a severeness I haven't seen in many days now. "I'm sorry," he says. "I wasn't saying that about you."

"But it applies to me." My cheeks burn hot.

He steps closer, lowering his voice. His scent and his heat and his skin and his breath envelop me too easily. "I will have to be more careful with my words in the future. I'm used to speaking without thought for others." A little furrow crinkles the smooth curve of his forehead. "For what it's worth, I consider you neither a drunk nor a fool."

I accept his explanation with a murmured, "Thank you." Though honestly, his apology alone would have sufficed.

"How are you holding up?"

I shrug. He has yet to put space between us. If I were of a more romantic nature, I might think this an attempt to shelter me. "I have good days and bad days." Last night was especially difficult. I called Orla into my room, begging for a bottle, a mouthful, a drop. Then she sat with me while I tossed and turned in my sweat-soaked blankets before switching them out for clean sheets with the dawn.

Turning away from him, I continue down the cramped road. Boreas falls into step beside me, avoiding the growing crowd easily with his grace. Softly, the words nearly lost to the clatter and din, he says, "Drinking may not be the healthiest coping mechanism, but it is far better than how I dealt with my grief."

My next step falters, but I keep moving. Once free of the market, the king guides me to a garden—quieter, thick with serenity and flowering plants, a little walking trail tucked among the broad, flat leaves. "What do you mean?"

He brushes his fingers against the greenery in passing. I'm almost positive he isn't aware of it, for his eyes have slipped behind a clouded haze. "When my wife and son were taken from me," he says, "the line between life and death blurred so much that I stopped living." We stroll side by side down the trail, passing yet another fountain. "I thought, if I could not protect the lives of people I loved, then maybe I didn't deserve a life anyway."

Something about his phrasing causes distress to spike in me. Surely he's not inferring what I think he is . . . though what other interpretation is there?

"I returned here, to the city, and I went to the Temple where the new gods held council. They, as the highest power, remembered me." There is a pause. "I asked them to end my life."

Shock roots my feet in the middle of the path. Boreas stops a few paces ahead, his back to me, but eventually he turns, and the churning emotion in his eyes, free for all to see, darkens with unspeakable grief.

This is a delicate—a very delicate—subject. I'm not sure of the way forward. Even at my lowest point, I never considered ending my life. I had Elora to care for, of course, but even if I hadn't, it's not in my nature to consider that an option. "What— I mean, obviously you're still here so . . ."

"They turned me away." He continues down the path, pushing through long, spindly threads of leaves from above. "Grief became my sentence, and I returned to the citadel, with its empty rooms, its memories."

Where he has been ever since.

We wander off-trail in the direction of a smaller plaza to the west, where bands of golden light burnish the pale stoned buildings. Gods of every color and size and manner of dress ease past, completely oblivious that one of their own has returned. One woman slips through the throng with a deer at her side, a bow slung across her back. A few blocks over, a god parades the streets atop his shining chariot, blood and gore sullying its sides.

I knew the North Wind had experienced loss, but I never realized how deeply it had impacted him. Enough to die. Enough to no longer exist, not even in memory. There have always been bright spots in my days, even if they grew more shadowed in the passing years.

"I suppose that's the burden of a mortal life," I say. The road curves, revealing a tiered vegetable garden to the left, another fountain to the right. "One day, our lives will end, and we move on, even if those we leave behind cannot."

~

Our meandering takes us to a small, outdoor seating area overlooking a park. While I settle in the shade beneath the overhanging second-story balcony, Boreas disappears and returns with two crystal glasses, setting them on the table, before taking the chair across from me.

"Wine?" I didn't expect Boreas to put me in a compromising position, especially one that would send me spiraling back to the sad, sorry person I'd been, peace and comfort found only in the dregs of a bottle.

"Nectar." He passes me my drink. The bright, gleaming substance, like liquid gold, clings thickly to the glass when I swirl it around. It smells of lemon and sugar. I take a sip, let it coat my tongue, and startle as the flavor becomes clear. "It tastes like chocolate cake with cherry filling and fudge icing." I gawp at the drink in bewilderment. "What is this sorcery?"

The corners around Boreas' mouth tick upward. "The nectar tastes like whatever your favorite food is." The glass looks comically dainty in his large hand.

I take another sip, because it's been so long since I've had my mother's cherry-filled chocolate cake. I've attempted to replicate it, but it never tastes the same. "What does it taste like to you?"

"A golden apple." At my intrigue, he goes on, "The fruit doesn't exist in your realm. They grow in a garden whose whereabouts are unknown, guarded by a large serpent."

Which makes me think of another particular garden hidden in the looming veil of a cave. "Are they made of gold?"

"Yes, but they taste like . . ." He ponders for a moment. "Like the best thing you have yet to taste."

"Hm." Settling back in the chair, I observe the cityfolk strolling throughout the park. No one seems to be in any particular hurry. The swelling backs of the mountains uproot the sky beyond the city, with its clean, elegant lines, ivy-grown balconies, and fluted marble pillars. "It's peaceful here. I like it."

"How does it compare to what you imagined it to look like?"

Truthfully, I hadn't given much thought to Boreas' home. It was far down the list of more pressing matters. "It's quieter than I thought it would be, but no less lovely." A slight hesitation before I take another sip of my drink. "I always wanted to travel places. I wanted to see the world, even knowing I likely never would." Despite wishing there would come a day when the earth warmed, I knew Elora would never want to leave Edgewood. And I could never leave Elora. Until I did.

The king studies me before taking a collective sweep of our surroundings. "But you have traveled places, haven't you?" At my puzzled expression, he elaborates, "In books."

Ah. "Yes, I have. But I long for a physical change of scenery as well. I want to see places with my own eyes. I want to experience the smells and flavors and colors of a new region." What I mean to say is that I want to feel present wherever I am, but I'm reluctant to voice that. "But books are a decent substitute."

The muscles of his throat flex with his swallow. I can't help but stare. "What else would you like to see?" Boreas asks. "There are theaters, symphonies, art galleries, libraries, the university, bookstores, the ballet—"

"Bookstore." I finish off the nectar, place the glass on the table. "And then the ballet. Oh, and maybe on the way back we can stop and get one of those pastries I saw in the bakery window earlier . . ."

～

Many hours later, I stand in front of the mirror in my bedchamber and wonder if my outfit is too much, too . . . vulnerable. This is becoming a habit—mirror-gazing. I should shatter the damn thing, but I don't shy from my reflection as I once did, and that is its own victory. My scar does not mark me as undesirable. It is but a memory wrapped in old, tough skin. Boreas has never shown revulsion toward it, but what does he see when he looks at me? Really, it shouldn't matter, and I shouldn't care. But it does matter. And I do care.

This is a problem.

"Lovely as usual, my lady."

Orla appears at my left shoulder in the mirror's reflection. Hours and hours Boreas and I spent in the City of Gods, wandering late into the evening until the shops closed, and although it is now the middle of the night, I'm not tired, not even a wink. I tug on the fabric nervously. The dress, cream fabric with a forest green trim, is on the looser side, allowing me to move about freely. My dark hair is unbound, falling in gentle waves over my shoulders. My eyes are dark, knowing, acknowledging the change that has come over me of late. I have to say, I don't dislike the person I see.

"Wish me luck," I say.

"I would," says Orla with a secret smile, "but you don't need it."

Oh, yes I do.

*Breathe.*

Nerves have no place this evening. The king and I have shared meals hundreds of times. But my palms prickle with sweat as I make my way downstairs to the dining room. The afternoon passed too quickly for my liking. Books, then the ballet, then the bakery, then the park, then back to the bakery. We later visited the university library upon my request to peruse the vast collection in the marble, column-lined building.

To my surprise, Boreas has already arrived and sits at the head of the table, his coat tossed over the back of his chair, tunic unbuttoned near the neck, black hair untethered and curling around his face. He stands upon my entrance, and I move toward my seat before realizing my usual place setting is absent. No plate, glass, utensils, or napkin. I turn to him in confusion, that faint, panicky feeling rolling as a single drop of sweat down the length of my spine.

Wordlessly, he gestures to the chair on his immediate right. My place setting has moved.

I'm proud that I only hesitate for half a heartbeat before taking my seat. This is certainly closer than Boreas and I have ever dined before, but it shouldn't be an issue. After spending so much time in his company today, I'm already used to the proximity.

"So," I say, taking a sip of water. "What's on the menu tonight?"

He lifts a hand, and the staff place six covered dishes onto the table. The silver domes bleed candlelight across their curved reflective surfaces.

"In the City of Gods," Boreas begins, "a meal is a communal affair. The divine love nothing more than to gorge, to connect with our more gluttonous natures, whatever form that might take." He uncovers the smallest dish, which sits farthest to the left. A round red fruit, cut in half, rests in the center of the silver plate. Red-orange juice pools beneath it.

"Eating is a tactile pursuit," he goes on. "A meal's purpose is to incite the senses. Thus, we feed the person to our immediate right."

I blink dumbly, certain I misheard him. "Feed? Like . . ."

He waits, his eyes very dark. The rings of blue around his pupils are so slender they appear nonexistent.

My lungs expand until the pinch near my ribs forces me to exhale. By then, the ground has solidified beneath my feet.

It is a dance, I suppose. Boreas offers me his hand, and I must decide whether to accept or deny him. I'm not a coward. I may be out of my depth, but I am not the only one taking a risk tonight. It's a strange, if twisted, comfort.

"Show me," I demand.

He moves without haste. He may be a sculptor for all the care and devotion he gives this task, peeling the fruit into sections, tearing free the rind. The knot in my stomach constricts. Patience has never been my strong suit, and hearing the slow, muffled tearing as Boreas separates the fruit is a unique form of agony.

And when he is done, he leans over the arm of his chair, his face inches from mine. My nostrils flare. His scent is darker on this night, rich with intensity.

"You need to open your mouth," he murmurs.

Right. That would be helpful.

My lips part in some deep-seeded reflex, and the fruit slides inside, slightly sweet, slightly musky. Boreas pulls back, though remains within my personal space, watching as I chew and swallow. A drop of fruit juice seeps from the corner of my mouth. He trails its winding path down my chin, gaze keen, jaw taut. I swipe it away with the back of my hand.

The knob in his throat dips. "Now you." A low, deep rasp.

My fingers twitch against my thighs, and my gaze falls to his mouth. I've always considered it the softest part of him. A mouth that does not belong to a man, yet somehow, it only adds to his allure.

"Scared?" He speaks the word like a croon, the points of his canines pronounced.

My eyes dart to his, narrowing. "Prick."

He chuckles. And I must be dreaming, because the sound is so rarely heard I scarcely recognize it.

I came to the Deadlands to kill this man. Instead, we are feeding one another.

I can do this. I *will* do this.

Readying myself, I select a section of the fruit and lean toward him. His fingers wrap around my wrist in the process, holding it there. The strength in his grip is too great to break. Heat pools between my legs as our eyes lock, my lips parting as, slowly, he draws the fruit, and my fingers, into his mouth.

My mind blanks. The hot, wet suction of his cheeks latches onto my fingers, and he takes a shallow pull, his throat working to ingest the mixture of saliva and fruit juice. *I can't breathe, I can't breathe, I can't breathe—*

He takes another sucking drag, gathering the last of the juice before swallowing. A flush ignites beneath my skin, scorching me from head to foot. I expect Boreas to pull away, but he doesn't. A low sound emanates from deep within his chest, the rough vibrations traveling up my arm. My core clenches in response of that sound, for it is something an animal might make, twined in madness and desire, the basest of natures.

The tip of his tongue flirts across my fingertips before sliding through the space between my pointer and middle finger. My breasts grow heavy as his tongue licks across my skin, leaving no area unmarked. Not once does he look away. Not once does he blink. He holds my gaze with bold daring, outright challenge, even. I'm perched on the edge of my seat, awaiting in painful anticipation of his next move.

But Boreas pulls away, and my gaze drops to his mouth. His lips gleam with dampness from where he sucked on my fingers. I realize we've somehow leaned toward one another, for I can see the striated slivers of blue, like fractures of light, in his irises. His breath grazes my parted lips.

His tongue on my fingers is only the beginning. I'm imagining it on other parts of my body. Across my breasts and between my legs, the hot seal of his mouth lingering in the places where I ache and ache.

As though he did not just rock the ground beneath my feet, Boreas leans back and removes the covering from the slightly larger second plate. A small cup of what appears to be broth sits on display, steam wafting upward.

"This is broth from the bone of the spotted elimna, which is similar to the grouse. It is a delicacy of my people." Smooth and cultured and dignified. I'm almost offended. Was he affected by that demonstration at all? "The fowl is harvested in the fall when the air begins to cool."

It takes effort, but eventually, my pulse drops from its careening high. If the king insists on maintaining composure, then I will, too. "You take a sip, then I take a sip?" The curl of the vapor is unexpectedly mesmerizing.

His short claws click against the glass as he brings it to his mouth, but he does not drink. "I take a sip," he says calmly, "and then I pass that sip onto you." At my blank stare, he elaborates, "Into your mouth."

"My mouth?"

"This is how it is done in the City of Gods." Cool and unperturbed.

Is it though? He's telling me all the gods partake in this sexually-charged custom, even close family members? "In case you haven't noticed," I croak, "we're not in the city anymore. We're in the Deadlands." And the thought of his mouth on mine . . . I've thought of it. I'm not a corpse. I've thought of that kiss in the greenhouse an embarrassing amount, despite it having been bestowed in comfort. This is not a comfort. This is something dark and raw and torn open, something that aches.

This is hunger.

"Ah." He sets down the glass. "So it is fear."

The king has learned exactly where to prod all those weak, soft places. If it's a challenge he wants, it's a challenge I will rise to meet. "Do it."

*I'm mad, I'm mad, I'm completely mad—*

Taking a small sip of the broth, he leans forward, cupping my head with both hands.

My heart staggers, and I lick my lips in anticipation of the kiss. My hands curve around his wrists. To steady myself. And to keep him close.

The sound of a horn cuts the quiet.

Boreas goes still.

The cry peaks, wavers, then dies. We remain locked in position as I whisper, "What was that?"

He swallows, leans back to put distance between us. I can't read the expression on his face. "There has been another breach in the Shade. My men call for aid." His hands drop, taking the warmth of his touch with it. "I must go." He stands.

The word howls through my mind, painful and unfulfilled. *Go.* The panic rears, a snarling mouth edged in teeth. There is no thought, only action, the desire to be near him longer than the day we have been given. I shove to my feet as well. "I'm coming with you."

# CHAPTER

## 32

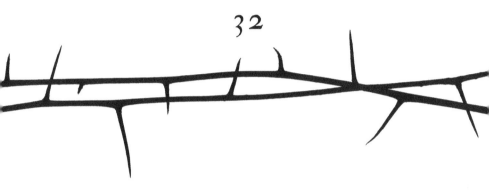

Boreas and I meet in the stables, where the air smells of hay and leather. Phaethon stamps inside his stall as if sensing the gathering beyond the walls, bodies laden with weapons, the clink of armor. Hundreds of battle-hardened men.

It's not yet sunrise. Dawn, with her rose-kissed fingers, will stir the dead trees into color within a few hours. As Boreas tightens the girth of Phaethon's saddle, I perch on a bale of hay, rubbing my hands together to keep them warm. I'm under the assumption I'll be riding with Boreas, but he surprises me by saying, "There's something I'd like to show you."

He sounds unsure. The king is never unsure.

"All right," I respond warily.

With a tilt of his head, he gestures me deeper into the building. The specter horses drop their heads over the stall doors in interest of the king's passing. At the end of the walkway, he turns left. The stalls near the back are empty—all but one. A lamp hanging from one of the support beams leaks light onto the creature that watches me with a single bright eye.

The mare is stunning, all long legs, an elegant, streamlined head, and a proud, arched neck. Her semi-transparent coat reminds me of wheat grass, a color shaded between the milk of a full moon and the brown of parched earth. Then there is the mane and tail, a paler cream against the darker coat. A white star shines on her forehead.

Reaching out, I offer the mare my hand to sniff. Warm breath coasts across my palm, and she nibbles my fingers curiously. The whiskers on her chin scratch my skin as I stroke the soft, velvet nose.

"She's beautiful," I say, and I mean that sincerely. Perhaps the most beautiful horse I've ever seen, even if she is a spirit. "Which guard did you bribe to lend me his horse?" And by *bribe*, I mean *threaten*.

The Frost King doesn't answer. I suddenly realize how quiet it is—his men must have moved off at some point—and I turn toward him. He stands with his arms hanging awkwardly at his sides, studying me with caution. Something shifts between us. Something grows behind my eyes, as if they are opening for the first time.

"This is one of your soldier's horses," I ask, taking note of any subtle reactions he might give me, "right?" I miss them if I'm not paying attention.

"She's yours."

My fingers tangle in the horse's mane, which feels like fog and light intertwined. I'm certain I didn't mishear him. "You bought me a horse?"

Boreas avoids my eye. "I bought her from a trainer in Neumovos so you wouldn't have to ride with me. He gave me a good price. It's nothing."

It is the furthest thing from nothing.

The chance to ride throughout his territory at will. A sign of his trust in me, belief that I will not attempt to flee. Boreas has gifted me something that, for the first time in my life, is wholly mine.

A hard knot of emotion swells in my throat. I sense a shift inside myself. Something soft taking place of all the hardness I've endured.

"Thank you," I whisper, lifting my gaze to his. "I will treasure her for the rest of my days."

He regards me for a long moment, perhaps in indecision. Then he crosses the distance separating us, tucking himself beside me against the stall. The mare sniffs his hair, and the Frost King's mouth curves. "What will you name her?" he asks, pressing a large palm to the horse's muscular neck.

The tip of his smallest finger rests a hairsbreadth from mine. For whatever reason, I'm fixated on that observation.

"Iliana," I say. "My mother's name."

"Iliana." Boreas tracks the path my hand makes as it smooths over the mare's cheek. "It suits her. You can choose whatever stall you like. And these are yours," he says, gesturing to her outfitting: saddle, blanket, bridle, halter. "The hosteler will care for her if you wish."

"That won't be necessary. I will oversee her care." Not that I distrust the hosteler—he is excellent with the horses—but it's important to shape the bond between horse and rider in those early days.

Since Iliana is already saddled, all that's left is to walk her out of the stable. Phaethon tosses his head, preening in the presence of a lady friend, and his shadowy breath streams out in dissolving tendrils. Soldiers gather beyond the gates. They are stoic and focused, reserved and unquestioning. The air hangs still around us. It hits me then, what awaits at the end of this trek, the long miles and many hours ahead.

"How dire is it?" I ask as Boreas mounts, directing Phaethon to my side.

He lifts a hand to his captain, signaling departure. Briefly, Pallas' gaze meets mine. I have not forgotten our first encounter in the practice court months prior, and he likely hasn't either. As long as he keeps his distance, I'll have no reason to spear another arrow through his chest. He's likely learned his lesson by now anyway.

"According to my men, the newest tear has expanded overnight."

"Then we'll close it," I say. Knit all those holes back together, and stop the humans from crossing into the Deadlands.

"We will do no such thing." He regards me from atop his mount. "The risk to your life is too great."

For the briefest moment, I sense an undercurrent of fear from Boreas. For *me*. And maybe more, if I am to look deeper. If I don't balk from the thought. "That's never stopped you before."

"That was then."

Tugging Iliana's reins to the right, I move toward the gates. "So what's the point of me traveling with you?"

"You tell me." Softly amused. "You volunteered to come."

He has a point. "This is war, is it not? And in war, there is always something to be done." I imagine there will be plenty to do once we reach camp.

The king inclines his head in approval. "Indeed."

Boreas and I ride abreast at the head of the campaign: two precise columns, the tail extending a half-mile behind. The journey takes the day. For the most part, I'm content to ride in silence, listening to the soldiers laugh and poke fun at one another—many have known each other hundreds of years, if that can be believed—but Boreas and I occasionally engage in small talk, which no longer makes me want to pull my hair out.

We reach camp before sundown. Tents, arranged in neat rows, dot the snow-patched clearing, white canvas pulled taut and staked into the ground. The air rings with honed metal and heavy, stamping hooves. Soldiers push carts of supplies down the muddy path, or gather firewood from the surrounding forest, or dig latrines. I spot servants among the group, men and women both. There is no laughter. There is barely conversation. Tension and uncertainty seep through the half-frozen soil.

Many of the soldiers and staff stare despite the hood covering my face. I dip my chin in acknowledgement. Regardless of what they think of me, I am here to help.

After being relieved of our mounts, the Frost King directs us to a voluminous tent situated on the northern end of camp, two men guarding the entrance. He dismisses them and pulls aside the flap for me to enter. Once inside, I halt in place.

I stare at the bed.

He stares at the bed.

Of course there is only one bed—again.

Of course.

The Frost King breaks the spell, striding forward with purpose.

Grabbing a pillow from the mattress, he tosses it in my direction. "You can sleep on the floor." He then proceeds to turn down the blankets, his back to me.

I gape at him, the pillow crushed between my palms, as the comment stirs in my memory. I said those exact words to him when we were forced to share a bed on Midwinter Eve.

"You bastard." I heave the pillow at the back of his head. It hits and falls harmlessly to the ground. "I'm not sleeping on the floor."

The king goes still. He makes a soft sound. At first, I think it's a scoff, yet it's quickly followed by a second, deeper exhalation. His shoulders tremble, his back shakes, his head drops forward, hair swinging to curtain his face. And then he turns, and I'm at a loss for words.

The North Wind is *laughing*.

And it is absolutely devastating.

His teeth are perfectly straight, perfectly bright. The edges of his mouth stretch all the way to his eyes, which crinkle with merriment. It completely transforms his face. It is as though he has shed an old skin. The laughter emanating from his chest flows like a slow current, and I stare. How can I not? In this moment, he is not the prickly, aloof immortal I've come to know. He is a man, in the flesh. My husband.

A pulse of pleasure quickens my blood. Against my better judgment, my mouth pulls. I snort at the absurdity of whacking a god with a pillow in a moment of irritation.

When the laughter trails off, the camp sounds intrude. I sniff with offense. "We'll share the bed like last time."

Boreas smiles, and it is free. "As you wish . . . Wren."

~

When light dies to the east, a bell clangs throughout the camp. Boreas rises from where he's been reading documents at his desk to tug on his boots. "Dinner," he announces.

I straighten in my chair, setting aside my pencil as he ties the laces up his calf muscle. "Isn't the staff going to bring you the meal?" I assumed that's why Orla and a handful of the other maidservants accompanied us.

"Everyone eats at the mess tent." He glances over in curiosity of what I've spent the last hour sketching. His eyebrows hitch upward. "Cake?"

"What?" I clutch the drawing of the elaborately decorated dessert to my chest. I'm guessing there will be no cake here. "You're fine with sharing dinner with the non-divine?"

"The soldiers work hard to protect my realm," he says, as if that's answer enough. For him, I suppose it is. He pushes open the tent flaps. "Coming?"

Every time I think I have Boreas figured out, he proves me wrong. He dislikes mortals, yet if they take up arms for him, he respects them. How can he respect them if this is their cage? A life of servitude to the king, whatever form that might take.

I haven't the energy to question the arrangement, so I let the subject drop. The long journey has made me hungry and sore, with no room for combative inquiries.

The Frost King leads me to a long, rectangular tent located on the other side of camp. Inside, soldiers gather at scuffed tables constructed of uneven planks of wood. My nose wrinkles. Thousands of unwashed bodies shoved into a small space? It stinks. I'm sure I smell less than delightful as well, after a day spent atop a horse.

As Boreas and I take our places in line for the meal, the boisterous conversation dies. Wood creaks as men shift in their seats for a better view.

"People are staring," I mutter.

"Yes," he says. "At you."

He's right. The soldiers watch me, not the king. Despite wearing a tunic and trousers, I stand as a woman in a man's world, boots sinking into soil soon to be soaked with blood. When the whispers begin, I bristle, searching for someone to blame. My attention locks on a man whose stare has slipped into leering territory.

"What?" I snarl. "You've never seen a pair of breasts before?"

Boreas sighs. The soldier looks away. Smart man.

The line moves quickly after that. When we reach the front, a man offers me a bowl of hot stew and a piece of crusty bread with a murmured, "My lady."

I accept it with thanks and follow the Frost King to an empty table. Eventually, the men return to their meals, as opposed to staring at me as if I'm an intruder. I focus on eating. It's simple fare, but I inhale it eagerly. The taste reminds me of home. As for these soldiers . . . they eat, but the food holds no flavor for them.

"Boreas." This spoken by a young man with dark facial hair and long, curling eyelashes who takes a seat on the bench across the table. "Glad you could make it."

*Boreas?*

No one in the citadel addresses the king so informally.

The man studies me curiously. His attention doesn't linger on my scar, which I appreciate. I'm sure he has his fair share of them.

I kick Boreas under the table. He hisses out a breath, glowering at me. I say perkily, "Aren't you going to introduce us?"

He mutters a few choice words that I choose to ignore. "Gideon, this is my wife, Wren. And before you say anything, I'd advise you to mind your tongue."

"Too soft-hearted?" Gideon teases.

"Actually," Boreas says dryly, "it's you I'm worried about."

My mouth twitches at the man's bewildered expression, and I feel a sudden wave of fondness for my husband.

"Wren," Boreas says, his hand brushing my lower back, "this is Gideon, one of the unit commanders."

Judging by the respect in Boreas' tone, he thinks highly of this man. That's a first. I offer my hand. "Nice to meet you."

He ducks his head. "My lady."

"Please, call me Wren." I continue eating my stew. "So how long have you known Boreas?"

Before he can answer, two others join our table. I stiffen. The first is Pallas. The captain spares me no attention, and I'm not sure if I'm relieved or irritated at being ignored. The second man is an ugly brute with a nose that sits on his face like a growth. He offers me a leering smile full of broken teeth. Ugh.

I turn to Pallas and say, "Aren't you going to say hello?"

"You've met?" the king asks.

"Once." I peer down my nose at the captain. "He knows where I stand about . . . things."

The brute growls, "If your wife is here, my lord, who's going to warm your bed while you're away?"

My hand remains steady as I spoon more stew into my mouth. There is no bed warming—from either of us. But as the soldiers chuckle at the age-old ribbing, my anger sparks and slithers through me. "Who says I'm the one doing the warming?"

The Frost King stiffens. I clamp a hand onto his thigh under the table, a silent request that he keep his tongue in check. I think nothing of the touch. It's a way to communicate my request without voicing it aloud. But when the muscle beneath my fingers flexes, I realize how hot his skin is through the fabric of his breeches, and I quickly remove my hand.

The ugly toad's upper lip curls. He looks to his king, then to me. "The woman always does the warming. Take now for instance. Got three wenches waiting for me back home."

How utterly fascinating.

I finish chewing a piece of meat. It's been too long since I've put a man in his place. Why, I'd almost say I miss it.

Planting my elbows on the table, I lean forward, staring the man down. I've met his kind before. Women belong in the kitchen, and if not in the kitchen, then on their backs in the bedroom. Pig. "You know what they say about men with big mouths, right?"

The man's gaze narrows like a viper's. "What?"

Bringing the bowl of soup to my mouth, I take the most obnoxious slurp possible. Chew. Swallow, because it's impolite to speak with your mouth full while doling out insults. Then I say, perfectly succinct, "Small prick."

The soldiers within earshot hoot and holler, slamming the tabletops with their open palms. Pallas shakes his head, mouth twitching. Even Boreas laughs. The only one not laughing is my victim.

Thankfully, the brute decides he's had enough conversation and barges off in a huff, reprieving us of his foul company.

With dinner complete, we gather our dishware and dump it in a bin on the way outside. While the men trudge to their tents, Boreas and I return to ours.

Someone built a fire in our absence. Orla, probably. I warm my hands against the flames as the king toes off his boots. There's a little washing station near the rear, and our clothing has been unpacked and organized in a small dresser.

When the sound of whispering cloth reaches me, I freeze.

I have been here before.

Whirling, I take in the sight before me. "What are you doing?"

The Frost King pauses in removing his tunic. He's already discarded his coat. "I should think that would be obvious." Another button slips through the opening, baring more skin. Firelight brightens the blue undertones of his hair, the ends wild and curled. "You've never seen a naked man before?"

Do I detect a taunt? "I've seen plenty," I reply breezily. "You've seen one cock, you've seen them all."

His lips thin, and time stretches into too long a silence. "I see."

In one liquid motion, he tugs his tunic over his head and tosses it aside.

I suck in air so fast I nearly swallow my tongue.

The groove bisecting his ridged abdomen cuts a pronounced line of shadow through the muscle, curling black hair trailing to the waistband of his breeches. Wide, powerful shoulders narrow to a trim waist. My gaze crawls over every bit of exposed skin, from the small, flat, dusky nipples, to the raised collarbones, to the hollow at the base of his throat where shadows gather. I've seen it all before. So why do I look at him as if for the very first time?

"You're staring."

Somehow, I manage to tear my eyes away from the impressive display. "And?" I cross my arms over my chest. "Am I not allowed to look at my husband?" Especially when he has the most delectable chest I've ever had the privilege of ogling.

"You may." His eyes darken. "So long as I'm allowed to do the same."

My skin tightens until my bones ache. What is happening between us? I don't want to think about the crumbling edge I toe. It would be far too easy to step forward and greet that abyss.

"I'm going to wash," I state, snatching my bag and slipping behind the divider where the tub sits. "And you're not invited."

With Boreas nearby, I don't linger in my washing. I'm scrubbed clean and wrapped in my sleepwear in less time than it takes to saddle a horse.

When I emerge from behind the divider, Boreas has changed into loose-fitting trousers. His chest is bare. His feet, too, are bare. The sight of his toes unnerves me as much as it did the first time. We study one another across the length of the tent, my skin humming, blood bristling with anticipation. I swallow to bring moisture to my mouth.

With effort, I move toward my side of the bed and slide beneath the blankets. Boreas blows out the lamps and follows suit. There's a healthy amount of space between us. It should suffice.

Except as soon as the blankets settle it becomes immediately apparent that they'll do little to combat the chill from the deepening night. Why did I agree to this? Stupid. Turning onto my side, I squeeze my eyes shut and burrow deeper into the lumpy mattress.

"We'll keep warm if we share body heat." The king's voice floats out of the orange-flecked darkness.

"The fire is warm enough."

"The fire will die."

"So? I'll be asleep by then." I hope.

But I underestimated the lure of a warm, solid body beside me. And I underestimated how much colder the night would be with only canvas for walls.

The fire dies an extremely quick death, from logs to coals in less than an hour. Winter's chill infiltrates the tent and slides beneath the blankets, razing my skin. I curl into a tighter ball, shivering.

Something brushes my leg, and I snap upright, breathing hard. "No touching." My teeth begin to chatter.

"I'm not the one who initiated touch last time."

He has some nerve. "That's not what happened. I woke up with your arm around my waist and your—"

The Frost King arches one eyebrow toward his hairline. I can barely make it out in the feeble light emitted from the red coals. "My what?"

My face heats. As if he doesn't know. "And your cock pressed against my ass."

His lips curve the slightest bit. He is definitely thinking it. *Filthy mouth.* "You're the one who turned to me in the middle of the night."

This again. "I wasn't in the right headspace, so keep your arms to yourself this time." Even if they are a spectacular pair.

He sighs. "Fine. Stay there, if you're so determined to freeze." He turns his back to me.

The hours crawl by with horrible cruelty. Even curled into the tightest ball, the cold manages to slither around my bones. My muscles contract in sporadic bursts. My eyes sting with exhaustion, but my mind cycles in and out of dark thoughts, snapping me awake every time I begin to drift. The camp has settled down, and there is only the occasional snore of a soldier to break the quiet night. I switch from lying on my side to lying on my back. Minutes later, I switch again.

"Wren."

I glare into the darkness. "What?"

"I can't sleep if you're tossing and turning all night." Boreas rolls onto his side to face me. His faceted bone structure is a study of shadow, his mouth the only softness. "Sharing body heat doesn't have to be sexual. My men do it in the field to conserve warmth. It's a survival tool, nothing more."

When he puts it like that, he has a point. Elora and I shared a bed the majority of our lives. Most people in Edgewood do, since the cottages haven't the space for additional rooms.

He must sense my reluctance, because his voice takes on a coaxing quality I've never heard before. "My frustrating, stubborn wife. Please. Just for tonight." His eyes glimmer with refracted light.

"Tonight," I concede.

The blankets rustle as I flip onto my other side and present him my back. Boreas eases closer, the mattress dipping beneath our combined weights. The well shaped by his body drags me backward. All at once, heat cloaks the entire length of my spine, shoulder to back. I flinch at the contact, biting my lip to muffle the embarrassing moan that threatens to fly free. The place where our skin touches practically sizzles.

One of his arms slides beneath my head. The other settles over my waist, fingers splayed flat against my stomach. The shadow of him tucked into the shadow of me.

"Better?" His lips brush my ear, and I suppress another shiver.

"Yes," I whisper. "Thank you." I'm not sure where to put my hands, so I tuck them under my cheek. My poor feet, however, are still numb with cold. I slide them backward until they touch hot skin.

Boreas hisses out a breath.

"What?" I'm so fatigued my voice slurs. Blessed warmth drags me deep into the folds of slumber.

"Your feet are freezing."

"Sorry."

I'm not sorry. I hate cold feet.

~

For the second time in many weeks, I wake in the Frost King's arms.

He is warm whereas the earth is cold. He is solid heat at my back and a beating heart thrumming against skin. Long ago, when Elora and I were children, I would often wake much the same: in comfort, knowing I was not alone.

Perhaps he was right. Perhaps I did turn to him on Midwinter Eve, and now. Deep down, I wanted connection with someone, even if it was only skin on skin.

Would it be so terrible to remain in the king's embrace, knowing everything I do, knowing I came to end his life, uncertain if that is where my path still leads? If I lie here, if I let myself feel instead of think, will something change?

Do I want it to?

Boreas stirs behind me. One of his legs is hooked over mine, anchoring me in place. "You're awake." His breath tickles my ear.

My eyes flutter shut. "Yes." It's easier to speak without looking at anything. Easier to pretend my response belongs to someone else.

As he shifts again, something hard pushes against my backside: the unmistakable shape of his arousal.

My eyes snap open on a gasp, and I roll over to face him. The blanket has slipped to his waist, and creases from the pillow mark his cheek. "You did that on purpose!"

He studies me through a bleary gaze, slightly perplexed. "What did I do?"

He has to know. He must. Unless insanity is an unfortunate side effect of marriage to a god. It's not completely out of the question.

"Never mind," I mutter. Maybe it was an accident.

Just like the first time was an accident . . .

Stubble lines his jaw and chin. It rasps as he runs his hand against it, regarding me with a frustrating lack of emotion.

"My lord?"

The Frost King swings his legs over the bed. At least he's wearing breeches. "Enter."

"What?" I squawk. "I'm indecent!"

"You're dressed head to toe and covered in blankets. I would hardly call that indecent."

Pallas enters, eyes widening momentarily. I keep my expression neutral. He wasn't expecting my presence. At least, not in bed.

"Pallas," the king snaps.

The man averts his gaze, clears his throat. "My lord, it is nearly sunrise. What are our orders?"

"Prepare the horses. We leave at once."

Pallas vanishes outside while Boreas shrugs on his tunic and reaches for his armor. I sit up in bed, the blanket held to my chest, though I'm aware it's pointless, considering I'm fully clothed.

Quickly and efficiently, the king prepares for departure. Armor buckled, straps tightened, boots tugged on, spear in hand. The North Wind, an inexorable force, and never more so than encased in gleaming metal.

"Stay at camp," he says as he adjusts his arm gauntlets. "It's the safest place for you." He then adds, as if in afterthought, "Don't do anything foolish."

I scoff. "When have I ever?"

He only stares.

Point made.

He's pushing through the tent flaps when I call out, "Boreas."

He stops, though he doesn't turn around.

"Be careful."

And then I am alone, the indentation of the mattress still warm from where my husband had lain.

# CHAPTER

## 33

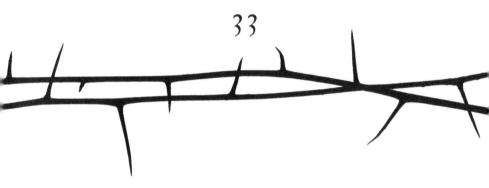

Boreas has not returned.

Maybe someone shoved a blade through his chest. It would serve him right after all the terrible things he's done. Yet the night deepens, and my heart does not slow its frantic pace. My feet carry me from one end of the tent to the other, again and again, until the lamps burn low, the space more shadow than light.

I shouldn't care.

I do care.

Well, shit.

Immortal or not, he can still be gravely injured. An arrow to the gut will deliver an intense, compounding agony until it is removed, his wounds bandaged. And that is not the worst these men, these darkwalkers, can do.

In minutes, I've changed into trousers, a long-sleeved tunic, knee-high boots, and a thick overcoat, my bow and quiver tossed over my shoulder.

Beyond the tent, the sounds of battle preparations greet me. Hammered metal and clinking armor. The snap of canvas tents. Whinnying horses. A group of men congregate around one of the small fires, speaking in low tones. No one notices me slinking around the back of the tent where Iliana grazes on brown, frost-bitten grass.

The mare greets me at my approach, nuzzling my shoulder in affection. The white star on her brow burns bright on this night.

"My lady."

I sigh. Of course it wouldn't be this easy.

Swinging into the saddle puts me at a height advantage, so that is what I do. "Yes?" I say, looking down at Pallas.

In the low light, the red of his hair matches that of the fire. He takes in my attire, my seated position atop Iliana, and frowns. "You're ordered to remain here until the king returns."

"Change of plans." I give him my friendliest smile. "Boreas has asked me to meet him at the field. Make sure he hasn't gotten himself into trouble." Sitting straight-backed in the saddle, I tilt my chin at a lofty angle. "Just doing my wifely duties."

Pallas grabs the reins, halting my forward motion. His armor clangs with the movement. "I can't let you do that. My orders were clear."

My mare tosses her head, fractious beneath me, eager to run. The smile is gone. "I am taking Iliana, and you are not going to stop me. Now unhand my mount, or I will do it for you. Or have you forgotten our last encounter?" I pat my bow, in case he needs reminding.

Two grooves appear to bracket his mouth, but I'm already pushing past him. He leaps back to avoid getting crushed by Iliana's hooves.

Pallas doesn't need to worry himself. A short visit to the field, just to make sure Boreas isn't bleeding out somewhere. I'll be back before my husband learns I've left.

I nudge Iliana into a trot. Once we reach the edge of camp, she explodes forward. The broken path left by Boreas' force leads me deep into the wilds. After a time, we slow to a trot, and then a walk until we reach the forest's edge.

I stand before a field of blood. And it is chaos.

Thousands of people teem beneath a swollen moon. Steam rises from the carnage littered far and wide. Mounds of bodies. Hills and peaks of blackened, shadow-torn flesh. A red-tinged fog descends, concealing much of the scarred, ruined ground. In the distance, the Shade flutters and croons, and people spill into the Deadlands from the Gray, wielding rusted swords and axes and pitchforks, and within minutes, their eyes flatten and their teeth crowd together. I gag, pressing the back of my hand to my nose and mouth.

Metal screams with ferocious intensity. There is so much movement I'm not sure where to look first. The king's force struggles to impede the outpouring from the Shade. New holes rip open and, just as quickly, knit together—the North Wind's power, fortifying that great barrier. But he is nowhere in sight.

It's impossible to stop the flow, the trickle squeezing between the cracks. The darkwalkers rise and the soldiers fall. The specters are already dead, but it seems they can die again. For that is blood coating their armor, open wounds giving sight to bone and tendon within.

Iliana prances forward, but I draw her back, behind one of the old dead trees. How many specters fight? Thousands? Boreas' force slashes luminescent blades across the darkwalkers' torsos, removing heads and limbs, black blood spraying. There must be some power to those weapons, a coat of salt, perhaps, that enables them to kill the beasts.

I scan the madness that spreads like a flood. My hands tighten on the reins. No sign of him. Not one sign—

*There.*

He is the dark blemish, the cold wind, the blackened stream, the vein that parts the battle-flood. He is the iron fist upon this realm.

The North Wind blasts a hole through the enemy with a spear whose point blazes white light. Another swing, and seven more darkwalkers are lacerated. Gray, snow-laden clouds drag their bellies across the spiked branches overhead. He must have sent Phaethon elsewhere, for there's no sign of the king's mount as he crosses the field on foot, his black cloak fluttering behind him, sweat-dampened hair clinging to his neck and face along with spattered gore. His eyes are two coals, blue as the heart of a flame.

Specters, darkwalkers, and half-corrupted mortals clash like a storm. Boreas swiftly ends those daring to rise against him. He wields explosive power with but a wrist flick, his very tread like the thunder above. What greets them is a cruel, ancient force, the might of winter blasting from a spear tip. Its force rips bodies in half, tears limbs from torsos.

The army's right flank buckles under a new wave of infiltration, and he hurries to aid the weakening margin, units of soldiers breaking and reforming around him. I lose sight of him as an upsurge of darkwalkers hits, seven at once. They fall and they fall, and still more take their place. With his back turned, Boreas does not see the enemy's force changing shape, an opening forming like a mouth to allow a single figure to pass through. He does not see a man, this simple village man, break through the crush of war-hardened bodies, closing the distance.

Boreas swings his spear, severing limbs, severing heads, pushing forward through the current that swarms. The enemy heaves like a wave crashing ashore, but he doesn't falter. Neither do his men.

And yet, no one is infallible. His soldiers do their best, but one falls from a dagger to the neck, followed by a second, then three more. The villager, corruption blackening his eyes, rams forward.

My lungs empty. My heart stills.

Bow in hand, wood cold and grounding.

The string, fully drawn, vibrating with a high, tinny pitch.

Aim, the arrow tracking the man's destination.

The man raises his sword, mouth open in a cry that's lost to the turmoil, one step, another, cutting in a fatal downward arc toward the king's unprotected back.

I release.

The arrow screams, slicing a clean path to embed itself in the man's chest.

Boreas whirls to find his pursuer dead in the mud, sword still gripped in hand. A hard yank rips the arrow from the man's front. Blood coats the tip in shining red. He holds it up to the light for a long, drawn-out moment.

At once, he's on his feet, scanning the area, but I'm too deep in the thicket for him to spot. With a whooping cry, I wheel Iliana around, and together, we flee back to camp.

≈

Hours later, I sit in our tent, mending a hole in my trousers, when Boreas barges through the flaps. His ghastly appearance startles me into dropping my clothes.

Livid scratches mark his face. Soiled tunic, dented armor, ripped breeches, scratched breastplate. The scent of death—split flesh and the copper tang of blood—quickly invades the space.

"What is this?" he demands.

My attention shifts to the object he holds in his leather-gloved hand: a blood-tipped arrow. The one I shot at the man who would have killed him, if my assumption is correct.

Calmly returning to my sewing, I reply, "It appears to be an arrow."

"That you shot."

My mouth purses in contemplation. "I'm not sure how that's possible if I've been at camp this whole time."

"You lie."

With a haughty sniff, I lift my chin. "Prove it."

If smiles could grow fangs, his would. A thrill runs through me at the sight, though I'm not sure if it's from fear or something more . . . carnal. "Pallas informed me of your midnight run."

"Pallas is an ass."

"Goose feathers? They bear your mark." He lifts the arrow shaft, presses the wood to his nose, and inhales. His voice deepens. "Lavender."

The scent of my hand soap.

Smart man. In that case, there's little point in continuing this charade. "So what if I shot it? Lucky for you I *was* there, otherwise that man would have cut you down."

"I told you to remain here for your own safety."

"You told me to remain here because you like everything in its place."

His eyes flare. "Vexing woman," he growls. "I knew you were reckless, but I didn't think you were a fool."

My spine locks, and the restraint of holding myself still twinges through my coiled muscles. "Why am I not surprised?" I snap, the comment driving deeper than I expect it to. That worries me. If he can hurt me, that means I've become far more vulnerable to him than I ever intended. I'm not sure when it happened. "You dare to insult me when I'm the one who saved you?"

"I am a god. I cannot die."

Yes, and he has the disturbing habit of reminding me so often I doubt I could forget it. "I was trying to help."

"Next time, help by following orders."

Anger sears like a small lump of coal in my chest. No gratitude, no words of appreciation. I should have let that villager carve him up out of spite.

He begins to turn away when I notice a dark stain spreading across his abdomen. The fresh blood glistens. "You're hurt," I say, grabbing his arm. "Let me see."

He attempts to tug free of my grip. I tighten my hold. "I'm fine," he growls, exasperated.

"You're not."

"Wife—"

"Sit down," I hiss, shoving him bodily into a chair. He stares at me in bewilderment as I unbuckle his breastplate, toss the blood-spattered metal aside, then peel away his tunic to reveal a grisly gash above his right hip bone. I suck in a sharp breath. It looks deep.

"It's nothing," Boreas says. "I barely even feel it."

Without taking my eyes from the wound, I shout, "Orla!"

My maid bursts into the tent, panting heavily. "Yes, my lady?" She glances between me and the king nervously.

"I need hot water, bandages, and wine." A flicker of what might be fear tightens Boreas' expression. "Lots of wine."

"No," he barks. "No wine."

I tense, recognizing what remains unsaid. "I'm not going to drink it. It's to disinfect your wound."

"I don't care—"

"I said I'm not going to drink it," I retort. "You either trust my word, or you don't. So which is it?" My cheeks burn with humiliation, the assumption that I might weaken when it comes to the bottle. It has happened before. Twice in the past eight years I've been sober, but never longer than six weeks. It's been nine days since I woke following my near-death ordeal. Each day has felt like a year.

His lips twitch, but he gives a curt nod.

Orla makes herself scarce. Boreas watches me as if I'm swinging around a sharp object. Blood and soil have caked his hair into long, ropy strands. "I'm going to examine your wound," I say, peering down at him. "You're going to sit there and deal with it. If you fuss, I'm going to make it hurt."

In answer, he leans back in the chair, grumbling about women and their penchant for petty violence.

I study the gash closely. Four inches long, by my estimate. "Your wound should have healed by now." Yet it looks as fresh as I imagine it had hours ago, the skin red and inflamed, the edges pulped. Whatever was responsible for this wound, it didn't sever cleanly.

He grunts a noncommittal response.

Orla returns with all the necessary supplies. I accept the bucket of hot water, cloth bandages, and wine with thanks from my maid, who makes a hasty retreat when the king growls at her for stepping too close.

I pinch his thigh.

His eyes cut to mine. "What was that for?"

"You're scaring Orla. She's trying to help, you ungrateful heathen."

He shifts in the chair, his attention flitting from me, to the bucket, to the wine.

"Afraid of a little pain?" I ask sweetly, batting my lashes. I think I'm going to enjoy this.

As I wet the cloth and reach for him, his hand snaps out, strong fingers shackling my wrist. His bare chest rises and falls fitfully. "Are you trained in healing?"

My lips purse. "Mm . . . no. But I know enough." A moment passes. "You need to let go of my wrist."

"It's nothing but a scratch."

"And this *scratch* should have healed by now, but it hasn't." Might that, too, be an effect of his weakening power?

Slapping his hand aside, I begin to gently clean the blood and grit from his skin. Once that's done, I grab the wine. My stomach twists in memory of the liquid sliding down my throat, but I made a promise. I want to be better. I deserve more than the half-life I was living. My mind has never been so clear.

"This is going to hurt."

A muscle pulses in his jaw. "Get it over with."

The scent of crushed grapes hits my nose, and my body clenches in longing the moment the red liquid pours across his open wound. Boreas stiffens, curses spitting from his mouth. His lips thin to the thinnest, whitest line before they peel back from his teeth, which have begun to lengthen, shadows rising to blot his skin. His hands clamp around the arms of the chair. I return my focus to the task at hand and work quickly, knowing how the sting ignites to flames.

Grabbing one of the clean cloths, I soak it in the hot water, then begin patting the area around the wound. His abdominal muscles contract, and he hisses out another vehement curse. "Wife."

"Oh, hush."

A tremor races beneath his pale skin, drawing out additional shadows. His eyes pool black, and his voice roughens to an animalistic growl. "You're killing me."

My mouth goes dry at the sight of him fighting the darkwalker's influence. Short, curled, ebon nails prick the ends of his fingers. "I already tried that," I say without a shred of remorse. "Multiple times. It didn't work. Hold still."

"Multiple times? How—" He expels an anguished groan as I douse the remainder of the wine over his flesh, killing any possible infection.

"Next time," I remark, "you should bring Alba. I don't know why you didn't insist on a healer."

"She is better served overseeing the health of my staff and w—" He breaks off.

After a momentary pause, my attention lifts from his stomach. "You were going to say *wife*, weren't you?" There must be something seriously wrong with me, to be intrigued by the possibility.

"And if I was?" That probing blue gaze locks onto mine, and its intensity squeezes the air from my lungs. "Your health is important to me."

"Mm." I completely fail at attempting to fight my smile. Gods, I'm sick.

It takes ten minutes to clean and bandage the wound. The injury isn't deep enough to warrant stitches—which is good, since I'm inept at them. Slumped in the chair, Boreas watches me through half-lidded eyes as I wind the cloth around his lower abdomen and tie it off near his hip. Faint scratches cover those rippling upper arms, and his chest bears a rash-like irritation from the press of his breastplate.

At last, I step away. My trousers stick to my skin where his blood has dampened them. "You should rest."

"I need to return to my men." Yet he doesn't move.

Seeing the depth of his exhaustion, something softens in me. "What happens if the specters die? I mean, they're technically already dead, they just haven't fully passed on, right?" That's what Orla told me.

"They will return to the Les to await their second Judgment." As if in response to an unspoken question, he says, "They can feel pain, and despair, same as the living. But those emotions are much darker, more difficult to shake. Physical pain can last long after a wound has healed."

He does not mention emotional pain, and I do not ask.

"Rest," I say. "I'll let you know if anyone comes looking for you."

The Frost King closes his eyes on a weary sigh. Within minutes, he's asleep.

While he rests, I wash the blood from his soiled armor and tunic, as a wife would do for her husband in battle. I do not feel less for doing it. The clothes need to be cleaned, and I am here. At the very least, it allows me to pass the time quickly.

That done, I change into clean clothes. I stoke the fire to a blaze. I lay a blanket over his torso and remove his boots. The air thickens with drowsy heat.

Perching on the edge of the mattress, I keep watch over the man who is my husband.

No one has disturbed us since Boreas' arrival. I could lend a hand elsewhere in camp, but I am reluctant to leave him. When I stabbed him in the stomach at Edgewood, the wound knit, quick and clean, before my eyes. Now, red bleeds through the white cloth. His skin, already pale to begin with, seems to leach color.

Boreas sleeps soundly, that full mouth softly parted. His long legs are outstretched, his lower torso hanging off the edge of the chair because it is too small to accommodate his large frame comfortably. At this angle, I'm given an unobstructed view of his cheekbone, the rounded end of his chin, the splay of those black lashes. It has been a long day—for us both. While I do not agree with the king's decision to bury the Gray in ice, I can understand wanting to protect his realm from invaders. Even if he is one himself.

I have pondered such things. The Deadlands, like Boreas, is not all darkened hollows. There is Makarios, his brightest star. These last few days he revealed to me a man who was not so aloof, whose soldiers regarded him with the highest respect, and whose sparse affections might soften beneath the right touch.

Deep night has now fallen. My eyes burn from fatigue. Before turning in, I decide to check his wound one last time.

Lifting the blanket, I take in the white bandage wrapped around his stomach, his chest rising steadily. I prod gentle fingertips around the edge of the cloth, testing the temperature of his skin. It doesn't feel hot or inflamed. That's a good sign. No infection.

When I lift my eyes, I find the Frost King watching me through a slitted gaze.

My heart dips, and I slowly straighten, for in his blown pupils simmers an unexpected heat. The silence brims and overflows, and the air draws taut between us. His gaze drifts down my body, all leisure. My skin pebbles in response.

"I was checking your wound for infection," I rasp out. "It's clean."

One of his hands curls around the arm of the chair. "I appreciate that." He has yet to blink. "How long was I out for?"

"A few hours. No one came by. No messages—"

He stands in one fluid motion. The blanket slips from his shoulders. I'd nearly forgotten how tall he is, how completely overwhelming.

He steps forward.

I take a step back.

"What are you doing?" I demand, voice shrill as his approach forces my retreat. One, two, three steps. My back hits the bedpost. He doesn't stop. His powerful legs eat up the last of the distance, and in a moment of panic, I push against his shoulders to stop his forward motion. There is nowhere left to go.

My arms tremble. His skin—hot, smooth—contours to the shape of my palms. My head is empty, frighteningly empty. Boreas is touching me. The king is touching me—

He leans into my touch, and my arms collapse from the added weight as his form presses fully against mine, chest to groin. A low hum brightens my blood.

He says, "Will you kill me for this?"

That hum surges with new intensity. My pulse escalates wildly as the question sinks in. "I should," I grind out.

The king lowers his head, brushing his nose with mine in a gesture of surprising affection. "Tell me to go." The words steam between us.

My hands return to his shoulders. Instead of shoving him away though, I curl my fingers into the hard muscle there and hold him to me. Staring into his eyes, I realize this isn't some act. His heart is open to me. He is letting me in despite that flickering fear.

I can't tell him to go because I don't want him to go.

"You want something from me?" I whisper hoarsely. "Then take it."

Never removing his eyes from mine, Boreas wraps the length of my hair around his fist and, gently, pulls my head back, baring my throat to him. A long breath shudders out of me. The position fuses my lower torso to his, the long, thick ridge of his arousal pressed to my hip bone.

Swift, glancing heat behind my ear, beneath my jaw and chin, trailing the arch of my neck. He returns to the place where my pulse thrums, a swipe of his hot tongue on that staccato beat.

I'm panting. If I were not so focused on the throb between my legs, I'd slap myself from embarrassment. He laves the pulse point, then latches his mouth there and suckles. My fingers dig harder into his shoulders as a soft noise slips out. His other hand splays against my lower back, anchoring me in place. Again and again, his wicked tongue dampens my skin, suckling, mouthing, and the first scrape of teeth has my fluttering eyes snapping open on a gasp.

Only then does he move on. Only then does he bestow nipping kisses along my jaw, closer to my flushed, tingling mouth.

The hand around my hair loosens. The roughened tips of his fingers fiddle with the bottom hem of my tunic before diving to the skin beneath. It is so small a thing, that touch, yet it feels as though an arrow has been fired after being drawn for the last three months.

As I straighten, our mouths align. His breath floats across my tongue, tasting of everything forbidden. My eyes sink shut. An invitation, if he is daring enough to accept it.

Boreas' mouth slides against mine, a gentle parting of lips. There is no haste, no messy drive to completion. His tongue teases out, licking the corner of my mouth, flirting across my full lower lip, slipping inside once I grant him entrance. Our noses brush. He pulls back, our lips clinging momentarily.

We come together again, gentleness edged in hunger. On and on the kiss goes, a lazy exploration that drifts like clouds through my body.

One hand clenches reflexively around my hip. Mine lifts to his chest, fingers splayed across the warm muscle and sleek skin, the bedpost digging into my spine. As his tongue curls around mine, suckling softly, he draws a sound of helpless need from my throat. I press closer, chasing the spiraling sensation.

*More.* The desire flares, and I think again, *More.* This isn't enough. His mouth, his taste, isn't enough. I want his body joined with mine. I want to push him to the very edge of insanity so that I may watch him break.

I want Boreas to lose control.

Fingers twining through the strands of his hair, I tug, urging him onward. Now there is teeth. Now there is racing, panting breath and wet sounds of suction as the kiss descends into one of unsatiated hunger. Our teeth clack and our tongues duel for dominance, my hands racing over every bit of flesh within reach. My body coils tighter with each penetrating stroke of his tongue. I've never felt this eager before. Never. Like chaos resides inside my body. Like my skin is the most insubstantial of barriers.

The Frost King bites my mouth possessively, and I match his carnality, reeling from the delicious abrasiveness of his cheeks against mine, his tongue plunging continually deeper, saliva slickening our lips and chins. My veins feel as though they are splitting open. And then he groans, deep, agonized, as I play with the roof of his mouth. The sound pulls at something in me. Husband and wife we may be, yet the affair feels illicit and forbidden.

My touch sweeps across his shoulders, fingers digging into flexing sinew. Hot like the fire that burns in the grate, smooth and supple beneath my hands. The curve of his neck draws my attention, then the ridges of his upper back, the wings of his shoulder blades. Standing on tip toe, body bowed toward his like a bowstring, I allow myself the pleasure of touching my husband for the very first time.

"Wren."

I like the sound of my name unfurling on his tongue. I like that his voice is gruff, breathy, resonant. I like knowing my touch is the cause of his unraveling. I like knowing this is just the beginning.

The kiss deepens further. He eats at my mouth, and the sweetness of his breath floods my throat while his hands, those large, capable hands, slide down my lower back to cup my backside, molding around the curves, fingers sinking into pliant flesh. One long, solid thigh slots between my legs, pressing upward against my folds. A moan flies out of me, and I tear my mouth away, panting.

Boreas studies me through hooded eyes as he shifts his leg in a subtle back and forth motion. The friction— My hands shake as they dive into his hair. I want this. It makes absolutely no sense. At this point, I'm past the point of caring.

"Harder," I rasp.

His only response is to relieve the pressure against my sex, slowing the motion.

"Husband," I say in warning.

His eyes crinkle with suppressed mirth. "Wife."

"Do you want to die?"

"I thought we've already discussed this." Leaning forward, he brushes his nose against the shell of my ear, eliciting a shaky exhale from me. "I cannot die."

My fingers find his nipple and twist—hard.

He recoils with an uttered oath, but I hang on, tightening my grip. "Do not underestimate an aroused woman."

His laughter erupts like the most beautiful song. "Never." His eyes, how they shine. The emotion there, plain as the brightest of days, makes my heart lurch uncomfortably. "Tell me what you want, Wren. No more secrets. No more lies."

Am I doing this?

I'm doing this.

"I want your fingers inside me," I say, a hitch in my breath, "as deep as they can go. Then I want you to fuck me with them hard."

Hunger ripples across his expression. "Filthy mouth," he murmurs, lowering his head to nip at my lips. Fingers digging into my backside, he moves me bodily against his thigh. Slow, gradually increasing the pace—faster, harder, punishing, pressure edged in pain. I grind mindlessly against his leg, no better than a dog in heat. The pleasure blooms bright within me, and I chase that feeling as far as I can.

"Good?" he asks.

"Yes," I pant. "Don't stop."

As I ride his leg, he fists the dark strands of my hair, then tilts my head to the side. I am a moth, pinned against a white light. The Frost King grazes his teeth across my nape. A sweep of chills pebbles my skin. He soothes the small hurts with dabs of his tongue, mouthing the areas into acute sensitivity until I begin to fight his hold. The dampness gathering between my thighs seeps through the fabric of my trousers.

At the next hard suck, he pushes upward against my core. Stars burst behind my eyes, and I whimper, trying to increase the friction. The ache in my pelvis builds. I never considered Boreas a particularly sexual being, but he absolutely knows what he's doing. He knows where I am most sensitive. He knows how to touch and stroke until the fever rises to the flushed edges of my skin.

"Hold on to me," he whispers. Brushing a final kiss to the side of my neck, he leans back and begins loosening the laces of my tunic collar. The fabric parts beneath his hands as I grip his waist. He pulls the collar opening to the side, baring the curve of my shoulder. There, he laves and suckles the skin so it pinkens beneath his ministrations. Meanwhile, his hot palms slide up my ribs, tease the curves of my peaked breasts, his gaze tracing the path of his hands. The rough fabric feels deliciously abrasive against my skin.

Is this his intention? To draw out my desire until I'm but ragged threads? The king strokes my skin with an expression bordering on awe. He cups my breasts beneath the band of fabric holding them in place, squeezes the aching flesh. Then he removes my tunic, pulls down the heavy banding. My nipples peak in the cold air. He circles around them, but avoids the turgid tips no matter how I shift in his arms.

I bite his left pectoral muscle. Just sink my teeth in and hold on.

"Shit!" Boreas barks.

I'm laughing through a mouthful of hard male flesh. And then I'm not. I'm smelling him. It's such a potent scent I have to fight the urge to rub my face against him like a cat. Snow and cedar, sweat and musk and man, the grit of battle. I swipe my tongue through the sweat gleaming on his neck. Salt and earth. Boreas groans and buries his face in my hair, trembling.

Power. It exists here, in the ability to send a god to his knees on the eve of battle, and I have taken it for myself. But there is no denying the power he holds over me as well. Even now, that wicked tongue traces the delicate curve of my ear. When he sucks the lobe into his mouth, my lips part wordlessly, and I arch my neck toward him, lured deeper by the desire firing between us. I want to see where it leads me, even if that is into the Frost King's bed.

Sweet, biting kisses dampen my jaw. He suckles the curve where my neck and shoulder meet before moving lower, across the swell of my breast, leaving a trail of dampness in his wake. "You are—" Another tremor. He sucks a nipple into his mouth, playing with the sensitive peak, flicking his tongue against it. His groan vibrates against my skin.

"Less talking," I pant, "more of—" He shifts his thigh harder against my throbbing core, and a mewling sound escapes me. "That. More of that."

The ridge of his cock strains against my abdomen. With every brush against his arousal, he grunts, the sound traveling through me as he crushes his lips to mine, unleashing an aggressive, open-mouthed assault that plucks at my every nerve ending.

My curiosity piqued, I trail my fingers along the length of him, root to tip. The fabric covering him is damp.

He goes still. His grip on my body tightens. Again, I touch him lightly, more suggestion than anything else. Boreas pulls back, watching me as though I've been sent to kill him. Little does he know, I have.

Here is my truth: I want to bury into his heat, I want to crawl inside his skin, I want his breath to become mine, and all the air he stole from me, I want to give it back. I want to destroy Boreas the way he has destroyed me: slowly, one toppled stone at a time. I want to bring him to the sweetest ruin.

Abruptly, he catches my hand in his, drawing it away from his erection, and returns it to his chest where his heart pounds. "Patience," he murmurs, and then his hand dives into the front of my trousers.

He probes the soft skin of my inner thighs, and my blood leaps to meet his touch. My legs begin to shake as he shifts higher, the heel of his palm brushing against my drenched flesh in a touch that feels so good my eyes roll into the back of my head. I bite my lip. I have to move, have to grind against his hand until the ache shatters, but—

*Patience.*

I want to please him.

Blunt fingers brush against my short curls. I widen my stance to give him better access, and he nods in wordless approval.

His touch returns to my thigh, up and inside where it joins with the torso. Slick coats the skin there, and his fingertips slide through it, gathering the moisture. His blue eyes smolder. Oh, mercy. I can't breathe. Gods help me, but I want this man. And if that means I'm going to hell, so be it.

"So you can touch me," I gasp as he lingers around the vee between my legs, "but I can't touch you?"

A momentary stall before he continues his indulgent exploration. "Does it upset you that I focus on your pleasure?"

"No." I grit my teeth. My core throbs fiercely. "Unless your aim is to drive me mad with desire."

A smile ghosts across his mouth. "Wren," he says. "That is exactly my plan."

And as his fingers slide through my wet folds, I moan. I moan so loudly I'm sure half the camp hears, a sound that comes from deep within me, eked out from a core of truthfulness.

He plays with me at his leisure. The wetness drenching his fingers allows him to glide along my sensitive flesh unhindered, sliding through my slit and tracing around my entrance. I grind against his hand, whimpering, my mouth latching onto the side of his neck. I suck the skin, hard. I want him to bruise, and I want to know that mark came from me.

As he skirts the place that throbs, I lick a path up his neck and back down, detouring to the slope of his shoulder and prominent collarbones. He nudges my face toward his. We kiss with deepening urgency, and for a moment, I swear our souls touch.

He's so focused on the kiss he doesn't notice my fingers coasting across his taut, heated skin. Down, down, trailing his lower abdomen to the ridge that stands proud. And as my fingers dive beneath his waistband, curling around his erection, Boreas emits a sound as though all the breath escapes his body.

Oh, he's big. His cock tents his breeches, the shape of the broad head visible against the rough fabric. My mouth dries at the sight. It's been so long since I've taken a man to bed. There are things I miss: the weight and strength of a man's body pinning me to the mattress, the fullness once we are joined. Sex is an animal, but it can be softened, with the right partner. I've witnessed it reducing even the most stoic of men to garbled pleas. And here stands the Frost King, warmed by desire. A flush reddens his arctic skin.

"I suppose," I drawl, pressing my thumb into the slit so his hips rock toward me, "you are adequate enough in size."

Glazed blue eyes snap to mine, narrow with disbelief. "You are not pleased?" The words are deliciously rough, base.

I shrug. My casual air would be much more convincing if I could stop staring at his mouth. In truth, it's not the size of a man's cock that matters, but what he can do with it. Though Boreas is probably the largest I've encountered.

A change overcomes him then. He seems almost pleased. "Wren," he whispers. "Why do you lie?" And he slowly slides one finger inside me, the walls of my sex stretching around the intrusion.

*Finally.* My fingers bite into his shoulders, and I groan, rising up onto my toes so he can sink his finger deeper, the clasp of my body drawing him in as far as he can go.

He pulls out, sinks back in, but only halfway. Not deep enough, and he knows it. And I think, *Two can play that game.*

A few precise tugs loosens his trousers, exposing him to my gaze. Lightly, I squeeze the thick, sparsely haired shaft, its flushed coloring and bulging veins. It twitches in my grip.

"Come on then," I taunt. Challenging the Frost King to a race toward climax is utterly ridiculous, yet I work him over, dragging my hand from base to tip, lingering around the fleshy head before plunging down with his early seed slicking my hand, quickening the motion.

Faster and faster, my hand flies. Boreas ruts against my hip, pressing my back into the bedpost, while his fingers play with my folds, liquid warmth sliding down the inside of my thighs. His fingers plunge into my core in a hard, continuous fuck that tightens my inner walls and, gods, I feel like I'm going to explode. His groan rattles my teeth as our mouths collide, hot, wet, messy. And when Boreas circles the engorged nub above my entrance tauntingly with his thumb, my hand falters as pleasure spikes and sparks burst behind my eyelids. The damn god smiles lazily as he breaks the kiss.

"Don't challenge me," he says, "if you haven't the ability to win."

I intend to win.

"Here's the deal," I croak, biting back another keen as he inserts a second finger and curls them against the front wall of my sex.

"Whoever holds out the longest—" The rapid pace escalates. Sounds of suction fill the air: his fingers fighting the clamp of my swollen flesh.

"Gets a favor of their choosing," he finishes for me, making a low, guttural sound as I gently squeeze his balls.

It takes a moment for the haze to dispel. A favor? I could do so much with that. "All right."

We push each other onward, spiraling higher and tighter and brighter. Boreas' breathing roughens as his pleasure peaks, but the wave doesn't break. It rolls over him, over me, in a continuous blanket of blossoming heat that sears me from the inside out. His thick fingers feel divine inside my body. His thumb works that pouting bud, circling and circling until my feet lift from the ground, until my pelvis cramps with budding ecstasy. So, so close. It's still not enough, but I have to hold out. I vow to win this challenge, to bring Boreas to his completion first.

And he is close as well. His inarticulate groans tell me he's especially sensitive on the underside of his shaft. I drag my nails lightly down the area until he bucks in my hand with a harshly rasped, "Wren." He pushes out the word through his clamped teeth. "You are—"

A bead of sweat slides down my nose. "Amazing?"

"The devil."

I laugh breathlessly and plant a sloppy kiss to his mouth. Heat clings to my skin like an impossibly warm rain. He fucks me with his hand and I'm nearing the peak, I'm lifting higher as my body tightens—

"My lord?" A voice calls from beyond the tent flaps.

The Frost King tears his mouth from mine, chest heaving. The fog clears from his eyes, and I touch my tender, swollen mouth in dazed wonder. We're plastered together, one of my legs curled around the back of his thigh, his hands down my trousers. "Yes?" he replies, that burning gaze fused to mine.

"The men are returning to the field. Another wave of darkwalkers has appeared." The man clears his throat. It sounds like Pallas. "S-sorry to interrupt."

Battle. War. I'd completely forgotten in my lust-drunk haze.

Boreas begins to step away when my hand whips out, snatching his arm and hauling him toward me. "You will not leave me here like this." My core aches with stymied pressure, failure to reach completion. His arousal presses into my lower belly in unfulfillment. I don't want to stop. I want to see this insanity through to its end.

Breathing heavily, he removes his hand from between my legs, curving it around the outside of my hip. "I must." Dampness transfers from his fingers to my skin, and cools there.

My stomach drops in unwanted hurt. In my mind, he is making a choice. And he is not choosing me.

The air between us grows cold. Maybe it's for the best we were interrupted before a mistake was made. "Very well." I'm utterly calm as I step back, adjusting my trousers, my breastband, pretending I didn't nearly climax with the Frost King's fingers deep in my core. I've made plenty of poor choices in my life, but this is one of the worst.

"Wren."

I turn from him, moving to stoke the fire to hide the evidence of my trembling hands. What a fool I was. What a fool I have always been. "Go," I say. "They're waiting."

I don't hear his departure. A glance over my shoulder reveals Boreas studying me, his clothes adjusted, the space between his eyebrows dimpled with his frown.

"Take care with your wound," I say. "You can't lose more blood."

His throat works. His eyes drop to my mouth and linger. "I'll be fine."

Then he is gone.

# CHAPTER
## 34

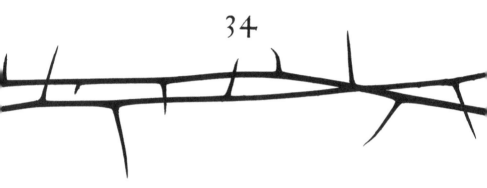

"My lady? Are you decent?"

My scissors pause at the edge of the square of fabric I've been cutting into bandages. The man's voice sounds from beyond the tent flaps. It's . . . pained? Hm. Orla sits beside me, washing Boreas' clothes in a pot of hot water that's been heated over the fire. "You may enter."

The captain, Pallas, lurches into the tent.

Orla gasps. I'm on my feet, the bandages slipping to the ground from where I'd stacked them atop my thighs. Just as the man lists to the side, I catch him by the arm. Blood, blood, and more blood. A long, ugly gash oozes from his shoulder. His tunic, stained black from the gruesome wound, squelches when he sags heavily against me, the metal breastplate cold against my skin.

"Orla," I bark in alarm. "Wine."

My maid darts to obey as I swing Pallas' arm over my shoulder and help him into a chair. He sinks into it with a pained grunt, his chin drooping against his chest as if it's too much effort to lift his head.

The wound looks serious, and of course Alba is back at the citadel where she is of no use. The only thing I can say is, "Don't die."

Pallas cracks a smile. "Thought you'd want that for me after the way I've treated you thus far."

"I may think you're an ass, but that doesn't mean I want you dead." Boreas mentioned how skilled of a soldier Pallas was on the ride over. They need all the help they can get fending off the darkwalkers.

He slumps deeper into the chair. "Don't plan on dying, my lady. At least—" He grunts. "Not today."

That's good. I've little desire to dig a grave. But I don't tell him that.

He's so translucent I fear he will dissolve straight through the chair. Outside the tent, the camp is suddenly alive with noise, the previous quiet shattered.

"I was sent," Pallas wheezes, shaking bodily, "to deliver a message."

My blood throbs against the confines of my skin, hot with adrenaline. The stench of battle infiltrates the space: iron and smoke. It makes my head swim. The unknown is a terrifying place to be. "What happened?" I think of Boreas striding from the tent hours earlier. What has become of him?

Pallas snatches the wineskin from Orla's grip, tilts the opening, and upends the contents into his mouth, seemingly unconcerned when half the liquid splashes down his front. The wine was meant for his wounds, but this works, too. Gently, I pry his fingers loose from the container. I set the drink aside before I'm tempted to take a sip myself.

"The message?" I remind him.

Pallas takes a shallow, quaking breath. I realize then how young he is. He was around my age when he died. He might even be a few years younger, toeing the line where a boy becomes a man, limbs unused to the weight of a new world.

Despite him glancing at the wineskin longingly, I remain strong and leave it out of reach—for both of us. "My lord was attempting to close one of the larger holes in the Shade when a new wave of darkwalkers hit from behind. It almost seemed as though the attack was an organized affair, but there was no leader anywhere that we could see." He coughs, and the sound is wet in his chest. "We weren't prepared."

If they were taken unaware, how many died?

And I realize something else. Pallas returned to camp alone. No fanfare arrival of the troops. "Where are the other soldiers?"

When he meets my gaze, my stomach drops in the vicinity of my lower pelvis. "My lord wants you to return to the citadel as quickly as possible, my lady."

He didn't answer the question. Why didn't he answer the question?

"Pallas."

His trembling intensifies. Another torturous glance at the wine. He looks so pathetic I give it to him. The drink manages to draw some color to his face, and he no longer appears as if he might vanish into the air itself. "Twelve. I brought twelve men with me, the worst of the wounded. I didn't want to come here." He speaks flatly. "Didn't want to leave my brothers-in-arms, but my lord made me go. To warn you so you'd have time to escape before the enemy reached camp."

"What about Boreas?"

"He was calling the men to retreat when I left. I can't be sure. I'm sorry."

I turn to Orla. Large, rounded eyes take me in, shimmering with dread, wisps of gray hair sticking to her sweaty neck. The space inside my chest shrinks, and I nod, though I'm not sure what I'm acknowledging, exactly.

"You must leave, my lady. Before it's too late."

Why didn't Boreas ask me to fortify the Shade? I can close the holes. I can stop the influx of darkwalker-turned-humans, at least temporarily. I suggest as much to Pallas, but the captain shakes his head vehemently. "He doesn't want you anywhere near the fighting. It's too dangerous."

Arguing is pointless. If Pallas was sent ahead, I imagine the darkwalkers travel with haste. "Then we need to gather what we can. Orla, let the staff know we leave within the hour—"

"My lord asked for your safety only, my lady."

There the words hang, and were I not so certain of Pallas' loyalty to Boreas, I would question their presence, my sanity, his impudence.

Boreas can fend for himself. So can the soldiers. But many of the accompanying staff aren't trained in combat. They can barely lift a sword. "What about the staff?" Those who haven't the privilege of a horse? Their lives will be forfeit.

"I just do as I'm told, my lady." His head lolls against the back of the chair, face drawn with fatigue.

"Maybe you are quick to abandon your own men," I seethe, "but I will not leave those who cannot fight as fodder for those abominable beasts."

Pallas' bloodless face twists, but he doesn't attempt to defend himself. The situation must be dire indeed if my anger drains as quickly as it ignited. The fault is not his. It is not Boreas' either. It is no one's.

"My lady," Orla whispers, grabbing my arm. "If the lord wants you safe, then that should be the priority."

"No." Many of these people have become my friends. I cannot abandon them. "If I go, we all go. We'll be safe behind the citadel walls."

Pallas attempts to sit up, but my maid nudges him back. "There are hundreds of people in this camp. It will take many hours to pack."

"We bring only what we can carry. Weapons and the clothes on our backs. Leave the rest. The extra weight will slow our progress." I demand, "Are you well enough to lead?"

And just like that, the last of his resolve crumbles. He may stand against me, but he will lose, and he knows this. My will is sounder than his, my purpose greater than retribution. Pallas responds, "Yes, my lady."

"Then we must hurry."

~

The peace of yesterday is gone, though I wonder if it had ever been. A storm is coming, a great storm. My skin itches as low clouds churn in the distance. We transfer the wounded to stretchers, douse the fires, gather and distribute weapons. Since there aren't enough horses to go around, some will have to walk. It is twenty miles of trudging through snow.

It takes the day. I help where I can, gathering provisions and securing them to the horses' saddles. Pallas, once patched up, organizes the party. Orla keeps the other maidservants calm, and for that, I'm grateful. She has lived with these people far longer than I have. To her, they are family.

By the time we're ready to move, the sun has long since vanished. The moon rises like a swollen pustule, and throbs from among its nest of scattered stars. It drags across the starved branches and heaves its bulk higher into a sky the black of a crow's wing. My stomach sinks at the sight. For night is the darkwalkers' domain, and we will be traveling with many wounded men.

Iliana stamps a hoof, ears pricked. Wind from the approaching storm drives the cold down thick. She senses it, as do I: something squatting beyond the rumbling veil, white dampening the world to the hiss of breath.

"My lady," Orla whispers. She sits behind me in the saddle. "What of the darkwalkers?"

My gaze flits from shadow to shadow. Wound as tightly as I am, everything looks like one of the grotesque, spindly creatures, although I've yet to smell smoke, evidence of burning.

"It will be all right, Orla." A dagger hangs at my hip. I've the bow in my lap, a quiver full of salt-tipped arrows. "I'll watch over you."

Her arms tighten around my waist in a brief embrace. "Thank you, my lady."

I pat her hand in comfort.

Gideon, the guard I met at dinner, directs his massive bay gelding to the front. His armor glints dully under the moonlight, as does the armor of the ten guards who flank us. "All is clear."

Then it is time to move.

I catch the eye of Pallas, who sits at the head of the campaign. Four hundred flee, including the wounded, yet there are only sixty able-bodied soldiers. The majority are blacksmiths, cooks, hostelers, laborers, and healers who have been assigned to the war camp for many weeks now.

At my nod, he lifts an arm, signaling our departure. We abandon the camp, the shell of its remains, as the storm's fringe grazes our backs and sleet begins to fall.

Progress is slow. The slowest, most debilitating plod in existence, though I try to keep my worry to a minimum, for Orla's sake. Many hours pass in the cold and the dark that never lifts, and the sleet that dribbles, then hurls into our party with grueling force. Every so often, Pallas will lift a hand, and the faction slows, listening. My clothes are completely drenched. I squint through the falling precipitation, teeth chattering, lips frozen.

Iliana prances sideways as something crashes to our right. My bow is up, arrow nocked, the arrowhead directed at an area of smudged darkness that seems to pulse with a primordial chill. At their core, horses are prey animals. The instinct can be smoothed over, as with animals trained for war, but it can never disappear completely. Something is out there. Something massive.

Someone, or something, screams.

I jerk Iliana around. The horses stamp, unwilling to move forward or backward. Paralyzed with fright.

"My lady—"

"Hush, Orla."

She falls quiet.

I suck in the air of another brutal gust of wind. Nothing. Cold and sleet. A storm can often mask scents, depending on its strength, but I don't smell ash. Not a whiff.

Nothing stirs. Dark clouds veil the moon. The tree branches appear as broken limbs, grotesque fingers, reaching. The men attempt to calm their restless horses to the best of their abilities, their swords unsheathed, agleam, but the fear bleeds out. It laps at the animals' hooves and drips from the sky above, and my pulse spikes from a branch snapping in the distance.

Orla trembles at my back. To my right, dense forest acts as a wall of tangled growth. To the left, a frozen creek runs parallel to the road. My every sense is heightened as I scan the area for movement. We need to push forward, but I'm afraid to take my eyes off the surrounding darkness.

Something brushes my arm. I whirl around, the arrow's sharpened tip pointing directly between Pallas' eyes.

"Shit," I hiss, lowering my bow. My heart pounds so ferociously I wouldn't be surprised if it suddenly gave out. "I could have killed you!"

"My lady. There are trees down ahead. We'll need to go around."

Get off the road, he means. Wonderful. "Didn't you hear that?" I squint into the dim over his shoulder.

"Hear what?"

"That scream." I wipe the freezing water from my eyes with my upper arm. "It came from the rear."

Thunder rumbles.

No, not thunder. Hooves.

Everyone in the vicinity wheels to face the back of the line. My bow is up before I remember darkwalkers don't have hooves. Well, Phaethon does. But he's an exception.

One of the soldiers emerges from the void beyond, veering in my direction. His pale, semi-translucent face shines. The sleet begins tapering off. "It's Gideon, my lady." He exhales sharply. "He's gone."

A chill drips down my already frozen spine. The beasts must be close, but I can't smell the fire and brimstone among the watery snow. Another gasp has me spinning toward the sound.

A darkwalker stalks from the shadows.

The group scatters in the presence of the beast. I turn as another blood-curdling scream erupts from somewhere in the huddle. "No!" I bark furiously. "Hold the lines."

A trio of servants flees into the forest.

Then two more.

Pallas maneuvers his mount forward, planting himself between me and the beast. His sword pulls free of its sheath with a hair-raising whine.

The creature's long, serpentine neck coils like an asp, then strikes. Pallas, even wounded, manages to dance away from the broken teeth and dripping maw atop his horse. Orla, rigid as a plank of wood at my back, whimpers in distress at the sight. I aim an arrow at the darkwalker, but I'm afraid of accidentally hitting the captain.

The soldiers snap orders, riding down the lines to try and contain the frightened staff members.

"Leave them!" I shout, eyes still on the beast. Those that fled are lost to us. I can't risk losing fighters to try and bring a few back. I need every sword. I need order. I need to reach the gates.

Pallas continues to slash at the darkwalker, and I realize he's attempting to draw it away from the group. The forest shadows begin to distort. The trees shake, though the wind has long since died. I recall very clearly Boreas mentioning once how the forest disliked his presence, but what of his people?

Another scream. Orla has begun to pray beneath her breath.

The soldier who informed me of Gideon's disappearance barks orders at his comrades. He says, "My lady."

He says, "What should we do, my lady?"

He says, "They are approaching. My lady, please!"

The screams are too many. My mind is a tangled mess, the demands piling higher, peace far from hand.

*Focus.*

Pallas is too preoccupied fending off the beast to give orders. Reaching the citadel safely is all that matters.

"Send any man with a bow to the outside," I reply. "You—" I point to a bearded soldier at the front of the line, whose vague form blends in with the surrounding night. "Lead the group around the fallen trees and continue toward the citadel." We shouldn't be far. We've been traveling the majority of the night. "Orla, you're going to want to hold on."

"I'm not sure I can hold on any tighter," she squeaks behind me.

While the group bolts for the citadel, I position Iliana at the side of the road. Pallas' men are spaced equidistance apart, their bows drawn, as is mine. A select few, those with swords or daggers, travel with the group ahead.

With the storm having passed overhead, the smell of ash hits at full force. I am waiting. The men are waiting. They are here. They have come.

"Show yourself," I hiss.

A beast lumbers from the wood.

It is larger than my cottage back at Edgewood. Its shoulders are lopsided lumps of shadow. Red, slitted eyes regard me above a squashed mouth stuffed with jagged fangs that drip black fluid. The air speaks in whispers, and it coaxes out another of its kin, and another.

The soldier to my right cries, "Take your mark."

A stream of them, slow and trickling, emerges to flood the space between our unit and the trees.

"Aim."

Five, six, seven more. Then eight. Twelve.

"Fire!"

Screeches echo throughout the valley. Those hit by the salt-tipped arrows explode into dripping ichor.

Two men, their backs to one another, fend off three at once. There, near the back, a guard on horseback leaps toward the sidling creature, slicing it through from neck to groin. Its airy flesh splits and bleeds, and an arrow to the chest brings about its end.

Nock, draw, release.

Head, eye, chest.

And they fall and they fall and they fall.

Yet still more come. There are too many. One melts away, and there's always another to take its place. The bow string slaps from how quickly I shoot. Four, six, ten. They fall, and they do not rise. And now I've run out of arrows.

It's a struggle to hold Iliana in place. The soldiers fight and fight hard, but the more men we lose, the greater the difficulty it will be in reaching the gates in one piece.

"It's no use," I call to Pallas. "We can't hold them off!"

"Retreat!" Pallas cups one hand against his mouth. "Retreat to the citadel!"

And then the air rings with horse screams as the herd gallops down the road, frozen mud flinging from their hooves. A break in the trees reveals the group ahead.

A glance over my shoulder. The darkwalkers give chase. They lack keen eyesight, but they're swift, using the surrounding darkness to aid their camouflage. They crash through the crowd, tearing into those who are too slow. One man is sprawled across the ground on his back, cowering beneath the darkwalker looming over him, its distorted spine rippling with eerie movements.

Digging my heels into Iliana's sides, I tighten my thighs around her girth as she leaps forward. I'm out of arrows, but I have my dagger.

Slicing the blade through my forearm, coating the cold, shining metal in my blood, I pull back and let the dagger fly.

It lodges in the center of the beast's chest. Scarlet veins slither through the smoke before it ruptures in a spray of night.

The man gapes up at me. I reach down and help him to his feet. "Move!"

We break into a clearing, and ahead lies the citadel, an eruption of black stone against the snow-topped mountain at its back, the promise of salvation.

"Open the gates!" I scream.

The army is a surge of man and horseflesh. In the chaos of the stampede, a man trips in his desperate run. He screams as a horse stamps on his arm. The crack of bone rings clearly, and I wheel Iliana around, positioning her like a boulder planted in the center of a river, the band rushing like water around it.

"Pallas," I shout, leaning down to help the fallen man to his feet. "Tell your men to maintain their formation. I will have no more unnecessary deaths tonight."

"Hold!" Pallas bellows.

The gates groan open at my back. A dry, rattling hiss expels from the darkwalkers surrounding us.

"Go!" I slap a nearby horse on its haunches, and it hurdles toward the safety of the courtyard. The remainder of the group rushes forward. Servants, then the wounded. Lastly, the guards.

When the last soldier slips past me, I drive Iliana through the gates. They slam closed with a resounding *boom*.

# CHAPTER
## 35

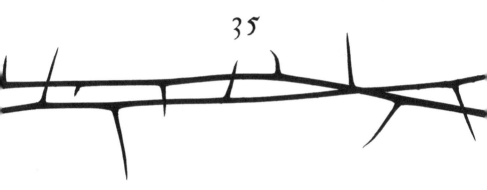

The entirety of Neumovos gathers inside the gates.

It is, to be certain, chaos. The courtyard is so crammed with refugees I cannot spot the gray stones underfoot. Even the smallest gap is occupied, either by an unruly child, a harried husband attempting to calm his family, a horse or goat or rickety cart piled high with sentimental goods. It is loud. Fear morphs the air into a weighted substance that slides like oil across my skin. The soldiers, with their battle-scarred bodies and blood-drenched armor, only heighten that distress.

Pushing through the crush, I call out, "Those in need of food, please head to the stables. If you require warm clothing, please go to the eastern courtyard."

"My lady." A young mother clamps her hand over my arm, halting my forward progress. "Is there any information about the missing soldiers?"

She's not the first to ask. I give her the same response I offered the woman before her, and the man before that. "I'm sorry, I won't know anything until the king's arrival."

It has been many hours, and still no sign of Boreas, no word. I worry for him, and it is a new, uncomfortable feeling I'm not used to.

Eyes wet, she nods, releases my arm. But I feel her gaze trailing me as I direct an older couple toward Orla, who is busy distributing woolen socks.

That familiar, buzzing panic has grown steadily overpowering over the course of the night. My skin itches in the cold. My throat tightens, and my nostrils fill with the scent of wine, a phantom memory. One sip would go a long way in banishing this feeling.

When word reached Neumovos of possible attack, they packed up and came here, to the citadel. Three thousand specters, hands empty of supplies, many partially clothed, desperate and afraid. I could not turn them away.

Boreas will be furious when he learns what I've done.

When the last blanket has been distributed, the vacant parlors and ballrooms and antechambers and sitting rooms and dining rooms occupied, I retreat inside the vast stone halls. It is dawn. My legs tremble. Twelve sleepless hours, gone in a blink. Now the citadel is overrun and who knows if there is enough to eat. But I can't be bothered by that. Somehow, I'll make it work.

My body is so drained I'm tempted to curl up on the floor, but I make the long climb upstairs to my room, only I don't stop there.

Instead of turning right where the hall bisects, I turn left, where four guards block my way into the north wing.

"I wish to visit my husband's chambers," I state.

"No one may pass but the king himself, my lady." This spoken by the largest of the soldiers present.

"And seeing that I am his *wife*," I say, "wouldn't have any bearing on that decision?"

"Let her pass." Pallas appears at the end of the opposite corridor, irritable and weary. "Lord's orders."

The men step aside, and I'm given a clear path to a set of sturdy double doors at the end of the hall.

For whatever reason, my footsteps grow heavier as I approach his quarters. I've been forbidden to enter this sanctuary of his, but today, I'm proven worthy of it.

My fingers wrap around the cool wooden handle, and I push.

Darkness. A void. It laps at my flesh as though alive. And from that darkness breeds frost, an absolute cold that respires from the obscured doorway. A high-pitched trill rings in my mind, warning me away. It is a cave, a crater, a cavity, a pit. The den of a darkwalker. And for whatever reason, I'm contemplating stepping foot inside.

I seriously doubt Boreas would set any sort of trap. After all, the staff enter to clean. Or rather, Orla does. She's never told me how often though and—

My teeth grind together. I'm no coward. This will not be the first time I've entered his rooms, but it's the first time I've entered via a door as opposed to a window. I see no reason why anything would change.

Into his chambers I go.

One of the first things I did in my bedroom was remove the curtains, but of course the Frost King would not have reason to do the same. After some fumbling, I manage to light a fire and the lamps. Much better.

The king's rooms are vast, of course, but I hadn't really studied the space in detail during my last *visit*, for lack of a better term. My attention snags on the largest piece of furniture—his bed. It is a panoply of blankets dyed the color of wine, too many pillows, and a gleaming headboard the size of a horse. Aside from the bed, the bedchamber houses a desk stacked with parchment, a bureau, and a sitting area before the fireplace with four armchairs and a couch.

Gently, I close and lock the door behind me.

The space is far less utilitarian than I thought it would be. It's marked by small touches of hominess, like a blanket tossed over one of the armchairs or an empty drinking glass abandoned on one of the side tables. The main room empties into a circular chamber edged with high bookshelves. Behind another closed door lies a bathing area. I search his rooms in the hope of finding a stash of wine, but there is none. He was not lying when he said he got rid of his entire cache.

I turn, and there again is his bed. It's far larger than mine. Probably more comfortable too, though mine is the most comfortable thing I've ever slept on. His must feel like clouds.

My curiosity gets the better of me. I launch myself onto the mattress, falling among soft, sinking pillows and feathery blankets. Oh, this is nice. Very nice. My body sighs at the contact and sinks down, down . . .

I don't remember falling asleep, but something startles me to wakefulness. A sound, a very strange sound. I can't put my finger on it. The fire is but hissing ash and smoke, yet a few coals still burn.

The door handle jiggles. Someone utters a curse from the other side of the door. Right. Because I locked it.

Leaping off the bed, I flip the bolt and haul the door open just as Boreas' weight slams into my front. We hit the ground, my body crushed beneath his.

He groans, his face mashed against my neck.

"Boreas." I shove his shoulders. He doesn't budge. "You're crushing me."

"Wren?"

The slurred question pricks my alarm. Where are the guards?

"Get up," I grit, and manage to shove him off me with one hard push. He flops onto his back and doesn't move.

"Boreas?" Kneeling by his side, I scan him from head to toe. There's a lot of blood. Enough blood that, were he a mortal man, I would be concerned. He could be a corpse for how still he lies. Oily black fluid drenches his legs.

*He can't die*, I remind myself. It does little to soothe my worry.

"The blood isn't mine," he slurs with his eyes shut.

The knowledge brings me a surprising amount of relief. However—

"Boreas." I poke him in the cheek. "Get up. You need to wash the blood off you."

"Can't. Too tired."

Hands on hips, I study him from my kneeled position with a weary sigh. Well, he's alive. That's all I care about. If he wants to sleep on the floor, then so be it. But first, he needs a bath.

"Orla!" She's around here somewhere. I swear I could call from the opposite side of the fortress and she'd somehow manage to hear me.

Less than a minute later, the echo of her quick footfalls reaches me. "Yes, my lady?" She crosses the threshold, face splotched red from exertion, and nearly trips over Boreas in the process. A sharp gasp follows. "My lord?"

"He's fine. Just tired." Exhausted is a more apt description, considering he would never display this level of vulnerability otherwise. "Can you bring someone to fill the king's bath, please?"

She rips her gaze from Boreas' prone form. "Right away."

For a middle-aged woman, Orla is extremely nimble when the situation calls for it. It seems as if only seconds pass before a group of servants scuttles inside bearing buckets of steaming water, which they pour into the wooden tub until it's full. They depart as quickly as they arrive.

"Thank you," I call to their retreating backs, shutting the door behind them. Then I turn, cross my arms, and study the Frost King. Could he be concussed? He says the blood isn't his, but this behavior is odd.

I kick him in the leg, though it's more of a nudge, really. He grunts, his face twisting. "Wife," he growls.

"Yes?" I reply patiently.

His eyelids flutter open. He squints at me. "I should have known you wouldn't let me sleep in peace."

"You realize you've collapsed on the floor, right?" When he doesn't answer, I add, "You need to wash. You stink like a corpse."

"Understandable, considering I killed many darkwalkers today."

The words ooze from his mouth, slow with fatigue. A shudder runs through him, and the tendons in his neck pull taut.

The first lick of unease moves through me. "Are you sure you aren't hurt?" Is it possible he was wounded but didn't notice in the heat of battle?

"I'm sure."

He still doesn't move. "Well?" I snap. "Get up before I kick you."

"I . . ." He glances around the room. The fingers of one hand twitch, then settle.

"What is it? Spit it out."

"I need help standing."

To admit that, he must truly be spent. I scrutinize him more closely. His skin is always pale, but now it holds an ugly pallor, a thin layer of sweat sheened atop it. Beneath his clouded gaze rests deep bruises. The Frost King doesn't fall ill. He can't die. He claims he is uninjured. So why does he look so terrible?

"My power was drained," he explains at my confusion. "Pain and fatigue are side effects of that."

I was not aware his power could be drained. Then again, what do I know of his power, its capabilities and extent? Very little.

Hauling a fully grown man to his feet isn't easy, but I manage. Boreas sags against me, one arm braced around my lower back, palm holding fast to my hip, while his other hand grabs mine for stability. Together, we shuffle toward the bathing chamber. He sits on a stool beside the wooden tub, then looks at me drowsily. I'm remembering a desperate, clinging kiss in the embrace of tent canvas; a fire smoldering nearby; hot, wet sounds of sucking mouths and eager tongues.

Had we not been interrupted, I would have climaxed around his fingers deep in my core, and I imagine he would have, too, with my hand wrapped around his stiff arousal. The way he touched me . . . No one has ever touched me with so much blatant want.

My pulse flutters, and I push the thought from my mind. What happened at the camp was nothing. Lack of physical touch, affection, sexual release. I was bound to kiss someone. Boreas just happened to be in the vicinity. And he just happened to kiss me back.

I realize Boreas is staring at me, as though he, too, remembers.

"I'm not stripping you."

He snorts. The sound is more vibration than sound. "I would not expect you to. My good fortune doesn't extend that far."

Good fortune? Now I know he has a concussion.

"You're right," I sniff. "Your good fortune doesn't even extend as far as your fingernails. Wash, then I'll help you into bed." Because for whatever reason, the thought of Boreas attempting to do so himself saddens me.

While he scrubs the blood and grime from his skin, I stoke the fire until it roars. Heat warms my stiff, aching joints, and I sigh gratefully. Then I take a seat in one of the armchairs, hands clasped, legs jittering. The hair on my body stands on end.

On the other side of the wall, water splashes, followed by a thump and a curse.

I still. "Are you all right?" I'm up, crossing the room. "Boreas?" I press a hand to the shut door of the bathing chamber.

His sigh reaches me. It's all the answer I need.

In hindsight, I should have braced myself for the sight that awaited me on the other side of the door, because imagining Boreas mid-wash is vastly different than witnessing it. His frame is so broad it dwarfs the tub, despite the basin being large enough for two adults to lounge in comfortably. He leans against the back curve, wet chest agleam in the lamplight, black hair plastered across his shoulders. Milky, rose-scented water veils what lies below his waist. A quick perusal reveals he's unhurt, just thoroughly frustrated.

He mumbles, "I can't reach my back."

Ah. That would be a problem.

I cross the threshold. A cool breeze brushes my cheek tentatively, and I say, without being fully aware of it, "I can help, if you want."

He does not appear at all thrilled by this. Meanwhile, I struggle to keep my eyes above his chest, with various success. His abdominal wound from earlier has healed. His nipples have pebbled in the cooler air.

When he fails to respond, I sigh and head for the door. "Fine. Flop around like a fish for all I care."

"Wait."

Mouth pursed, I slowly pivot to face him. As much as I'd like to ease his struggles, I'm not going to knock on a door that refuses to open.

With obvious reluctance, he offers me a bar of soap. Boreas looks so miserable I have to fight a smile. He doesn't want help, but he is asking for it regardless.

Pulling over a stool from the corner, I position myself behind him, wet my hand, and lather up the soap I pluck from his fingers. Black hair slicks his scalp. At the moment, he leans against the back of the tub, so only his shoulders and neck are visible. Wide, *very wide* shoulders streaked with remnants of battle. It's just a body. Skin and blood and veins and tendon.

Upon the first touch, the king tenses. Sweat and grime slough from his corded form, darkening the water further. I imagine it is an old crone I bathe. Someone whose presence does not change the rhythm of my heart. But I quickly learn how pointless those visualizations are. The give of his skin beneath my questing fingers, the slide of the soapy water, feels highly sensual.

Once I've lathered the back of his shoulders and neck, I begin to move down his arms. My palms glide over the contours of his musculature. His skin is fever hot. Or maybe that's me.

A light splash sounds as I pull back. "Lean forward, please."

Boreas is rigid as hardened bricks. I fight the undeniable pull to round his front, to see his expression out of fear of what I'll find. Distaste? Surely my touch doesn't repulse him. He kissed me with the hunger of a man starved.

Prying his fingers from the lip of the tub, he leans forward, the motion sending the gray-tinged bath water lapping at the curved sides as he bares the arch of his spine to me, each hilly vertebra.

And every scar marring his back.

I go still. I've seen the scarring before, but never up close. His skin doesn't even bear resemblance to skin. More like heaping eruptions, jagged topography, craters of earth spilling out. The rise of some areas looks as if the skin healed, only to be broken open again.

It is a horrible sight. I can only imagine the extent of his suffering.

With the gentlest touch, I smooth my soapy hands over the scarred, uneven expanse. His breath hitches, then shudders out. His head bows forward in a sign of trust that tightens my throat.

"It was my idea to join the resistance that overthrew the old gods," he slurs.

I wipe away streaks of dirt, the places where the straps connecting his breastplate had pressed into his tunic.

"I was convinced this new life, under new rule, would allow us greater freedoms and influence." He swallows, then goes on. "I was wrong, obviously. Prior to our banishment, my brothers and I were to be flogged. The new gods wanted to make an example of us, to show what happened to those who conspired against them.

"I asked to receive the lashes meant for them. They agreed to my compounded agony. Above all, the divine are vain and power-hungry. They slowed my body's natural healing abilities so my skin would scar. So that I would always remember my failure."

He falls quiet after that. I process the information, slotting it into the blank spaces between what I know of the king, and what I thought I knew of him. "Does it hurt?" I ask, cupping water in my hands to cleanse the suds, which sluice down the divots straddling his spine.

His head bobs against his chest. "The scarring tugs occasionally, and my back aches if I do not stretch before intense exercise." The last word is barely audible. He's falling asleep in the bath.

"You need to rest. You're dead on your feet."

"I cannot rest." He straightens, turning his head in an attempt to look at me. "There is too much to do, too many wounded, too many deaths. I managed to patch the Shade, but I don't know how long it will last. It's as if the mortals are compelled to enter the Deadlands. It doesn't make sense." He adds, "I will need to fortify the barrier surrounding the citadel, but that will have to wait until my power is restored. And I need to tally the dead." He struggles to stand, but he's so drained he only succeeds in slopping water over the tub's edge.

If the Frost King will not listen to me, then I must entice him into sleep. A body too fired with adrenaline, the mind circling and circling without end? I understand what he needs.

"You're too tense," I whisper, brushing my fingertips across the slope of his shoulders. He is watchful as I reposition the stool against the side of the tub so I'm given a view of his front. "Might I offer a suggestion?"

As though sensing a shift in the air, Boreas searches my face, lingering on my mouth. His eyelids droop lower, slitting the blue gaze beneath, whose color blazes despite the fatigue. "Go on."

"The body, after release, tends to relax."

His lips part in surprise. "Sex?"

The deep rasp tugs on something low in my pelvis. As my attention drops to the murky water where his legs are spread, I spy the faint outline of his protruding erection lying against his abdomen, its slight upward curve.

"Not sex." The words are coarse. Gods, I need water. I mean wine. "I would focus on your pleasure only." Because if I am to burn in whatever hell exists, then I want Boreas to burn with me.

The silence drags on. We stare at each other, and I wonder if he recognizes that this suggestion is born of my own selfish desires. I want to touch him, to feel his body come alive, to watch him sunder, damn the consequences.

Carefully, he replies, "How would this work?"

Well, he's not saying no. That's something. "You don't have to do anything. Just sit there while I touch you."

He searches my face as though anticipating a trap. If it is a trap, it is one of my own making.

Eventually, he leans back, wary in his surrender. A glint of tension rises in him and is stymied.

Trailing the fingers of one hand through the surface of the water,

I let him settle. Knees bent and legs spread, he is a king in every battle-honed edge and every unexpected curve.

My fingertips brush his abdomen beneath the water, and he flinches. Bumps scatter across his flesh in the wake of my touch. My mouth is painfully dry as I continue the trailing path, up the ridged abdomen, across his sculpted chest, down, ending with my hand wrapped around his hard, jutting shaft.

Boreas groans, and his body curves helplessly around my hand.

Every thought trickles through the sieve of my mind. The feel of him is exactly as I remember. A throbbing, compact heat beneath the give of flesh. I give a slow, experimental stroke from root to crown and back. The king's hips twitch even as he swells in my grip, and his arousal ripens the air, stealing the last of my sanity.

I watch my hand work him over beneath the surface of the soapy water. He, in turn, watches my face, a hiss escaping whenever I give additional attention to the head. A pulse darts through his length, and he hardens further.

"Good?" I ask, catching his eye.

No. Slower.

Shadows have lengthened his fingers into claws. And when my strokes aren't enough, his hips begin to rock, easy and deliberate, pushing his shaft through the opening my hand makes. Water splashes, a distant sound. My body feels scorched. To touch him without restraint, without limit. He is masterful.

Fizzling heat spreads and climbs my throat. When I reach the very base of his cock, Boreas breaks off with a panting curse. And I realize he's trying to show me something.

"Like this?" I repeat the motion.

One of his hands pries free of the tub's edge to wrap around my wrist. The dark shadows tickle my brown skin. He guides my hand, widens his legs, tilts his pelvis, throws back his head. A slow, rolling motion. And again. When I complete my third pass, his fingers spasm around mine, and he thrusts faster. His hand falls away to rest on his submerged thigh, fist clenched. "Yes," he breathes, eyes fluttering shut.

Red colors the rise of his cheeks, deepens his lips to blush. A bead of water, or maybe sweat, trickles down the side of his jaw. I lean forward to lick it clean. He grunts but doesn't open his eyes.

There is something highly erotic about bringing Boreas to that knife's edge. To watch the compulsion—*sex*—overrule all reason. My touch is the dream and the reality.

Yet another twisting glide, and he gasps. My tongue sticks to the roof of my parched mouth. He is the indomitable force of so many lives, a hammer to shape molten metal, but tonight, I might watch him break.

Water sloshes from the rapid motion of my hand. My grip tightens on the upward drag, fingers loosening around the wide head. I trace the slit and push in gently, and his body arches beautifully, the hard set of his jaw revealing how rapidly his control frays. Boreas is beautiful. A cut body and the blackest hair plastered to his cheeks and neck, pale blue eyes that smolder. His hand covers mine again, but I'd like to think it's simply for the pleasure of touching me, skin on skin, for he doesn't guide my movements.

The closer he approaches completion, the more I fight my own urges. To climb into the tub and spread my legs across his lap. To grind against his length until my body shatters. I could do it. He would likely not stop me, might even invite me to go further and sink onto him completely. But I meant what I said before. This is for his pleasure only, and sleep, tenuous sleep, awaits at its end.

Feeling bolder, I shift back toward the base and gently play with his balls. Boreas jerks with a vicious curse. "Wren." Mouth partially open, lips red, red, red.

My hand quickens. Impetus builds as he ruts against me, his cock pushing free of the water, baring the flushed, ruddy head I *really* want to suck on. He throws his head back with a drawn-out groan, rough and guttural. The corded tendons in his neck flex with his swallow. One of his hands is white-knuckled around the tub's edge, the other on my upper arm.

"More," he whispers. A labored, breathy plea. Strain locks his limbs into wooden carvings. My lips part in response to his prurience, the hunger that swells black in his pupils, that fists in my gut in unending ache. Just as his hips begin to stutter, I lightly squeeze his shaft and Boreas erupts in my hand with a hoarse cry, his seed spurting into the water and slickening my grip around him further, mindless thrusts chasing his pleasure to completion, every drop sucked dry.

My strokes slow as his body sags into the water. Utterly spent. His grip on my arm loosens, and he caresses the skin for a brief moment before releasing me.

I wash off my hand, satisfied by the sight of his drooping eyelids. He will sleep well tonight. As for me, I ache and throb in the most secret places, but I force myself to stand and reach out my hand. "Out."

The Frost King is barely conscious as I snag a towel and wrap it around his waist. Then I help him shuffle into the bedchamber, toward the bed. Pressed body to body, the scent of soap rising from his skin teases my senses. Muscles shift seamlessly beneath my hand.

"Thank you," Boreas says.

"For?"

He gestures to the fire.

"Oh." And why should it matter that he noticed I lit a fire? The room was cold. Anyone would have done the same. "You're welcome."

His attention shifts to my right, and awareness sharpens in his gaze. For whatever reason, I'm afraid to look, as if, subconsciously, I know what he's focused on.

I turn. He's looking at the bed. More specifically, the indentation in the center of the mattress, undeniable proof that a body had lain there.

My face grows hot. Boreas stares at the bed as though it is a flower sprouting in the snow. He asks, very carefully, "Were you sleeping in my bed?"

"No."

"No." Spoken like a question, yet not. He takes me in at his side, a lingering study.

"I was . . . testing the support."

"I see." He returns to staring at the indentation. "What about this?" As if the indentation isn't embarrassing enough, he gestures to the enormous spot of dried saliva on the pillow.

"That," I say with whatever shred of dignity remains, "is a mistake."

"Mm."

"Lie down, Boreas." I nudge him toward the mattress, where he sits and collapses with a bone-weary groan. The towel manages to cling to his waist by sheer will alone.

"You don't need to stay," he manages. "I know you would rather be elsewhere."

He assumes things of me I'm not sure are true anymore. But let him think what he will. It's easier to maintain distance. Easier not to think of how he so effortlessly unraveled me and took things I did not realize I wanted to give him.

I pull the blankets over him. In seconds, he is out. And since there's no reason for me to linger, I return to my rooms.

Boreas was right. I didn't *need* to stay.

But I would have, had he asked me to.

∾

Boreas is not at breakfast the next day. Either he is avoiding me after our latest sexual encounter, or he has reason not to attend, which makes me believe he lied the previous night about being unhurt. He was breathing when I left him, and I didn't see any open wounds on his body, but I don't know the consequences of draining one's divine power.

Either way, he will be hungry. So I gather a plate of food and bring it to his rooms while the staff busy themselves passing out meals to our many guests. This time I'm allowed to enter the north wing without incident. As I lift my hand to knock, the door opens. Boreas, dressed in a tunic the color of the sea in winter and loose trousers, halts in surprise.

"Hello." I lift the plate to draw his attention to the food rather than the blush warming my cheeks. "You weren't at breakfast, so I brought you this. In case you were hungry." Because what else would he do with a plate of food? Stupid. So, so stupid. In any case, his health appears much improved.

Boreas looks to the food, to me, back to the food. "There are people in my citadel."

I lift an eyebrow. "There are."

"The entire town of Neumovos, if I'm not mistaken."

"You are not."

A dark glower demands I explain myself.

Brushing past him, I set the plate on an end table, saying, "I didn't have a choice. They asked for refuge, and I couldn't turn them away. I wasn't sure how dire the threat was."

At this, he nods, as if he would have decided the same, and plucks a piece of toast from the plate. "The darkwalkers are scattered at the moment. I'm not sure how long until they retaliate."

"I wanted to talk to you about that, actually."

"Oh?"

"I'd like to go through with the party."

He pauses with the toast halfway to his mouth. Blinks. "You're aware we sit on the eve of battle, yes? We cannot afford a distraction."

"How quickly do you think the darkwalkers will reorganize?"

He chews in thought. "It is difficult to say. Someone or something is controlling them, but I've yet to learn what or who. We cannot lower our guard, not for a moment. We must prepare for when they strike back."

Arms crossed, I study him with the confidence of one who knows what they're doing. Sometimes it works. Sometimes it doesn't. "Why can't we do both?"

Boreas offers me a slice of melon. I already ate, but I accept the offering, as I'm feeling particularly amicable this morning. He watches me chew, and his focus is so acute I have to turn away.

Of course, my attention falls to the bed. Rumpled blankets and pillows tossed to the floor tell me Orla hasn't been by yet. Then I peek at the door leading to the bathing chamber, behind which sits the tub. I glance away, but Boreas' nostrils flare as though scenting the spike in my arousal, even though that's impossible.

*Focus.*

"Thinking about something?" he murmurs knowingly.

"No."

He steps closer. "Your cheeks are flushed."

My gaze dips to his chest, lower, to the unmistakable erection constrained by the seam of his trousers. I could reach out and touch him if I wanted to. But that would be a terrible idea. Probably.

Clearing my throat, I glance up at him. His fingers lift toward my face, and he tucks a strand of hair behind my ear, the gesture tender and, dare I say, heartfelt.

"Are you thinking of last night?" he asks lowly.

"I," I announce firmly, chin thrust out, "am a delicate flower."

Warm laughter helps drive back the chill the room holds. "I have never heard something so untrue." His eyes crinkle. I don't think I'll ever get used to the sight.

"Look, I know what you're going to say about the party." My hands ball into fists. "You'll say you don't want people in your space, but your men are weary. The townsfolk are frightened. I think a celebration would help lift everyone's mood. We can have it tomorrow. The decorations are still in place, and there is enough food." I checked with Silas before breakfast. "Surely the darkwalkers can't regroup so quickly after so much loss—"

He sighs. "Wren."

"—however I really think it would help boost morale, and let's face it, eternal winter is hard enough without the poorly decorated interior—"

"Wren."

"—and even though you're mad at me for hosting this party in the first place and not telling you I invited the entire town—"

"*Wren.*"

"What?" I snap.

"The answer is yes."

"You—oh." My arms fall. "Really?"

He dips his chin. "On one condition."

Of course it would not be that easy. "And that is?"

"You must invite your sister."

# CHAPTER 36

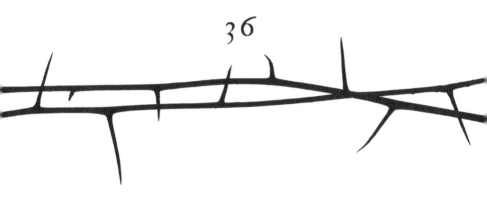

"No."

That's my answer. No further elaboration needed.

No.

Boreas watches me pace his room. "Care to explain?"

Of all the requests I expected from the North Wind, this was the least anticipated. "You know why." After the humiliation of my first visit, I'm uninterested in repeating it. I crawled back to the Deadlands with my tail between my legs, and licked my wounds, and suffered in silence. To have my own sister treat me so poorly . . . It broke something in me.

Near silent footsteps pad toward me. The heat and breadth of the king's body blanket my spine, as though I might be free to lean against him, to borrow strength in this moment, should I choose to do so.

Boreas sighs. "Wren."

"Elora doesn't want me in her life," I snap, voice cracking on the last word. "She made that perfectly clear." After all, I was only there to fulfill her selfish needs, right? Food on the table. A roof over her head. Gathered firewood. Sweets, when I could scrounge up enough coin to trade for them, which usually involved sleeping with the weaver's cruel nephew. Nothing ever sullied her pristine hands.

In the end, Elora didn't choose me. She never chose me. And therein lies the difference between us, because I chose her every day despite the fear that everything I did wasn't enough, would never be enough, because she never reassured me otherwise.

I stride to the bed, to the window, back to the bed, then to the fireplace. "It doesn't matter. I don't need her. I don't need anyone. She has her beloved Shaw. She has the baby in her belly." I grip the top of the wooden mantel. "You must think me a terrible sister."

"I said no such thing."

"But you think it," I burst out, whirling around. Up my throat, out my mouth, into my eyes—the fury consumes me with breathless speed. "I should be happy for her. But the truth is, I want Elora to feel the way I do. I want her to feel my hurt, anger, and betrayal. I want every weight I have ever carried for our family to be passed onto her shoulders, and I want her spine to break from it." The words fall, vicious and unchecked, from my mouth. I'm no longer aware of them.

"Sometimes—" I stop. Boreas watches me steadily, without judgment. That is the only reason I push forward. "Sometimes I think about returning to Edgewood and burning her stupid house down, or spoiling her food cache, or cutting holes in her hats and coats. But mostly," I say with a half-crazed laugh, "I wonder if the fault is mine, to have thought so little of myself for so long that I squandered my own self-worth."

And as the tears come, as my face folds, my hands lift to shield my expression from Boreas, the pain I struggle to snuff out. The crying will end, right now. Right . . . now.

Still crying.

"It's all your fault, you know," I manage in a wobbly tone. "Pretending like you care about my feelings. Why can't you toss me into the dungeon like old times?" Despising him the way I once did is no longer an option. It is, in fact, impossible.

His large hands cup my shoulders. One tug, and my forehead rests against his chest without resistance. A deep breath pulls his winter scent into my lungs, and I delay my exhale for as long as possible so as to not lose its trace.

"There is no pretending, Wren. I do care."

Life was so much easier when we hated each other. Easier than whatever this thing is that's developing between us.

And since the North Wind does not lie, he must be telling the truth.

He goes on in a low rumble, "You need closure. This visit will give you that."

Deep down, I knew it would come to something of this nature. But I'm not sure if I'm ready. "Will you come with me?"

He squeezes the back of my neck. "You need only to ask."

～

Later that evening, Boreas and I stand at the entrance to Edgewood, our boots toeing the line of salt that encircles the town. It appears much smaller than I remember. I have seen the world, and my mind is open, my worldview broadened. And yet, this is the place where I was born. It represents all that I was. And those earliest memories will forever stay with me.

"I feel ill," I mutter, eyes trained on the square in the distance. I inhaled a slice of cake prior to our journey downriver. For courage.

Most have bedded down for the night, but a few windows glow with lamplight. How tired the cottages look. The wood warps and bends. The handful of surviving livestock huddle in their pens, old skin and frail bones, unlikely to survive the next few months. It saddens me. I want better for Edgewood, but that's out of my hands.

"If you must be sick," the Frost King quips as he surveys the town, "try to avoid my boots."

"I make no promises."

He turns to look at me. "You do not have to address her now. We can come back later when you are ready. In the end, the choice is yours."

But the party is tomorrow, and as much as I want to avoid this meeting, I can't. This is something I must do for myself.

Stepping over the salt barrier, I stride down the deserted street, past the square, to where a narrow path of trampled snow leads to Elora and Shaw's home. Meanwhile, our old cottage sits vacant, the chimney cold, the front porch concealed by a dumping of snow. Doubt begins to creep in on me. Here I am, arriving unannounced in the middle of the night with the Frost King in tow. A glance in his direction confirms he looks as dangerous as his previous visit, wrapped in his long cloak, cruel features having been sculpted with a precise hand.

"Do you think you can make yourself look a little more approachable and less . . . this?" I gesture toward his frown.

"That's my face." Bland.

"Right. That." I attempt a smile, but it falls flat.

Boreas huffs, squeezing the back of my neck affectionately. With a gentle nudge, I'm pushed along, nearer to Elora's home.

My heart pounds sickeningly fast. "Don't scowl," I say. "Don't move too quickly—you might frighten them." What else? "Keep your spear out of sight. Make sure you chew with your mouth closed."

"I always chew with my mouth closed," he clips out. "You should take your own advice."

I ignore him. "Don't take off your gloves. Oh, don't—"

"Wren." He stops me prior to reaching the porch, his grip sure, yet gentle. It's a combination I've grown to appreciate from him. "There is nothing you or I need to change. Either Elora accepts the circumstances, or she doesn't. That is not something you have control over."

"If she tells me to leave . . ." I can't finish the thought. It hurts too much.

Something in his expression softens. "Then you and I will go." He brings my hand to his chest. His heart thumps beneath my palm, and the rhythm grounds me. "But at least you will have closure. You will know you tried. You fought for her when she would not fight for you."

*And you,* I nearly say. *You fought for me, too.*

How we managed to reach this point in time, this place, I will never understand. But I do know one thing.

"I'm glad you're here."

Boreas squeezes my hand, then releases it. "Me, too."

A rush of renewed courage steels my spine. I climb the rickety stairs onto the equally rickety porch. Lifting my fist, I knock twice, then wait.

Elora, dressed in a simple beige gown with her dark brown hair contained to a bun, startles upon opening the door. "Wren?"

Then she spots Boreas. Her face drains of color so quickly she sways, and I reach out to steady her.

She recoils from my touch, stumbling backward. Her hip rams into a small table, and the vase resting atop it tips, shattering upon hitting the floor.

"Elora?" Hurried footsteps thunder from the back of the house. Her husband, Shaw, comes into view. To his credit, he doesn't balk at the sight of the North Wind standing on his doorstep. But he is instantly wary.

"What do you want?" Shaw bites out, planting himself in front of his wife. I don't blame him. We hardly know each other. But Elora doesn't attempt to stop him, and *that* hurts.

Lifting my chin, I say, "I'm here to speak with my sister."

"In the middle of the night? It seems a most inconvenient time." Another cutting glance at Boreas, who stiffens at my back. "And rather dubious."

"I could hardly send a letter across the Shade," I reply with false sweetness. I'm already reconsidering the no-spear rule. A bit of fear never failed to inspire. "Don't worry. Boreas isn't looking for another bride. He already has his hands full with me." And anyway, I'm not interested in sharing.

A huff of air stirs the crown of my head. It sounds suspiciously like laughter.

Elora peeks around her husband's shoulder. Her soft, slender hands clench the fabric of Shaw's tunic with white-knuckled strength. Small, timid, faint-hearted. An oily feeling squirms up my spine, for

I was once like her. I once looked at the Frost King as she does now, with room only for terror on my face. "May we come in?" I ask.

She glances between me and the king. "What do you want?"

The answer snaps out of me. "For you to speak with me face to face. For once in your life, Elora, try not to act like a coward."

And there's the fury, so like mine. It's not often I witness it, but it is a thing to behold when she frees it from its tightly woven tether. She shakes from the force of that rage. But so do I.

"This goes too far," she grinds out, both hands cupped around her considerable girth. In her eyes, I have betrayed her trust. I have brought peril to her doorstep. It is one dagger to the heart after another. "I invited you into my home last time, but that was when you came alone." She swallows. "You are no longer welcome here. I'm sorry, Wren, but I can't risk the baby."

When I last visited Elora, I looked into eyes the same color and shape as mine, and I wondered who, exactly, had changed. It is obvious to me now.

"Do you actually think I would ever harm your child? Your husband? Anyone who matters to you?" My rage is total. It closes my throat, burns red behind my eyes. Not even Boreas' reassuring presence is able to calm me. "How can you possibly think that?"

"Look," Shaw begins.

"I wasn't talking to you," I spit at him. My attention returns to Elora. "Well?"

Elora's gaze flits to Boreas, as though afraid he will strike without warning. But it's not my husband she needs to be concerned with.

Her lips part, trembling, then press flat. "I don't have to explain anything to you. This is my home now, and I . . . I decide what is acceptable or not. My reasoning stands. So please, just go." She begins to shut the door when Boreas moves.

A shriek erupts from Elora. He is behind me, and then he is filling the doorway, that immortal grace allowing him to move between blinks, like shadow and wind.

He sticks his boot against the jamb, his height and breadth engulfing those unused to it. Elora gasps and falls back against Shaw's chest. Her husband's arms come around her, hands crossed over her stomach protectively.

Boreas says, slow and cold, "I will remain outside, if that is what you wish, but you will speak to Wren. As her sister, you will give her the courtesy and respect she deserves."

Elora looks close to fainting. And I have the ridiculous urge to cackle until my lungs shrivel up.

I rest a hand against the king's back, and he retreats, giving me space to step forward and retake control of the situation. "In case you were wondering," I tell Elora, "you do not have a choice in this. I'm not leaving until you've heard what I have to say."

"Fine." She huffs through her nostrils, having regained some dignity. "Wren, you are welcome inside. We can discuss whatever it is you wish to discuss."

"If you expect my husband to wait outside in the cold—"

"He's the *Frost King*—"

"I don't care!" I bark, vibrating from the ferocity lashing through my bloodstream. I am burning, I am raging, I am fighting, at last, for my voice.

I am born anew.

Elora's eyes widen. She is afraid of me. She does not know who

I am. For so long, I kept all those sharp edges hidden away. I was too rough, too forward, not gentle enough, not obedient enough, not kind enough, not soft enough. I was the woman with the scarred face and willing body. I was confined to the shade while Elora was granted the sun. But no longer.

"You've changed," she whispers.

"Have I?" Or am I at last set free?

Shaw glowers at me. I ignore him. So long as Boreas is present, he wouldn't dare strike against me.

"All my life I cared for you," I whisper to my sister, my twin. We shared the same womb. "It was my greatest pride, providing you a good life. There was nothing I would not do for you. Nothing. I sold my body for coin. I risked life and limb fighting darkwalkers. I hiked hundreds of miles every month searching for food. I never complained, not once in all those long, difficult years." My voice thickens. By the gods, I will not break. Not until I am far away from here, not until I've said my piece.

"You called me selfish," I continue. "You, who have made no attempts to lift a finger your entire life, dared to call me selfish?" My mouth curls.

Something like guilt flashes through her eyes, and I wonder if she knew these things. If Elora made the conscious decision to remain quiet, ignorant of my choices so that she could avoid living a burdensome life. Before, I would not have believed it. Now I am certain it is true. What else have I been blind to?

"That you can stand here and judge me for the choice I made—a choice to protect *you*—reveals how weak and selfish your character is. Yes, I lied to you. Yes, I left without saying goodbye. But I was willing to die so that you could live, because I loved you more than anything in the world. Can you say the same?"

Elora disentangles herself from Shaw's hold. "I tried, Wren. I really did. But over the years, the drinking grew worse—"

My stomach drops. Boreas growls at my back.

"—and caring for me seemed to give you some stability—"

"No." My hand cuts the air. "You do not get to shame me. You do not get to use my faults as a scapegoat for your selfishness and inaction. I have reflected on my past behavior, my destructive tendencies, and while I understand it caused you pain, you refuse to take accountability for your actions, and that is the reason why I am standing here. Not my sobriety."

Boreas moves to stand by my side. Quiet, restrained, loyal, unflinching. Elora's expression tightens. Her mouth quavers, and she bites her bottom lip, clearly pained.

She says tentatively, "You're right. My comment was uncalled for. If you wish to make amends, then let us discuss."

"I'm not here to make amends." I am far beyond that. "You have a choice. If you cannot accept the reasonings for my actions, accept *me*, then I see no reason to continue this relationship. I will leave and not return. You can live your life bearing the guilt of having turned away the one person who has always loved you." My voice hardens. "If, however, you wish to keep me in your life, you will accept our invitation to attend a party tomorrow evening."

Elora swallows. "In the Deadlands?"

"Yes. Shaw is welcome, too, of course."

They exchange a wordless glance. Shaw then asks, "How will that work?"

"A boat will meet you at the Les. Once you cross through the Shade, you will be provided mounts that will take you to the citadel. You need not worry about your wellbeing, or of your child's wellbeing. As my guests, you will be granted the highest of protections. Should you decide not to attend," I say, "then we no longer have anything to say to one another." And that will be something else I must carry, something I must grieve.

Elora's face falls. "Wren—"

"I wish you happiness in your life. It is all I've ever wanted for you. I only wished you wanted the same for me."

The woman who left Edgewood, bound for the Deadlands atop a darkwalker's back, is not the same woman who leaves now, standing with the North Wind as his equal. With one last look at Elora's face, I turn, picking my way down the stairs. Boreas wraps an arm around my shoulders, tucking me against his side as we stride through the deserted square.

"I'm proud of you," he murmurs, mouth dipping near my ear.

For a moment, I allow myself to lean into his side. A few tears trickle down my cheeks, hot against my frozen skin. "I'm just happy I didn't vomit."

A chuckle rasps out of him. And despite the feeling of my chest cleaving open, I manage to laugh as well.

"How do you feel?"

Our boots click against the bare, moon-brightened stones. Phaethon awaits in the trees, and I look forward to returning to my rooms, where I imagine a hot bath awaits me. "Sad, but I'll be all right."

The choice is hers. If Elora wants to save our relationship, she will bridge the distance, not I. It's time she carried her own weight. And while she may not have supported me in this, someone else certainly did.

Taking a shaky breath, I say, "Thank you for being here. I'm not sure I would have had the courage to face Elora without you."

Again, Boreas squeezes me around the shoulders. "You would have." His certainty is unbending. "Let's go home."

I glance at him, startled, but he only smiles down at me. "Home," I agree, and take his hand in mine.

*You've changed*, Elora claimed, and she was right. Months ago, I chose my sister.

This time, I chose myself.

# CHAPTER

## 37

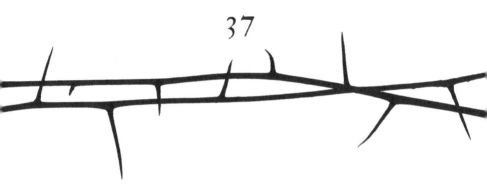

The North Wind paces like a chained dog. His gaze narrows at every passing server, every child rushing underfoot, every circling couple, every clinking glass. His eye twitches from the wild, drunken laughter, the bubbling, effervescent happiness of a party full underway. His upper lip curls each time someone *dares* approach him.

He is, quite simply, a terror.

Loitering by his side near one of the wide, arched windows, I sigh. "You're scowling again."

His scowl deepens, if possible. His petulance makes fists of his hands, which he's shoved into the pockets of his black overcoat, the high collar adding to his reserve. In the glow of soft lamplight overhead, his cheeks cut like knives.

The ballroom has been transformed for the event. Swaths of pale blue fabric drape the walls, the windows, the folds like ripples in a clear mountain stream. White silk intermingles, pooling in the corners where it crisscrosses the ceiling. The center of the room has been cleared for dancing, and there is plenty of it thanks to the small chamber ensemble—courtesy of volunteer musicians from Neumovos. A lovely, trilling melody skips atop the deep basso continuo, and every so often, the harp's resonance twines with that of a flute.

I happily sip from my cup of fruit juice, despite the amount of wine being served. Just because I must avoid alcohol, doesn't mean the townsfolk can't enjoy themselves, though I thought long and hard about the decision before asking that wine be stocked.

"You're sure?" Boreas asked me only hours ago.

"I'm sure."

He accepted that without argument, and behold, the wine flowed.

I glance at him from the corner of my eye. He's removed his hands from his pockets and idly taps a finger against his thigh. "Clench your jaw any harder," I remark, "and you'll crack a tooth."

"It'll heal." The tapping quickens until I capture his fingers. His face jerks toward me in surprise, but I drop his hand as though it burns. No gloves tonight. I wonder if that is a mistake, considering how wound-up he is. At least his spear is absent. *That* would be grounds for concern.

"Relax," I soothe. "There is much to be grateful for." The specters are dressed in whatever they managed to carry after fleeing Neumovos. Most wear trousers and tunics, but a few women have donned their finest gowns. Despite their haphazard manner of dress, they didn't hesitate in jumping feet-first into the festivities.

I crane my head, searching for someone in particular. Boreas says, "Any sign of her?"

A shallow twinge near my heart. I ignore it. "No."

Elora is not among the crowd. It was to be expected. I take her absence, and I hold it close one last time. I'm disappointed, but more than that, I'm tired. Tired of fighting for someone who refuses to fight for me. It's time I accept that.

"My lady?" A servant appears, a tray of bite-sized fruit pastries placed artfully atop. Dollops of sweet cream garnish the miniature desserts.

I snatch two with a heartfelt, "Thank you."

"And you, my lord?"

Boreas glares. The man flinches, retreating a step, and scampers away as if the king shot ice from his fingertips.

I shove the first pastry into my mouth. "You're incorrigible."

The denizens of Neumovos are having the time of their lives, and the soldiers, and the staff. Everyone except Boreas.

Why does this not surprise me?

I turn to him in curiosity. "Why is it so hard for you to enjoy yourself?" I'm not trying to put him down. I honestly want to know. Maybe I could help him climb that hurdle, should he let me. "You said I could host the party."

"And I regret that decision."

That is apparent. "Why?" For perhaps the first time ever, the people of Neumovos are not treated as though shunned. They do not look at Boreas as though he is the enemy. How can they when he has allowed them refuge from the darkwalkers?

Before he can answer, a group of townsfolk approach us. Boreas stiffens beside me. I touch his arm, which helps loosen the tension. We stand quite close, and the heat of his body warms my side. I remember how that body moved against my hand, the helpless sounds he made while I brought him to climax.

"My lord." The tallest man steps forward and bows low, first to Boreas, then to me with a softly uttered, "My lady."

I smile at him. Boreas does not.

A sharp elbow to his ribs has him uttering a low curse.

"Don't be rude," I hiss.

He grumbles, but manages a smile that is only half as vicious as I expected. We will have to work on that.

"Thank you for opening up your home to us." The gentleman's eyes glow with a rare affection toward the Frost King. "I admit, we were surprised by your wife's invitation, your desire to begin healing the wounds between us."

"That's because it wasn't my idea—"

I slam my heel against the toe of his boot. He grunts, teeth clicking shut, and glowers at me. My smile is as serene as the most placid of lakes, but my eyes spark a warning. *Don't cross me.*

"Please, enjoy the party," I tell the group, before pulling my husband over to a secluded corner.

"Drink," I say, plucking a glass of grape juice from the tray of a passing server and shoving it into his hand. He examines it as though it is poisoned.

"Boreas." I sigh. "For once, just . . . let go. Eat, dance, enjoy the festivities. Tonight, you are no king. You are a man—"

"God," he corrects me, sipping from his glass.

"God," I relent, watching how the liquid sheens his upper lip. "You can let go of control for one night."

"They will vandalize my property."

I burst out laughing, mostly because I know he's serious. "What do you think mortals are? Vermin?" Their spirit forms flicker between various shades of opacity in the shifting firelight as they dance and flirt and mingle, but I imagine Boreas will always see them as they once were. "No one is going to vandalize anything. I promise."

"See that woman?" He points to the subject in question. She is elderly and hunched, and currently stokes the fire in one of the fireplaces. He studies her as if her existence is a personal affront. "She will burn down my home."

The woman is barely strong enough to lift the poker and is far more likely to accidentally stab someone with it. "Perhaps you should go talk to her."

His mouth thins. "No, thank you." I hear the unspoken words. *I would rather be hung up by my bleeding entrails.*

I sigh, set my glass on a nearby table, and rest a hand against his lower back. The heat of his skin pools against the fabric and sparks against my palm.

Boreas stiffens. "What are you doing?" The words emerge strangled.

"Distracting you." I toss him a sly smile and shift lower to where his backside curves. My heart thunders, but I keep my hand where it is, as though I have every right to touch him in any way I wish. "Is it working?"

His fingers twitch around the stem of his glass. His tongue darts out to wet his lips.

"Ask me to dance," I urge.

Something in his expression softens. Then his hand, rough and wide of palm, curves around the base of my neck, his thumb gently tipping up my chin. "Will you step on my toes like last time?"

The affection in his voice pulls heat to my face. "Only if you give me a reason to."

"Very well." Boreas sets down his glass and swings me onto the dance floor, a delighted peal escaping me at the smooth, snapping motion. His eyes crinkle with a rare joy. We come together, one of my hands curled over his shoulder, the other caught against his much larger palm. His remaining hand rests on my waist.

The music slows and wends through the paired couples. And for a time, I pretend that I can have this. I can have this dance. I can have this sense of belonging. I can have this man and this night. We sway to a pulse entirely of our own making while the flourish of skirts unfolds around us. My nose brushes his chest, and I inhale his crisp scent, my thoughts spiraling.

Boreas tucks me closer, and I welcome it. I'm not sure if I've ever been more frightened of this growing thing inside my chest. I can't look at it too closely. I can't ignore it either. Most days I give it a brief acknowledgement before the wall comes down, the feelings muted behind its adamant shield. But the king's gentle touch manages to weaken that barrier.

"You haven't commented on my outfit." Indeed, it took days for Orla to stitch the dress, not to mention the hours spent on my hair and makeup. The only indication of my husband's pleasure was how his pupils dilated when he saw me enter the room. Aside from that, nothing.

"That's because I fear the consequences of overstepping your boundaries."

Boreas is warm beneath my hands, sturdy. "A god, fear me?" My mouth curves at the sheer ridiculousness of it.

"You underestimate your wrath, Wife."

His cheek brushes mine, and my eyes flutter shut at the acute pleasure of skin on skin contact. "Perhaps I just like to torture you."

My breath hitches as his mouth touches the line of my neck. "You are quite good at that," he concedes.

An impatient, grumbling heat fizzles between us. Boreas digs his fingers harder into my waist, as though to steady himself. Two steps forward, two steps to the right, until we complete a small circle in clockwise motion. I let him lead as the music swells against my ears, a sound so beautiful I know I can never forget this night, if only for the music.

"I was thinking," I whisper, resting my head on his chest. "There are a lot of doors I've yet to explore. Maybe you could show me which ones are worthwhile."

Even though I can't see his face, I sense his surprise and, more tentatively, his pleasure. "I would like that. Very much."

Then it is done.

On and on and on, we dance and dance and do not stop. I once thought his heart a rigid, cold thing, without the capacity to love. But it beats as steadily as mine, and quickens as his hand curls around my hip. As for my heart . . . it changed its beat to him over time. I wasn't fully aware of it until now.

"Tell me this is real."

The voice is mine. But I do not recognize its tremulous hope, the slight trace of fear that this might all be ripped away.

"My lord?"

Boreas curses under his breath, then pulls back to glare at the guard who interrupted us. "Yes?"

To the man's credit, he does not flinch in the face of his king's irritation. How many hundreds of years, I wonder, has it taken to desensitize himself to the king's surly nature? "A couple awaits at the gates. They are mortal, my lord."

*Mortal.*

I gasp. "She came." My hands tighten on Boreas' shoulders. The excitement builds until I fear I will burst from it. "Elora came!" But with excitement comes a heavier emotion, and I bite my lip to hold it in. "I didn't think she would."

He says to the guard, "We will meet them at the gates."

Grabbing his hand, I lead him down the front steps and across the courtyard, where the gates stand open, two silhouettes cut like dark cloth against the moonlit backdrop. Elora and Shaw step forward. They wear heavy cloaks, their hands intertwined. Looking upon my sister, I can't help the smile that spreads across my face. "You came."

Brown eyes offset by long, thick lashes lift to mine, black kohl swept atop the lids, drawn to points at the corners. The delicate muscles of her throat work, and she licks her red painted lips. "I hope we are not too late."

That she decided to show at all . . . I feared Elora did not care enough about our relationship to bother mending it.

But she braved the Shade, the Deadlands, for me. I will not

soon forget it. "You're here now," I whisper hoarsely. "That's all that matters." After a moment, I reach out to squeeze her arm tentatively. "Let me show you to the ballroom."

"Wait." She lifts a hand. It shakes. "I need to say this."

Boreas is a solid presence at my back. I wait patiently for Elora to continue.

"I'm sorry. You were right. I was selfish and inconsiderate. I have been for a long time. You spent so many years caring for me, choosing my happiness and comfort over your own, and I never lifted a finger to change that. And I am ashamed."

It's strange to see my own face break, tears streaming down an unscarred cheek. I cannot go to her. I cannot relieve this burden from her. And I no longer want to.

"Mama would be so disappointed with how I treated you when she was gone, when Papa was gone. I treated you like . . ."

"Like shit?"

Elora blanches at my choice of words, but she sniffles, and nods. "Yes. And I misjudged you and your . . . husband. I know your heart, Wren."

"And what is my heart?" The claim will only go so far. If she can peel back another layer, if she can prove that she sees me, it will do much in healing that which is broken between us.

Elora looks to her husband. He nods in encouragement.

"Your heart," she says, "is stronger than mine ever was or ever will be. You make the difficult decisions. You give, whereas I only take. I allowed fear to twist my perception of you, and I regret not realizing that sooner. When you left, I realized what I would be losing, and I can't bear not having you in my life, my children's lives. So I'm sorry. Deeply, sincerely sorry. If you can accept that I obviously have much growing to do, I hope we can start over."

She bows her head meekly. I want nothing more than to gather her in my arms, but that will take time. That she decided to show . . . it's a step.

"Elora," I say, "I'd like you to meet my husband, Boreas. Boreas, this is my sister, Elora, and her husband, Shaw."

Her eyes widen as she takes in the North Wind, a god of devastating presence. He wears a tunic of pale silver, unbuttoned at the throat. The air stirs as he takes her delicate, glove-clad fingers in his own large hand. "A pleasure." She shivers from the cool, flowing power of his voice.

He then accepts Shaw's hand. Elora's husband studies the Frost King with a shuttered expression before pulling away.

They follow us up the front steps, where I have the absurd pleasure of watching my sister's mouth drop open at the vast entrance hall with its colorful tapestries and glowing lamps. Granted, she is seeing a polished version of it, free of cobwebs and stifling air, but it is no less remarkable.

"How was your journey?" I ask. Pallas would have met them at the river's edge before leading them through the forested region safely on horseback. "Are you hungry? Would you like a drink? Here, let me take your coats."

"Thank you." Elora watches as I hang up her coat in the entrance hall closet. Boreas takes Shaw's. "It was fine, thank you. We ate before arriving, but I'll have a drink if you are."

"Sure. Shaw?"

"Wine, please."

I turn to Boreas. "Can you please find our guests some wine? Juice for me."

Once alone, Elora says, studying me as if she's never seen me before, "You do not drink?"

A slow, creeping flush spreads beneath my skin, but I do not lower my eyes. Shame, my old foe, has come knocking. And I slam the door in its face. "Not anymore, no."

"How long have you been sober?"

Not that it's any of her business, but I'm allowed to take pride in my accomplishments. "Twenty-three days."

My sister's eyes sheen, and she grips both of my hands. My knuckles creak in the might of her grip. "I'm happy for you, Wren. And proud. So, so proud."

"Thank you. I appreciate it." After a moment, I disentangle my fingers from hers. "Why don't I show you around? This is the entrance hall." I point to various locations as we move past the great spiraling staircase, blue ribbons wound around the gleaming oaken banister. "Down that corridor is the east parlor and the drawing room. Through that door is one of the studies."

"How many studies are there?" Elora asks.

"I've counted over thirty so far. I'm sure there are some I've yet to discover."

"Thirty!" She sounds scandalized.

Shaw trails us to the ballroom entrance, the magnificent, gilded doors opened wide. My sister sucks in a sharp breath at the sight. I'm proud enough to preen. She probably assumed the citadel would be a dark, creepy, horrid place. Weeks ago, it had been. "It's beautiful." Then she halts, as though having run into an invisible wall. "The guests." Horror fills every crevasse and curve of those stuttering words.

I wait.

"I can see through their bodies." A dull, breathless statement.

Shaw attempts to tug Elora against his side. She ignores him, watching the whirling couples in mounting distress.

"They're specters," I explain calmly, as if watching a bunch of spirits dance is nothing out of the ordinary.

She lowers her voice before speaking. "Dead?"

No need to remind her that this is the Deadlands. And anyway, I've not forgotten my first encounter with Orla. "Yes, but they haven't fully passed on. They eat and sleep just like us, and their bodies are solid, despite their transparency."

My sister frowns in distaste.

A change in subject is definitely in order. "The citadel houses thousands of doors leading to other realms. I've seen so much, Elora. Cities and parks and theaters and mountains. One door took me to a secluded cove with all these tidal pools. I'd never seen anything like it."

Slowly, Elora turns, peering at me with an intensity I would expect from Boreas, not her. I cross my arms over my stomach, suddenly uncomfortable. "What?"

"You look happy. The happiest I've seen in a long time."

I'm not sure how to respond to that. I feel lighter, certainly. But happy? I'm so unused to the sensation I suppose I never considered it.

"He treats you well?" she asks quietly. At my withering glare,

Elora explains, "I would ask this for any man you marry. You deserve the best."

He did lock me in the dungeon. Even if that was before, well, everything.

But Elora doesn't need to know that.

"He does," I assure her.

"Good. Otherwise I might have to hurt him." A twinkling smirk. "Your husband looks happy, too," she adds. "Though not at the moment."

I look to where she gestures. Boreas has been stopped near one of the food tables, drinks in hand, his expression stamped into one of polite interest as a man speaks to him about something he most likely cares nothing for. I snort. "I imagine he needs saving. Why don't you and Shaw take a look around. I'll come find you when I'm done."

Once they wander off, I turn, accidentally ramming into someone in the process. "I'm sor—"

Disbelief hits me like a slap across the cheek. For the face peering at me from beneath the hood of a green cloak is familiar. "Zephyrus? What are you doing here?"

"I could ask you the same question," he says in an odd tone. It lacks the pleasant, rounded flow I've come to expect. His green eyes glitter, pale and distant.

"I'm not sure I understand." I watch him guardedly. "I live here."

Zephyrus sighs, a sound of utter disappointment that manages to deflate me. "Why didn't you respond to my note?"

The note I've been hoarding in my pocket all this time. The note I stare at every night before bed, waging an internal battle I'm not sure I can win. "I've been busy, is all."

"Busy. I see."

A glance from the corner of my eye. Boreas still hasn't noticed me, or my companion. If he discovers Zephyrus here, I'm afraid he'll kill him.

"You're squandering your chance, Wren," Zephyrus whispers. "You might not get another."

Right. To kill my husband. "Things change."

A few dancing couples flow around us, forcing Zephyrus and I into closer proximity. Beneath the cowl of his hood, his mouth curls with displeasure. "All this time, I've been trying to help you. I risked a lot sneaking into Sleep's cave—"

"So did I."

He ignores that. "I've been working on this tonic for weeks. And now you're saying you don't want it?" His lips pinch and his eyes narrow. "That's quite selfish of you, Wren."

The word bristles in me. *Selfish.* It's not true. I know in my heart it's not.

Tonight was going so well, and now . . . this.

"Zephyrus." I sigh. "Boreas isn't who you think he is. He isn't vindictive." He's actually rather sweet. Remote, yes, and most definitely awkward, but he's warmed toward me in ways I could have never imagined. To think I needed to drink my way through our first dinner together. The memory brings a smile to my face.

"Oh, Wren. Oh, no." The West Wind shakes his head, a hand pressed to his brow, cupped over his downcast eyes. "You've fallen in love with him."

That wrenches my spine straight. "No!" I cry, startling myself. Zephyrus quirks a brow. "I mean . . ." *Do* I love him? Is that even possible? "He's my husband. I care for him, yes. But—" Love? I look away. "Even if I went through with the plan, even if I returned to

Edgewood, I don't think I would be welcome there anymore. My sister was so cold toward me when I visited. We're trying to move past that, but she has a family now. I would just get in the way."

Zephyrus considers me with a prying gaze. It takes everything in me not to retreat. "Have you ever considered why she was so cold toward you? As long as you are connected to this place, your sister, the people of Edgewood, will never see you as one of their own." He steps closer, and the urge to remove myself from this situation, to find shelter in Boreas' embrace, vibrates in my limbs. The Bringer of Spring is not a threat to me. I know this. So why do I feel as though something between us has changed?

"See that?" He gestures toward where Elora and Shaw have taken refuge in one of the corners, as far from the specters as possible. "This is not her world. She fears it. And as long as she fears it, she fears you."

"My sister doesn't fear me."

"How do you know she came here to make amends and not because she was afraid of what my brother might do if she didn't?"

"That's not— Elora wasn't forced to come here. She made her choice. She wants me in her life. She told me." And Elora is not a liar.

"Are you sure?"

I keep silent, my stomach lurching as the words sink in. What if he's right? Elora is here, but only because she's afraid of what *she'll* lose. And that's . . . fine. That is something my sister and I will work through, in time.

"Wren." His voice softens and soothes. The tension in my shoulders seeps away, but not completely. Zephyrus is my friend, I remind myself. He wants what is best for me. "This could be your only opportunity to return to your old life. What if you pass it up, then change your mind weeks later? It will be too late. Can you live with yourself knowing you chose your captor over your remaining family?"

He passes something into my hand: a small glass vial filled with scarlet liquid—essence of the poppy flower.

"The last thing I want for you," Zephyrus whispers into my ear, sending a chill down my spine, "is regret." Pulling away, he studies my face, then nods and moves off, vanishing down a shadowy corridor before I can call him back.

My skin flushes hot, then cold. The glass grows sweaty in my grip. I consider everything Zephyrus said. I look to where Elora and Shaw stand, apart from everyone else. I look to where Boreas is still engaged in forced conversation, and I remember what it felt like to observe him for the first time, black terror looming inside me.

That promise? To kill the North Wind? I'd made it months ago. But what if Zephyrus is right? What if I change my mind, in time? What if Elora returns to Edgewood and I never see her again? I thought I could live with that separation, but what if I can't? Is risking the chance of returning to Edgewood, free of the Deadlands' taint, worth the pain I'll cause myself, and Boreas, if he ever learns of my deceit?

I don't know. But if I do not make this choice with a conscious effort, awareness of everything I could lose, then was the choice ever really mine?

My feet are already moving. Down the hall, up the stairs. Calm. I am calm.

The party's clamor stretches thin and faint. Distance—it grows and grows. My chest cinches tighter, as though my feet send me in one direction, my heart another, tearing a cavity straight through me.

But I push onward. This choice, brought to me on a knifepoint, will give me clarity. I can decide without outside influence. I can choose for myself at last.

I tell myself this—yet as my legs grow weighted, as sweat springs to my hairline, as the twisting in my stomach shreds my gut into tiny, tiny pieces, I wonder if I already know the answer.

"Pallas." The guards barring my entry into the north wing bow in my presence. "I left something in Boreas' rooms."

"What is it, my lady? I will grab it for you." Since tending to him in the war camp, he has warmed up to me considerably.

"I don't think that's the best idea." I make a show of shuffling my feet, the mark of a woman having been put in a compromising position. It is an effort to maintain the charade, to keep the distress from my voice and face. "What I left is, well . . ." My eyes flit to the men. Cupping a hand to the side of my mouth, I whisper, "My undergarments."

He blanches, pale cheeks darkening with his blush. "Oh." He looks to the other guards, who are doing a spectacular job of ignoring him. "In that case, yes, you may grab it. But be quick."

And just like that, I'm through the last line of defense, the door handle biting into my palm.

I slip inside and seal my fate.

# CHAPTER
# 38

Unexpectedly, darkness does not shroud the king's rooms. A fire burns low, alighting the walls in a deep amber glow, and moonlight spills through the windows, the curtains having been tied off, allowing a glimpse of the nightscape beyond. With the warmer weather of late, much of the snow has melted to reveal patches of dirt, dead grass. The Deadlands is changing—perhaps for the better.

The door clicks shut behind me. A quiet sound, full of lurking premonition. The rug muffles my footsteps as I move farther into the room, toward the tray placed on a low table that supports the kettle for his tea, awaiting heating. My head throbs as if in sickness. The glass vial squeezes in the clamp of my sweaty fist.

When I first met the Frost King, I knew him only as a banished god, whose cruelty crept like ice over everything it touched. But Boreas is not like that. He is a man who has lost much, who clings to his power because it is the armor encasing his bruised, grief-stricken heart. By acting on my promise, Boreas will fall into a bottomless sleep, allowing me the opportunity to slip into his room like a phantom, slide a knife into his heart. And I will be free.

*Free.* Somehow, the word no longer holds its allure.

What changed? Because I may be a coward in some respect, but I've learned, above all else, to be honest with myself. To look into my own heart and see.

The plan was to return home. The plan was always to return home—until it wasn't. Elora is married, a child on the way. She has Shaw, a new life carved from its old shell. It hurt, but I came to terms with the choices she made. I let go.

But a tide always returns. This time, it brought Zephyrus, the means to revive a crushed hope. Another chance, if I was willing to follow through on my initial vow. The West Wind claimed my true life awaits me out there. In the Gray, not the Deadlands. But Edgewood has faded, as do all things, given enough distance and time.

These are my lies:

Boreas is my enemy.

Elora comes first.

I want to return home.

These are my truths:

Boreas is my husband.

My needs come first.

I am already home.

I grip the draught as though it is an arrow drawn, the string pulled taut.

I did not choose this life. It was forced upon me. But I've come to understand my place here, this feeling of belonging. I've learned I am brave and rash and selfless and compulsive and angry and wounded, and I feel no shame for who I am. I do not think about what I lack, as I once did. Rather, I recognize all that I've found in these derelict halls: companionship, passion, trust. And yes, even love.

So maybe I did not choose this life in the beginning, but what if, instead, it chose me?

"Why do you hesitate?"

I gasp, whirling around as the fire gutters to embers. The voice came from the back wall, but the area is naught but amassed, bleeding shadows where the moonlight is unable to penetrate.

Gradually, a shape refines into focus: a silhouette, broad-shouldered and trim. Shadows scatter and reform around its approach. I spot the curve of a thigh, the rise of a pale cheekbone, and lastly, the glint of a single, unwavering blue eye.

Saliva floods my mouth on a surge of fear. Two ragged heartbeats pass before I'm able to speak. "How long have you been standing there?"

Boreas steps into the puddled, dying light. "Long enough."

Red fires the curled ends of his black hair. The tips of his canines peak out, sinking into his lower lip, and the smooth skin of his gloveless hands darkens.

"I was—"

"Planning my demise?"

Boreas rounds the low couch. He nearly reaches me before my body remembers the danger of an approaching predator. I retreat toward the fire, but the air sears the backs of my legs, so I pivot, skirting the enormous bed with its multitude of pillows. His long legs eat up the space, and the way he moves, the fluidity, reminds me he is no mortal. My back hits the wall, the air tightening between us with an undeniable pull.

"My wife," he says coldly, his mouth a hairsbreadth from mine. "The liar."

There's no refuting my presence in his bedroom. He knows. His lack of surprise is evidence enough.

"I will ask you again," he says. "Why do you hesitate?"

How to explain when even *I* don't know the reason? A drowning man clings to any lifeline.

Boreas lifts his hand. I'm so tense I revert to my first memory of him, the creak of the battered wooden door upon his arrival at Edgewood, those thunderous footfalls, and I flinch.

He goes still, his hand near enough to my cheek that I feel its heat. "Is this how it will be?" he asks quietly. "Do you fear me?"

My throat squeezes as hot shame washes through me. I did, once. But that time is past. "No," I whisper. "I know you wouldn't hurt me."

"And here I thought the same."

The pinch in my chest morphs into an undying agony. More than anything, I wish to tell him I was not going to harm him, in any manner, was not going to strike against him, but I doubt he would believe me.

His gaze falls to the vial clutched in my hand. One by one, he pries away my fingers to reveal the scarlet liquid contained within the glass. Nothing but shoots and leaves, a means to end his life. The idea rooted inside me. I tried to kill it, yet it revived itself.

He says, in a tone heavy with fatigue, "Zephyrus."

The lie crawls up my throat and pools hotly in my mouth. It

tastes strongly of stomach bile. If he knows, there's little point in denying it. I could blame all of this on his brother, but I must take accountability for my own actions. I am the one who approached Zephyrus about a sleep tonic. Only me.

"You mentioned Zephyrus needed herbs from the Garden of Slumber," Boreas says, "but you never mentioned who the tonic was for." He stares at me. "Who needed the draught so desperately you were willing to risk your life entering Sleep's territory to steal the plants?"

It's hard to breathe. The way he looks at me, with so much mistrust . . . But I've lied enough, I think. To him, and to myself. "I did."

Another stretch of silence passes. It feels as though it frays against my skin. "I knew my brother would attempt to poison you against me. I have known this from the moment you met him. He did the same with my late wife."

The one killed by bandits. The mother of his child.

"You remind me of her," he says.

My head snaps up. When our eyes meet, I'm surprised by the affection there. Surely I am imagining it.

"Rash?" My voice wavers.

"Loyal and brave," he says, "and bearing the heart of a lion."

His words warm the place behind my sternum. Is that how he sees me, truly?

"My late wife was not afraid of me either."

"What makes you think I'm not afraid?"

"Are you?" he asks, brows creeping toward his hairline.

"At first I was, yes. You terrified me, with your black countenance and your spear. I thought you cruel."

"Ah." The skin around his eyes pinches, like furrows in cloth. "You hid it well."

With that, Boreas drops my hand, steps away, and I swear the moment he does, a thread inside me snaps. He moves to the chair before the fire, gripping its back as he watches the wood blacken and crumble within the hot coals. "The first time we met, she called me a pompous ass." A sound escapes him. Whatever it is—laughter, a scoff—it is fractured. "I knew then I could not kill her."

It's absolutely pathetic of me to envy the life of a dead woman. But I hear how wholly he loved her, how it destroyed any shred of humanity he might have possessed when she and his son were taken from him. I suppose I'd hoped I might fill that void. Stupid.

"The Shade needed her blood. She fought like a wildcat, threatened to cut off my manhood." He gives me a sidelong glance. "Another similarity."

I clear my throat. "Fond times."

The shadows in his eyes are also the shadows in his face, and they begin to turn inward. "I had never let a sacrifice live. I didn't know what to do with her. She likely didn't know what to do with me either." A shake of his head. "I gave her free rein of the citadel. The first two years, she tried to poison me at every turn. She ran away more times than I can count. Her purpose was to bring about my end, and I cannot fault her for that.

"About five years following her arrival to the Deadlands, however, she grew severely ill. Alba did her best, but whatever sickness had taken hold, it was impervious to her remedies."

There is a pause, but I don't bother filling it. Boreas gathers himself before pushing onward.

"Many months were spent by her bedside. My wife managed to

recover, after a time, and by then, we had formed something of a tentative friendship. And then that friendship deepened," he says, voice softening, "and I fell in love with a mortal."

My heart slams so hard against my sternum I'm certain it's audible. I never thought I'd hear that word from the North Wind's mouth: *love*. He is capable of love just as he is capable of compassion, kindness. This, I nearly saw too late.

"When I learned she was with child, my life changed again. I did not think there was anyone happier than I. It had been so long since I'd had a family, and we would build one together."

The urge to approach him, comfort him, is so strong I have to physically restrain myself from doing so. It's in his voice, the pain. His voice and his posture and the skin drawn tight across his face, the white press of his lips. For I know how this story ends.

"Zephyrus would visit occasionally," he continues. "Naturally, he spent time with my wife while I was away. I didn't think anything of it. I had no reason to."

The hair lifts on the back of my neck. I wasn't aware Zephyrus had known Boreas' late wife. He'd never mentioned it.

The king's fingers flex around the chair. A hard, heavy breath punches past his teeth. "I should have known his intentions were selfish. At his core, he is a trickster, driven by jealousy and greed. My wife grew distant in the years following the birth of our son, Calais. Then one day, I discovered her missing. Abducted, as it turns out. And our son . . ." His throat bobs.

Disbelief clangs through me. It's not possible—

"There was an ambush. Bandits in the mountains. By the time I reached them, it was too late. They were gone, and Zephyrus was nowhere to be found."

I stare at him, completely horrified. "Zephyrus abducted your wife and son?"

"He did."

My stomach feels like it's moments away from expelling bile up my throat. He never told me, but why would he? All this time. All this time, Zephyrus had been using me. He never cared about being my friend. He only cared about hurting Boreas in unspeakable ways. And I nearly fell for it.

"I didn't know," I croak painfully. My heart aches for him, for I, too, know what it is like to lose those who are most precious to you. "I'm so sorry. I had no idea."

His fingers clench further, the tips sinking into the cushioned chairback.

"So you see," he continues as if I hadn't spoken, "that is why I cannot trust my brother. And why I could not trust you completely. From the beginning, I feared he would turn you against me. It seems I was right."

That may have been my original intention, to end him, but I've changed. Yet how can I prove he is wrong when I stand here, evidence in hand?

His attention drifts to the fire before shifting back to me. The chill in his gaze is depleted. There is only heat and the fiery core of yearning. "Tell me what would have happened had I not followed you."

Really? He wants a step-by-step account of his attempted murder? It can be no more twisted than finding I haven't the strength to refuse him. "I would have added the tonic to your tea kettle."

Boreas nods. After all, he already knows what would have occurred. "Go on."

Sweat springs to my open palms. "Look, we don't have to do this—"

"Go on." A demand of unbreakable iron, a focused blow to the gut. A punishment, worse than anything that has come before.

In a hoarse whisper, I manage through a tightening airway, "After, I would have returned to the party."

"We would dance."

Yes, I suppose we would. I would step on his toes, and he would step on mine, and we might share a moment of laughter between us. "It would be expected, so yes." I swallow. "Afterward, you would retire to your rooms and make yourself a cup of tea." My voice shakes. I feel as if I'm being lashed by a harsh wind. "Once the tonic took effect, you'd fall asleep. I would . . . sneak in through your window." I'd have to due to the guards posted outside of his rooms.

"I would be asleep," Boreas offers, moving toward me. "Unaware."

"Yes." I swallow to moisten the inside of my mouth. His nearness, his heat, clouds my head. Pulling away grants me space, allows me time to gather every stray thread and weave them into something resembling a whole and unbroken thought. "I would take your dagger," I whisper, turning to peer out the window. The land, even cold, is beautiful. I have learned this too late.

Slow, careful footsteps. "Then what?"

"Then I would—" Pain tears into my insides at the thought of what comes next. "S-stab you in the heart."

There is a long moment of silence.

Then:

"I see."

I have failed him. I have ruined this green, growing thing between us, having crushed it beneath the heel of my boot. My eyes sheen as abject terror courses through me.

"And when I lay dead?" Boreas murmurs. "What then?"

Obviously, I would not be able to stay here. Once the guards discovered their king dead, I'd have to run. "Then I would return to Edgewood." My chin lifts a notch. It's all bluster, considering I never found the door leading from the Deadlands, and stopped looking long ago. "Return to my life."

"Because that was always your intention," he says with a close study of me.

The air feels fragile—too fragile. "It was, yes."

This pause is significantly more torturous. A single unending stretch derived from lack of sound. "That is what you want? To return to Edgewood?"

"That was my intention," I say again.

"You did not answer the question. Is returning to Edgewood what you want?"

He wants the truth. It would behoove me to give it to him. So why can't I just say it?

Without giving me a chance to respond, he steps around me, pushing aside a heavy tapestry hanging from the wall to reveal a plain wooden door. I blink in surprise.

The king lays his palm against the dark-grained wood and says, "I know you've been searching for a way out of the Deadlands." Though he does not look at me, I sense the weight of his sadness. "This door will deposit you on the other side of the Shade, a few miles west of your home." His shoulders sag, dragged down by too many burdens, and I fear I am one of them.

He turns the handle, opens the door to reveal a snow-laden field. "Go."

I stare at that field. White, sparkling, pristine. I inhale the gust of cold air that breezes through the opening, glimpse the silver band of a frozen brook nestled in the hills. But I don't move.

"This is what you want, right?" he growls. "Your freedom?"

He's letting me go? I could have never imagined . . . "Just like that?"

A curt nod. "I won't go after you."

Instead of moving toward the door, I stride toward the window. "I don't know what I want," I whisper, palm pressed to the icy glass. My skin sears at the contact, but it helps clear my head, helps ground me in the here and now. This is where I am. This is where I've somehow managed to build a life I'm proud of. The Deadlands, against all odds, has become my home.

The door shuts with a muted click, and the tapestry hisses as it falls back into place. "I think you do." Boreas comes to stand behind me. Heat against my back and breath stirring the crown of my head. "But I think fear tells you otherwise."

How is it this man is suddenly an expert on what I fear? I've mentioned a few things, in passing, but some things one must look within to see, to understand, and I fear Boreas has seen those things. He understands that Edgewood *was* my home, but it never allowed me to flourish. As ridiculous as it sounds, being trapped in this citadel under no obligation to someone else, I was allowed to discover my own needs for the first time in twenty-three years.

But who likes discussing weakness? No one. And so my chin lifts in preparation of this conversation. My sweaty palm squeaks as it slides across the glass. "You would know, right?" I turn. The window blazes a line of cold down my back. "I understand you now. Why you're here. Why you lock yourself in these walls with the curtains drawn. Why you have a greenhouse full of green things, when all the world is laid to waste in cold." I level him a stare of flint and steel. "You're afraid."

He flinches. The blow lands precisely where I want it to.

"You're afraid of letting others get close to you. You're afraid of getting hurt again. It's why being in control is so important to you. Why your power is so important to you."

And yet the land is changing because Boreas is changing. As he learns to trust in others, his cold black heart thaws.

Blue eyes hold fierce to mine. "And you?" he demands. "You, who fear weakness, who fear you are unworthy. Are you not, too, afraid?"

Somehow, we've shifted and now stand nose to nose. One of his hands braces against the windowpane near my head.

He speaks the truth. I am afraid.

But not of him. Afraid of what I feel *for* him.

My voice grows strained. "I didn't want this." *Don't*, I correct myself. I *don't* want this.

"This," he says, lifting the dagger he's removed from his belt. "This is what you want." Firelight limns the edge of his god-touched blade.

The Frost King draws my hand forward, closing it over the hilt. The leather crinkles beneath my sweaty palm as he positions the dagger point to rest over his heart.

My pulse throbs in the roots of my teeth. My heart, which has crawled into my mouth, pounds to the very edges of my skin. I feel ill—worse than ill. My hand trembles beneath his, but he will not release me, no matter how hard I tug.

"You could not follow through the first time." Boreas steps closer, forcing the tip deeper into his skin. His head lowers, and when he next speaks, his cool breath slips into my parted mouth too easily. "You had so many opportunities, too. If not with this blade, then the bow my brother gifted you, its arrows."

The bow. I never considered using it, even knowing it was god-touched.

"But you are here again. So what now?"

Everything is different. Were I to shove the dagger into his heart, as was originally planned, Boreas would die. I would have my vengeance. And I would truly be alone.

"Now—" My stomach churns. The lies surge with rising demand. It is easier that way. "Now—"

"Be forthright, Wren. For once."

It is never easy letting go of what once was. But that is what I must do. Elora and I will always be sisters. I will always love her. I will always wish her happiness. But I know my place now, and my place is here, in the Deadlands, beside the reticent god who rules it, the man I love.

There will be no death tonight, not from me, not ever. I will be all right, as long as I trust in myself.

"I don't want to go." I choke with emotion. "I don't want to return to Edgewood." I haven't wanted that in weeks.

His throat bobs, and he lifts his hand, cupping the scarred side of my face gently. "Then what do you want?"

Why do the simplest questions have the most trying answers? I have given the North Wind every part of myself save my heart, and now I give him one more thing. "You," I whisper hoarsely. "I want you."

# CHAPTER 39

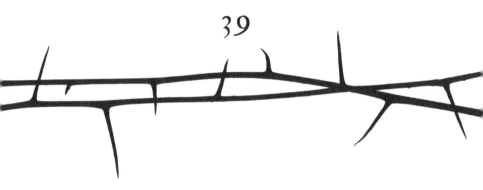

Boreas presses his forehead to mine, our noses brushing affectionately. "Then you have me."

Gripping my waist, he tugs me close, and it is the greatest relief to slip my hands over his shoulders, curl them around the back of his head, and sift my fingers through the silken strands of his hair. He tucks his face into the curve of my neck, inhales deeply, breathing in the scent of my skin. His large hands roam my back, tracing each vertebra of my spine.

Damp, glancing heat on my collarbone. Another kiss marks the swell of my shoulder through the fabric of my dress. As though sampling the finest of silks, he maps the dip of my waist, the winged shoulder blades, before drifting south again. When I chase his mouth, he angles his face away, denying me that pleasure. "Bastard."

Warm laughter drifts over me. "Patience, Wife." The hand at my hip squeezes.

Patience is for those who know little of what they want. I tell him as much.

His mouth twitches. His eyes sparkle with the light of dying stars. I fought this for so long, but I can fight no longer. I feel seen with this man. The heart wants what the heart wants.

Boreas licks a pathway to my ear, sucks the lobe into his mouth. "It will be well worth the wait," he whispers. "I assure you."

"You will not abandon me, should one of your guards come knocking?"

He pulls back, his expression carefully blank. A low blow, yes, but I'm not interested in starting something unless it reaches its finish. Unless I reach my completion. And Boreas, I suppose. I'm feeling rather generous this evening.

Cupping the side of my face, he hooks his thumb beneath my jaw, tilting it upward so I'm forced to meet his apologetic gaze. "I regret leaving you that night and have regretted it every night since. My hand is a poor substitute."

A dark thrill runs through me at the thought, and I lean forward. "You touched yourself thinking of me? How often?"

"That," he clips out, "is none of your concern."

This is the best thing I've heard in days. I'm now imagining a half-naked Boreas in bed, in the bath, fisting himself until he spills. "But—"

He digs his teeth into the soft lobe, dragging a moan from me. The sting whips down my spine, and I tilt my head to allow him better access, growing drowsy from the marvel of his hot mouth, his clever tongue, his blunt, grazing teeth. It's so . . . I don't even have words.

"Is this your plan?" I whisper against his skin. "Push me as far as you can? See how long it takes until I break?"

Boreas draws away slightly. His breath puffs against my sticky skin where his saliva has dried. "You've been pushing me since you arrived here." He sinks his thumb into my chin. "It's only fair that I return the favor."

Suddenly, his palm skims my backside, lifting my leg below the thigh to hitch it around his waist, skirts and all. He sinks his hips into mine, and the ridge of his arousal presses against the part of me that *aches*.

"Gods," I pant. Heat crackles through my veins, and the air, perfumed with our sweat, thickens. "Damn it all, kiss me." Clamping my hands around his head, I draw it down to mine, lifting onto my toes to meet him halfway. Boreas laughs. I don't think I'll ever get used to the sound.

Except my kiss falls to the wayside, brushing his chin instead of his mouth. Before I can remedy that, he tracks a slow path to the space behind my ear, where his teeth nip. The bright sting dulls beneath the brush of his lips. As much as I love the feel of his mouth on my skin, I want his mouth on mine, deep and thorough.

My hand dives between us, cupping his prominent erection. I give a warning squeeze.

He stills.

"Kiss me," I demand. "Or else." I tighten my grip to make a point.

He begins to pant as I trace its shape, circling the head, around and around and around, feeling dampness seep through the rough cloth, slicking the tips of my fingers. He shudders and bows his head, fighting his body's reaction. At the next brief squeeze, Boreas bucks his hips.

"You, Wren—" Each word a sharp point. "—are the devil."

I gesture wiping away an imaginary tear. "I think that might be the kindest thing you've ever said to me." Then I begin to stroke, slow and easy. "Doesn't change what I want." His lips on mine, his breath flooding my throat, his tongue in my mouth—and other places, eventually.

A coarse rumble fills his chest. It makes my skin pebble, a sound of unadulterated desire, anguish and need and hunger. Cupping his hand around mine, he begins to guide my movements, showing me the pace and pressure he likes. I linger around the head, working the heel of my palm in a circular motion against the flesh. To witness Boreas succumb to pleasure . . . My stomach flutters in anticipation as I continue to touch and explore until, with a feral growl, he drops his hand and crushes his lips to mine.

His mouth, full of hot pressure, a quickening tongue that licks at my teeth, draws a moan from my throat. I plaster myself against him. Every sharp edge molding to every subtle curve. My head spins with wicked thoughts of what he might do now that I'm at his mercy. My hand falls away to grip his hair, his neck, anything I might reach. I chase his tongue with mine and when they clash with a savage thrust, he deepens the kiss until our mouths are so closely mated I grow dizzy from lack of air.

Boreas breaks away for a brief reprieve. My lips, swollen and red from the onslaught, tingle. "How do you get this dratted thing off?" he growls, yanking on the laces crisscrossing my back.

I slap aside his hands. "Let me." All that's needed is a short tug, and the laces loosen, allowing Boreas to drag the garment over my head. He takes me in: breastband, underwear, naked brown skin warmed by a flush. My makeup is smudged and my hair is a horrible mess, but deep hunger darkens the blue of his eyes.

"Delightful," he says.

My cheeks warm at the fervent desire lacing his tone. I've been called many things by men. Never delightful. "You're saying that to get on my good side."

"Wren." He smiles, his hand skimming my lower stomach. "I'm already on your good side."

For a time, his calloused hands roam my exposed skin, the abrasive sensation raising gooseflesh on my arms and legs. He skirts my breasts, choosing to explore my back, lower. Palming the curves of my rear, hooking his thumbs around the sides of my underwear. Two heartbeats later, I'm rid of my undergarments.

His nostrils flare at the sight, but I step close again, fingering the sleeve of his coat. "My turn."

Undressing Boreas is a joy I didn't expect. It must be savored. The stiff fabric of his coat splits open like a shell across his chest. One hard shove, and it falls away from his shoulders. Next, his tunic, the fabric warmed from his skin. He removes his boots and socks, allowing me the opportunity to loosen the ties of his breeches. My fingers brush his stiffened cock in the process, and I smile sweetly at him. A little torture never hurt anyone.

Then he stands naked before me. He is, to be clear, magnificent. A body of pure brawn: lean, ropy muscle coated in a light layer of black hair, enough, but not too much. My body temperature creeps upward just from staring at him.

I press my palms to his pectoral muscles, sweep them low across his abdomen. Then I move around to his back to stare at the scarred ruin that somehow healed. If I could, I would take these hurts from him. But I only press a soft kiss to the worst of the crisscrossing scars, feeling his muscles tense beneath my mouth.

Boreas snags my arm to draw me back to his front. His face, those blue eyes, everything is open to me. Vulnerability simmers among the banked heat, and affection, and something stronger and pure, something too frightening to name.

Catching me around the waist, he tosses me onto the bed with ease.

The mattress sinks beneath my weight. The sheets feel like air against my skin. Scooting back against the headboard, I take my time surveying every inch of his magnificent shape. The muscles of his powerful thighs bunch with each step of his approach. A thatch of dense, curling hair rests at the base of his jutting cock, the length darkened by raised, crisscrossing veins.

Flipping onto my knees, I crawl to the edge of the bed and wrap a hand around his shaft. Boreas shudders and tangles his fingers in my hair, tugging gently so tingles skitter across my scalp. I stare at the pearly bead of liquid that seeps from the ruddy crown and swipe my thumb across it, delineating a small circle there.

He releases a slow breath. "Wren."

I bury my face in his groin and inhale. Dark, thrilling, part sweat, part musk, part crisp of cedar. Boreas continues to massage my scalp, fingertips pressing into the base of my skull, and a wave of calm combats the incessant buzzing beneath my skin. Pulling back, I lap at the flushed head experimentally. The flesh gives beneath the pressure of my tongue, and I repeat the motion simply for the pleasure of tasting him.

Those sturdy legs lock, muscle flexing as he releases a short, hissing breath. The notch beneath his cockhead draws my attention, and I tickle the small indentation, mouth the surrounding area, loving how he swells and stiffens even further beneath the weight of my wandering tongue. He tastes better than any man I've slept with before. I lap up the trickle leaking from his slit, peering at him through my lashes, waiting until his eyes latch onto mine. Then I suck him down to the root.

He stiffens, his voice cracking on a groan. Filthy expletives spill from his mouth, each dirtier than the last. My entire body lights up with pleasure. It's been an age since I've done this. Men have their preferences, but for the most part, I'm familiar with the more sensitive areas and use that to my advantage, stoking the Frost King like a fire that burns hotter over time.

I suck him hard upon my retreat, ensuring his entire length is wet. He wants to move. His body craves it. But he should not have allowed me to touch him, because now I will take him apart, piece by piece, with agonizing slowness.

The underside of his shaft, I quickly learn, is especially sensitive. So that is where I linger in the breaks between lavishing attention on the head. My saliva gleams against his skin, growing sticky in the air.

His legs begin to shake. I lap at his crown and suckle it for a time, curling my tongue languorously there, drawing another pained sound from deep in his chest.

"Enough," he hisses, attempting to pry me free. But I grab his thighs, slow my strokes. His body heaves for air. I slow further. The tip of my tongue brushes the slit, just a slight caress, a prelude of what's to come. His early seed flows across my tongue like the sweetest wine.

"Wren," Boreas growls. His hands tangle in my hair and tug.

I ignore him.

"Wren."

A small *pop* sounds as I pull away. "Patience," I croon with a flash of teeth.

The fire has all but died. The hollows of his bone structure bleed shadow, though the moonlight outlines the broad planes of his body impressively. Then there is his mouth. That soft mouth, unfairly feminine, lush. Pointed canines sink into his bottom lip. In his eyes, only black remains.

A bolt of desire takes me by surprise. What might happen were I to test his patience? I'm looking forward to finding out.

A slow glide as I add my hand to the mess, so no part of his erection is untouched. On the upstroke, a sound of pure torment fills the room, and fractures. The fingers tangled in my hair tighten, holding me in place, my scalp stinging with a welcome pain. A brief image flickers in the dark recesses of my mind. A fantasy, really. That I might demand him to fuck my mouth as hard and deep as he can go, thrust after thrust, until my throat is wrecked, contracting painfully around him, saliva and tears dripping down my face. Punishing and ravenous.

As if Boreas senses what I want, he begins to pump in and out. Slow though. And that's nearly as good.

"Tell me to stop and I will," I mumble around his girth. Glancing up through my eyelashes, I meet the fiery blacks of his eyes. "That is, if you can fight it."

He stills. "Devil." Gripping me under the arms, he pulls me upright so I'm braced on my knees. His mouth parts mine, diving in deep, plundering every sweet drop. My head falls back. He takes and he takes and he takes, and when I am spent, dizzy from lack of air, my limbs pliant and my breasts tender, he sucks one of my nipples into his mouth.

I cry out, pressing closer. His tongue. He shifts his attention to the other breast, plumping it with his hand and bestowing the pointed tip with damp, languid strokes. My core pulses impatiently.

"Harder," I grit out.

The king nibbles with his teeth, then soothes. Not hard enough. Not even close. Every time I arch toward him, he mouths the skin around my nipple, and suckles, and traces the curves of my hips with his hands, indulgent and slow. Meanwhile, that dull, insistent throb begins to climb.

Pulling away with a frustrated growl, I draw him down onto the bed. It's the perfect position to place doting kisses along his neck and collarbone. I anticipated Boreas rushing toward the finale, but he seems to enjoy the touches that are more comforting than sexual. I'm reminded of the centuries alone he's spent in this citadel. When was the last time he had the touch of compassion, of caring?

When my mouth grazes the corner of his, I pull back, one hand cupping his jaw, and take him in. His hair falls in messy clumps over his shoulders, the true black of a night sky.

"You hide it well," I whisper, "but you are not so cold a man."

Turning his head, he brushes his lips against my palm. "I am not a man," he replies, equally soft. "I am a god."

And then he moves. Down, down, the trail of kisses leading south. As Boreas shoves his shoulders between my legs, smoothing rough hands up the plane of my stomach, I stare up at the darkened ceiling, wondering how I found myself in the Frost King's bed. It was a slow, reluctant fall. Even now I wonder how he can choose me—a skinny, scarred mortal woman—when he can have his choice of anyone.

"I'm—" I grapple for the blanket beneath me as the need to shield myself takes hold. "My chest is small. I'm bony. And my scar . . ."

He lifts his head. Our eyes meet, his softened by tenderness. "I like that your skin is not perfectly smooth. I like the shape of your body. I like every part of you, Wren."

"I'm not perfect."

"Perfection is an impossible expectation. You did not shy away from my scars. Why should I shy away from yours?"

My lips tremble. It's hard to overthink this when he is being kind. So I lie back in the blankets, loose a breath, and allow myself to feel.

His teeth nip the curve of my waist. One hand pins down my hip, the other reaching upward to cup one of my breasts. His thumb plays with the nipple: red-tipped, painfully sensitive. A gentle pinch sends tingling heat branching through my limbs.

And then his mouth is between my legs, wet, sucking heat tearing a moan from me, and I snatch a pillow and slam it over my face to mute the embarrassing noises. Boreas' wide shoulders prevent me from closing my legs. Another tug on my drenched folds, and I cry out brokenly, my hips moving instinctively to prolong the flaring pleasure. He spreads my thighs wider. The cool air hits my heated flesh, and I flinch.

Suddenly the pillow is gone. "What—" I blink in confusion at where he kneels at the foot of the bed.

"Don't hide from me." That wintry gaze pins me against the headboard. "Not after everything."

Everything. As if we have traveled through hell and back to get here. I do not think he is wrong.

"Yes," I whisper, my head falling back and my eyes fluttering shut.

His mouth returns to its cruel ministrations. As he plays with that small, tender bud, his lips sealing hotly over it, he stretches two fingers inside me, scraping them against my front wall. I buck against his mouth with a garbled plea, delirious with the pleasure scorching my veins. Wetness streaks my inner thighs. Boreas makes a sound of indulgence as he licks my skin clean, and I clench around his fingers in reflex, trying to draw them deeper. His fingers move inside me, blunt and heavy. I'm barely aware of the words falling from my mouth. *More. Please. Faster. Yes, there.* My skin tightens as the tension crests and, with one last suck, I come undone.

A wild scream claws through me as my back bows and my hips snap upward, and I'm spiraling, grinding against his mouth as he continues to pluck my every nerve, peeling me open like a ripened fruit. My toes curl and my heels dig into the mattress. My sight whitens momentarily. I'm yanking at Boreas' hair while moving through the throes of a beautiful, life-altering, shattering pleasure, carried far on the wave until it loses momentum and deposits me ashore.

I stare at the ceiling, sated, skin prickling with sweat.

Am I alive?

The king bestows a gentle kiss to the inside of my thigh before crawling up my body, nuzzling the warm, soft areas. He kisses the subtle curve of my breast, the sweaty dampness of my neck, my temple, and finally, my mouth. This kiss is the best one yet. A tender, hungry thing.

"You almost killed me," I whisper when we break apart.

The corners of his eyes crinkle. "But you're still alive. So you're saying I failed?"

"I'm saying we still have a ways to go."

Time spins out. With our mouths fused, our hands stroke and our fingers bite into pliant flesh, and together, we begin to climb.

Later, much later, Boreas positions himself at my entrance. His gaze meets mine, and holds.

"I don't want to hurt you," he says.

I lift an eyebrow. I've bedded men who treated me roughly before. Not that I believe Boreas will do the same, but sometimes passion gets in the way of care. I trust him.

"You won't hurt me," I say. "I'll tell you if you do."

He dips his chin somberly. "Very well."

"Wait." I press a hand to his chest before he can enter me. "What about pregnancy? I don't have a charm to prevent that." I'm not ready to bring a child into the world. And I'm not sure Boreas would want one anyway, given the death of his son. We've never discussed it.

He tugs on a lock of my hair, smooths his thumb along my jaw. "There's no worry. Alba can provide you with a tonic until we're able to secure a charm." The concern in his gaze gives way to something else. He studies my face carefully. "Would you want children? Not now, but someday?"

I see it now, the hope. And the fear.

I'd never given much thought to children because I never saw myself in a position to raise them. All my focus went toward survival. Additionally, I never felt a particular inclination to bear children with anyone at Edgewood. But I can see that future with Boreas so clearly. I imagine he would be a wonderful father. He thrives when he has something to care for, like the greenhouse.

But it can't be that simple. One day, I will grow old. Boreas will outlive me. What of the children? Will they, too, be immortal?

"I don't know," I whisper honestly. "I suppose I never saw children as an option in my life. Things never felt stable enough." I say, "Your son. Was he immortal?"

"Calais was mortal, but he possessed traits that revealed the divine blood in his veins. He was very strong for a child." His smile fades. "You are worried about the child's lifespan?"

"One day, I will die," I murmur, touching the corner of his mouth. "If the child is mortal as well, what will happen when that child is gone?" I don't want Boreas to grieve alone. And the thought of him taking another wife after me . . . I fight down a surge of jealousy.

He considers this. It's hard to read him.

"I'm not saying no, but I would like time to consider the implications." For my body will age while Boreas remains a man in his prime. How is that to work? Will he still want me when my skin begins to sag? When my teeth rot? It's too unpleasant to think about at the moment. "But you should know that if I thought of bearing and raising children with anyone . . . it would be you." The immortal who stole my heart.

He closes the space, fitting his mouth to mine for a long moment. I feel his smile, and that in turn makes me smile.

With one hand braced near my head, he uses the other to guide himself inside me, a blunt heat, rocking his hips forward bit by bit, sinking deeper each time as my body stretches to accommodate him. When he's fully seated, I manage, "You are rather, um . . . large."

Boreas sulks, as if he'd never considered this to be an issue. "And this displeases you?"

How have I never noticed how funny he is? I snort and wrap my arms around his neck. "Not in the slightest." We kiss. It's brief, sweet, and quickly forgotten in the heat of our coupling.

The North Wind draws out and sinks in with languorous ease. His abdomen contracts with the motion, and the muscles of his flank flex beneath my hand. Sweat drips from the tip of his nose to spatter on my chest, which he licks clean with swipes of his tongue.

The citadel lies in deep silence around us. The ragged edge of his breath rises and falls depending on his thrust or retreat. Boreas increases the pace, shifting onto his knees with my legs splayed over his hard thighs, before taking my legs and wrapping them around his waist so we're locked groin to groin. Fingers digging into my hips, he lifts me, angles his cock, and sheaths himself in one perfect slide.

Full, deep thrusts. I gasp as he fucks me harder. Our bodies sink and rise in harmony, and we move in tandem as though we have been doing this our entire lives. He pounds into me, drawing out my pleasure until our scents merge and there is no beginning and no end, only my name in his mouth, his taste upon my tongue, togetherness.

This man, who saw the wounded, lashing creature in my heart, who coaxed it out of hiding, who praised me for what I was, not what I was not, who didn't flinch at all my sharp edges, sees all of me. My captor, my husband, my enemy, my lover, my friend.

A dream I did not dare to dream.

Mine.

Boreas whispers my name. My hands glide across his damp skin, which gleams with an iridescent sheen. I fist my hands in his hair and hang on for the filthy rutting of our bodies, a pleasure so acute it spears through me. It burrows and spirals higher, tighter, drilling down deep and setting my blood alight. I'm climbing. I'm moving leaps and bounds even as I grow smaller, my skin shrinking, bones bending, potential that has yet to be unleashed.

I gasp as the pleasure spikes, and suddenly I'm that much higher and nearer to completion. I'm at the very cusp, and Boreas slams into me with complete madness, his mouth agape, and I'm right there with him, toeing that edge.

"Wren." He grunts and sucks hard on the curve of my neck. My nails dig crescent moons into the skin of his back. It breaks his rhythm momentarily, but he picks it up, the smell of sex rising to encompass us.

"Whatever you do," I gasp, "don't stop."

Boreas chokes out laughter. I can't laugh. I'm too busy trying to remember how to breathe properly as, hand in hand, we bring each other to a higher place, one uniquely ours. And then I shatter.

With a hoarse cry, I bow upward, consumed by the fire splitting my skin, tearing open my core and deeper insides. The world is a wave, and I'm carried upon that wave, carried far and wide, Boreas pounding out his own pleasure.

Abruptly, he stiffens. Sharp-edged emotion explodes in those dark pupils, and he shoves me onto my back, fucks me like an animal, skin slapping wet skin and the musk of our arousal sitting like a fog in my head and feeding through me, and on he goes, and on, until his hips stutter against mine and he spills his seed deep inside me before collapsing atop my chest.

Boreas' dead weight presses me into the blankets and pillows. I'm utterly spent. Boneless beneath him. I couldn't move even if I wanted to.

"You're crushing my lungs," I mutter into his neck.

He huffs a laugh, wraps me in his arms, and rolls to the side, tucking me into the curve of his larger body. One of his legs hooks over mine, trapping it beneath the warm, solid weight. I feel small, but safe. Cherished. At peace.

There we remain while our hearts slow and our bodies cool. He traces the swell of my hip in idle strokes.

I turn to face him. He wears the stony mask, the one he clings to so ferociously, but it's of little use now. I see the cracks.

The lines on his face smooth. Leaning forward, he nudges his nose with mine. My hands lift to cup his jaw, my thumbs sweeping across his cheeks.

"I like feeling close to you," Boreas says, quietly and with feeling.

My throat tightens. I can have this, I realize, if I am brave enough to take it. "Me, too," I whisper, then lean forward to brush a kiss across my husband's mouth.

# CHAPTER

## 40

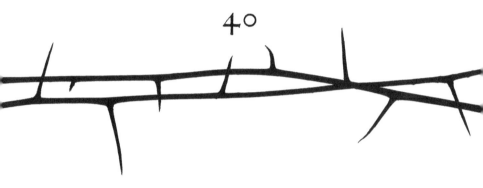

A warm hand on my thigh jerks me awake. Boreas leans over me, dark hair in disarray, blue eyes narrowed with intensity. He presses a finger to his lips to signal my silence.

Senses prickling, I slowly sit up, squinting through the darkness. The fire has long since died. We fell asleep hours ago after another round of intense lovemaking, our sated, boneless bodies pressed as closely as possible, lazy kisses and wandering hands.

"My guards sounded the horn," he says, voice low and warm in my ear.

The first wave of alarm crests in me, and I lean into his chest without realizing it. There's been a breach to the citadel. "Darkwalkers?"

He nods grimly.

"How did they get past the barrier?"

He brushes two fingers down the side of my face. "I don't know." The furrow between his eyebrows deepens, a sooty line in the vague shadow of his mien. He's told me time and again the barrier cannot be weakened, for it is sealed over every portion of the high stone wall. The gates open only at his command.

My attention darts to the window. He would have a view of the courtyard, and of those guarding the wall. A bird's-eye perspective could give additional insight into how the darkwalkers managed to infiltrate, the numbers we are up against. If it's any comparison to the bloodbath of the most recent battle . . .

"Don't," he says, sensing where my thoughts have gone. "No one can know your location. You must keep out of sight." He begins to pull away. "Stay here."

As if. "I'm coming with you." I swing my legs over the side of the mattress, my nightgown hanging off one shoulder.

"No." He stays me with a hand to my arm. I've never seen him so grave. "I'll return for you when it's safe."

The chilly darkness slithers down my spine. I shiver, grasping for my husband's hand. Boreas is immortal. He cannot die by a mortal-made weapon. As far as I know, he cannot die from a darkwalker either, considering he is one himself. Yet when he was last wounded, he couldn't properly heal. Something prevented him from doing so.

"What if they take you?" I whisper.

Gently, he squeezes my fingers. "It is not my life I worry about."

My heart, which is already fragile to begin with, completely disintegrates at his words. Who knew Boreas could be so romantic at so inconvenient a time?

He slides from the bed and dresses in his discarded clothing. "Lock the door behind me. There's a hidden passage in the study, behind the tapestry. It will take you to the stableyard. Grab Iliana and flee as far north as you can. I will find you as soon as it's safe."

I lunge, catching his wrist. He turns. His face is lost to shadow, but the blue of his eyes glimmers with fierce resolve. He cannot go. There are things I must say to him. The emotion pinches between us, fearful and new. I thought we'd have time to speak of such things, yet it has been snatched from us.

He says, in a quiet tone, "Wren. Please."

"But—"

He silences me with a kiss, our lips clinging. "Stay." Then he is gone, little more than a shroud of memory.

With peril prowling the grounds, I'm not about to fight darkwalkers in a nightgown. I need a weapon. And trousers.

My chambers, however, are located in a completely different wing. But without my bow, I'm a sitting duck.

My hand quivers as I grasp the door handle. This measly lock, my only protection—I flip it and ease open the door.

The hallway is deserted. The guards have abandoned their posts to keep the infiltrating darkwalkers at bay. The wall sconces gutter from a sudden wind that streams down the stone corridor. An icy, white cloud puffs from my stiff, frozen lips.

I run. I do not stop. The fabric of my nightgown flutters around my legs, and I keep my ears pricked for any unusual sounds. The passageways are empty, each branching arm, so I reach my rooms in a flash, bursting through the doors to change into trousers and a tunic, gloves and boots and coat, and to grab my dagger, bow, and quiver. Twelve arrows. I will have to make them count.

A crash from one of the lower levels brings an end to the quiet. Discordant noise, like shattering glass or a blood-curdling scream that startles the body into wakefulness, follows. A *boom* echoes through the bones of the citadel: a door being smashed open. Blood thrums in time with my racing heartbeat. How many? How quickly do they move? A beastly roar sounds as though the air itself is shredding into pieces. The screams that follow send me toward the door. I must find Elora.

She and the other guests are being housed in the south wing, but when I arrive, I find everything in disarray, doors ripped off hinges, specters running left and right. The stream of refugees clots the entryways, preventing escape. Only by sheer will am I able to squeeze through the press of bodies. It's a riot, a stampede. The citadel, cracked open like an egg, the insides scrambled.

At the end of the corridor, a massive dark shape lurches from around the corner, half a torso dangling from its enormous maw. Men and women in various states of undress throw themselves out of the way, mindless with the terror that has taken hold of their bodies.

I snag a woman's arm. "Have you seen my sister?" But she yanks free, sobbing, and stumbles onward with the masses. The crowd jostles me in its rush to flee the darkwalker. I aim the arrow toward the ground so as to not accidentally impale someone on it. "Has anyone seen Elora? She's a mortal, brown hair and skin like me."

Screams are the only answer.

A giant of a man with slablike shoulders rams me against the wall. My skull cracks against the stone, momentarily darkening my vision, and stinging pain sears all the way to my neck. I drop my bow with a startled cry.

The air reeks of ash. I cough heavily, my hand flying to the back of my head. Shit. My fingers pull away coated in blood.

A throb pulses through my skull, and my stomach twists in

response, nausea burbling in warning. Fumbling for my bow, I snatch it up, along with the fallen arrow, and reset, pressing close to the wall to avoid the worst of the rush. The darkwalker drops its meal, the body now a soulless husk, and releases another bone-rattling roar.

My fingers tighten around my weapon. I need to find Elora, but first, to deal with this ilk.

Slicing my palm with the arrow, I dip the stone tip in blood. One of the guards appears to give aid, but I spare him no mind as I draw and release. It hits the darkwalker in the center of its barrel chest, and red veins swim through the black as it recoils, screaming. It explodes in a spray of dripping ichor moments later.

Pivoting, I shoot a second arrow into the eye of another beast that lumbers behind the first. A woman, skirts gathered in both hands, rushes past in blind terror, knocking into my shoulder.

The darkwalker stumbles, allowing the guard to slice a line from belly to sternum. Another arrow punctures its other eye. A shriek pierces my concentration. It's blinded. "Kill it!" I cry to the guard. He darts forward and shoves his blade through the darkwalker's heart. That's two down, but three more have appeared, scuttering and snatching specters with rapid, lightning-quick strikes.

"Wren!"

My head snaps around. "Elora?"

No response. Nothing but the interrupted cries of those being trampled, mutilated, their flesh torn. Did her voice come from ahead or behind?

Too many bodies. I join the current that barrels toward the stairs. All the while, I'm scanning the chaos for brown skin, the flush of blood beneath. I spot a head of dark hair in the distance, then a large man at the woman's side that can only be Shaw. "Here!" I scream, waving a hand as I attempt to shove toward them. Like wading through muck.

"Wren!" My sister's terror-stricken eyes find mine. No blood anywhere that I can see, only the rumpled appearance of those forced to dress hastily. Thank the gods she's unharmed. "What's happening? The darkwalkers—"

"Come." Grabbing her hand, I haul her in the direction of the king's rooms, Shaw bringing up the rear. The screams trail us, reach terrifying heights. Then a rolling force quakes the fortress, and I stumble against the wall as a new upsurge of screams heaves and crashes downward. My grip tightens on Elora's small fingers. Nearly there.

Once inside Boreas' quarters, I slam and lock the door, tear away the tapestry that conceals the exit leading to the Gray. Elora rests a trembling hand on her round stomach. Shaw cups her slim shoulders as they gape at what the doorway reveals: the sucking, icy breath of the world.

"This leads back to Edgewood," I rush to say. "See the creek in the distance?" I point to a glimmer of ice through the trees. "Keep traveling east until you reach the town. You'll be safe there." Safe inside the ring of salt.

My sister turns her head slightly, taking me in. Sweat dampens her face. "What about you, Wren?"

"My place is here." I meet Shaw's gaze, see the understanding there. "With my husband." As it should be. "Now go. You don't have much time." With the amount of darkwalkers infiltrating the grounds, I fear something has happened to Boreas. Why isn't his power pushing them back?

"Wait!" Elora latches onto my hand. The slender bones, the

delicate blue veins. For so long, she was my purpose in life. But I have a new purpose now: myself. "Tell me you'll be safe."

I cannot promise that. The Deadlands has never been safe, likely will never be safe so long as the North Wind reigns. But I chose him. And by choosing him, I chose the beasts and the snow and the lifeless rock. His inheritance is now mine.

"Elora." Shaw's deep voice is nearly drowned out as another scream rents the air. One of the staff? The voice is too high-pitched to be Orla, but in the dark, people sound different, especially when afraid. "We're wasting time."

My throat bobs, and I pull Elora into the first real embrace we've shared in many months. If, for whatever reason, I do not escape this night unscathed, I want her last memory of me to be one of love. "We'll see each other soon."

She clings to me as she did when we were children, sharing blankets to keep out the chill. Another moment longer, and I pry Elora loose.

Once they've stepped foot across the threshold, I close the door and hurry to the study, the tapestry, yet another concealed door.

Down the passage I flee. If these darkwalkers managed to find a way through the barrier, I wouldn't put it past them to know the secret passages as well. Cool packed mud leads me deeper into the earth's belly. The battle sounds grow muted and eventually fade. There is only my breath, sawing in and out of my burning lungs. There is only the terror that looms black before my eyes, the stuttering, shuffling footsteps of one trying to find their way in the dark.

By the time I reach the exit—an old door set in stone—a layer of sweat coats my body. The wintry air pricks my skin, the hair along my arms beneath my coat rising, seeking any bit of warmth. There is none. This is winter at its cruelest. I sense Boreas' control over the winds, the temperature dropping in rapid increments. Every inhale scours my insides.

I nudge open the warped, crooked door and peer through the crack to the stableyard beyond.

Blood and bedlam and devastation. It is a swarm, a colony, a shredding storm. I'm protected behind a pile of rocks where the tunnel empties out, but the battle is moving, spreading. Soon, it will touch my tentative refuge.

For the darkwalkers have amassed. The horde of beasts rips into the armed guards, whose orders are to stand firm, to not buckle, to not yield, to break the crashing wave, to allow time for the denizens of Neumovos to flee to safety.

But their orders have doomed them to unspeakable horrors. They watch their comrades break until they themselves find their bodies crushed between enormous jaws, reeking black fluid trailing from their open wounds.

It is a slaughter.

But where is Boreas? I would have thought he'd be where the fighting is thickest, the need most dire. One of the tower windows shatters, raining broken glass as one of the maids leaps from the fourth story, a darkwalker's head lunging for her through the open window. Her body breaks on the ground below.

"Check the south wing. Leave no stone unturned."

I go utterly still. That voice is all too familiar.

Crouched behind the rock pile, I peer into the distance, past the worst of the bloodshed, seeking out the voice's owner. Moonlight saturates the snow beyond the open gates. Nothing. Just soldiers frantically trying to staunch the darkwalkers climbing the outer wall.

One figure, however, does not move like the rest. Light catches the gold strands in the head of curls, and gleams against the curve of his bow as he scans the surrounding area from his station near the stable doors, studying the butchering with cold calculation.

A gnawing sensation eats at the enlarging pit in my stomach. I know how the darkwalkers were able to enter the citadel unseen. I know, because I told Zephyrus about the hole in the wall. When I was a different person who felt nothing for the Frost King. When my singular mission was to remove him from this earth so that my people and the rest of humanity could live in peace, free of winter's devastating fist. When I was lonely and in denial about my needs. That woman was driven by vengeance and resentment, and that woman is no more.

"Zephyrus." The demand cracks out, hoarse with rage. "Zephyrus!"

My head snaps in the direction of the shout. My heart clenches, the fear noose-tight around my throat. I see nothing, nothing at all. But then a darkwalker steps into the light, carrying a thrashing figure by one clawed hand.

I audibly gasp. Boreas' hands and ankles are bound, and a sack covers his head. How did they manage to catch him so soon? And why isn't he using his powers to fight back?

"Calm yourself, Brother." The West Wind watches Boreas struggle in boredom. "It will all be over soon."

Zephyrus and the darkwalker round the stables. I follow, keeping low and quiet, moving amongst the shadows. If need be, I will kill Zephyrus to save Boreas. If he harms one hair on my husband's head . . .

"Take him north," Zephyrus says to the beast. "I will meet you when I am done here."

The creature gallops through the front gates into the dark forest, Boreas clutched in its grip. I watch him go, my heart carried off with him. I'll never be able to catch up with them on foot.

I need a horse.

With the West Wind's attention turned elsewhere, the way to the stables is clear. I throw open the door to enter the lamplit space, hurrying to the stall that holds Iliana. She blows hot air into my palm.

The unmistakable whine of a bow string being drawn has me retaliating in turn. I'm well aware of who threatens my life. Wherever he goes, the smell of green things follows.

With my own arrow nocked, I turn, aiming at Zephyrus' chest, just as his arrow is aimed at mine.

Our eyes meet across the heavy dim. My pulse climbs as a lick of cold moves through me.

"Hello, Wren."

His irises are the bright green of new growth, and cut like cold gemstones. Mud sullies his normally pristine tunic, his breeches torn at one knee. Sweat clumps his boisterous curls.

"You made a mistake in coming here," I say, tone level. The fear is but a shade, incinerated in the fury of my anger. He took something that did not belong to him. He took my husband. He lied and he lied, and he made them sound so sweet upon his tongue. Those actions cannot go unpunished.

"Mistake?" His mouth slants into a lopsided smile. A thin scratch across one cheekbone oozes blood. "My only mistake was in not arriving sooner."

He shifts closer. My fingers twitch around the string. The irony does not escape me, that I might shoot the god who gifted me this weapon. The gift, as it turns out, meant nothing. Merely a way to earn my trust, a bond that has been tarnished since its deceptive beginning.

"One more step," I warn, "and I'll shoot." Both the bow and arrows are god-touched. And I rarely miss.

He frowns, but stops. "I suppose that's fair."

"I should have listened to Boreas. I didn't believe—"

"That I am as depraved as he claims?" A mirthless smile. "Despite what Boreas thinks, I do not want his death. I only want his spear. His power has grown so unchecked that it is beginning to affect my own realm, as you are well aware, and I cannot have that. His power threatens to unbalance that which is balanced, and it must be stopped. Am I to stand aside while my realm, my people, die?"

"There are other ways. Choices that do not take the lives of innocent people."

"They are already dead."

"As you will be, if you don't give me the answers I want. Is that why you killed his wife and son? Because you felt his power grew unchecked?"

"Technically, bandits killed them."

Only years of discipline keep my hold on the string. An arrow to the heart—he deserves nothing less. "Are you honestly that cold-hearted?"

"Wren." He sighs, as if he's had this conversation before and has grown tired of it. "It was not purposeful."

Right. And I have a third eye. "Enough with the lies. You purposefully poisoned Boreas' wife against him. You took advantage of her, betrayed your brother's trust." *And me*, I think with a spike of fury. *You betrayed me.*

"It is not my fault she was unhappy," he replies with a careless shrug. I could stab him for it. "I gave her an out, just as I gave you one, and she took it."

"She wasn't unhappy. She loved him." But Zephyrus, with his treacherous, cunning mind, managed to crawl under that woman's skin, hone her into a tool used against her husband. Like he nearly did to me. I can't help but think Zephyrus must be lacking in some core moral to do something so malicious. "Why is that so hard for you to believe?"

"Because love," he says, expression contorting with sudden rage and grief, "is cruel. It takes something from you, and when that person is gone, you are never getting it back. I never wanted this, you know." He gestures to the stable around us. "I was happy in the City of Gods. And then my brother thought it a good idea to mutiny against our ancestors, to join the new regime in their quest for power. Because of his actions, I can never return, though I doubt you care."

I glare at him. "You're right. I don't."

But I am not thinking of Zephyrus. Strangely, I am thinking of sweet Thyamine, empty-headed Thyamine, forgetful Thyamine. She had sensed something was amiss during our trek to Sleep's cave. Then, I thought she feared for my safety, but it's possible my assumption was wrong. I never learned why she had drunk from the River of Forgetting.

"Thyamine," I say. "Did you tamper with her memories? Did she see something she wasn't supposed to?"

The West Wind rolls his eyes. "The woman was too nosy for her own good. She noticed that I began spending time with my brother's wife, and I feared she would say something. I took care of the problem."

Bastard. Self-serving bastard.

Zephyrus offers me his hand. "Be that as it may, I like you, Wren, so I will give you this chance. If you come quietly, I will not hurt you."

The ghost of a smile threatens. So he can use me for leverage? I don't think so. Months ago, I would not have believed the Frost King to care for my life. Yet Zephyrus, somehow, sensed that might change. He only had to bide his time.

"Zephyrus," I croon. "I've never done anything quietly in my life."

I release. The arrow sinks deep into Zephyrus' shoulder. He shrieks, drops the bow, and I'm vaulting over the stall door, unlatching it from the inside, and scrambling atop Iliana's back. No time for a bridle or saddle. She tosses her elegant head. The body beneath me, pure, untapped power, springs forward, and we lunge through the open door, galloping out of the stable and into the night.

# CHAPTER
## 41

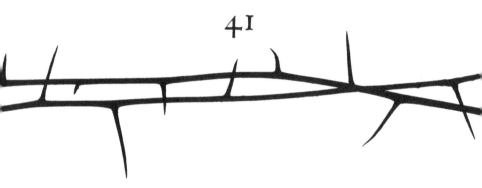

The quiver of arrows slams against my back. We fly like we've never flown before, through melting snow and gray slush, over streams that trickle from the remnants of an ice-encrusted land, descending into wide, flattened valleys and flitting upward to meet the rocky, pitted hills. The earth thunders with the hoofbeats of what sounds like half a dozen horses behind me. For that reason alone, I dare not look back. As soon as I tear my gaze away from what lies ahead, I'll be thrown off course.

"Hurry, Iliana." My fingers tangle in her mane. She's pushing as hard as she can, but she can't keep the pace for long. The darkwalker carrying Boreas had a head start. Eventually, it will hit Mnemenos. Will it attempt to cross, or will it follow the river's slithering path westward? Is that Zephyrus' intention? To take Boreas across the

Shade into his own territory? His power is, after all, weakened in the Deadlands.

The trail of broken branches dips into yet another valley. Iliana pants hard from the flight, yet continues to push. Zephyrus might be a traitor, but he isn't a fool. He'd want to return to the safety of his home, wherever that might be.

No, the fool was me. My own bias toward Boreas blinded me to the truth, and the truth is this: the West Wind is a snake, a fraud, a thief. I only pray I am not too late.

An arrow screams past my ear. I jerk Iliana to the left, off the marked trail, plowing deeper into the foggy, wooded interior. Curved over her neck, cold wind drying out my tear-filled eyes, I focus on the ground ahead. It's pocked with dangerous cracks, fallen trees, snow drifts. Any wrong move could sprain one of my mare's legs.

A fallen tree blocks the way. Iliana coils and springs, clearing the protruding branches nimbly. Ahead, slots of brightness appear through the tangled copse, and then the trees vanish. The world stretches before us—a flat, snowy ground set ablaze by the light of the swollen moon. I give Iliana her head. She blazes a path forward, carries me across the open plain with little effort. Then—more trees. We dive inside and disappear.

But eventually, Iliana begins to lag. We slow to a trot. The moon's positioning informs me we're traveling north, yet I direct us south toward Mnemenos so I can track the darkwalker. Its ashy stench has grown faint, and that worries me. I am praying, beseeching to gods I abandoned long ago, to keep Boreas safe. I am pouring every shred of my soul into a single request, a wish that the wind might carry my voice to him: *hold on*.

Miles later, a prickle at the base of my spine alerts me to company. Glancing over my shoulder, I spot a handful of figures illuminated by moonlight, all on horseback, closing the half-mile stretch between us in rapid pursuit.

I push Iliana into a sprint until we reach a river. It's not Mnemenos. The coloring is all wrong, red and pink rather than blue. My fingers twitch around the reins. Another glance over my shoulder. Those hunting me have closed the distance. I'm wary of touching the water when I'm not certain of its properties, but I haven't a choice. I'll have to cross.

"Let's go, girl."

I let Iliana pick her way across the water. The current races over the smooth, rocky bottom, a sound I've heard so rarely it takes a few moments before I'm convinced it is real—flowing water, free of ice. The air is warming. The earth begins to stir with life.

Once across the river, I dismount. My legs wobble beneath me. They want to move, for to stand still is to be prey, but I must keep my head. First, deal with those in pursuit, likely humans who are half-transformed. Then find my husband. I will rip the world apart if that's what it takes. That these individuals stand in my way? They will not live long enough to regret it.

Leading Iliana with soft clicks of my tongue, I trudge through the soft snow as far as possible before leaving her hidden behind a clump of trees. Then I hurry back to the river, crouch behind a snowbank, and place an arrow to the bowstring.

A breeze stirs, plucking at the individual voices of the approaching group like strings, high and low and those in-between. There is at least five men approaching. Then another voice adds to the mix. Six, at the minimum. Fools. They will die for their idiocy. I have seven arrows remaining in my quiver. Each shot must count.

The first man tops the rise, mounted atop a specter horse. I'm already adjusting my aim, a slight shift to the right. The man lifts his hand, and his companions fall silent. A little late for that. The string groans as I pull it back in a full draw, aiming for his chest.

But as his horse picks its way down the incline, the haze of survival clears.

It's Pallas.

My knees fold, and I cling to the lowest branch of the tree beside me to avoid planting face-first into the ground. I've never been more relieved to see him. The captain and I have had our difficulties, but I've never doubted his loyalty to Boreas. I scramble out from behind the tree. "Pallas."

The captain startles. A quick head-to-toe perusal as he surveys me. "My lady. Are you injured?" He directs his horse to the bottom of the hill. The dark bay gelding snorts, its white breath clouding with shallow pulses from its nostrils. In the shadowed light, the tips of the captain's hair appear red as flame.

"I'm fine." As he comes closer, alarm sends me forward a step. "You look unwell." And that's being kind.

"Oh." He glances down at the gore smeared across his breastplate. Chunks of skin, splatters of black fluid. The darkwalkers never fail to leave their mark. "It's not mine."

He reaches the opposite bank as more soldiers appear atop the hill. Six of them, all uninjured at first glance. They lose their opacity crossing through a beam of moonlight, yet reappear once they hit the shaded darkness beneath the trees. Exhausted, grim with defeat.

It was to be expected. Three I recognize from camp a few days prior. All six are heavily armed—swords, daggers, axes, bows. They scan the area warily.

"So few?" I ask, searching Pallas' face, and the dread, the *dread*. There must be a reason they are only seven total.

"My lady." His expression is the gravest of the grave. "I have never seen so many darkwalkers. We were quickly overwhelmed."

I knew that. And I had already anticipated the answer. But I'd hoped for something different. "What of the citadel?" My voice drops to a whisper.

Pallas glances toward a middle-aged soldier with a black mustache, who bows his head gravely. "It is out of our hands, my lady. The darkwalkers have taken it for themselves."

And that was another thing I'd hoped: for the fortress to have been spared, despite the darkwalkers' destructive tendencies. For that is my home now. The thought of it forever out of reach . . . "What of the guests? The staff?"

"We were able to get most of the townsfolk out through the tunnels. The staff as well."

That means Orla is probably safe, far from the bloodshed. And Silas. And Thyamine, too, blast the scatter-brained woman. "Is this all that remains of the army then?"

Pallas nods grimly. "Aside from those who helped lead the townsfolk to safety. And those on border patrol, but they are too far to call for aid. We won't know who survived until everyone is accounted for."

So few to fight against Zephyrus. It's hard not to give in to despair when hope continues to drain through my fingers, along with the time I cannot spare. I tell them, voice wobbly, "A darkwalker took Boreas captive. I couldn't reach him in time." My hand flies to my throat. Failure. What an awful, crippling thing. "I don't understand. He should have been able to fight back, but he didn't. Is there a reason why that may have happened?" Was his power drained that quickly? If that's the case, how will he ever be able to free himself?

Pallas and his men share another silent exchange. Then the captain shakes his head. "I'm not well-versed in my lord's power, but if he has not drained it, then something must be impeding his ability to use it."

And I haven't any idea what that *something* could be.

Shaking my head, I return to the matter at hand. "I was on my way to Mnemenos to see if I could pick up the darkwalker's tracks. I imagine you lost the trail as well?"

"We were not looking for the king," says the mustached man. "Our orders were to stay with you." The other soldiers nod in agreement.

Of course. Boreas would not care about his own safety. Frustrating immortal.

But it does offer me a greater advantage. Seven fighters total, armed, hungry for vengeance. They know the land. And they're well acquainted with the enemy. I will need every weapon at my disposal, blades whetted and agleam.

"The West Wind has taken Boreas," I state, looking each soldier in the eye. "I'm going after him, but I can't do it alone."

"My lady." Pallas smiles, and it bears an edge. "We aim to serve."

$\approx$

The men build a fire. After hours exposed to the wintry chill, the warmth thawing my frozen fingers as I hold my hands to the licking red flames is welcome.

Night infiltrates every crack and corner, dropped like a cloth overhead. I, along with Pallas and his comrades, congregate around the fire, perched on rocks or logs to discuss the next step. Time is not our ally. I may be an excellent shot, but I know little of warfare, battle maneuverings. The guards' extensive knowledge on the subject has been invaluable. Tonight, I am their most eager pupil.

"History shows us the darkwalkers congregate in small bands," says the mustached soldier as he tosses more sticks into the flames. Sparks crack and scatter against the darkness. "Five, six, at times ten to a group. Any more than that and there is infighting."

"So wherever Boreas is," I say, connecting the dots, "we can expect a group of darkwalkers." In addition to Zephyrus.

"Yes, my lady."

Needless to say, this does not bode well.

According to the guards, there are a few places Zephyrus could have used to hide Boreas. Caves to the east. A canyon to the southwest. Then the deepest recesses of the forest, which lie a day's ride north. They sent two scouts hours ago, one to the caves, one to the canyon. If they return with no sighting, then we'll travel north.

One of the younger soldiers, a squat man with a square face, asks, "How long do you think Zephyrus can maintain control of the darkwalkers?" He peeks sidelong at me, then drops his eyes. "Begging your pardon, my lady, but if my lord is in their grasp, who is to say they will be able to fight those instincts until we're able to rescue him?"

My stomach twists. A darkwalker's instinct is to drink living souls, drink them down and lap at the life-giving force. Specters may whet their appetite, but the North Wind is a full-blooded immortal, power beyond measure, the sweetest nectar.

"He's not dead," Pallas states, picking at a stray thread on his breeches. He speaks with wholehearted conviction, which eases the snarling knots within me. I'm inclined to agree. Zephyrus may have a misdirected sense of justice, but he wouldn't harm his brother. At least, not yet. "Though I can't say he'll remain that way for long." An apologetic glance my way.

It's what I fear most. Zephyrus wants his brother's spear, to put an end to this cold. Boreas refuses to give it to him. Which of the Anemoi possesses the stronger will? What will reign, in the end? Love, or vengeance? Winter, or spring?

The moon sinks as the night deepens, and panic spikes intermittently, my fear compounding, nightmarish scenarios of how, exactly, Zephyrus will punish his brother. Approximately three hours have passed since I fled the citadel and I fear that is three hours too late. If he hurts him . . . I force myself to exhale, my heart to stabilize.

I should have killed Zephyrus when I had the chance.

"How should we approach this?" I ask the captain.

"Difficult to say without knowing what we're up against." He pokes the fire. "I've dealt with Zephyrus before. He's tricky. And with all those darkwalkers on his side . . ." He shakes his head. "We are only eight. We cannot fight the horde. But the darkwalkers look to Zephyrus for guidance, however he has managed to assert his control over them. If we can remove Zephyrus from the situation, we can cut the snake off at its head."

Kill the snake, he means.

Something he said snags my attention though. "What do you mean you've dealt with Zephyrus before?"

The light flickers in his eyes—then is extinguished. "I accompanied my lord to the mountains when his wife and son had been abducted. And when we found them . . ." Pallas' mouth flattens.

He can't say it, but I know. We all know.

One of the men chimes in, "Once Zephyrus is dead, do you think the darkwalkers will return to how they were before? Corrupt, but lacking intelligence."

The question gives me pause. The men aren't aware that Boreas is a darkwalker. They know the Shade, and his power, have weakened, but they do not know why.

The captain's noncommittal grunt gives the impression he hasn't a clue. No one does.

But I remember something I read in a book once. A flower, unable to flourish, often withers. The flower being a metaphor for love. So I wonder if the Frost King's stagnation in his grief has caused his own demise. The torn Shade, the multitude of corrupted souls. And I wonder if love, trust, belonging have caused the earth to warm, have lurched time forward again. A salve to heal Boreas' wounds and restore balance.

The sound of approaching footsteps snaps everyone to attention.

A scout breaks from the shadows and steps into the ring of light. Muddy snow sops his breeches below the knee.

"I've found him," he pants. "I've found the king."

# CHAPTER
## 42

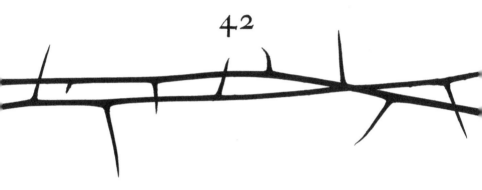

We crouch in the deepest shadows at the clearing's edge—the men and I. We left the horses tied a mile east and traversed the remaining distance on foot. Before us lies the cave. Its mouth is wide and dark, veiling what lies inside, perched atop a sloped, snowy hill. The scout was right. Darkwalkers guard the entrance. They prowl and shuffle in the surrounding vicinity, at least twenty of them. Who knows how many linger inside. We are only eight.

"My lady." One of the guards kneels at my side, having returned from surveying the area. "There is another entrance around the back of the cave. It's small, but you should be able to squeeze through it."

I meet Pallas' gaze. He nods. The other men are positioned nearby. While they engage the darkwalkers, I'll enter the cave alone. "Noted."

"You're sure you don't want me to accompany you?" murmurs the captain.

If he does, he will likely be killed. Zephyrus may hesitate to end my life, but not a specter's. "I'm certain. If I'm not back within the hour, then something has happened to me. Take your men and flee." Either I emerge from the cave with Boreas, or I do not emerge at all.

"We will not abandon you, my lady." Resolute.

"I am your queen, and that is my final order, captain. We're wasting time."

Pallas' expression folds into one of discontent, but he gives the hand signal.

It is time to move.

I creep around the forest's edge, keeping to the darkness, until I spot the back of the cave. There, I wait. One of the men loaned me his dagger. I'm not as skilled with a blade compared to a bow, but it's better than entering this situation empty-handed.

It doesn't take long. Silence deepens, then shatters all at once.

Six, seven, eight howling cries rent the air. The darkwalkers round the front of the cave with earth-shattering roars, leaving my way clear. Another shriek lifts the hair on my arms, a sharp, shrill sound that screams violence. Pallas' shout is lost in the sounds of battle. I count backward from ten in my head, then make my move.

My palms hit the smooth rockface, coasting along the surface, searching for any opening where moonlight pools onto the cracks. Something thuds to my right. An arrow, missing its mark. I push forward, seeking high and low for an opening. These caves are all formed from limestone, which is an extremely porous substrate. With the amount of snowfall, there would have to be another opening, but I'm not seeing it—

My hands fall into nothing. A fissure in the wall. It's large enough for me to squeeze through, and I push into the long, narrow crack that delves into the cave's innards. My shoulders and back scrape against the walls, and my hip bones. The opening narrows further. Another hard push.

A slot of deeper darkness pulses up ahead. I reach forward and am relieved to find that the opening has emptied out into a large chamber.

The air is warmer than aboveground, yet my throat still sears with each chilly inhale. Within the darkness, a light flickers ahead, a lamp maybe, or a torch.

Resting my gloved fingers against the cool, damp wall, I follow the tunnel into a shallow descent among the stale, earthen corners, my heart quickening as my soft footfalls echo in the space. The uneven surface of the rock beneath my hands grounds me. The path steepens. It spirals downward without end. I can feel the weight of the earth pressing upon my head. It's too heavy.

Meanwhile, darkness slithers across my skin, and I am thinking of blood, of broken bones and vacant eyes, of Boreas gone, Boreas dead, Boreas dismembered, Boreas in pain. Gorge rises. My feet begin to drag, and I have to stop and breathe until the tremors pass, dabbing at the sweat prickling my hairline.

But the light beckons. Water drips nearby, and air rushes against me as though there's an opening somewhere beyond sight. I hasten my pace, turning a corner, and step into a small niche with a single torch flickering on the wall.

At first, I think the space is empty. But that's a body on the ground.

Light limns the edge of Boreas' jaw. Eyes closed. Skin wan.

His hair, splayed out, caked with gore. His poor face, nearly unrecognizable. Nothing but puffy, inflamed skin darkened by blood and blotting shadows.

That is not even the worst of it. I gasp upon spotting the multiple arrows protruding from his body. His fingers are bent at odd angles, as if each one had been individually snapped.

He doesn't move.

My knees fold, cracking against the stone ground. Something collapses in my chest. My lungs, or my heart. My vision grows dark.

His chest isn't moving.

His skin is cold.

He cannot be dead.

"Boreas." My breath hitches as my eyes well. "Please wake up. Please." I bow my head, brush his swollen cheek with a gentle hand. I kiss his slackened lips. Breath in my mouth—his breath.

He's alive.

Bits of me crumble and cave, but I do not break. I can't. His life depends on my lucidity. What must be done? Escape. Healing. That leaves Zephyrus to contend with. How does one defeat a god?

"Wren?" One eye cracks open. Black. Not even a sliver of blue.

I glance at his hands. Clawed. And the shadows wreathing his neck don't derive from the darkness of the cave. They live beneath his skin.

"I'm here," I whisper, peeling away the bloody strands of hair sticking to his face. My hands shake. I will them to settle. I can't let my worry over his physical state—the injuries, his beast so near— cloud my judgment. "I'm going to get you out of here."

"No." He fumbles for my hand despite the broken fingers, squeezing it so hard I'm surprised the bones don't crack. The points of his curved talons dimple my skin. "You have to leave. Zephyrus is here. He could . . . hurt you."

Zephyrus has already hurt me in the one way that truly matters. "I'm not leaving you."

"You must."

"I will do nothing of the sort. Now stop arguing with me. You should know by now it's a useless endeavor."

"Stubborn woman," he manages, each word spoken with a harsh, tearing sound.

"You're the one who married me."

"Yes." Temporarily, the fog clears from his eyes. "And I have not regretted that decision for a moment."

Now is not the time to melt into a puddle of feelings. That he is able to speak this truth aloud . . . it is the greatest gift I could have received from someone I could not imagine being without.

I scan his body. One of his legs is bent at an unnatural angle. "Can you stand?" I'm too exhausted to carry him, but if he's able to use the wall for support, we can make it work.

"Wren." The sound of my name, drawn up from a great depth, spills from his bloodied lips. "You must listen to me. Zephyrus cannot get his hands on you. Run. As far and as fast as you can. When this ends, I will find you. I swear it. But I need to know you're safe."

Calmly, I wipe the smeared dirt from his jaw, though I have never felt closer to hitting someone so dense in their understanding. "Do you think I will abandon you, Husband? Or perhaps that has been your plan all along." I sincerely hope Pallas and his men have dealt with the darkwalkers by the time we reach the outside.

"Blast you, woman. Can't you see how I love you? Is that not enough to fulfill my request?" He attempts to sit up, only for his expression to crumple in pain. The blacks of his eyes shine wetly against his pale white face. "Please. For my own sanity."

I snatch my hand away, mouth agape. It may have been the echo of the fight aboveground, or the thunder of blood in my ears, but I do not think I misunderstood him.

"You can't say things like that when I'm trying to save your skin." I wonder if he even means it. He is delirious. Likely suffering from extensive blood loss. "We're not discussing this. Stand up. We're leaving." I tug on his arm.

"It's a lovely sentiment, truly," a voice drawls from the darkness, "but I'm afraid it's too late for that, Wren."

Zephyrus peels away from the shadows.

The West Wind. The Bringer of Spring. I have only ever seen him perfectly groomed, yet here, now, he looks as though someone took a switch to his face and enjoyed it.

Those boisterous curls hang sweaty and limp. A bruise grows on one cheekbone like a blight, his right eye swollen shut. As for his tunic, it's slashed to shreds, the skin beneath scabbed and bloody. Ruined.

I plant myself in front of my husband, despite Boreas' slurred cursing, hand wrapped around my dagger. If Zephyrus wants his brother, he'll have to cut me down where I stand. My hands twitch, eager for the fight.

"You can change your mind," I growl. "You can make the right choice. Let us leave unharmed. You've done enough damage this evening."

His nostrils flare with budding fury. I can't believe I ever thought the West Wind pretty. He is ugly to the core. His heart is a rotten, black, twisted amalgamation. How could I not have seen it? I have been blind, so blind.

"It never had to come to this," he replies. "I approached Boreas with a reasonable request. Had he agreed to kill the winter intruding on my lands, we would not find ourselves in this situation."

"Doubtful. The selfish are never satisfied."

Zephyrus shifts, fingers alighting casually on the dagger at his waist. Where is the bow he is never without? "Everything always came so easily to my brother. Boreas, the North Wind, the eldest of our father's sons." His teeth glow with a white luster, the ends sharpened to points. "Why should he not be punished for failing to take accountability for his actions?"

"So that gives you justification to ruin his life? He—" No. I will not describe the ways in which Boreas was destroyed by that loss. Zephyrus does not deserve an explanation, and he likely cares not. "You're just a spoiled, petty, selfish, jealous prick. By the gods, I hope one day you experience the depth of his suffering. I hope it destroys you."

He traces a finger over the hilt. "Charming." But he appears unsettled by my vehement tone.

"Let us go," I say, "and I promise your realm will be restored to its former state." As I talk, my mind races through possible solutions to the issue of being trapped underground. How are we supposed to get past him? Maybe I shouldn't have ordered Pallas and his men away. But I did not want their deaths on my hands.

"The time for reconciliation is past, I'm afraid." He curls his hand around the knife hilt.

I need to keep Zephyrus talking. Time—I need time.

Zephyrus says with a long-suffering sigh, "Hand over your spear, Boreas, and your wife will walk out of here with nary a scratch."

"Don't give it to him," I snap, my gaze never straying from the West Wind.

Zephyrus ignores me. The entirety of his focus remains on his brother, who lies prone at his feet. "What will it be? Is your power so important you would sacrifice your wife's safety?"

"Don't listen to him. I can protect myself." I've been doing it long before I arrived in the Deadlands.

He appears saddened by my unwillingness to cooperate. "Then you have made your choice."

A green vine lashes out, wraps around my throat, and snaps me back against the wall. My scream chokes off as the vine cinches my airway shut.

Boreas roars, struggling into a seated position. But his face whitens from the motion, and he sways. He is holding on to consciousness by sheer will alone.

Again, Boreas attempts to sit up, but he cries out and flops onto his back, panting. The talons at his broken fingertips lengthen and curl. As he weakens, the darkwalker within begins to manifest.

The West Wind watches his struggles stonily. "It is your life or your wife's. Choose, or I will do it for you."

"You're despicable," I spit. Hot, furious tears cloud my vision, smudging the flickering torchlight. It would be the cruelest irony to die after having discovered a life worth living.

"Wait."

A shallow hiss from where Boreas lies on the ground.

Something begins to take shape atop his chest. A smooth wooden haft, the stone tip. His spear.

"Here," chokes the Frost King. He picks up the spear—picks it up with those crooked, splintered fingers—and holds it out, his breathing wet and ragged, hand twitching in pain. "Take it. Just let Wren go."

"No." I struggle against the binding, but another vine wraps around my waist, pinning me in place. "He'll kill you!" The scream wrenches out, the blackest of torments.

Zephyrus flicks his gaze skyward. "How many times must I repeat myself?" he mutters. "I do not want my brother's death. I want balance restored to the world. A remnant of Boreas' power will remain, never fear."

I go still. "What are you talking about?"

The West Wind looks to the North Wind expectantly. But Boreas twitches as the beast begins to surface, as those shadows begin to rise, blackening the pale of his skin. He arches off the ground with a furious shriek. I watch the transformation with a deadened pulse, sickening dismay. "Boreas," I whisper. If he makes the change, I fear he will be unable to turn back, weakened as he is.

He slumps, teeth gritted, black eyes wide.

Without removing his attention from his brother, Zephyrus explains, "Our power is tied to our immortality. To give up our power is to choose a mortal life."

Mortal? He'd never mentioned that. I'd always assumed his power and immortality were separate. But if they are linked . . . I try and fail to wrap my thoughts around this newfound discovery. Boreas, a mortal man. Boreas, powerless, spear gone.

A gruff breath seethes from the North Wind's mouth. After a moment, he seems to regain control over the change, because there is no fear in his eyes as he offers up his spear, the repository of his power, the source of his immortality, to Zephyrus. If it is a choice between his life and mine, then it is not a choice. It is forced. He will hate a mundane, mortal life. What will he cling to when that power is gone? How will he view himself? What purpose will he have? Who will he become once his life is stripped away?

"Don't," I plead. "Just . . . think about what you're doing."

A shudder runs through him, and the black veins slither up his neck, across his cheeks. His voice, when he speaks, is guttural. "This is my choice, Wren. I am certain."

"But that will throw everything out of balance." The land needs winter just as it needs spring. If he loses his power, who will call down the snow, the bitter cold?

Zephyrus responds for him. "Don't fret, Wren. The earth is older than the oldest gods, its gifts bestowed upon the divine eons ago. The seasons will return to their normal cycle in your realm, as it should be. A brief winter, and then respite, regrowth."

Boreas continues to hold out the spear. Zephyrus is so intent on the weapon he doesn't realize the vines have loosened around my torso. My feet slide to the ground.

The spearpoint glows in strengthening intensity. The light is searing. Then it dulls, throbbing like a weak heartbeat.

And it's as if Boreas has funneled all that power—power tainted by that darkwalker within—into the spear, because the shadows gradually recede from his skin. My husband's eyes, having returned to their unclouded blue, flick to me as Zephyrus steps forward, reaching for the weapon. And I understand what he wants me to do.

The West Wind's guard is down.

We will have one chance.

As soon as Zephyrus closes his hand around the haft, it vanishes and reappears at my feet. I snatch it up. An electric pulse surges through my body, alighting my bones, shredding my veins to dust. Warm, fervent power, leaking from my pores. Is this what it feels like to be a god?

The stone point flares with light, and Zephyrus' eyes widen. I bare my teeth in a snarling grin.

"You, Zephyrus of the West," I spit, "are an ass."

The spear crackles. Blazing light floods the small space as, with a mighty heave, I swing the weapon in a wide arc.

Ice ruptures from the tip, arrowing toward Zephyrus' chest. He flies backward from the impact, smashes the wall with so much force it cracks, and another shudder rocks the cave, a groan trembling in its wake. The ground lurches as the spear disintegrates in my hands. All that power, mere dust. And as the first chunk of rock crumbles overhead, I lunge toward Boreas, fling my body over his, and bear the weight of a ceiling collapsing over me.

# CHAPTER
## 43

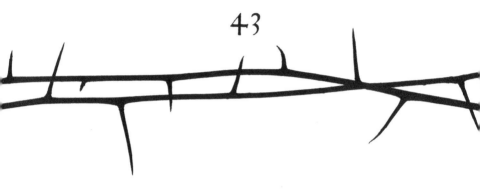

Love (noun): a profoundly tender, passionate affection for another person. Attraction that involves sexual desire. A person you love in a romantic way. Eternal devotion.

# CHAPTER

## 44

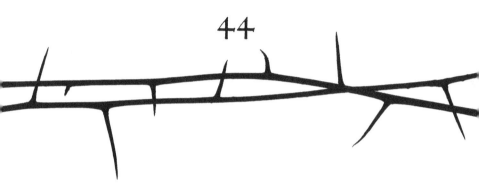

A knock sounds at my door, a rapid *tap-tap-tap*, sharp and immediate. "My lady?"

I sit curled in a chair, head leaning against the window, watching the clouds dissipate with the sun's rising. It's how I've spent the last few mornings. My breath makes steam against the frosted glass. Hot, spreading condensation that evaporates within moments, because nothing lasts—including the walls around my heart, now in ruin.

Three days have passed since I found Boreas in that cave, and I have yet to visit him.

The memory of that dark place haunts me. Boreas, his bruised, beaten face and body. And the broken arm and collarbone, and the lacerations to his skin, and the horror of his hands, and the arrows embedded in his thighs, his arms. Then there was Zephyrus, expression blank and cold as he stood over him. Brother. Liar. Traitor.

My stomach pitches dangerously. I close my eyes until the dizziness subsides and press my forehead against the searing glass. I should eat something, but every time I try, my body rebels.

I am a coward.

A touch on my arm draws my attention to the hand that rests there. Orla says, her eyes swimming with worry, "My lady? Did you hear me?"

"Sorry, Orla. I was thinking, is all." Or rather, trying not to think.

My maid and friend cups my hand between both of hers as if to shelter it, the warmth of her translucent skin thawing the dead chill of mine. "You are sad."

It is true. It is the truest thing about me. I think a part of my heart died in that cave. "Orla," I whisper. "I need help."

"Of course you do," she says kindly, as though having expected this all along. "There's no shame to it."

"I don't know what to do. I'm confused."

Following the collapse of the cave, Pallas and his men dug me, Boreas, and Zephyrus out of the wreckage. They carried me to Alba, who healed my broken leg and wrist. Zephyrus, they tossed into the cells beneath the citadel. Orla told me yesterday Boreas had freed his brother, for whatever reason. In my opinion, he should have ended his miserable life.

The things Zephyrus did to Boreas in that cave . . . The horrors will not vanish. Every time I close my eyes I relive his suffering, the choice he made: his life, or mine. And he chose me. It was never even a question.

Why would he do such a thing? Stupid fool. I would barge into his room and slap him if it didn't mean emerging from the shelter of my quarters.

Orla wipes my face with a clean cloth. "You love the lord."

Her words nearly stop my heart. But there is no denying it. "Yes."

"Well." She clucks her tongue in a motherly fashion, and even in my distress, I feel a wave of fondness move through me. "Then you must tell him."

My head snaps up. "Tell him?" The thought makes me want to do something rash like, oh, toss myself from the window. "I can't do that."

"And why not?"

"Because he doesn't feel the same way." I will not think of the declaration he made in the cave. Boreas would have said whatever he thought I needed to hear in order to leave him behind. If our positions had been reversed, why, I would have done the same. No hesitation.

"I have worked for the lord for a long time." She smiles, and it's so gentle I might weep. "I have to disagree with you. Since your arrival, I have seen him come alive again. He may be a man of few words, but I believe what he feels for you is plain."

"He can't." The idea strikes me like a fist to the heart. "He's just being nice."

She huffs. It sounds suspiciously like a laugh.

"Orla," I snap. "This isn't funny."

"I'm sorry." She does not sound the least bit apologetic. "But you are so stubborn sometimes. And blind. Stubborn and blind." A wistful sighs escapes her.

Stubborn? Absolutely. But I see fine. Boreas doesn't love me. He can't. I've caused him nothing but frustration, misery, and harm since I arrived.

I burned his curtains.

"You are worthy of love, you know," my maid whispers.

My throat tightens around the lump of feeling that lodges there. It's far too early to start crying, even if she touches on a deeply-buried hurt. I'm a mess, always have been. My emotions are too tangled, my edges too rough. And that is when I'm completely sober.

"I've tried to kill him," I point out. "Multiple times, I might add."

Orla doesn't even appear fazed by this. Has she known all along of my deception? "And?"

My face twists in confusion. "And that's a problem, I think." No, it's definitely a problem. What if I had succeeded? What if I hadn't realized in time how wrong my prejudice had steered me? I could have killed the only man I've ever loved and—

"Breathe, my lady." Orla's warm, soft hand settles on the back of my neck. My breath stutters in its attempt to slow. "People show love in different ways. I'm certain if you went to the lord and told him how you felt, he would return the sentiment. Your hearts are one and the same."

My eyes pinch shut. And what if he doesn't? How humiliating that would be. "You speak as though love is a simple concept. It's not! It's complicated." Quite complicated. Frustratingly complicated.

"Accepting love, maybe. But how you feel should be simple. Think about your sister. You love her, don't you?"

Yes, I do. And thankfully, she is safe in Edgewood, where she will remain until she gives birth. An occasion I wouldn't miss for anything. Yesterday, I wrote her, and Pallas was kind enough to deliver the message. It's my hope she writes back, when she's able to. But I only say, "It's not the same."

"Is it?" Orla challenges. "Will you hide in your chambers for the rest of your days?"

I mean, I could, technically.

"My lady," she warns.

Slowly, I uncurl my spine and sit taller in the chair, leveling a glare at my maid, whose eyes twinkle with much knowing.

"Go," she whispers. "The lord waits for you."

Those words give me the courage to stand and shake out the wrinkles from my dress. Orla is right. I cannot hide in this room forever. I cannot—will not—hide at all.

The number of sentries guarding the north wing has increased to ten. After the breach, I imagine they are reluctant to leave the king so exposed.

Pallas is nowhere in sight. A younger man with a scraggly beard has taken his place, and he states, "My lord is not taking visitors at this hour."

"Then it's a good thing I'm not a visitor," I say flatly. "Now get out of my way before I gut you with a fork. I promise, I will make it hurt."

The men exchange a worrying glance, as if wondering how unbalanced I have become these past few days cooped up in my rooms. As it turns out, quite unbalanced.

They shuffle aside, allowing me to pass. My heart gallops as I close the distance, the dark-grained wood of the massive double doors all that separates me from the truth. Two heartbeats—two heartbeats is all I allow myself to hesitate.

*Death to fear.*

Steeling my nerves, I barge into the king's rooms.

Boreas springs to his feet, booming, "What is the meaning of—"

He turns, and the fury pinching his face melts away. A book slips from his hands onto the armchair he'd just vacated, the fire roaring at his back. "Wren."

The orange light may soften his features, but it cannot erase the horrible sight before me. A man, a god, in distress, torment. The slight hunch of his posture due to injury, the bruising and swelling on his face, a reminder of how much he suffered to ensure my safety, the gray pallor of his newly-mortal skin, and I can't pretend I do not care. Anguish rises like gorge in my throat, and something caves in my chest. What have I done? I am the fool who fell in love with my enemy.

The Frost King has neither a heart of ice nor a heart of stone. He has a heart, a big one. Bruised and weary it may be, but I'd like to think it is healing. I'd like to think I am the reason for that healing.

The silence squats between us. Like a complete dolt, I stare at him. Every scratch, every patch of skin. Nothing escapes my notice. Even purpled and smudged, he is beautiful. "I—"

Words turn to ash in my mouth. There is so much I want to say, but I'm not sure where to begin.

Boreas clears his throat. He wears breeches and a loose white undershirt that falls to mid-thigh. "Would you like to sit?" He gestures to an empty armchair awkwardly.

As if I am able to sit at a time like this.

"I'll stand."

He takes a step toward me, then stops. Unruly clumps of hair poke from his skull, which he attempts to smooth over in a rare display of self-consciousness. "How are you?"

I bite the inside of my cheek so hard I draw blood. "Fine." Which is about the biggest lie in this room at the moment. I have missed my husband these last three days. I'm here now. So why do I still miss him?

He goes quiet. Thinking, perhaps, of a way to bridge this gap. If I were more emotionally available, I would ask him how he's been. How my husband has been.

We speak at the same time.

"Have you—"

"I was thinking—"

Another gaping hole where the sound falls through. I cross my arms over my chest, shivering despite the heat from the fire. "You first."

"No," he says. "You go."

There he goes, being kind to me. Being considerate and *good*.

"This was a mistake." I rush for the door. "I'm sorry to have disturbed you."

The moment I touch the door handle, Boreas intercepts me, his hand engulfing mine to stop my escape.

"Please." My eyes sting from the agony in his voice. "Don't leave."

But there is an unspoken word.

Don't leave *me*.

I stare down at our hands. No shadows darken his skin, and his nails are blunt, human. His touch—tender, grounding—slides through me like water carried downstream. There's an effortlessness to the gesture. A tentative hope.

Pressure builds behind my eyes. I have been strong my entire life, but I cannot be strong about this. Boreas suffered in that cave—to protect me. No one has ever put my needs before their own, as if I am worthy of such a thing. That I might have once killed him, the only person who has ever loved me unconditionally, tears me apart. I cannot lie. I cannot hide what I feel.

The world melts, hot and stinging. "I'm sorry." A sob tears out of me, a fracturing sound that quickly descends into hysterics. Fear of my own developing feelings led to me abandoning my husband when he needed me. "I wanted to see you. I couldn't . . . I thought . . ."

Boreas squeezes my fingers. I sense his desire to pull me close, yet there is a line. I wish he would, damn it all. More so, I wish I were not so cowardly in the face of love.

Peering up at him through damp, spiked eyelashes, I whisper, "They hurt you." But it's more than that, isn't it? *I* hurt him. Zephyrus knew how to enter the citadel because of me. I informed him of the hole in the wall. I requested the sleep tonic. I picked the poppies. Me. It has been my doing since the very beginning.

The sight of the sickly green tinge around his right eye sends another wave of shame through me, and fresh tears course down my face.

"Bones heal," Boreas whispers. "The bruises will fade."

And what of those internal scars? "I could kill Zephyrus for this."

He says, with quiet restraint, "That will not be necessary. I've dealt with my brother. He has returned to his realm and is barred from the Deadlands, and the Gray, forevermore. He will soon learn the consequences of his actions." A satisfied little smile that sparks my intrigue.

"What did you do?" I breathe.

"Let's just say Zephyrus will have an interesting time growing comfortable in his new skin."

I have no idea what that means, but whatever plague he cast upon his brother, it is well deserved.

"What about the Shade? The darkwalkers?" How will his sacrifice affect those connected to this land?

He nods as if he expected certain inquiries. "The Shade is restored to its natural balance. As for the darkwalkers, they have been cleansed, their souls returned to the Les in pure form."

"But—" It can't be that easy. What of the ripple effects of this change? Is there to be a great cataclysm? Will I be struck down by the gods? "There has to be something else, something more—"

His expression smooths into one of concern. "Wren."

My knees wobble at the sound of my name in his mouth, crafted so lovingly. "It's my fault. I can't forgive myself."

"You don't need to forgive yourself." He tugs me against his chest, then rests his hands on my hips, anchoring me in place. "I forgive you. Whatever you have done, I forgive you."

"No." I shake my head and push away from him. My hands go to my tangled hair, then drop. "It's all wrong. You . . . you forfeited your immortality. For someone like me?" Why can't I catch my breath? "Zephyrus could have killed you. You had no protection, no means to defend yourself." My blood ices over from the devastating possibilities. What could have been.

"Wren." Lifting my hand, Boreas presses it to his swollen cheek, eyes fluttering closed and an expression of quiet agony passing over him. "I would do it all over again, give it all up, if only to spend another day in your company."

It's official: the North Wind is insane. "You don't know what you're talking about. You're concussed." Yes, that explains it. "Your power is gone. It's not coming back." Along with the eternity he was promised by his immortal blood. "You gave it up like it was nothing."

"What need have I of power when my life is full? You mean everything to me," he whispers hoarsely. "My beautiful, stubborn, thoughtful wife, whom I love."

"*What?*" I wheeze for air. "You can't . . . say things like that. It's not nice and I know you don't mean it and—"

He takes a step closer. "Stop talking, you frustrating woman." Those soft eyes rest on me. His thumb presses into my chin, tilting it up so that I meet his gaze. "Did you think I lied to you in that cave?"

"Yes, actually. I did."

He laughs endearingly. How odd. "You don't believe me? But I suppose that is to be expected."

"Listen to me. There's a chance we can reverse this, right? Maybe if you went to the City of Gods and appealed for your power, they would return it to you." If his power is derived from nature's cycle, it can't truly be gone. "We can go right now—"

His lips brush mine, stealing the remainder of my thought. A second, less tentative pass has him slanting his mouth over mine, sucking in my shaky exhale. My mind blanks as a low, delicious rumble vibrates through me. Then I'm arching into his touch, arms wrapped around his neck, starved for a taste as his tongue plunders my mouth. Deep, worshipful strokes, wet and messy, everything we cannot say. Eventually, it dissolves into something slow and tender and sweet, his grip loosening enough to cup my face in his large hands. Boreas breaks the kiss, our lips clinging momentarily.

"Was that your plan?" I whisper, searching his gaze. "Kiss me in hopes that I'll forget about your power?"

"Did it work?"

My chest cinches tighter. "Boreas."

"I need you to listen to me, Wren. Can you do that?"

Since he asked so nicely . . . I nod glumly.

"You," he says, catching my chin before I can look away, "are the most important person in my life. There is nothing I would not do for you. I would conquer cities in your name. I would lay waste to the world and place its greatest treasures at your feet. I would cross realms and topple empires and alter time, all for the promise of an eternity spent by your side."

A tear slips down my cheek, which he wipes away with the pad of his thumb.

"I don't want my power." He brushes a strand of hair from my cheek. His tone warrants no argument. "I want you. That's all I want. A life with you, an entire life, not just a flash amidst eternity. Your mind, your body, your trust, your laughter, your carefully guarded heart. I want it all. I will accept nothing less."

At this, my throat bobs. I will not fear what he offers me freely. I will not fear his heart, just as I will not fear mine. "You seem certain I will give it to you."

"Won't you?" At my scowling features, his warm, deep laughter curls around my bones, and he keeps laughing, gathering me close, one hand buried in my hair, the other snagging around my waist. The blue of his eyes dazzles. "Say it," he murmurs. "Be free."

"And if I don't?"

"Then I will have to convince you otherwise." The hand at my waist slips to the curve of my backside, squeezing playfully. "Mm." My cheeks flush. "How does a slice of cake sound?"

He knows me too well. "All right, drat it all. Yes, I love you," I hiss. "Is that what you wanted to hear? Are you happy now? How dare you make me fall in love with you!" I beat my fist against his shoulder. He captures my balled fingers, brings them to his lips, and kisses the knuckles, then my temple, my cheek, my mouth. There, he sinks in, teasing my tongue with languorous ease.

When we break apart, I bury my face against his chest, eyes squeezed shut. "I love you." Something loosens inside me at uttering these words, so I say them again. "I love you. So, so much. It frightens me how much I love you." Boreas is a fire in the hearth, warmth in my soul, peace at long last. Home. He is home.

"There," he murmurs into my ear. "Was that so difficult?"

Insufferable prick. "I can still stab you," I warn. But I press closer to him. I will accept not even a sliver of space between us. "What does this mean?"

"It means," he says, nuzzling my neck, "that one day you will grow old, as will I. It means the seasons will change, and winter will come to pass, and the rivers will flow once more. It means we can build a life together, and tend to it for the remainder of our days."

"I thought we were already building a life." I peer up at him with a lopsided grin, warmed by the adoration in his gaze, the tenderness. Immortal he is no longer, but for me, Boreas will always be the North Wind, the Frost King, the man I love, and from whom I never wish to be parted.

# EPILOGUE

## IN WHICH THE NORTH WIND ATTEMPTS TO BAKE A CAKE

Boreas had never baked a cake before.

And why would he? He was a god. *Was* being the pertinent word. For five millennia, he'd lived by a single task: to call down the snows, the winds, the cold. But only in the last three years had he learned what it meant to walk in a mortal's skin, to experience the enormous and frightening range of human emotions, and to love as he had never loved before, a woman with a vivacious spirit, whose heart never wavered.

The point was, as a god, he hadn't needed to bake. Silas cooked. The staff maintained the citadel and its grounds. The hostlers cared for the horses. This was the natural order of things.

Today, however, was special. It was Wren's birthday. He'd left his wife dozing in their bed while dawn's rosy fingertips warmed a land livened with soft green grass. At long last, winter had released its relentless grip on the Gray. The snow had thawed, the air had shed its chill. Birds and flowers everywhere. Despite his absolute despisal of Zephyrus, he could admit spring was quite beautiful.

A choice he had made: power, or love. Eternal death or a brief, yet fulfilling, life. How he had feared the loss of control, but he needn't have worried. Sharing a life with Wren was enough. More than enough.

He'd risen early because he needed the day. At this hour, the kitchen was deserted, the air tinged with yeast. Watery sunlight dribbled through the eastern windows, spreading gold over the wooden countertops.

Days before, when he'd approached Silas with his intentions, the man had kindly explained the process in great detail. He had then collected all the necessary fixings: flour, eggs, butter, milk, sugar, baking powder, vanilla, salt.

Boreas stared at the ingredients as though they were enemies of war.

He had until dinner this evening to complete his task. It shouldn't be too difficult.

Step one: add two cups of flour.

But which measuring cup to use? The smallest one? The largest one? Silas must have mentioned it, but he couldn't remember, damn it all.

In the end, he went with the largest of the four available. It seemed like an appropriate amount.

As the flour hit the glass mixing bowl, however, it bloomed outward, coloring the air and coating the front of his clothes. Boreas sneered at the mess.

"My lord, if I could offer a few suggestions?"

His head snapped up. Silas stood in the doorway, peering at his work with concern. Since spring had become a semi-permanent fixture in the Deadlands, the majority of his staff had exchanged their heavy woolen breeches for thinner stockings and light tunics. In an effort to move in a positive direction, he'd revoked the sentence that bound his staff into service. Many had returned to Neumovos to live out their days in content, but surprisingly, many had requested to stay on, including Orla and Silas, claiming they grew bored when unoccupied.

Then he noticed what the older man held in his hands: an apron.

"I don't need an apron," he stated calmly.

"My lord, I would strongly suggest—"

"Silas."

The man dropped his arm with a nod and hung the white apron on a hook attached to the wall. "Do you need assistance?"

Boreas brushed his flour-coated hands onto his breeches. "I'm perfectly capable of conquering this cake."

Silas stared at the flour-dusted surface of the counter with a pained expression. "My lord, I do not know if a cake can be, well . . . conquered."

Anything could be conquered with the right leverage. "Everything is under control, Silas. This cake will yield to me. You'll see."

The man offered him a tremulous smile. "Of course, my lord. If you're sure then." He turned to go.

"Wait."

Silas stopped in the doorway.

"How many eggs do I use?"

"My lord—"

"How many?"

He sighed. "Two. And do not overbeat them." He grabbed an apple on his way out, leaving Boreas to wonder what *overbeat* meant.

Silas had shown him this as well: how to crack an egg. So he didn't think much of it as he slammed the egg against the side of the bowl, where it shattered in his hand, the sticky insides sliding to the bottom. Pieces of white shell sat in the runny yellow yolks, mocking him.

He swore and began to pick out each shard. In a moment of frustration, he ended up tossing out the egg, grabbing a fresh bowl, and cracking another egg—more carefully this time. Only a few pieces of shell fell into the yolk. A vast improvement.

The morning passed too quickly for Boreas' liking. The air was more flour than not and powdered the counters like snowfall. After pouring the lumpy batter into a baking dish, he placed it into the oven to bake and began cleaning the mess he'd made. Wren had most likely woken by now, but their son kept her busy in the mornings. And she would never think to search for him in the kitchen.

After a time, the air began to smell almost pleasant. When the bell chimed, Boreas pulled the cake out of the oven.

His stomach fell. It looked like a burned, lumpen, misshapen head. He sneered at it. Not good enough. Not nearly good enough, but it might taste satisfactory.

Breaking off a piece of the warm, yellow cake, he slipped it past his lips and promptly spit it out. Inedible. Why did it taste so salty? He'd added two cups of sugar, just as the recipe demanded.

Time to start again.

The morning waned. His second attempt resulted in nearly burning down the kitchen. Silas materialized in the doorway, breathing hard. He took in the scene: smoke belching from the oven, flour coating the counters, the floors, the walls, even parts of the ceiling, Boreas' black hair now ashen. In a timid voice, he asked, "My lord?"

Boreas glared out the window from his position near the sink. "Don't fret, Silas." He would conquer this cake if it was the last thing he did.

For the third time, he mixed the ingredients—quite aggressively— and poured the batter into a pan, and set it into the oven where the fire burned low. He checked the cake every ten minutes or so until the air smelled slightly sweet.

Removing the pan from the oven, Boreas scrutinized the warm, bread-like food, poking the spongy texture experimentally. It certainly looked like a cake. It wasn't nearly as lumpy as its predecessor, or as burned. It also smelled like a cake, like sugary flour. The strain around his eyes and mouth lessened in relief. It had taken the day, but he had done it. He, Boreas the North Wind, had baked a cake. Now to decorate.

Fresh flowers arranged in a nearby vase caught his eye. Perfect. Boreas ripped the white petals off the stems, sprinkling them over the top. There. Wren liked flowers. Thus, she would like this cake. The sweet concoction had been a worthy adversary, but he had prevailed, in the end.

"Orla," he called.

Wren's maid appeared in the doorway. "Yes, my lord?"

"Please inform the staff that Wren and I will be dining shortly. And please take this cake to the table."

The older woman looked at him curiously as she hefted the plate bearing the decorated cake. "My lord, did you make this for Lady Wren?"

"I did, but I'd rather it be a surprise."

"Of course." Her eyes twinkled as she vanished into the hall in a rustle of skirts.

As it was nearly dinner, he hadn't the time to wash. So he went in search of his wife.

He found Wren descending the central staircase, their son cradled in her arms. She wore a simple green dress with white trim and pearl earrings he had gifted her for their anniversary last month. The green complemented the warmth of her brown skin, her dark hair and darker eyes. She was lovely. A jewel. There was not one part of her he did not love with the whole of his heart.

Her gasp rang throughout the echoing space as she caught sight of his ghastly appearance. "Boreas? What in the world—" She blinked as he climbed the stairs until he stood two steps below her, their eyes level. "Is that flour in your hair?" She touched a strand paled by the flour dust.

Taking her hand, he kissed its palm, her scarred cheek, her temple. Something about her presence never failed to calm him. Nose pressed to his wife's hair, he inhaled deeply, taking the scent of lavender into his lungs. The baby squabbled between them, reaching for his papa.

His smile broke free as he tucked their son against his chest. "Did he sleep?"

"Well enough." Wryness dimpled her cheek.

Leaning in, he pressed a kiss to his wife's mouth, resting one hand against her swollen belly where their next child grew. Then, because he had every right to, he deepened the kiss until Wren was left gasping, her cheeks flushed and her eyes fever-bright.

"Where have you been?" Wren demanded. "I thought you would come back to bed."

"Busy."

She scowled. Boreas laughed. All was right in his world.

"Come." With their son perched on his hip, Boreas drew Wren downstairs to the dining room. The fireplaces sat empty, but come autumn when the air began to cool, they'd light the fires. Currently, a warm breeze ruffled the white, gauzy curtains framing the open windows. Various works of art decorated the cool stone walls, and patterned rugs livened the space. Last week, Elora had visited with her husband and daughter, and she and Wren had spent the day rearranging furniture. After the growing pains Wren had experienced with her sister, he was glad they remained close, calling on one another every few months.

"What's this?"

Wren stood near her chair, her attention having fallen to the petal-decorated cake in the center of the table. She blinked, clearly bewildered by the sight. "I thought Silas had the day off."

There was a silence. Of course she would assume Silas had baked it. "He does," he said, and something in his tone must have revealed the truth.

Lifting her eyes to his, Wren asked, very carefully, "Boreas, did you bake me a cake?" She bit her lower lip, a sure sign of suppressed laughter.

"I did."

Her mouth opened, then snapped shut. Her gaze returned to the sweet. "It's very . . . floral."

His chest puffed out with pride. "It is." The epitome of spring.

His wife spent every free moment in the greenhouse, often carrying their son in a sling on her back while tending to the flower garden that expanded year after year.

After a moment of studying the dessert, Wren brightened. "I can't believe it. No one has ever baked me a cake before."

That wasn't entirely true. Wren had asked Silas to bake her a cake their second dinner together as husband and wife. She'd then proceeded to eat the entire confection herself. An appalling, if impressive, feat.

"Well, *you've* never baked me a cake, is what I should have said," she corrected.

His eyes warmed. His palm curved over Wren's backside and began to wander. She lifted a questioning eyebrow, glancing at the baby from the corner of her eye.

He removed his hand with some effort, pressing a kiss to Wren's forehead. "Will you try it?"

Wren sat. Their son banged his chubby hands against the tabletop between them. He had his mother's coloring but, Boreas noted with pride, his father's eyes. In four months, their family would grow again. Boreas hoped it was a girl.

"What's the flavor?" she asked.

"Vanilla."

Wren forked a bite into her mouth, chewing slowly.

Boreas found himself perched on the edge of his chair.

"It's—" She lowered her fork. "—interesting."

He straightened. Interesting. That was good, yes?

"Mm." She coughed and took a dainty sip of water. "Very." Then she smiled.

Boreas' chest swelled in satisfaction. He had done it. He had baked a cake for his wife, and she had liked it. He must try this masterpiece.

Snatching his fork, he sunk the tines into the dessert, brought a piece to his mouth, and gagged.

It tasted like literal horse shit.

Wren's eyes shone with mirth, and her mouth began to twitch. The longer he chewed, the more forcefully his gag reflex kicked in. But he fought it. After the many hours spent toiling in that kitchen, this foul piece of sustenance wouldn't conquer him. So he chewed and chewed and chewed some more, the horrid bite congealed to a paste across his tongue.

But he could bear the revolting taste no longer. Boreas spit the offensive dessert into his napkin as Wren's howling laughter climbed all the way to the ceiling rafters.

His wife laughed so hard and for so long tears streamed down her face. Boreas couldn't help himself. He laughed, too. Even their son giggled, screaming and waving his hands from his highchair.

"I'm sorry," she croaked, her laughter tapering off. She swiped at her damp eyes, color having climbed high into her cheeks. "You were so hopeful, and it must have taken you the entire day to make this. I didn't want to hurt your feelings." A pause. "Even if it is the worst cake I've ever tasted."

Pushing back his chair, he knelt at Wren's side. Sometimes it struck him anew that this woman loved him, that he loved her, would love her until the end of his days. They had built a beautiful life together. He would never be lonely again. "You could never." Boreas gathered his wife and son in his arms—his family. "Happy birthday, Wren."

# ACKNOWLEDGEMENTS

*The North Wind* began as a NaNoWriMo project and somehow morphed into a (metaphorical) beast, a much deeper and layered story than I originally intended to write, but I'm proud of the book it has become.

As a child of the 90s, that pretty much makes me a child of Disney, and I believe all the fairytale princess movies I watched growing up had an effect on my writing of this story, whether consciously or subconsciously. So thanks, Disney!

Thank you to Kate for beta reading an earlier draft and giving me some great feedback concerning Wren's sister.

Thank you to Beth, my critique partner, for the awesome, awesome feedback, as always. I'm still so sorry it turned out to be such a long novel! I swear I'll read whatever you want, whenever you want.

My thanks to my family as well for their support. And a very special thank you to my mom for listening to all of my ramblings. Love you, Mom.

Alexandria Warwick is the author of the North series, the Four Winds series, and *The Demon Race*. A Florida native, Alexandria spends much of her time performing in orchestras, drinking tea, or obsessing over *Avatar: The Last Airbender*. To find out more, visit alexandriawarwick.com or follow @alexandriawarwick on Instagram.

CPSIA information can be obtained
at www.ICGtesting.com
Printed in the USA
LVHW041315080722
723038LV00003B/337